The Moonlit Garden

The Moonlit Garden

Corina Bomann

Translated by Alison Layland

amazoncrossing

Text copyright © 2013 Corina Bomann and Ullstein Buchverlage GmbH
Translation copyright © 2015 Alison Layland

Previously published as *Der Mondscheingarten* by Ullstein Buchverlage GmbH in Berlin in 2013. Translated from German by Alison Layland. First published in English by AmazonCrossing in 2016.

Published by AmazonCrossing, Seattle

www.apub.com

Amazon, the Amazon logo, and AmazonCrossing are trademarks of Amazon.com, Inc., or its affiliates.

ISBN-13: 9781503950641
ISBN-10: 1503950646

Cover design by M. S. Corley

Printed in the United States of America

Prologue

London, 1920

Helen Carter gazed in bewilderment at her reflection in the mirror. Her deathly pale cheeks were marbled by rivulets of tears mingled with makeup, and her exotic, amber-colored eyes gleamed strangely below thick layers of dark eye shadow, making her look like a silent movie star.

Helen had never been particularly interested in the cinema—her passion was for music alone—but at that moment she really did feel like a character in a movie. The scene that had just played out could easily have been penned by one of those scribblers who hung around outside film studios, screenplays in hand, in the hope of catching the eye of a producer.

Helen laughed bitterly before letting out a brief sob. Once again, her eyes filled with tears, which were stained black before sliding down her cheeks.

A few minutes ago everything had still been fine. Her glittering career as a violinist beckoned; the world was her oyster. She had been due to play Tchaikovsky on the stage of a London concert hall in half an hour. King George V would be present with his queen consort, an honor they only rarely granted to musicians.

Helen had always been lucky. She had been discovered as a child prodigy at the age of seven, and now, having just turned eighteen, she was fêted as one of the best musicians in the world. In Italy, the newspapers were already declaring her, an Englishwoman, to be the true heir of Paganini. When her agent had shown her the headline, she had smiled. Let people believe what they would! She knew to whom she owed her success. She remembered only too well the promise she had made.

And now that woman had turned up. She had followed her like a shadow almost everywhere she went for three days now. As Helen walked the streets of London, she caught glimpses of her. Whenever her gaze wandered out the window while practicing, she saw her across the street. The first day Helen had thought it a mere coincidence, but as the sightings were repeated over the next two days, she began to feel nervous. Every so often she encountered crazy admirers, women included, who would do anything to get her on her own for a moment.

Trevor Black, her agent, had dismissed her concern when she told him about it.

"It's only an old woman, harmless, if a little mad."

"Harmless? Mad people are never harmless! Perhaps she's hiding a knife in her bag," Helen had replied, but Trevor seemed convinced that the old woman meant her no harm.

"If she's still bothering you after the concert, we'll inform the police."

"Why not now?"

"Because they'd only laugh at us. Just look at her!"

Trevor had pointed through the window to where the stranger could be seen at the end of the street. Her figure was a little stooped, her clothes old-fashioned, and her features Asiatic. Helen had no idea why this woman should be stalking her. She was momentarily reminded of her childhood, but she quickly pushed the thought to one side.

She was now sure that the stranger really had been watching her, waiting for an opportunity to speak to Helen alone. She had somehow managed to worm her way into the dressing room shortly after Helen had sent Rosie off to see how full the auditorium was.

Helen's first instinct had been to call for help, but there had been something hypnotic about the woman that made it impossible for her to cry out. What the visitor told her during the brief conversation made something give way inside her, and Helen shouted at the woman to leave.

She had obeyed, but her assertion still hung in the room. Of course it was possible that she was lying, but something told Helen that was not the case. Everything fit together. Long-forgotten images, memories of words spoken, thoughts—they all suddenly made sense.

Helen looked at the violin lying nearby. Before her visitor had appeared, she had wanted to practice a couple of particularly difficult passages one final time, but there was no hope of that now.

With shaking hands, Helen gripped the instrument and turned it over. As her fingers slid over the rose burned into it, a face appeared in her mind's eye. The face of the woman who had given her this violin. Was it really possible?

As the door behind Helen was pushed open, the violin made a strange, hollow sound. A broken string lashed her skin, leaving a red welt. Shaken, Helen watched drops of blood well up along the cut as the memory of her cruel music teacher stirred a surge of anger inside her. In her rage she felt like jumping up and throwing the violin into a corner, but Rosie's kind face appeared behind her in the mirror.

"We have a full house!" Her smile faded. "My goodness!" Her dresser's hand flew to her mouth in shock as she saw the blood oozing from Helen's wrist. "Are you all right?"

"It's nothing," Helen replied, summoning her self-control. She hardly felt the pain, as the anger inside her was stronger, drowning out all physical sensation. "One of the strings broke. I was careless."

She should have dealt with the violin right away, but she was unable to rise from her stool. She doubted she would ever be able to rise again.

"Can I fetch you anything, Miss Carter?" Rosie asked helplessly, but Helen shook her head.

"No, it's fine, Rosie, I don't need anything." The words felt heavier on her lips than they should have.

"But you're due on stage soon, madam. The violin."

Helen nodded absently. Yes, she was due on stage. Just as the woman's visit had changed something deep inside her, it had also stolen her confidence. Perhaps it would mean the end of her career, but at that moment all Helen wanted was to be away from there and rid of that damned violin—the instrument that had been given to her by a dead woman—which had now injured her as her music teacher had.

With the violin in her hand, Helen rose and, head held high, walked out of the dressing room. She ignored Rosie's call, just as she ignored the broken string that swung against her calves. From the concert hall she could hear the sounds of the musicians tuning their instruments. A wasted effort since the concert was not going to take place. The expectant murmuring of the audience was also in vain.

She made her way determinedly to the rear exit, ignoring the astounded looks of the stage crew. I don't belong here. I don't want all this. I only want peace; I want . . . clarity.

As Helen pushed open the door, the violin in her hand gave out a grating note, like a warning. Clammy, cold air rushed against her. At this time of year the London nights were particularly unpleasant, but she didn't care. The cut on her wrist throbbed; the violin was suddenly heavy. The dead woman's eyes haunted Helen, driving her to run into the street outside the concert hall.

Helen heard a bloodcurdling horn blaring. She froze and raised her arms to shield herself against the glaring lights that sped toward her.

1

Berlin, January 2011

With the hands of the big grandfather clock showing just before five, Lilly Kaiser was sure that no one else would be coming into her shop. Huddled beneath turned-up coat collars, with caps pulled down over their faces, people were hurrying past the window without so much as a glance at the display.

No one was interested in antiques during the first few weeks of the new year. Purses and bank accounts were empty, and people weren't looking for special pieces for their loved ones. Things would improve in spring and summer when the tourists began to return. Until then she had to find a way to get through the slack period.

With a sigh, Lilly sank down on a small Louis XV stool and looked up through the window at the sky. Snow had been falling incessantly for days. Her gaze fell on the reflection of her face in the shiny polished side of a little cupboard that belonged to her growing army of unsold items.

Her delicate, almost girlish features looked pale and drawn, with her red hair and green eyes providing the only spots of color. The Christmas holidays had not done much to revive her—her annual visit to her parents had once again ended with them entreating her to find herself a new man.

However much she loved her parents, that had been too much for Lilly. She returned to Berlin, her nerves in shreds, to spend New Year's alone in her apartment before carrying out an inventory of the stock in her shop.

That was now done, leaving nothing to do but wait for customers. Lilly hated to be idle, but what else was she to do? She wondered if she should simply close up shop and go on an eight-week vacation. On her return, the snow would be gone and the shop full again.

She was torn from her thoughts by the sound of the bell over the door, a piece from a country house that always conjured up the image of servants scurrying hither and thither.

An old man stood on the threshold as if wondering whether to come in, snowflakes glistening on his coat and slowly melting in the warmth of the room. His weathered face could have belonged to a salty sea dog from a commercial. Under his arm was an old violin case, battered and worn. Did he want to sell it?

Lilly rose, briskly brushed down her knitted cardigan, and moved to greet the man.

"Hello, what can I do for you?"

The man studied her, then smiled hesitantly. "I assume you own this shop?"

"Yes, I do." Lilly smiled as she tried to size up her customer. Was he an elderly musician on his way home from a recital? A violin teacher who fought weekly battles with mediocre pupils? "How can I help you?"

The man looked at her again as if searching for something in her face. Then he took the violin case from under his arm.

"I have something for you here. Will you permit me to show it to you?"

Lilly did not want to buy anything else that month, but it was so rare for someone to offer her a musical instrument that she was unable to refuse.

"Could you come over here?"

She led the man to a simple table near the counter, where she sat the customers who came to offer her items. There was usually little she could use—people tended to think that the trinkets they found in their attics or inherited in relatives' wills were more valuable than they turned out to be—and she was all too often subject to a torrent of reproach when she claimed that a precious porcelain figurine was merely bric-a-brac.

But as the old man lifted the cover of the violin case, Lilly suspected she was about to see something special. The threadbare, moth-eaten lining, which must once have been deep red, cradled a violin. An old violin. Lilly was no expert, but she estimated that the instrument must have notched up at least a hundred years, if not more.

"Feel free to take it out," the old man said, watching her closely.

Lilly obeyed a little hesitantly. She had the greatest respect for musical instruments, even though she did not play anything herself. As she curled her fingers around the neck, she thought of her friend Ellen, whose profession and passion was restoring treasures like this. She would have been able to estimate the value of this one in seconds.

As Lilly gazed at the violin—its beautiful varnish, its uniquely formed scroll—she noticed a drawing of a rose on the back. It looked sketchy and very stylized, almost as if it were the work of a child. Though it was definitely recognizable as a rose.

What violin maker would decorate an instrument with an ornament like this? Lilly made a mental note to call Ellen that evening. She was sure she would be unable to afford this violin, but she nevertheless wanted to tell her friend about the image—and perhaps the man would allow her to take a photo.

"I'm afraid I probably don't have enough money to buy this from you," she said as she laid the instrument carefully back in its case. "It must be worth a fortune."

"There's no doubt that it is," the old man replied thoughtfully. "I detect a note of regret in your voice. You'd like this violin, wouldn't you?"

"Yes, it's . . . it's so special."

"Well, what would you say if I told you I'm not here to sell it?"

Lilly raised her eyebrows in amazement. "So why are you here?"

The man smiled briefly. "It belongs to you."

"I beg your pardon?" Lilly looked at him in confusion. Surely she had misheard him? "You want to give me this violin?" She realized she had spoken this absurd thought aloud.

"No, that's not strictly true, since you can only give something away if you own it. This violin belongs to you. At least it does if the registry office is to be believed. Unless you're not Lilly Kaiser."

"Of course I am, but—"

"Then it's your violin. And there's something else that goes with it."

His warm smile did nothing to dispel Lilly's bewilderment. Common sense told her that the whole thing must be a trick, or at least a mistake. What reason could this man have to give her a violin? She had never seen him before in her life.

"Look beneath the lining," he persisted. "Perhaps you'll find something there that explains things."

Hesitantly at first, then with trembling hands, Lilly drew out a piece of mildewed paper and unfolded it.

"Sheet music?" she murmured in surprise.

The title of the piece was "The Moonlit Garden." The notes looked shaky, as if they had been written out in a great hurry. There was no composer's name.

"Where did you get the violin?" Lilly asked. "And how did you know—"

She was interrupted by the doorbell and looked up from the sheet music to see the man striding quickly away, like a thief about to be arrested by the police.

At first Lilly just stood there, frozen, but then she ran to the door, tore it open, and ran outside to the accompaniment of the bell's angry clanging. But the old man, whose name she didn't even know, had vanished. The frost bit hard into her cheeks and hands, mercilessly penetrating her clothes and eventually driving her back into the shop.

The violin was still lying there in its case, and it was only then that Lilly noticed she was still holding the page of sheet music.

What was she to do now? Again she looked out, but there was no sign of the old man.

A shiver ran down her spine as her gaze fell on the distinctively colored violin, its taut strings against the slim neck, and the delicate lines of the scroll. What a wonderful instrument! She still couldn't believe that it was really hers. And what about the sheet of music? Why had he drawn her attention to it?

A bang startled her. She turned around in fright to see a crowd of kids running noisily past the shop. A snowball clung to the first letter of "Kaiser Antiques" on the window.

Lilly breathed again, and her gaze returned to the violin. I ought to show it to Ellen. She may know who made it—and with a bit of luck she'll also be able to find out who composed the piece.

Now certain that no more customers were about to appear, let alone another old man with some mysterious musical instrument, she went to the door, turned the sign to "Closed," and fetched her coat.

2

With the violin case under her arm, Lilly climbed the steps to her apartment on Berliner Street. The house was old and stood next door to a boarded-up theater that had been vacant and waiting for an owner or tenant for several years.

The steps creaked beneath Lilly's feet, her familiarity with the house enfolding her. A variety of smells hovered on the staircase, a different one for each floor. On the ground floor it was cats; on the middle floor, cabbage; and at the top, the musty smell of damp laundry, even though none of the tenants hung their clothes out to dry on the landing. Here and there the smells faded at the edges, but they were regularly renewed as someone cooked a Sunday dinner, let the cats out, or did whatever else caused that floor's characteristic smell.

Lilly's floor was the one with the hint of damp laundry. She had four more sets of stairs to go before she could block out the mustiness by closing her door behind her. As she climbed, the feeling slowly came back into her frozen cheeks. Her hands were also numb, despite her gloves. Lilly could hardly wait to make herself a cup of coffee and ring Ellen.

She was halfway to her sanctuary when she met Sunny Berger, the twenty-year-old tattoo-covered student who sometimes helped out in her shop and had a very good eye for antiques. Customers would occasionally look askance at her when they noticed the images on her skin, but Sunny usually won them over quickly with her charm.

That had happened immediately with Lilly—she had befriended the student within a week of her moving in.

"Hey, Sunny, how's it going?" Lilly asked, once again toying with the idea of treating herself to a little vacation. If there was anyone she could ask to hold down the fort for her, it was Sunny.

"Fine, thanks. You?" The young woman gleefully drew up the sleeve of her sweater. "Look, this is my latest."

The tattoo depicted a pinup girl riding a black eight ball. Lilly had no intention of decorating her own body with images, but seeing them on Sunny filled her with amazement at the work of the artist and the image itself.

"It's very good. Where did you have it done?"

"In a shop on Torstrasse," Sunny replied, a smitten smile crossing her face. "The tattoo artist was really nice—I think I'll be going there again."

"You? Making a commitment?" Lilly smiled—unlike her tattoos, Sunny's relationships were anything but lasting.

"Well, for the next tattoo, anyway. After that . . ." With an expression of regret she tapped the ring finger on her left hand, the one tattooed with the fine lettering of the word *Love.*

"Ah, married," Lilly observed, and Sunny nodded.

"Yes, unfortunately. It would be something to land a tattoo artist. I could get my tattoos for free."

"And within a year you'd have no space left on your body."

"True enough. And how boring would that be? But Dennis *is* very nice."

"Get to know him a bit better, then—he might give you a discount."

"We'll see. How are things looking with you—will you be needing any help in the shop?" Sunny asked as she rolled her sleeve back down.

Lilly smiled inwardly. It was a question Sunny always asked when she'd just had a tattoo. The body art regularly tore a hole in her budget, though it never stopped her from treating herself to new ink when she wanted it. Lilly was about to turn her down when she remembered her thoughts about a vacation and escaping from snow-covered Berlin.

"I may," she replied, knowing that if she didn't stay in Sunny's good graces, she might have no one to call on if she really needed to. "Perhaps in a week or two. Could you help out then?"

"Of course," Sunny said. "I'll hold the time for you as soon as you tell me how long you need me for. I've got some study leave coming up."

Lilly thought back to her student days. Although, like Sunny, she had always been on the lookout for a job to bring a little money in, she had loved the freedom and flexibility of student life.

"I don't want to spoil your leave, but maybe you could arrange to help out for three or four weeks?"

"Are you planning to go away?"

"Perhaps." Lilly felt the hint of a smile on her face as she absently stroked the violin case beneath her arm.

"And you're going to learn the violin while you're there?"

"No, this is something I got today, and . . ." If Ellen showed any interest in it, Lilly would take it to England. But she wasn't going to tell that to Sunny. Not yet. "We'll see."

"OK, just tell me when you need me. I'll drop everything for your shop."

"Thanks. I'll let you know in the next couple of days."

"OK!" Sunny flitted past her and disappeared down to the cats' floor. Lilly trudged on up until she was engulfed by the smell of stale laundry.

"Ah, hello, Lilly!" called out Martin Gepard, who was just closing the door to his apartment.

He had moved in about a month after Lilly and worked in a nearby supermarket. Although they were both about the same age and each knew that the other was single, there had been no further contact between them. Lilly greeted him briefly before disappearing into her apartment, free at last of the landing's mustiness. Within her four walls the air smelled of vanilla, wood, and books.

She had never been tempted to fill her rooms with antiques from her shop. Before, in another life, she had owned a lot of antique furniture, but since her husband had died, Lilly preferred modernity in her home. Her furniture was new—nothing special, just the usual ubiquitous items from Ikea. The only thing she had brought with her from her former home was a painting of a woman standing by a window and looking out over a rather indistinct garden.

Especially in the early days of her new life, Lilly had imagined herself in the scene. The woman in the portrait also had red hair and looked a little lost. It was impossible to tell what she could see in the shadowy garden, but whatever it was, it didn't please her. She seemed to be wondering what she should do and whether it would be worth moving on, leaving the garden behind.

It was a question Lilly often asked herself. The apartment suited her fine, and the existence of the shop made any idea of running away impossible. For a few days or a week, it could be done, since she had Sunny for that, but she couldn't imagine leaving Berlin. Where would she go? She had never had many friends, and their number had decreased further since her husband died. She really only had Ellen now. But that didn't make Lilly sad; on the contrary, it was good to know that there was one person who would always be there for her.

Lilly took the violin case straight over to her desk, where she set it down carefully. She clicked on the desk lamp, and its glow lent the old leather and the tarnished handles a mysterious gleam.

"What do you think?" she asked the photo of a man smiling out at her from a simple frame. "Should I let myself get drawn into another adventure?"

Her husband had always believed she should seize every opportunity that came her way. And now, too, he seemed to be smiling his encouragement. Lilly could hardly believe that three years had passed since his death. She still sometimes caught herself waiting for him to come into the shop, bringing her an ice cream or a coffee and admiring her latest acquisitions.

Peter was a novice with antiques, but his taste was faultless. He would have loved the violin.

She ran a hand lovingly over the portrait, but as she felt the tears welling up in her eyes, she turned to the phone.

The conversation with Ellen was bound to distract her. As she dialed the number, she conjured up an image of her lively, cheerful friend. She was in her late thirties with sparkling blue eyes, a pert nose, and a tendency to jut out her chin slightly too determinedly. Although they were both the same age, Ellen had always seemed more mature. And that was still the case: Ellen was strong and self-assured, and Lilly, childlike and doubtful.

"Hi, Ellen—it's Lilly," she said as a husky voice answered.

"Lilly, what a surprise! We haven't talked in ages!"

"Too long," Lilly said as she thought back over the weeks. It must have been three months since they last spoke. They e-mailed regularly, but that was a poor substitute for the long, heartfelt conversations they used to have.

"You're telling me." Ellen laughed with her characteristic gurgle. "To what do I owe the pleasure of your call?"

It sounded like Ellen was in the kitchen; Lilly could hear steaming pans hissing in the background. In London it was a little before seven o'clock, just the time Ellen would be preparing dinner. Although she could have afforded it, Ellen didn't employ a cook but insisted on cooking for herself in the evenings—at least when she was home.

"I had a very strange encounter in the shop today," Lilly said, finding it difficult to hold back from blurting out everything about the violin at once. But she knew Ellen liked a mystery and would have been disappointed with a mere account of the bald facts. Besides, Lilly found the whole thing so strange that she was beginning to doubt it had happened at all.

So she gave such a detailed description of the man's appearance, the words he spoke, and the gift he gave her that she knew she must have been running up a hefty bill for the international phone call.

"He *gave* you a violin?" Ellen's voice was full of disbelief.

"He did. And the strange thing is, he said the violin was meant for me, even though I've seen no indication of that anywhere on it. All I found was a sheet of music under the lining with the title 'The Moonlit Garden.'"

"'The Moonlit Garden'—how pretty," Ellen said. "So you got no address for your benefactor?"

"No, he didn't even tell me his name. Before I even noticed, he was gone."

Ellen clicked her tongue in disapproval. "Let that be a lesson to you. Next time you need to ask more questions. Someone could be palming stolen goods off on you."

The thought had never occurred to Lilly. It was one of her principles that she never asked her customers' names unless they wanted a detailed receipt for the sale. Now it hit her like a ton of bricks, and she chided herself for being so naïve.

"You really think it could have been stolen?" She looked at the violin case with suspicion.

"Well, we can't rule it out," Ellen said. "But on the other hand, he did give you the violin and say it was yours. If I were a thief, I'd try to get as much as I could for it, and if I couldn't get anything, I'd throw it out the car window."

"You certainly would not!" Lilly said, now feeling a little pacified. No, the violin wasn't stolen. There was clearly something remarkable about it, but it wasn't stolen goods.

"OK, you're right. I wouldn't throw any musical instrument out the window, but then I'm not a thief. So what does this treasure look like?"

Lilly described the violin to the best of her ability: the curve of the scroll, the length of the neck, the position of the f-holes, the size, the color. She saved the rose on the back until last. When she said that it looked like it had been burned into the wood by a pyrographer's tool or soldering iron, Ellen gasped in disappointment. There was a rattling behind her; something was probably boiling over.

"Sorry."

She excused herself briefly, the receiver clattering down onto the kitchen table, and Lilly caught a juicy curse, footsteps, and more sounds. After a minute the phone was picked up again, and Ellen's voice rang out.

"Sorry, that stew almost boiled over."

Lilly grinned. Ellen was not a particularly good housekeeper—her prodigious talents lay elsewhere—but it never stopped her from trying things out in the kitchen.

"So? What do you think of the rose?"

"Well, I must admit I'm a bit surprised," she replied. A chair scraped on the floor, and Lilly knew that her friend had sat down. "You're saying the drawing's burned into the varnish? What ignoramus would do something like that?"

"Calm down." Lilly looked over at the violin case. "It's branded into the wood beneath the varnish. Almost as if the violin maker had decorated it before varnishing it. Kind of like a signature."

"If so, it would be extremely unusual. Violin makers don't put signatures on the outside of their violins. The only ones who would do that these days are a few eccentric musicians who think their talent makes them gods."

"But it seems as though our violin maker wanted to make his violin something special. Are there really no violins with any kind of design on them?"

"Yes, of course you get decorated violins, but they're not by the great masters. I'd like to see how Guarneri or Stradivari would have reacted if someone had asked them for a painted violin."

"If they'd been paid well enough, I'm sure they would have done it."

"No, you're wrong there. They made instruments to order, but nothing that would put their prestige at risk. If someone wanted a violin with a rose decoration for their daughter, whether or not it affected the sound, they could be sure that the masters would refuse and pass it on to a less talented colleague. I can assure you that the only instruments to leave the workshops of Stradivari and his like were those that would have brought their makers the greatest glory."

"So you're saying that I've been given a completely worthless violin." Lilly was unsure whether or not she was disappointed by this. To be given a valuable instrument would have been even crazier.

"I'd have to see this baby first. Why don't you come over and let me have a look? And bring the sheet music with you."

"You mean that? I'm sure you must have a lot to do."

"And then some!" Ellen sighed but quickly added, "Though you're welcome anytime. I'd love to have a look at your violin and the music and drag you around to some of the sights of London. We haven't seen each other for so long, and to be honest, I've spent the last few weeks trying to think of an excuse to entice you over here."

"So it was you who sent the old weirdo with his violin?"

"No, I swear it has nothing to do with me. But I'll bear it in mind for next time. So when are you coming?"

"You're sure I'm not making work for you? I don't want it all to—"

"Don't be silly!" Ellen interrupted. "You're not making too much work for me, and it won't be the least bit stressful—I promise. I desperately need a change, and in any case, I'm dying to see you. I miss you like crazy, Lilly! And Dean, Jessie, and Norma would love to see you again. You know how my daughters are besotted with you."

"I do. And I look forward to seeing you all, too."

"So that means you're coming?"

Lilly was overjoyed. "Yes, it does. I just have to find someone to stand in for me at the shop. And you're sure the time's right—you're not about to jet off to New York?"

"Don't worry, it's fine. I suspect there's a really interesting story behind your violin. Perhaps even a mystery we can solve together. Do you remember our treasure hunts in your attic?"

Lilly smiled broadly. "I remember. Except we never really found anything mysterious at all."

"Just a whole load of junk. Perhaps that's what laid the foundation for your love of antiques."

Yes, that was highly likely. Lilly had always been drawn to old things. The attic of her parents' house had been a rich playground for her, one she enjoyed exploring with Ellen all too often. Old trunks and furniture everywhere. Objects that had survived the war, others that had become outmoded, and others still that had simply been forgotten. Ellen had liked to hide behind the trunks, jumping out and scaring her. Lilly, on the other hand, could have sat there for hours, losing herself in the carvings on an old chest, pictures whose meanings had eluded her then. But now she knew the frieze had depicted a dance of death.

"And perhaps it was where you discovered your love of old musical instruments," Lilly said, pushing the memories aside.

Ellen laughed. "Of course! Do you remember that old accordion?"

"Do I? You used to plonk away on it, making a terrible racket."

"Maybe so, but I've been fascinated by instruments ever since, the older the better."

There was a brief pause, as if each of them had to free themselves from the memories to return to the here and now.

"OK, I can count on you, then?" Ellen said finally, and Lilly could almost hear her peering across at her stew. Half an hour had gone by, and Dean was bound to be home from work soon. Not to mention the fact that Lilly's phone company would be rubbing their hands together with glee.

"You certainly can. I'll just figure out what's going to happen with the shop, and I'll let you know."

"Great! Take care of yourself in the meantime, you hear? And don't forget to e-mail me tomorrow."

"Sure. Say hello to Dean and the girls for me."

"I will. Bye."

After hanging up, Lilly sat for a few minutes, embracing the silence. The few moments of that telephone call had opened up a window in her soul. Since childhood, she and Ellen had been friends—no, almost sisters, a relationship those around them had often envied. They stuck together like glue, and if they ever did argue, it wouldn't be long before they made up. When Ellen had met a young Englishman while on vacation in Britain, Lilly had been the first to hear how she had fallen head over heels in love with him. Years later she had stood beside Ellen as her witness in a small church in London. She cried almost more than the bride herself. These wisps of memory always succeeded in conjuring up a little sunlight in Lilly's heart. Not the sun in all its blazing glory, but a few rays of light piercing the clouds left by Peter's death.

Finally she rose and went over to the violin case on the desk. The light softly caressed the leather of the lid. Was it worth anything or not, and what did it matter? Lilly only wanted to know why the old man had been so convinced that she was entitled to this violin—and why he had made such a quick getaway.

She carefully drew out the sheet of music and looked it over. "The Moonlit Garden." It sounded so incredibly romantic! Which garden had the composer intended to immortalize in the music? Who was he? Was the music the key to the origin of the violin? And what did it have to do with her? So many questions . . .

She was determined to find the answers.

3

"Remember to lock up the shop if you take a break and go out. People may not be particularly interested in antiques most of the time, but if they see the opportunity to grab something for free, they'll be happy to take what they can."

"Of course," Sunny said, visibly repressing the urge to roll her eyes. Justifiably so, as she'd proved herself to be completely reliable every time before. Even when she took the opportunity to do some studying at work, she always kept an eye on what was happening in the shop.

"If someone comes in to ask you about selling something, give them our card and put them off till the week after next. I'd like to look at any new pieces myself."

"Sure. After all, you know more about prices than I do," Sunny said without the slightest hint of taking offense.

Lilly nevertheless felt obliged to add, "I do think you're quite capable of estimating the value of an item, but sometimes we get things that we're stuck with for life." She indicated the little cupboard that she had secretly christened "the Unsellable." "See this one here—it's lovely, but for some reason nobody wants it. As if it has bad karma."

"I think it's gorgeous," Sunny blurted out, then pressed her lips together and gave an embarrassed smile.

"If that's the case, I could always give it to you as payment for standing in for me. What do you think?"

Sunny shook her head dismissively. "Nah, Lilly, I'd rather take the five hundred you offered me. You can always give me the cupboard as a wedding present."

"You're not referring to the tattoo artist, are you?" Lilly winked.

"Whoever. I have no intention of marrying for at least ten years, but if the cupboard's still here then . . ."

"If that cupboard's still here in ten years, I'll give it to you for your birthday."

For no reason, Lilly was suddenly painfully aware that she could have had a daughter Sunny's age. Well, not quite. She had met Peter when she was twenty-one, but if fate had been kinder to her, she could have had a teenage daughter by now to help her out in the shop and help her get over her loss. Sometimes she noticed herself feeling almost motherly toward Sunny. She would quickly pull herself together—she liked the girl a lot, but she didn't want to burden her with all her woes, and she probably wouldn't be interested in any case.

You're still young, she told herself. Young enough to find a new man. Young enough to have a child. Over the sound of her own comforting thoughts, Lilly could hear her biological clock ticking, but she still didn't feel ready to get involved with another man.

"Well, in any case, you'll be in charge of the shop, and I'm trusting that when I return I'll find everything—except for the items that have sold—still here and in one piece." Lilly took her wallet from her purse and handed her a hundred-euro note. "Here, a small down payment. I'll give you the rest when I get back."

"Thanks, that's great." Sunny stuffed the note into her jeans pocket. "So, are you all excited?"

Lilly glanced at her baggage, which was waiting for her by the door.

She had intended to travel light but had gathered an increasing number of "essentials," gifts and other small things, until she was now taking a wheeled suitcase and a travel bag stuffed to bursting. And of course the violin case, which had resisted all attempts to stuff it in a suitcase or bag, as if it wanted all passersby to see it in Lilly's possession.

"Very. I haven't seen my friend for quite a while now."

"And you're taking the violin with you?"

"Yes, I want Ellen to cast her expert eye over it."

"So you think it's worth something?"

"No idea, but I'm interested in finding out who might have owned it. Maybe we can figure that much out."

"I'm sure you will. It certainly won't be lying around here for ten years before someone buys it!"

Lilly refrained from telling Sunny that she had no intention of selling the violin. Later, when she was back, she would perhaps tell her the story—if there was one.

Lilly looked around one last time, as if implanting the appearance of her shop in her memory, shouldered her travel bag, clamped the violin case under her arm, and with her free hand grasped the suitcase to drag it behind her.

"Have a good one, Sunny!"

"You too, Lilly!"

The bell rang above her head as she stepped out into the wintry cold.

Lilly found it amazing how fast things happened sometimes. No sooner had the idea of a trip occurred to her than she was off. The day after her phone conversation with Ellen she had rung Sunny's doorbell. The young woman had been delighted at the idea of starting immediately, especially since she needed a refuge away from her roommates where she could get some studying done.

Everything else had fallen into place like clockwork. A call to Ellen, booking the flight, packing her bags. Her inquiry to Ellen about a good hotel had been brushed aside with a heartfelt "Are you crazy? You'll be staying with us, of course!" And now she was on her way to London, her flight due to leave in a few hours.

She felt butterflies of anticipation in her stomach as she trudged toward the suburban railway station. The frost bit her cheeks and, as if the weather were telling her she was doing the right thing, the sun shone brightly in a cloudless morning sky. The heaps of snow that lined the streets and made parking almost impossible shone like innumerable diamonds, and it even seemed as though the faces of passersby didn't look so sullen.

Lilly felt a pang of regret that she didn't travel often enough. She used her shop as an excuse, but deep inside she knew the real reason was Peter. The fear of being alone on a journey, failing to find company, and being plagued by memories and homesickness that threatened to spoil everything was so strong that if she ever felt stirred by wanderlust, she would satisfy herself with a walk in the Botanical Garden.

After three-quarters of an hour Lilly arrived at the Berlin Tegel Airport and checked in immediately. As she did so, her cell phone rang, but it stopped before she had a chance to answer it. Once she had handed over her baggage and was finally able to look, she saw a message from Ellen in her in-box.

Ellen's voice mail instructed Lilly to make her way straight to their house on arrival, since she had prepared something for her.

Lilly smiled to herself as she hung up. Even when she was under stress, Ellen never failed to have everything planned out.

As she boarded the plane, the flight attendant gave her a look of surprise when she caught sight of the violin but said nothing, merely resorting to a polite smile. Lilly couldn't bring herself to hand over the lovely instrument with the rest of her baggage, and fortunately it was small and light enough to be taken on board.

Lilly struggled to heave the case into the overhead bin since she was not quite tall enough.

"Can I help you?" asked a man's voice in English.

Lilly turned her head, and her eyes fell first on a dark gray shirt before moving up to the face of a man of about forty, framed by curly, lightly graying hair. Like a man from a commercial, Lilly thought fleetingly. Although she was confident that she would manage to stow the violin case away somehow, she nodded and replied, also in English, "Thanks, that would be very kind."

The Englishman tucked the violin case safely away and then asked, "Are you a musician?"

Lilly shook her head. "I received the instrument as a gift, and I want to get an expert opinion on it."

"You don't play yourself?"

She shook her head again. "No, I sell antiques."

"What a shame. I'm sure you'd look good onstage."

Was that a compliment? Lilly felt herself blushing.

"I think I'd have to stand on a stool so people could see me," she said in an attempt to hide her embarrassment. It had been so long since a man had said anything nice to her.

The stranger laughed warmly. "And people say the Germans don't have a sense of humor!" He held out his hand to her. "I'm Gabriel Thornton, and I'm looking forward to spending the flight in your company."

"Lilly Kaiser," she replied, still a little embarrassed as she noticed he had a seat in the same row as she did. There was a spare seat between them, but when the man who was supposed to be sitting there arrived, the Englishman worked his charm and persuaded him to swap places. A good exchange, since he was offering him a window seat. A seat he was prepared to give up to talk to her.

Shortly after takeoff, Lilly had already found out that Mr. Thornton was head of a music school in London and also taught musicology. He had been in Berlin to give a series of guest lectures, which had finished the previous day. As he spoke, she caught herself looking at him—his mouth, his nose, his eyes. Trying not to appear obvious, she lowered her gaze, but his hands were also worth looking at. Strong but supple, and above all well cared for. He had the hands of a musician.

"What did you like about Berlin?" Lilly asked, once again feeling butterflies in her stomach, but of a different kind from the ones she'd felt on her way to the railway station. She was still full of anticipation about her visit, but now she had the added pleasure of finding her companion very pleasant company.

"It's a lovely city. And it's good to see it no longer divided by a wall."

"It hasn't been for twenty years," Lilly said with amusement. Could it be that foreigners still expected to find a no-man's-land running through the city?

"Believe it or not, my last visit was in 1987—the Berlin Wall was still standing then."

"So you were a student here?"

Thornton nodded. "Yes, full of hopes and dreams. And full of curiosity about German girls." He winked at her, and she felt her cheeks growing warm. Was she blushing? The man only happened to be sitting in the next seat. Perhaps he was married, with a pretty wife and children. Perhaps she would never see him again after they landed.

"How about you? Were you born in Berlin?" he asked her.

Lilly shook her head. "No, I'm originally from Hamburg. After the reunification of Germany, my husband and I moved to Berlin and opened a shop there."

"Your husband's a lucky man to have such a delightful wife."

Lilly pressed her lips together. It was not her usual way to tell people what had happened, but since this man seemed so friendly, she made an exception.

"He was—perhaps."

A pensive frown appeared between Thornton's eyebrows.

"He died?" he guessed correctly. "I'm sorry."

"It was three years ago," Lilly replied, her head sinking. She didn't tell him that her husband had suffered from a brain tumor.

Thornton pressed his lips together in consternation as Lilly tried to think of something to fill the silence. When the flight attendant came to ask if they would like anything, Lilly ordered a glass of water and Thornton a tomato juice.

"Did you know that tomato juice is the most popular drink on planes?" he asked her, the smile back on his face. "And that even people who don't otherwise drink it will order a tomato juice?"

Lilly couldn't help returning the smile. "Has there been a study about it?"

"No, I read it somewhere. Don't ask me where."

He laughed winningly, finally dispelling the dark cloud that had settled over their heads.

"How about you? I'm sure your wife will be pleased to have you back after such a long trip," Lilly remarked as the flight attendant served their drinks. She stole a quick glance to the side and noticed four other glasses of red juice along their row.

A fleeting, enigmatic smile crossed Thornton's lips. "I'm sure she would—if I had one."

"You're not—" Lilly broke off in embarrassment.

"No. Not anymore. We parted amicably. We still see each other once in a while, but that's all."

Another silence followed, several minutes long, before Thornton resumed. "So you want to have your violin examined?"

"Yes, that's right. I don't think it's particularly valuable, but it's got . . . sentimental value."

"Was it given to you by a relative?"

"No, from a passing acquaintance. A man came into the shop and gave it to me. Just like that. Then he vanished, and I have no idea where to look for him. Now I want to know to what I owe the honor."

"Sounds exciting. Who are you getting to look at it?"

"Ellen Morris. I'm sure you won't have heard of her, but—"

"Oh, I have! She's one of the best restorers. I've never had the pleasure of meeting her myself, but I'm always hearing good things about her."

Ellen would love to hear that, Lilly thought. If he's serious. But she had not detected a trace of irony in his voice.

"How did you find out about her?" he asked. "I mean, there must be plenty of experts in the field in Germany."

"We've been friends since our school days. She's German, but she married an Englishman and, thanks to her name, people always think she's a native."

Thornton raised his eyebrows in surprise. "Is she really? I don't think anyone has any idea. Thanks for the info; perhaps it'll come in handy sometime."

"You think?" Lilly made a face. "I doubt that any of it would move her to accept any less for her services."

"No, but I'd have a readymade topic of conversation if I see her. I can simply ask her how her lovely friend is and let one thing lead to another."

The pilot's announcement that they would shortly be landing at Heathrow brought their conversation to an end. Seat belts were fastened and flight attendants swept once more down the aisle as they readied for landing.

A pity, Lilly thought. I would have enjoyed getting to know this man during a long-haul flight. She was sure they still had so much to say to one another.

But there was no time left for that. They said good-bye after landing and lost sight of one another at baggage claim. Lilly felt a little sad.

4

Lilly took it as a good omen that London was not showing its clichéd face of dull clouds and rain. The sky above the airport was postcard blue, and there were only a few feathery clouds to be seen. It seemed as if she'd brought the good weather with her from Berlin.

Ellen had offered to pick her up from the airport, but Lilly had declined. She knew only too well what a heavy workload her friend had. After briefly wondering whether to rent a car, she decided on a taxi. The driver was in his fifties and, judging by his accent, Scottish. With his slightly baggy tweed jacket, cord pants, and peaked cap, he looked like a typical pub regular from every British TV series.

"Are you a musician?" he asked as they left Heathrow behind them, gesturing with his chin toward the violin case that lay across her lap.

"No, I'm an antiques dealer." Lilly silently asked herself how often she would have to explain.

"So do you play as a hobby?" he persisted. "My son sends his little girl to a music school in Belgravia, thinking that one day she'll be a top violinist." The man sniffed scornfully.

"Doesn't your granddaughter play well?"

"Yes, she does—for a seven-year-old. But I believe that kids should play outside, mixing with others of their own age."

Of course the man had a point, Lilly thought. If the girl were forced to play the violin, she would probably suffer for it and reject the instrument as soon as puberty injected enough rebellion into her. But maybe she enjoyed it. There were many artists who knew from an early age what they wanted to do; those were the ones who didn't care whether or not they were considered normal. Not all children enjoyed romping in the mud or climbing trees after all.

"Perhaps she really might be a star one day," she said eventually. "And if she doesn't enjoy it, she'll stop soon enough, believe me."

As the conversation with the taxi driver petered out, Lilly's thoughts returned to Thornton. It suddenly occurred to her that something about him reminded her of Peter. They were completely different in appearance—Peter had blond hair and blue eyes, while Thornton had graying hair and dark eyes—but in retrospect she discovered a few similarities in the Englishman's mannerisms. The way he spoke, the way he smiled as he looked at her . . .

"My goodness, that's quite a place!" The driver's whistle of amazement tore Lilly from her thoughts. As she looked up, she saw they had arrived at Ellen's house.

"Are you really going there?"

"Yes, that's where my friend lives," Lilly explained, beginning to feel warmth flooding through her. All at once her nostrils were filled with the scent of a Christmas she had once spent here with Ellen and her family. The whole house had smelled of toasted almonds, sugar candy, raisins, and plum pudding.

The taxi stopped in front of the tall wrought-iron gates that must have dated back to Elizabethan times. Lilly paid the driver, who heaved the suitcase and bag from the trunk before roaring off. The taxi's radio had called for his attention with an impatient stream of noise while they were still on the way, so he had no time to stare at the property for any longer than it took to unload the bags.

Lilly was under its spell immediately. She peered through the railings, enchanted but pierced by more than a little stab of envy. Her friend had always been the lucky one. Not only was she pursuing her dream career, but she also had a wonderful husband, two adorable daughters, and this house. Though the word *house* was a bit of a misnomer, as this truly was a mansion.

Frosted with rime, the house bristled with gables, turrets, and chimneys, and the blue winter sky was reflected in the ancient windows.

Ellen and her husband, Dean, had bought the house around ten years ago from an English businessman with noble roots. It had been rather neglected at the time, as the businessman had cared little for it and was happy to be rid of the "pile."

In just six months Dean, who owned a large building firm in London, had transformed the eyesore into a real gem, which, despite all the modernization, still transported visitors back to Tudor times.

Lilly regretted not having come here more often since Peter's death. Dean and Peter had gotten along really well. Perhaps she had been afraid that Dean, and even Ellen, would drown her in excessive pity. But those times were past, and Lilly now felt that this visit would change something within her. She pressed the button on the intercom.

Her ringing triggered a deep, threatening-sounding bark, and two Rottweilers came running. The massive animals hurtled down the narrow gravel path, jostling for position and baring their dangerous-looking teeth. But as soon as they recognized Lilly, they jumped up against the gate and panted hot breath over her. This made them look no less threatening, but Lilly, despite taking a cautious step back from the gate, knew that they would only actually bite if commanded to do so. Probably.

"Yes, hello?" A child's voice could be heard over a loud crackling. Lilly recognized the voice immediately, although it was a little more mature than it had been on her last visit.

"Norma? It's me, Aunt Lilly."

"Hi!" the voice said in delight. "Wait, I'll open up."

Lilly heard the gate spring from its catch, and she gave the dogs a skeptical look. What were they called again? Skippy and Dotty?

Lilly decided not to speak to them as she carefully pushed the gate open.

Then she heard a shrill whistle. "Hey, you two, leave the lady in peace!"

Rufus, the gardener, was waving at her. Lilly gave a sigh of relief. The dogs always listened to him. After glancing once more in her direction, they charged over to him in giant bounds.

As she came nearer, she saw that he had gathered a few branches together for the shredder.

"Hello, Mr. Devon!" Lilly greeted the gardener, who drew a small ball from his bag and flung it, leading the dogs away from them in a rush.

"Hello, Mrs. Kaiser," he replied, hurriedly wiping his hand on his pants before holding it out to Lilly. "Mrs. Morris told me you were coming. I'd hoped to have everything ready before you arrived, but these two rascals keep holding me back."

Rufus Devon was a joker—and crazy about dogs. Somehow he managed to win over any dog, from the most timid to the most boisterous. He was from a family of dog breeders, and the animals were in his blood.

"I don't think even David Copperfield could conjure violets from the snow," Lilly said. "The fact that you're here and looking after the garden this early in the year is plenty good enough—the growing season won't really begin for a few months yet."

"True, but I want to have everything ready by the time it does. I want this park to look good again."

"It will, I'm sure."

Lilly took her leave of Mr. Devon and turned toward the house. She breathed in deeply, savoring the air that was so different from that of Berlin. It smelled of wood shavings and humus, of rotting leaves and old snow. Pine needles, old beams, reeds, and pond water.

The shredder started up again behind Lilly with a noise that sent goose bumps down her spine. It was time to go inside. Fond though she may have been of Rufus Devon, she was almost allergic to noise. As she reached the steps leading up to the front door, she was relieved to know that it would soon be a little quieter.

Once again she felt something like envy as she looked up at the two turrets adorning the front of the house. She wondered if Queen Elizabeth I had ever used it as a hunting lodge. The distant past was still tangible.

Lilly had little time to think about it since she had hardly begun to climb the steps when the front door flew open. Ellen's daughters rushed out toward her as if she were Father Christmas.

"Aunt Lilly!" they called as if from one mouth, embracing her so forcefully that she had to take care not to fall back down the steps. The girls had grown since she last saw them, but she held back from saying it out loud, remembering how she'd hated such remarks from her own aunts.

"It's so lovely to see you!" she said in English, although she knew that Ellen had made sure they both spoke good German.

"It's lovely to see you too, Aunty," Jessie replied politely in German, causing Lilly to smile. "Mum said we should show you to your room as soon as you arrived."

"Yes, you need to have a little rest before anything else," Norma added.

"But I've been sitting down all this time—I didn't swim the Channel, you know."

The two girls giggled at her joke, then turned and ran on ahead.

As she followed Jessie and Norma through the house, Lilly noticed one or two pieces of furniture that had not been there on her last visit. The sugary candy smell of that distant Christmas had gone, replaced by a smell like glue that filled the hallway. One of the girls had probably been sitting down to a project for her homework.

The way the two girls ran down the corridor to her bedroom reminded Lilly of herself and Ellen when they were younger. They, too, ran with echoing footsteps through the halls of her parents' house—the young girls not quite sisters, but something close to it. Ellen, with her long legs, had always been a little ahead, with Lilly sprinting to keep up.

"Mum said that we shouldn't bombard you with questions," said Jessie, the oldest. Although only eleven, she was almost as tall as Lilly.

"Well, isn't that a strange rule?" Lilly replied. "That's why I'm here, to be bombarded with questions. But I'm afraid I won't be able to help you if you want to know about the latest bands in Berlin."

"Mummy said you have a violin," said Norma, who was not at all interested in bands and clothes. "Is that it there? Can I see it?"

"Of course, I'll show it to you later. Let me unpack first."

The girls stopped in front of a carved door, one of the few that had been preserved in their original condition. Lilly's heart thumped for joy. It was the room where she always stayed when she was here. It reminded her so strongly of her grandmother's house that she had a strange feeling of returning to one of her childhood haunts. The high bed, the rough beams, the old furniture.

The two girls opened the door, and Lilly saw that hardly anything had changed. The big, heavy bed that she remembered had not changed, and the antique wardrobe that had come from Dean's deceased parents' bedroom was still there. The room was watched over by an old stag's head, "Henry" as Lilly mockingly called him after a children's book she had bought in East Berlin a few years before the wall came down. Standing before this stuffed monstrosity for the first time, she had thought it creepy, but now the sight of it hardly fazed her. It was merely a part of this room, like the wainscoting or the red silk wallpaper that had been restored by a specialist from Oxford.

What was new was the long box that lay on the bed.

"That's a present from Mummy!" Jessie said with as much pride as if she had chosen it herself. "She brought it yesterday and told us not to look inside."

"Can we look now?" Norma asked immediately.

"Yes, you can. But first let me put my things down."

The girls stood expectantly by the bed, watching with curiosity as Lilly set her suitcase down in front of the wardrobe. Lilly had to smile. She could hardly believe that they were both obeying their mother's instructions. She, and Ellen, too, would most likely have taken a peek as soon as their mothers' backs were turned. Or were the two only bluffing now?

Whatever the truth, Lilly turned her attention to the box and opened it carefully. Nestled in lime-green tissue paper patterned with leaves was a bottle-green dress—the very color that went best with the red of her hair. It took her breath away.

"Oh, doesn't it look pretty?" Norma said in amazement.

"Please can I try it on?" Jessie asked.

At first Lilly didn't know what to say. She usually dressed rather simply; she didn't need more than jeans and a blouse, or a black turtleneck sweater in winter, and maybe the occasional pantsuit for when she visited trade fairs. She felt best in jeans and T-shirts.

Shining in the afternoon light, the dress was better than anything she had in her wardrobe. She would feel hopelessly overdressed in an ordinary pub or on the street.

"Don't you like it?" Jessie asked as if she wanted to make off with the dress herself.

"Yes, it's . . ." Ridiculously expensive, she thought, but quickly added: "It's wonderful!"

She carefully ran a hand over the fabric. It felt every bit as soft as it looked. She could comfortably have been seen in Buckingham Palace in it, or at Ascot. Ellen was probably planning to take her to such places. All right, perhaps not to the palace, and it was a bit early in the year for the races, but who knew what she was planning?

"When I'm grown up, I want one of those!" Norma said, clapping her hands. "Or will you lend me yours, Aunt Lilly?"

"By the time you're old enough to wear something like this, I'm sure fashion will have moved on." Lilly gazed at it once more before replacing the lid on the box.

The two girls looked at one another, and then Jessie asked, "Should we bring you something to drink, Aunt Lilly?"

The perfect hostess.

"Thank you, that's very kind, but first I've got something for you two."

She went to her suitcase and got out their gifts. She had found some hand-printed T-shirts and bags in a lovely little shop. The sales assistant had assured her that this kind of thing was popular with young people at the moment.

"What's in there?" Norma asked, feeling the parcel.

"Berlin air," Lilly laughed. "You'd better open it and see—and try it on, of course."

Her suggestion obviously appealed to the girls, since they disappeared into their bedroom with the booty. Lilly was once again reminded of herself and Ellen. They had always opened the Christmas gifts from Ellen's foster mother together. That was probably what the children were doing now. Unusual children, Lilly thought as she moved the box to one side and put the violin case on the bedcover—a handmade quilt with dark red roses. Polite, unlike so many in Berlin.

As she laid out her things on the shelves of the wardrobe, Lilly wondered what Peter would have said about the dress. He never liked to see Ellen giving her expensive gifts, but Ellen had managed to convince him that she expected nothing in return.

"Lilly and I have known one another much longer than you two," she had always said.

Peter had been won over in the end by her charm. And he would certainly have liked the dress, even though she still had no idea when she would wear it.

The humming of an engine and crunching of gravel beneath approaching wheels pulled Lilly from her thoughts. That must be Ellen! She went over to the window and pushed the heavy curtain to one side to confirm her suspicions.

With a smile, Lilly watched Ellen get out of the car, hurry around to the trunk, and pull out two packed shopping bags. With her arms full, she climbed the steps and disappeared into the house. Jessie and Norma were bound to tell their mother immediately that she had arrived.

Lilly moved away from the window and left her room, carrying the gift she had brought for Ellen. Out on the landing she heard Ellen puttering in the kitchen. She had clearly returned so early because, as always when Lilly came to visit, she wanted to cook for her.

"Hi, Ellen."

Her friend started and almost dropped the package of meat she was stowing away in the fridge.

"Lilly, you're awake? I thought you'd want to lie down for a while after the flight."

"Why should I need to? I haven't flown in from Singapore. And I'm far too wound up to sleep—I wanted a word with you . . ." She looked at Ellen reproachfully but couldn't hold the expression for long before breaking into a broad smile and giving her friend a hug.

"Ah, you found it," Ellen said, holding Lilly tight. "Go on, you can say it—you don't like it."

"Of course I like it! But it must have been ludicrously expensive. And when do you think I'm going to wear it?"

Ellen released her, a broad grin on her face. "Come on, do you think I'd miss an opportunity to take my friend, whom I only see once or twice a year these days, to the Ritz? Or we could go to one of those outrageously expensive shops that have opened recently. There are some really stylish restaurants around here where you've a good chance of bumping into a celebrity or two."

Was that what she wanted? At that moment, strange though it might seem, the only person Lilly wanted to see was the man from the airplane, whether in a pub or a chic restaurant.

"Well, the gift I've brought for you looks a bit shabby in comparison." Lilly handed her the box she had wrapped in paper decorated with real pressed flowers she had collected years ago during a trip into the mountains.

Ellen shook her head as she took the box over to the table. "Nothing's shabby to me—you know that. What have you brought me, then?" The tone of Ellen's voice sounded like the fourteen-year-old she had been once.

Lilly had spent a long time wondering what her friend would like. Bringing something from her own shop seemed cheap, so she had gone to the competition and bought a silver candelabrum that would look good on the long table in the dining room. Now she was a little doubtful whether Ellen would like it, but when she opened the parcel, a genuine smile sprang to her lips.

"It's wonderful. Is it from your shop?"

"No, from a competitor downtown. It's a wonderful shop. I'm amazed I still have any customers."

Faint worry lines appeared on Ellen's brow. "Isn't your shop doing well?"

Lilly waved away her concerns. "Just a temporary lull. It's usually like that after Christmas. Things will pick up when the tourists arrive.

I've wondered about ordering heaps of cuckoo clocks—the Japanese are particularly keen on those."

"Naturally; they're typical of Berlin." Ellen laughed, then wrapped her arms around her friend. "I've missed you so much. Next time you're not going to leave it as long as six months, OK?"

"I'll see what happens. If the shop gets busy, I can hardly leave Sunny there alone."

"Is she still helping you?"

"Yes, she's back. It's a pity she's got other ambitions. She seems born to be an antiques dealer."

Ellen knew Sunny from her last visit to Lilly. It had been summer then, and so many customers had been pouring through the door that Lilly would never have coped alone. She would have been in a real fix without Sunny. And thanks to her, she had even been able to enjoy Ellen's surprise visit a little.

"Then try and convince her. I'm sure the prospects for arts students don't look any better over there than they do here. At least she'd have a job."

Lilly nodded. "I'll see. If business picks up, I certainly want to employ an assistant so that I can visit you."

"And don't forget seeing the big wide world."

Lilly lowered her head sadly. "Yes, the big wide world . . . If only Peter were still alive." She stopped short, thinking it was the last thing her friend wanted to hear. But Ellen laid an arm around her shoulders in sympathy.

"Let's go for a little walk before the sun disappears completely."

5

The crunching of the gravel under their boots sounded loud in the winter stillness. Rufus Devon had finished his work with the shredder and there was now no sign of him or the dogs. As the sky turned a deeper shade of violet and the air grew colder, all that could be heard was a light rustling of the bare branches and the distant cawing of crows on the breeze.

Neither of them had spoken a word since leaving the kitchen.

Peter's death had also shaken Ellen deeply, as if she had lost a brother. Whenever he was mentioned, they fell into a silence that could last awhile, as if any mention of him conjured up images in their heads that they needed a moment's peace to contemplate.

Lilly almost regretted saying his name out loud. Yes, of course she missed him, with particular melancholy whenever the conversation turned to traveling. But the time was long since past when she felt unable to talk about it.

As her friend continued to say nothing, seeming to need the time to reflect, Lilly also stayed silent, regarding her instead.

Ellen didn't look her age, and she exuded from her very pores the self-confidence that Lilly so envied. Lilly was often struck by the idea that fate seemed compelled to compensate her friend for all she had suffered when she was young.

When Ellen, whose name had then been Ellen Pauly, was a year old, her mother and brother had been killed in a car accident. She had never known her father, because her mother had never revealed his name, even to her own parents, and the secret had gone with her to the grave. The man himself probably didn't even know he had a daughter.

Ellen had initially been brought up by her grandparents, but they had soon become too old and infirm to take proper care of their grand-daughter. The fact that Ellen had been fostered had proved a stroke of good fortune, both for her and for Lilly. The two girls met at school in third grade. Whenever Ellen spoke of her foster mother, she called her Mama, although she knew she had had another mother. But Miriam Pauly and Ellen's brother, Martin, were no more than a faded photo to her and, as was her way, she gave her unreserved affection to those who were there for her and who had given her a feeling of security.

That was probably the reason their friendship was so unshakeable. Although it now felt as if Lilly was the one who was more in need, that had not always been the case. Lilly had once been the one who helped Ellen in difficult times and protected her from troublemakers. She and Ellen had a deep conviction that they were soul mates, a feeling that Lilly felt in full when she stepped out from the house onto the gravel path by her friend's side.

"A penny for your thoughts," Ellen said as she noticed Lilly watching her.

"I'm thinking how lucky you are in your life. You've got Dean, the girls . . . the house . . ."

Ellen put her arm around her. "And you'll soon have similar luck, I promise. One day your prince will come, whisk you away from your beloved shop, and take you off to travel the world."

"Yes, perhaps," Lilly replied with a trace of bitterness.

"Perhaps? You have to believe it will happen!" Ellen hugged her tightly. "How can you expect it to happen if you keep doubting?"

"I'm only human. I'd just like to be able to see the solution, to know where I'm heading."

"But there are times when you simply can't know. You can take an unexpected turn in the road and find something wonderful waiting around the corner for you."

Or something awful, Lilly thought. That was how it had been with Peter. When he had encountered difficulties, he would keep them from her. Until the diagnosis, which had struck Lilly like a bolt out of the blue.

"Everyone has their own cross to bear," Ellen added after a brief pause. "Of course some people's load is a little harder to bear than others', but we all have our problems. You should hear the way I curse the company sometimes! And sometimes even Dean when he's up to something. The important thing is that, whatever rubbish the world throws at you, you don't lose heart, and you make sure you always find a way to rid yourself of the bad stuff."

"I wish I could," Lilly said dejectedly. "It's been a while now, but I still find myself waiting for Peter in the evenings, wishing I could talk to him."

"That's only natural. And I'd be heartless if I advised you not to. But maybe you really should get out more, meet new people. The fact that you're here with me now is a step in the right direction, but there must be some great places to go in Berlin."

"Of course, but . . ." Lilly pressed her lips together. Ellen was right, but whenever she was out and about, she found it difficult to enjoy herself. It hadn't always been like that.

"But what?" Ellen insisted.

"But everything feels wrong without him. If I walk in the park, I seem to see happy couples everywhere, and it tears me apart to see them kissing in each other's arms. I see families and think, that could have been us."

Ellen thought for a moment in silence. Lilly was aware of a raven's croak and the beating of its wings as it flew overhead.

"I don't want to sound harsh, but what has happened is something you can't change or ever get back," her friend finally ventured. "Peter would have wanted you to carry on, to live your life. He would have wanted you to see the world, for as long as you're able. He wouldn't have wanted you to get bogged down in memories."

"But how can I free myself from them? How can I get him out of my head?"

"You can't and you shouldn't. But perhaps there's a way of . . . of getting your life back."

Getting her life back? At first Lilly wanted to protest, but she soon saw that Ellen had a point. She breathed, she saw the world around her, she existed. But with Peter she had felt completely different—more full of life.

They walked on through the garden for a while in silence, circled the small well that was surrounded by a cast-iron fence and covered with boards, and passed two elegantly painted benches that waited for the snow to melt so the house's occupants could once again sit and enjoy the sunshine.

"Have you really not found a man you could be interested in?" Ellen said, restarting the conversation.

Lilly shook her head. "No, no one. I only seem to meet old men who give me some mysterious gift before disappearing without a trace."

"Well, that's something I've never experienced. I'm really looking forward to seeing your treasure. I've told Terence to rearrange an appointment I had tomorrow morning to give me time for you."

"Terence?"

"My secretary."

"What are you going to do?"

"My usual procedure. I'll examine it closely and then send a few samples of the varnish to our laboratory. We'll see what happens then."

"And if it's only fit for the flea market?"

"Then we'll have an amusing story to tell. Anyway, we ought to be getting back now so I can start on dinner."

Ellen linked her arm through Lilly's and led her back to the house.

***

An hour later, the meal was ready. Ellen had succeeded without major mishap in conjuring up something involving meat, herbs, tomatoes, potatoes, and white wine, to be followed by a rice pudding flavored with vanilla, cinnamon, and muscatel.

Sitting on the broad window seat in the kitchen, Lilly felt comfortingly enfolded by the warmth and the wine that she had drunk with Ellen as she cooked. The effects of the wine came on quickly, making her head feel light and pinning her body to the seat. I could stay here, she thought.

From the kitchen window she had watched the light disappear behind the bare trees, the violet sky turning deep blue and revealing thousands of frosty stars. Back home the nights never looked like this; in Berlin there was light, light everywhere, light that swallowed the stars and gave the sky an orange glow, even when the skies were at their clearest. Lilly wondered if she had noticed on previous visits how beautiful it was outdoors in this place.

A pair of headlights sliced through the darkness as they approached the house.

"Dean's on his way," Lilly announced and set her glass down on the table.

Ellen untied her apron. She threw Lilly a hesitant glance as if to make sure it would be all right for her to give her husband her usual cheerful greeting. Lilly smiled at her, the same conspiratorial smile they used to share in school when they had covered up for each other's silly mistakes.

As Dean came through the door, he greeted Ellen as warmly as he always did and gave her a kiss before turning to Lilly with a broad grin.

"It's so lovely to see you. I was beginning to forget what you look like."

"Oh, it's not been that long, surely," Lilly countered, accepting his brief hug.

"Well, it's been long enough. If I were an elderly aunt of yours, I'd be remarking how much you've grown."

"Then it's a good thing you're not my aunt or I'd have rolled my eyes in irritation."

Dean led her into the living room, where they chatted about this and that, especially his construction business, until they were called in for dinner. The table was laid with stylish simplicity, Lilly's candelabrum taking pride of place alongside an arrangement of artificial flowers that looked deceptively real.

"Now, tell us all about your violin," Ellen said after they had cleared away the main course and were starting on the pudding.

Lilly cleared her throat, put her spoon to one side, and considered how to make the story as exciting as possible for Dean and the girls. She quickly realized that the very fact of a total stranger placing a violin in her hand before disappearing without a trace was actually exciting enough in itself. She began with the afternoon when she had been about to close up shop and finished with the moment when she realized that the old man seemed to have vanished into thin air.

"It sounds as though someone mistook you for a spy," said Dean, who was known to have a weakness for stories of Her Majesty's Secret Service. "You have checked that there are no plutonium rods hidden away in the lining? Or any secret messages?"

Lilly grinned. "You think the sheet music is some kind of code?"

"Why not?" Dean replied, as if it were the most normal thing in the world.

"My husband's obviously wanting to start a new career as a crime writer," Ellen said, laughing.

"Is it such an absurd idea? There have always been secret messages smuggled into the possession of people who know nothing about them so they can unwittingly get them to the right place."

"But then the man would have had to tell me where to take the violin," Lilly replied.

"Perhaps to Sherlock Holmes!" Jessie chipped in. "I've read about him."

"You've read Conan Doyle?" Lilly asked, a little surprised.

"At school," Jessie said. "A story in which Sherlock Holmes played the violin."

"I don't think I've been drawn into any conspiracy with this violin. It's more likely to have been a mistake. If the old man realizes it and comes back, I'd definitely give it back to him."

"Maybe there's a dark secret in your family," Dean said, clearly unwilling to be diverted from the idea of secret agents. "Perhaps you had a musician among you?"

Lilly shook her head. "No, not that I know of. The only musical person I know is your wife. My parents and grandparents had no musical appreciation, and that's a good thing, too, or I'd have been a huge disappointment to them."

"And yet a stranger believed the violin belonged to you. Weird."

Dean took a drink of wine and pensively studied the liquid clinging to the sides of the glass.

"Oh, just leave Lilly in peace," Ellen said finally. "After all, that's why she's here, to find out about the instrument. Now, Jessie and Norma, you haven't told me anything about school yet. I didn't know you'd been reading Conan Doyle."

As the two girls began on a report of their day at school, Lilly leaned back, completely at ease and enjoying being part of the family. The girls were both wearing the T-shirts Lilly had given them, and she was pleased they fit so well.

"We're going to take the bags with us to school tomorrow!" they said in chorus, as their account brought them to the time of Lilly's arrival.

After the meal, when the girls had gone to watch TV, Ellen asked Lilly to fetch the violin so she could take a look. Dean asked if he could be there, which Ellen found a little strange, remarking that he was usually only interested in somewhat larger timber structures.

Lilly carried the violin case in front of her as if it contained a valuable relic. She had tucked the page of music back under the lining. She wanted Ellen to have the same experience she had had when opening up the violin case.

In the living room Lilly laid the case on the side table next to the chesterfield. Ellen had put on a pair of white cotton gloves that looked like something a butler would wear.

She lifted the lid carefully and stepped to one side. The light from the central fixture above them gave the red-hued varnish a deep glow so that it almost seemed to pulsate. For the first time Lilly noticed that the strings looked a little worn, and the violin seemed to be showing its age a little more. Lilly was not only interested in the age and value of the instrument but also wanted to discover why the old man believed it should be hers.

When Ellen saw the violin, she sucked air through her teeth in anticipation. "At first glance it looks perfectly normal, apart from the unusual varnish. May I?"

Lilly nodded, and her friend gently lifted the violin from the case. "A beautiful, delicate sound box," she stated as she turned it in her hands. "And there it is."

Ellen lightly ran a hand over the spot where the rose lay beneath the varnish.

"Completely undamaged apart from the usual signs of use. The rose must have been applied to the wood before it was varnished." She plucked the strings. "Totally out of tune," she remarked, and slowly began to tighten the strings. "But the pegs are in incredibly good condition."

Once she was satisfied with the sound of the strings, she removed her gloves and picked up the bow, tightened the horsehair fibers, and applied some rosin before setting the instrument under her chin.

"Could you play from the sheet music perhaps?" Lilly asked.

Lilly drew the page from beneath the lining, and Ellen put the violin down again.

"'The Moonlit Garden,'" she murmured. "No composer's name. Perhaps your old man wrote it."

Lilly shook her head. "I don't think so. The paper appears to be quite a bit older than that, and look at the writing. I sometimes get books with handwritten inscriptions or dedications. Just look at the ink! Black, but browning at the edges. If you ask me, this music is at least a hundred years old."

Ellen stuck out her lower lip, frowning. It was a clear sign that she was trying to absorb the melody. Lilly watched her for a moment in anticipation as Dean refilled their wineglasses. After a few minutes Ellen lowered the page of music.

"So?" Lilly asked. "Does it make any sense to you?"

"Yes, it does, but it's very unusual . . ." Ellen turned the page over, but apart from a few spots of mildew there was nothing on it. "You may be right about the paper, but if a composer of the late nineteenth or early twentieth century wrote this, they must have been very progressive."

"Then I'd suggest you play it for us, love," Dean said. "Who knows, perhaps we'll be the first in a hundred years to hear this piece."

Ellen had at first seemed determined to try out the violin, but now she hesitated.

"Please, Ellen," Lilly said. "I've been wondering ever since I got it what it would sound like."

Ellen picked the violin back up and drew the bow across the strings. She played the first note, and a strange feeling ran through Lilly. The piece sounded very exotic, but at the same time strangely familiar. It was not as if she had heard it before, but the sequence of notes somehow gave her a warm, safe feeling.

Perhaps the title had something to do with it. She suddenly had a mental image of her first date with Peter. It had been a spring evening, and they had sat, hugging each other close, beneath a magnolia tree with a pale moon shining down on them. The fleeting impression vanished as quickly as it had come.

Lilly listened, enraptured, to the end of the piece.

Ellen lowered the violin reverentially. "Wow!" she said, staring at the instrument in wonder, as if the melody had magically played itself. "I haven't heard a sound like that for a long time."

"So it's not a bad instrument, then?" Lilly was still moved by her friend's performance.

"No, it's not bad at all. The person who made it must have been a master craftsman. Just like the person who wrote that piece."

"It reminds me a bit of a Pacific island," Dean said. "But as you know, I'm totally uncultured."

"No you're not," Lilly said. "I thought it sounded exotic, too. Like . . . like a night beneath a blossoming magnolia tree."

Ellen smiled again. "Listen to your vivid imaginations. But perhaps the composer really did want to evoke the feel of a garden. You know Vivaldi's *Four Seasons*? The *Spring* Concerto—it's almost like you can hear the birds and the storm."

"My favorite of *The Four Seasons* is *Winter*, but I know what you mean," Lilly said.

"I'm dying to know more about it—for two reasons. Firstly, to find out about the composer, and secondly, to discover who made this beauty." Again Ellen turned the violin over and studied the rose beneath the gleaming varnish.

Lilly looked across at Dean, who was sitting on the sofa gazing at his wife in fascination, as if her musical side were completely new to him.

"He was probably a total unknown," Lilly said, a little disappointed.

"There are many excellent violin makers who have been forgotten with the passage of time. Let's have a look whether its creator has left a mark inside."

Ellen took a small flashlight from a drawer and shone it through the f-holes. It was not long before she clicked her tongue in disapproval.

"No label and no mark. The guy can't have been proud of the instrument."

Lilly knew that by *label* Ellen meant the manufacturer's mark on an instrument, in the form of a strip of paper inserted into the finished violin with pincers and glued in place.

Ellen looked at the violin once more, then carefully laid it back down in the case.

"Ah well. It could be difficult but isn't a hopeless task, I'd say. Come with me tomorrow, and we can take it further. The lady may be keeping herself aloof, but I'm sure we'll succeed in unlocking her secret."

***

That night Lilly was unable to sleep on her soft mattress and lavender-scented linens. With the moon's pale light streaming in through the window, she stared at the ceiling and felt she could still hear the tune of "The Moonlit Garden."

What was all this with the violin about? According to Ellen, it was a good instrument, but why should she have any claim to it?

Lilly thought long and hard, trawling her memory for stories from her mother and Grandma Paulsen, but she could think of no indication that anything strange had happened. Her grandparents were solid, respectable people, good citizens of Hamburg. There had been a wealth of mementoes in their attic, but with an adult's hindsight she could see there was nothing mysterious about them.

Her grandparents had both been dead for a few years now, her grandfather passing away a little before her grandmother. The keepsakes in the attic had been sold along with the house. Had the violin been one of them? She had never heard any mention of either of her grandparents playing a musical instrument. And even if the violin had been found hidden away somewhere in the house, why would the purchaser have had any reason to give it to Lilly? He could just as easily have sold it.

Lilly frowned, her thoughts once again roaming through the attic. Was there a family secret unknown even to her parents? Valuable artifacts weren't kept in an attic—they were perhaps hidden in a safe place, but one the owners knew about. At least that was what Lilly had always done if she had something she didn't want anyone to find.

Perhaps she should call her mother.

Then it hit her. The video surveillance camera! Three years ago, at the request of her insurer, she'd had one installed in her shop. The old man must have been recorded by it. Why hadn't she thought of it before?

Lilly immediately sat up in bed. Sunny! Perhaps she could ask her to upload the camera footage onto her computer and send it over to them.

She instinctively reached for her cell phone, which was on the bedside table, but remembered that Sunny would probably be in bed. She would have to wait until the morning and call her at the shop.

With a sigh she lowered her head back onto the pillow. She felt even more on edge now. If the old man had been caught on video, it might be possible to trace him and ask him about it all. Lilly still had no idea how she was going to pull it off, but she was sure she would find a solution somehow.

At last she grew sleepy, and as she fell into her dream world, she thought she could detect the closing strains of "The Moonlit Garden."

6

Padang, 1902

"A wonderful view, don't you think?"

Paul Havenden, young lord and, since the recent death of his father, head of an extensive, extremely prominent family of English aristocrats, breathed a deep lungful of the warm air laced with the rich scents of the harbor.

The view of the sea was magnificent.

The water was a magical mirror lying beneath a cloudless sky. A few palms swayed in the warm, moist onshore breeze that whispered through the city. The buildings around the harbor were predominantly colonial in style, with a clear Dutch influence. He had seen plenty of houses like these, with their broad columns and sweeping roofs, in Amsterdam, but here they were interspersed with the exotic vernacular buildings that gave the city its special charm.

Since their arrival here his troubles had eased considerably. Almost by the hour he could feel his body recovering its strength, his skin shedding all the problems that had plagued him in the cold English climate. How he had longed for this warmth, especially during the last few months.

Yet Maggie, Paul's new bride, seemed to see things differently. Stretched out on a chaise longue, she stirred the air with a Chinese fan, since the one on the ceiling failed dismally to mitigate the heat. A monsoon seemed to be announcing its imminent arrival. The air was incredibly humid—exactly the right weather for someone suffering from skin problems, but hell on earth for his wife, who felt at her best in cool London parlors and refused to go without a corset beneath her clothing even in the tropics.

"I could tell from the ship that it's really beautiful here," Maggie replied with a forced little smile. "But I'd prefer it if we were still in the cabin on board. This heat is unbearable. I'd have to abandon all sense of propriety to make it more bearable."

Paul laughed. "Oh, darling, you'll soon get used to the climate here. After a couple of weeks you'll not want to leave, I assure you. How can gray England compare to this sparkling jewel? Have you seen the colorful garb of the people around the harbor? The merchants? A rainbow of color as far as the eye can see! An oriental bazaar couldn't be more magnificent."

Maggie smiled affectionately at him, but Paul knew she was anything other than delighted that he had accepted the invitation of the governor here. The ball season was just beginning in London, and she must feel completely cut off from the society in which she shone.

But Paul had been unable to turn down Governor van Swieten, not only because he was a friend of his father's but also because he had offered him the prospect of some extremely lucrative business. Sumatra was famous for its sugar and tobacco plantations, over which the Dutch still had a monopoly. Van Swieten's offer of a share in a thriving sugar plantation whose owner had a tendency to let money slip through his fingers sounded extremely attractive.

Of course he had told Maggie nothing about the proposal, since it annoyed her when he burdened her with a journey she did not want to make, for the sake of business. Granted, he could have left her behind in England, but van Swieten had insisted on meeting the new Lady Havenden.

She had appreciated this, and in order to persuade her to agree to the possibility of a longer stay, he had told her that he was seeking inspiration for a book, a travelogue, that he wanted to write. This had delighted Maggie, as there was hardly anything London society valued more than stories from distant lands.

But the prospect of having to wait long hours in the hotel for Paul, of having no entertainment to look forward to, no tea with society ladies, had caused Maggie's spirits to flag since their arrival. Suddenly the heat, which had been manageable on board the ship, became unbearable, and she lost all interest in this place that had such wonderful sights to offer.

"At least gray England is a place of culture," Maggie replied. "And it's a place where there are things to do. You could at least find me a guidebook to read so I could discover whether there's anything worth visiting here."

"I'll get one for you as soon as I can," Paul said kindly. "And I promise that, until the governor gets in touch, I'll take you anywhere you want. How about a trip inland to the jungle?"

"Jungle?" Maggie's eyes widened with indignation. "You must be joking. You're pulling my leg."

"Not at all. I'm sure there are ways of seeing the jungle in safety and comfort. Perhaps an elephant ride, like in India?"

"You know I'm afraid of such heights!"

"Then we can sit you on a buffalo," Paul said, laughing.

The thought of Maggie allowing herself to be placed on a water buffalo was hilarious to Paul, but his wife was not amused by his attempt at humor.

"Paul Havenden!" she scolded. "I don't know what I've done to deserve being the butt of such a ridiculous joke."

"I'm sorry, darling—I didn't mean to offend you. But perhaps you really should think about seeing the jungle. You'll certainly have an adventure to report back to your ladies."

A bell rang, interrupting their conversation.

"That will be the governor's lad," Paul said as he hurried to the door.

He saw a dark-skinned boy in white baggy pants and a short, dark red jacket standing there. As soon as the boy set eyes on Paul, he took his hands and touched them to his forehead. Paul knew this was a gesture of courtesy used by children to show their respect toward adults.

"What brings you here?" Paul asked in Dutch, the language of his mother, who was the daughter of a wealthy Dutch merchant. She had gone to considerable pains to ensure that he was equally fluent in both languages, which she insisted were the languages of world trade.

He could tell from the boy's expression that he had understood him.

"Mijnheer van Swieten has sent me to give you this," the boy said, using the Dutch word for *Mister*. He held out a thick envelope marked with a few stains here and there. Clearly the messenger had made a small detour via a market on the way.

Paul slipped a few coins to the lad, who bowed and swiftly vanished.

"What was that about?" asked Maggie, who was now sitting upright on the chaise longue.

"The governor has sent us a message," Paul replied after closing the door. With the knife he always carried in his boot when traveling, he carefully slit the envelope open. Polite as ever, van Swieten had written the text in English.

"We've been sent an invitation. Mijnheer van Swieten is asking us to attend a formal dinner at his residence, Welkom, this weekend."

"He calls his house Welcome?" Maggie asked, amazed.

"Yes, the Dutch are very hospitable; he must want to emphasize that."

Maggie became visibly more animated. The prospect of spending an evening with cultured people made her eyes shine. "Who do you think will be there? Any notables from the local area?"

Paul could see Maggie's mind working. She was probably wondering how to find a good dressmaker here to sew her a dress in five days that would cause the other women to go pale with envy.

"It'll probably be friends of the governor's—and of course a couple of sugar and tobacco plantation owners."

"English?"

"Certainly. Dutch and German, too. And they'll all have their wives with them, so you've no need to fear being bored."

"Indeed I won't," Maggie protested, rising from her seat. "I simply fail to find the idea of spending weeks among monkeys and palm trees particularly appealing."

"But you haven't seen anything of those monkeys and palm trees yet." Paul suddenly had a brilliant idea. "How about a little stroll around town? I'm sure there will be plenty of shops here to take your fancy. You must want to look for some new jewelry, or even a new dress, for a reception at the governor's."

The light now shining in his better half's eyes told him he'd hit the mark.

"Oh yes, a new dress would be wonderful. And I've heard that Sumatra is supposed to be the island of gold. Perhaps I'll find some really gorgeous jewelry here."

"All right, go and freshen up. We'll head into the city and find you the perfect dress for the reception."

Maggie disappeared into the bathroom, and Paul returned to the window to observe the comings and goings on the street below. His attention was drawn by a group of women clothed in gleaming white. Among all the bright colors they looked like daisies in a bed of roses, but that was what made them so attractive. As was usual in Muslim countries, their hair was bound beneath long head scarves, but their faces were beautifully radiant.

His father had always enthused about the Balinese dancers he had seen during visits to van Swieten's house. Did the governor plan to put on a similar entertainment for them? With an indefinable yearning in his breast he gazed after the women until Maggie emerged from the bathroom.

The promise of the imminent company of other foreigners made her a little more gracious. Neither the traders at the sides of the road nor the gaggles of children who would suddenly appear before them and beg with their customary respect seemed to bother her. When the muezzin from a nearby mosque called the Muslims to prayer, Maggie remarked, "It's almost like being in Egypt, except it's not so dry and dusty here."

When she had been a very young woman, Paul knew, she and her mother had accompanied her father on a research trip. He had been the financer of an archaeological excavation in the Valley of the Kings, which had unfortunately not proved a particular success. They had spent most of the time in tents, and Maggie would often enthuse about the wonderful desert sunsets or complain of the cold of the nights.

The call to prayer meant that within a few moments they were caught up in a dense crowd of people and could do nothing but allow themselves to be swept along until they were able to extricate themselves from the throng into a small side street. Maggie gripped Paul's arm tightly the whole time, looking around with fear in her eyes.

The quarter in which they now found themselves seemed to be a preserve of the locals, as many of the houses were built in the traditional style, on stilts. Palm trees rose above the houses, and washing lines stretched between a few close-standing trunks. It was prayer time and there were no men to be seen, only women who were either sitting with their children on their verandas or busy with housework.

They all stared at Paul and Maggie. Some of the women put their heads together, talking in a language Paul did not understand. He noticed that at that moment they were the only Europeans on the street, and moreover their clothes were slightly different from those of the Dutch. Their fashionable dress made it clear that they were only visitors.

"I think we should turn back," Maggie murmured, but Paul stroked her hand reassuringly.

"There's no need to fear these people. They're only curious. My father was never harmed on the streets of Padang. Especially not by women."

Maggie did not seem to doubt him, yet she did not trust these women an inch. They seemed to sense it, too, as any children that were eager to run up to them were held back by the hands of wary mothers.

Paul gave them an apologetic smile and led Maggie on.

After they had followed the street for a while, a familiar scent reached his nostrils. It was not long before Paul recognized the source.

"Look, darling, there are cinnamon trees growing over there."

There was a kind of cinnamon-tree plantation behind one of the larger stilt houses. Beyond it rose rice paddies in terraces, with the jungle crowding up against them.

"That's the Padang cinnamon my father used to go into raptures about," he said to Maggie, indicating the trees. "He always said it was better than the cinnamon from Ceylon. And beyond them you can see the rice paddies. Rice is the staple here."

Maggie still seemed as if she would prefer to flee, but Paul was fascinated by the way Padang fit seamlessly into the surrounding natural world. It was unlike any other capital city he had ever seen. The rich green of the paddy fields filled his vision, and the scent, which seemed to get stronger with every step, was intoxicating. He understood now what had led his father to return here again and again. After only a few hours this country was addictive. Perhaps Maggie just needed a little more time.

At last they came to an alleyway where they saw only a few scattered houses. Between them were numerous palm trees, their crowns rustling mysteriously and strange cries emanating from them.

"Why haven't the Dutch settled in this district?" Maggie wondered, looking around a little anxiously.

"I'm sure it's not because this place is dangerous," Paul said. "A lot of Dutchmen and Germans have plantations here, and a few Englishmen, too. Their houses are outside the city. I bet the cinnamon trees belong to one of the plantations."

Something suddenly shot out of the bush in front of them. Paul saw only reddish-brown fur before the animal disappeared from view again. Maggie started with a brief shriek.

"Can we go, please, Paul?" she said as she pressed up against him.

Paul laughed. "Darling, I can't understand why you're so afraid. It was only a monkey. Look up in that palm—there he is!"

Maggie was paralyzed.

"You've traveled with your father—why are you so timid here?" Paul kept on. "There are monkeys in Egypt, after all."

"It's not because of the monkeys," she replied finally. "I simply don't feel right. And I've heard there are supposed to be tigers here."

"There are indeed, but they wouldn't dare come to places where there are people. Since they're hunted here, like they are everywhere, I'd venture to suggest they're more afraid of us than we are of them."

Paul's words did nothing to pacify Maggie, as all desire to continue their walk seemed to have abandoned her.

"All right, we'll head back to the city center," Paul said, turning her around. "We're sure to find a boutique or dressmaker's, and I'm sure there'll be no tigers there."

"Please don't be cross with me," Maggie said in a small voice. "I . . . It just makes me nervous, all these animals and strange people . . . It was the same in Egypt. I had to spend some time getting used to it all. I hope you can understand."

Paul took her hand and kissed it. "Of course, my love. Perhaps I'd feel similarly if my father hadn't told me so much about this country. I loved his stories—maybe that's why so much of it feels familiar."

As they walked back down the street, the people stared at them again. Maggie was visibly trying to ignore them—a shame, Paul thought, as the looks were not at all hostile. The women seemed curious and were probably whispering about them in their language, but they did not appear derogatory or unpleasant. Maggie only relaxed once they had found a dressmaker's shop. The window display was truly impressive, and inside they found a helpful young Chinese woman. When one of the women present remarked that this shop was a favorite of the plantation owner's wife, Maggie seemed appeased.

Paul whiled away the wait by watching the activity out on the street, smiling as he recalled his father's tales. What a shame that he was no longer alive! Paul realized how much it would have meant to have accompanied him on his travels while he was alive.

***

Surabaja, 1902

Dressed only in a corset, chemise, and long drawers, Rose Gallway sat, legs apart, on a chair. The croaking voice of Mrs. Faraday, her old music teacher in London, was ringing in her ears. "A lady just doesn't do that kind of thing! It's utterly indecent!"

Rose could see nothing indecent about it, as she thought it the most comfortable position for fitting new strings to her violin and tuning them. She had left Mrs. Faraday's Music School behind, and although she was haunted every so often by the memory of her exhortations, she now merely smiled at them.

For a few years now Rose had been on course to become one of the best violinists in the country, perhaps even the world. Her career had been remarkable. Despite her English name, she was originally from Padang, the daughter of a warehouse supervisor who had taken a native woman for his wife.

Although her father was a very parsimonious man, he had set his own rules aside when it became clear that his daughter possessed a special musical talent. One of the Dutch teachers at her school in Padang, Mejuffrouw Dalebreek, had visited her parents in a frenzied state after a music lesson and begged them to let their daughter learn an instrument.

Her father had given Rose a violin, the instrument she had secretly craved for a long time. From that day on, her life changed, and the lessons with Anna Dalebreek had ultimately been followed by an invitation to Mrs. Faraday's Music School.

Rose remembered well how her cheeks had glowed with excitement—and her stomach had cramped with fear.

At first her father had not wanted to allow her to go, since his wife was pregnant again after a long gap and needed help around the house. Yet it had been her gentle but strong-willed mother who had made every effort to change his mind. She could not have known that she would suffer a miscarriage three months later.

On the ship to England, Rose had cried herself dry, and more tears followed when she found out that the conservatory was populated with over-ambitious pupils and over-strict teachers. Eventually she grew accustomed to it all—to the cold, to the gray weather, to the taunts of her fellow pupils, and to the malicious remarks of Mrs. Faraday. She ended up as the school's best pupil and became a firm favorite in the English concert halls.

The lessons in Mrs. Faraday's conservatory had taught Rose a lot, but even her strict teacher had been unable to scrub her clean of all her idiosyncrasies. This was something she was proud of—she was not one of those English dolls who were likely to hang up their violins as soon as they got married.

Once she had finished her tuning, she drew the bow lightly over the strings. She was still not happy with the sound, so she reached for a tuning fork and tapped it. With a few turns of the pegs she was satisfied. She was about to position the violin under her chin when the dressing room door flew open.

"Miss!" Mai, her Chinese assistant, waved a piece of paper excitedly. "I've just been given this from Mijnheer Colderup. He said I should pass it on to you immediately."

With a deep breath, Rose took the letter and threw a loaded look at the girl. "Next time, I'd rather you entered the dressing room more quietly, or do you want me to drop my violin?"

"No, miss, but I . . ." Mai blushed. She was actually a very quiet servant who worshipped her mistress beyond all measure, but every now and then she forgot herself.

"No buts, Mai. This violin earns not only my living but also yours. Without my instrument I can't play; if I don't play I have no money; and without money I can't afford a dresser, so remember: pianissimo, not forte!"

Mai nodded eagerly, but Rose doubted she had any idea what the words meant. Her annoyance subsided immediately when she read the name of the letter's sender.

"A letter from Governor van Swieten?" she wondered aloud as she broke the seal and opened the envelope. "What can he want?"

"He must want you to play for him!" Mai cried in excitement.

Rose gave her a stern glare, causing her dresser's face to fall. But Mai's guess was correct.

Dear Miss Gallway,

It has come to my attention that you are currently giving a guest performance in our city, and I would like to take the opportunity to invite you to give a concert in my house on the twenty-fifth of this month.

I have admired your playing ever since I heard you at the conservatory in London, and I would consider it a great honor to receive you for a recital at Welkom. If you wish to accept my invitation, please contact my secretary, Westraa, who will clarify the details with you.

Yours in admiration,
Piet van Swieten

Rose whistled in amazement. She would never have counted Mijnheer van Swieten among her admirers. He had been governor of the island when she was a child and would not have cared one jot about Rose Gallway. Things had changed since then.

"Mai, will you please bring me my calendar," she asked her dresser, who darted away as quick as a flash. Appointments were usually her agent's business, but Rose wanted to be certain, and noted it down in her own diary.

She checked that she had no prior engagements on the evening in question, though even if she had, she would probably have dropped them like a shot for this more important appointment. She looked forward to spending a few days in her hometown, which would at last give her a chance to visit her parents.

"It looks like we're in luck," she said cheerfully to Mai, who was making herself useful by gathering together all her mistress's things that were scattered over the room. Mai knew only too well how her mistress hated idleness and only rarely allowed herself moments of peace and quiet. If she was not about to go on stage, she was either tuning her violin or playing, playing, playing. "We're going to play at the governor's residence—isn't it wonderful?"

Mai nodded dutifully but immediately returned her attention to her work.

Rose stood. After carefully laying her violin back in the case, she went over to her desk, where she composed a reply to the governor and gave it to Mai together with a note for her agent, who was bound to be somewhere with the owner of the concert hall where she was to play the next day.

"Don't lose it, you understand?"

"Yes, miss." Nodding eagerly, Mai stuffed the letters in her jacket pocket.

"And hurry up. I'll need you again soon to prepare for the concert."

"Yes, miss, I'll be back right away."

As the door closed behind Mai, a smile spread over Rose's face. The governor of Sumatra had invited her to play. It was almost as good as playing personally for the sultan himself. No, it was actually better, as it was well known that the sultan hardly held any power on the island anymore. The more influential people would be at the governor's house. And who knew, perhaps she could make a few contacts to help give a boost to her international career. She would like to tour Europe and Asia perhaps, but her dream was America. To play there really would make her the best violinist in the world.

7

London, 2011

The next morning, Lilly rode into town with Ellen to begin their investigation. As her friend drove, Lilly stroked the violin case absently, Ellen's recital from the previous evening running through her head. What wonderful sounds she had coaxed from the violin!

"Why did you never take your violin playing any further?" she said, thinking out loud. "When you played yesterday . . . I'd never realized that you could play so brilliantly."

"You call that brilliant?" Ellen shook her head with a laugh. "No, all you heard yesterday was technique. Merely recalling finger movements I learned as a child and have never forgotten since. Any serious critic would have put their hands over their ears and dismissed my playing as totally wooden."

That was not what Lilly felt. "It sounded wonderful to my ears. Anyway, it was a completely new piece. You played as if you'd been practicing it."

"It's like riding a bike—there are some things you never forget," Ellen insisted.

They were both silent for a few moments until Lilly asked, "And you really have no idea who could have made this violin?"

"No, I wish I did, but I don't. The sound reminds me a bit of a Stradivari, but it's quite a bit softer. I don't know of any violin maker whose instruments could produce a sound quite like it. But perhaps Mr. Cavendish knows something."

"What does he do?"

"He's my head conservator."

They had arrived at the institute, and Ellen drove into the parking garage beneath the building and parked in her reserved space.

Lilly had never been to the Morris Institute before, and she was full of anticipation, eager to see where her friend worked.

The elevator brought them to the third floor, whose walls were adorned with modern art and floors covered with simple but expensive-looking carpets.

"This is where I receive my clients. The second floor is where the restoration workshops are housed."

"I'd really love to see those," Lilly said, feeling like a small girl walking through a museum, amazed by all she saw.

"And so you shall—but first I'd like to show you my office."

Ellen led Lilly to a door at the far end of the corridor, which opened onto a kind of lobby, where they were greeted by an extremely well-groomed young man.

"This is Terence, my secretary. Terence, this is my friend Lilly Kaiser."

"Pleased to meet you."

Not only was Terence incredibly good-looking, but he also had an incredibly masculine handshake. Lilly was bowled over. How long had it been since she'd laid eyes on such a fine specimen of a man, let alone been introduced to him?

"Terence, you've kept my schedule free for this morning, haven't you?"

"Of course, Mrs. Morris. And this time I've even managed to keep Mr. Catrell of Sotheby's at bay. He'll call back tomorrow."

"Oh my goodness, that means another three-hour conversation." Ellen groaned playfully. "Thanks very much, Terence, for sparing me that today at least!"

As they disappeared into Ellen's office, Lilly pointed back at the door, her mouth agape and eyes wide.

"I don't get it. How have you managed to get yourself Brad Pitt's double as secretary?" The first time Ellen referred to Terence, Lilly had imagined an elderly man with elbow patches on his sleeves.

"Yes, Terence does look a bit like him, doesn't he? I admit, if I were single I'd find it hard to keep my mind on track. But unfortunately there are other factors, quite apart from my wedding ring, that would make a relationship with him impossible."

"You're his boss."

"Oh, that wouldn't really be a reason."

"He's gay?"

"Bingo! Good fortune for the men, bad luck for us."

Ellen led Lilly over to the tall windows that offered a good view of the Thames and London Bridge.

"It's wonderful," Lilly exclaimed.

The telephone rang, and Ellen went over to the desk to pick it up. Lilly was unable to hear who was calling, but she could tell that her friend had been expecting the call.

"That was Mr. Cavendish. He's ready for us. We should go down to his office now."

Lilly was fascinated by the way Ellen spoke about this man, her employee. He was clearly an eminent authority in his field, and she felt her excitement mounting as they hurried past the workshops.

Ellen knocked briefly, and when a deep male voice called "Come in," she opened the door.

Lilly had imagined a restorer's workshop to look completely different from this, and the restorer himself. In films such people were depicted bustling around sterile rooms in long white coats. This room may not have been crammed with antique furniture, but it nevertheless had a certain cozy feel to it. A tall bookshelf stood against one wall, and behind the desk was an old, well-worn chair. A jumble of books and papers lay on the desk. On the workbench near the window was a white cloth, and on it a violin that did not appear to show the slightest sign of damage. Tools were stowed neatly to one side, indicating that the work on the instrument was complete.

At first glance, Mr. Cavendish reminded Lilly a little of the actor who played Q in the old James Bond films. Slightly stooped, he was wearing a tweed jacket and cords, with a snow-white starched shirt and elegant tie. All that remained of his hair was a gray fringe at the back, but the light in his dark eyes behind tasteful, silver-colored glasses recalled the young man he had once been. Lilly was sure he must have been a real ladies' man, and he still looked quite good now.

"Good morning, Ben. May I introduce my friend Lilly Kaiser?"

"Ah, the lady with the strange violin." With a smile he looked her in the eyes before turning his attention to the violin case under her arm. "I'm pleased to meet you. You and your violin."

The hand he extended to Lilly was warm and gentle.

"If we were playing by old-school rules, now would be the time to exchange a few pleasantries, but the old times are past and, as Ellen can confirm, I'm not known for my patience. As an old man, I've no time for patience anymore, so I'll merely confess that I'm incredibly curious about the violin and can't wait to look at it."

"Of course." Lilly glanced at Ellen, who moved over to the workbench.

When Lilly opened the case, Cavendish moved to stand beside her, his hands already sheathed in white gloves. She wondered briefly whether to tell him the story, but in the end stepped to one side without a word.

He carefully lifted the violin from its case and studied it with his keen eyes. "Do you intend to play this violin, or lock it away?"

"To begin with, I'd like to know why it's in my possession in the first place. Someone gave it to me because he claimed it belonged to me, but I haven't the faintest idea why."

Cavendish turned the violin in his hands and then gasped audibly. "Well, well, just look! What have we here?"

"Does it mean anything to you?"

"Oh yes, a lot. You've gotten a good catch here. This violin is in very good condition. A few parts could be replaced, but it's not really necessary. It only needs cleaning and polishing. I estimate that it dates from the early eighteenth century, but I couldn't say for certain until the varnish has been analyzed."

Lilly looked at Ellen.

"Don't worry," she said, "we won't remove it all. We only take a tiny sample—after it's been cleaned and polished, the scratch will be practically invisible."

"Yes, I can assure you of that," Cavendish said, now holding the violin beneath the workbench lamp. "A very beautiful piece."

"And the rose? Do you know what that signifies?" Lilly asked.

Cavendish considered before replying. "No, unfortunately I don't. It's certainly unusual, and the way the rose has been drawn confirms my suspicion that the violin dates from the start of the eighteenth century."

Cavendish called something up on his computer before inserting an endoscope into one of the f-holes. An image of the inside of the violin appeared on the monitor. Lilly thought it must be the perspective a mouse would have if it skittered around inside the instrument.

"No maker's mark. And if I'm right, there's never been a label, either."

"So would it be possible that the violin was an embarrassment to its maker? He didn't like it and so didn't want to associate it with his name?"

"Or someone stole the violin from its maker before he had a chance to insert his label." Cavendish withdrew the tiny camera. "But it's good craftsmanship in any case."

Lilly thought for a moment, then on a whim produced the sheet of music.

"Mr. Cavendish, could I ask you to take a look at this? This sheet of music came with the violin. Neither Ellen nor I know the composer, but perhaps you will have an idea from the style."

Cavendish took the music and looked at it briefly. "Well, if you ask me, you'd be better off getting Gabriel Thornton's advice. He's head of a music school in London that was once a very famous conservatory. As far as I know, he likes to research its former pupils. Perhaps you'll be in luck, and he'll be able to recognize the style as that of someone who used to attend his conservatory. Of course it would be rather incredible if a previous owner of the violin was the composer."

Lilly was briefly unnerved by the mention of Thornton's name. Could it be him? Perhaps it was just a coincidence, and the man sitting next to her on the flight merely had the same name as the head of this music school . . . But it seemed rather unlikely that two men with the same name both ran music schools.

"What's up?" Ellen asked, clearly taken aback by her expression.

"I met Thornton yesterday on my flight to London. Sounds crazy, I know, but it's true."

"Well, what a coincidence!" Mr. Cavendish clapped his hands in delight.

Ellen raised her eyebrows. "You didn't tell me anything about that."

"Why should I? I didn't know who this Thornton was. I thought he was any old music teacher."

"Oh, he's much more than a music teacher," Cavendish said. "He's an outstanding musicologist. And, what's more, an authority on any instrument played by the conservatory's former pupils."

"What exactly do you know, Ben?" Ellen asked. Lilly could tell she was near to bursting with curiosity. She was, too, even though she still wasn't sure what excited her more—the violin itself or the question of why it should belong to her.

But Cavendish remained completely unperturbed. "Well, there's a story I heard many years ago. I'd stowed it away somewhere in the recesses of my brain without giving it much thought, but now, given this violin and the music—"

"Don't keep us on tenterhooks!" Ellen said, beginning to pace agitatedly up and down.

Lilly was watching Cavendish, who seemed to be combing the depths of his memory.

"The story goes that a pupil of that conservatory had a very special violin, one with a rose on the back. I don't remember what she was called, though I'm not sure if that's because I didn't pay enough attention or because time has eroded my memory—who knows? But I'm sure Mr. Thornton will be able to tell you plenty more."

8

After they had photographed the violin from all angles, printed out the images in their office, taken a copy of the sheet music, and handed it all back to Lilly, Ellen called a taxi to take Lilly to the Faraday School of Music—Thornton's "music school" that had formerly been a kind of conservatory.

"Grill the man about everything he knows, and report back to me," her friend said as she sent her on her way. She waved, and Lilly hurried out to the taxi, which was already hooting impatiently.

On the way, she couldn't help shaking her head. How was this possible? First the violin and now this coincidence with Thornton! Could the theory be true that the beating of a butterfly's wing could set off a chain of events that trigger a storm? Had the old man's appearance been the beating of that butterfly's wing? And what kind of storm was about to strike?

"Is everything OK, ma'am?" asked the driver, whose dreadlocks reminded her of a young Bob Marley.

"Yes, of course, I was just lost in thought."

"Very strange thoughts, from the way you're shaking your head."

Had she been so obvious? Lilly smiled, then asked, "Do you believe coincidences have meaning?"

The taxi driver laughed. "Of course. They make the world go round. Yesterday I met an old friend, quite by chance, whom I hadn't seen since we were at school. It was only the day before that I'd been wondering what had happened to Bobby, and the very next day we more or less bumped into one another."

"Perhaps you'd summoned him with your thoughts?"

"Could well be, but I believe that coincidences happen for a reason. And sometimes they change something in us. When I spoke to Bobby, it was as if the ten years we hadn't seen each other hadn't happened. Now I've found out that he's moved to London, and this weekend he's coming to visit me and my girlfriend. Amazing, hey?"

"Yes, really amazing," Lilly replied.

"What about you? The way you were shaking your head, it was as if you couldn't believe you'd seen him again."

"It's more the case that I can't believe I'm about to see him again." When the taxi driver raised his eyebrows in anticipation, she added, "I met a very nice man on the airplane yesterday. And now I've just discovered that he's someone who could help me with something. A strange coincidence, isn't it?"

"Oh, that's no coincidence," the driver said meaningfully. "My grandmother would say that's fate. God's will. I'm sure this man will be able to help you, whatever it is you need."

Really? Lilly wondered. Could Thornton really have an answer to how she had come by this strange violin?

The driver eventually stopped in front of a two-story classical-style building.

"Here we are!" he announced superfluously. Lilly paid the fare and got out. "Good luck, lady!"

"You too," Lilly said as the taxi roared away.

She shivered in the icy breeze as she looked up at the facade bathed in the midday sunshine. It looked just as she would have imagined a music conservatory to look, but as she approached, she saw that the building also housed two other organizations. According to a sign in the foyer, the ground floor was shared by a property-management company and a concert agency. The second floor housed the Faraday School of Music.

She immediately started up the marble stairs, which must formerly have been ascended by all kinds of well-heeled gentry. Once at the top she began subconsciously to appraise an old bureau, which must date back to the period in which the house was built. The piece was now used to display brochures about the conservatory and notices of forthcoming events.

All she had to do now was find Thornton's office. She marched down the long corridors, the muted sounds of violin, cello, and piano music reaching her from behind the doors. She even came across an opera singer working on an aria.

I should have phoned, she thought. He won't be too pleased about me simply turning up like this.

After wandering past a few doors, she finally spoke to a young woman who had clearly just been to a music lesson, as she was carrying a violin case under her arm.

"You're best to go round that corner; Mr. Thornton's office is half-way along the left-hand corridor," the young woman said. Lilly thanked her and continued.

The door was open, which she took to be a hopeful sign, but as she entered, she realized it was only a lobby—complete with secretary. She was blonde and looked around forty, and although she was very attractive, she had all the charm of an icicle.

"Hello. I wanted to ask if it would be possible to speak to Mr. Thornton," she began, trying to ignore the fact that she had cold feet about this. "My name is Lilly Kaiser."

"Do you have an appointment?" the secretary asked sharply.

"No, I don't, but I've just come from Ellen Morris's institute. It's about a violin I'd like to show to Mr. Thornton."

There was no doubt from the dragon's glare she gave Lilly that she thought her boss's time could be better spent than by looking at some old violin.

"I'm sorry, but Mr. Thornton is very busy at the moment. The best I can do is to make you an appointment for April."

Lilly thought she must have misheard. April? In Germany you could get an appointment to see a medical specialist sooner than that!

"I'm sorry, but I'm afraid I'll have left London by April. Is it not possible to speak to him sometime this week or next? I only want him to take a look at the instrument, nothing more."

The secretary's expression didn't melt in the slightest.

"Then you'll have to find someone else. Mr. Thornton's calendar is completely full this week and next."

Lilly sighed, wondering how she could engineer a meeting with Thornton so he could examine her violin. Perhaps it would be worth lying in wait for him in the parking lot.

"What's up here?" came a voice from behind her.

Lilly whirled round. Thornton was leaning on the door frame with a boyish smile on his face. It seemed his secretary had only just noticed his arrival, as she breathed in sharply, but she soon started in again.

"This lady would like to make an appointment with you," she gasped out, but his eyes had already betrayed his recognition.

"Well, if it isn't my recent companion from the Berlin flight! Do you want to arrange lessons with me?"

The blood shot to Lilly's cheeks. She was so embarrassed that words failed her. Thornton gave her an encouraging wink, then looked across at his secretary, who seemed at a loss as to what was happening.

"Yes, I mean, no, I . . . I'm here about something else," she managed to say. "I promise I won't keep you for long, but I'm afraid I can't stay in London for long, and I'd really appreciate it if you could help me."

Thornton regarded her for a moment, then turned to his secretary. "How does it look, Eva? Do I have anything urgent?"

From the corner of her eye Lilly could see that Eva was also blushing now, which made sense when she replied, "No, Mr. Thornton, your next appointment is at half past one."

"Great! Have you any objection to me taking you for something to eat in our award-winning cafeteria, Mrs. Kaiser?"

"Thank you, that's very kind."

Forcing herself not to throw the secretary a malicious glance, Lilly followed Thornton.

"I must confess that 'award-winning' was a joke," Thornton said as they strolled down a long corridor, "but the food here is actually very good. I recommend the steak and mashed potatoes."

Lilly felt as if she were back in her college days as she stood before the service counter with a tray. At the same time, she was touched by the way Thornton mixed in with his employees and students for his meals. Her university rector would never have been seen in the cafeteria.

Lilly was not particularly hungry but nevertheless went for the steak he'd recommended, which turned out to be rather good.

"So, how can I help you?" Thornton asked after swallowing a hearty bite of steak.

Lilly pushed her plate to one side and took out the photos. "You know Ben Cavendish, who works for Ellen Morris? He knows you and thinks you can help me with this."

"Fire away!"

"You remember the violin you kindly stowed in the overhead bin on the plane for me?"

"Yes, the one you were seeking an expert opinion on."

Lilly nodded and pushed the photos over to him. "This is it."

Thornton frowned briefly. "You don't have it with you?"

"No, Ellen's got it. She's going to examine it. I'd like to know who it used to belong to so I can perhaps find out how it came to me. It was handed over to me as a kind of inheritance."

Thornton leafed through the pictures. When he came to the one showing the back of the violin, he stopped short.

"My goodness," he murmured, laying the photo almost reverently on the table in front of him. "I thought it had been destroyed."

Lilly raised her eyebrows. His words had no meaning for her—at least not yet. "Don't tell me you know this violin!"

Thornton nodded, staring at the rose for a few moments in silence.

"Come with me," he said finally.

"Where to?" Lilly asked.

"To our archive in the basement. Unless you want to polish off the rest of your steak."

Lilly had lost the meager appetite she'd had. Her heart was beating wildly, and her face felt flushed. She jumped up so fast she made her chair rock dangerously, but she reacted quickly and managed to grasp it before it fell and drew the attention of the whole cafeteria to her.

"Take it easy." Thornton smiled. "What I'm about to show you isn't going to run away."

Embarrassed, Lilly gathered up the rest of the pictures and followed Thornton out of the cafeteria.

"There was a time when disobedient pupils would have been threatened with being locked up down here," Thornton remarked as the elevator carried them down. "Nowadays that wouldn't scare anyone, since there are some very interesting things down here. Ancient recordings, instruments, sheet music, pupils' files, and the like."

Sheet music. Lilly felt like whipping out the photocopy of the sheet music on the spot, but she controlled her impulse.

"And photos?" she asked instead.

"Yes, a lot of photos. We regularly employ restorers who bring battered instruments back into good condition, and we keep photographic records of all of them. And of course all of our collections are digitized. At the moment we're busy making MP3 recordings of wax cylinders and old shellac records. That's not such an easy task since these machines sadly don't have USB ports."

Lilly laughed—the thought of a gramophone with a USB port was so absurd. There had once been an old gramophone in her shop, and she had always regretted not keeping it for herself.

"Here it is!" Thornton indicated a glass door with "Archive" on it in antique lettering. Inside, it was anything but an old dusty storage area. The air was kept at a pleasant temperature and smelled of old paper and wood.

"I hope you're not too cold down here. As well as old instruments, recordings, and photos, we've got a collection of sheet music, some of it very old. Some items even date back to the time before the Great Fire of London in 1666. I have no idea how they managed to survive the fire, but it's absolutely fascinating to hold in your hand, for example, an original from Henry VIII's time, and play the composition."

"I can imagine," Lilly said, practically bursting with enthusiasm. "I also get very excited when I'm offered a really old piece."

"What was the oldest piece you ever had in your shop?"

"A seventeenth-century bureau. The owner had found it in a barn and thought it was worthless. I had it restored and sold it at a very high price. It really was a wonderful specimen; it wouldn't have been out of place in a museum."

"That could well be, and it's a good thing that museums preserve these treasures. But objects were originally made to be used—just like musical instruments. It makes my heart bleed to hear of someone placing a valuable Stradivari in a safe in Switzerland so it's never played. Apart from the fact that this isn't good for an instrument, the best virtuosi in the world would kill to be able to play it. And there'd be no better way of getting big names into the audience."

Thornton opened a cupboard and took out a kind of index-card box. It didn't appear to contain much, but the name "Rose Gallway" was printed on the front.

"Unfortunately, this is all we have," he said apologetically as he took out a photo. "The violin that's come into your possession once belonged to a former pupil of this conservatory. I'm sure of it."

The picture showed a young, dark-haired woman in a high-necked, severe-looking white dress. Her features were a little faded, but it made the violin in her hand all the clearer. Lilly found the way she held it very unusual, turning it so the back could be seen. Musicians generally always posed with the fronts of their instruments showing. It was as if she wanted to show that her violin was something special.

"For many years now we've collected photos and paintings of the men and women who studied here. They're usually holding their instruments, which means we can readily identify them if they're still in our possession." Thornton tapped the photo lightly. "This young woman was a minor legend in her circles. She was one of the best violinists of her age. Sometimes, though, when stars shine too brightly, they soon burn out. Rose Gallway was one of those for whom fame was all too brief."

"What happened?"

Thornton shrugged. "No one ever really got to the bottom of it. She was on a concert tour and disappeared without a trace. The newspapers at the time indulged in wild speculation. There was talk of abduction and murder—some even say that she married the ruler of some exotic kingdom, but nothing certain was ever discovered. What we do know is that she played a most remarkable violin."

"My rose violin," Lilly said without moving her gaze from the photo. "Did Rose Gallway have any children?"

"No one knows. As I said, she simply disappeared. And the violin materialized in the possession of another young woman. Helen Carter."

Lilly needed a moment to take this news in. Her violin had belonged to a famous violinist! But how had it come to her?

"Who was this Helen Carter?"

"The daughter of an English couple who lived on Sumatra. Helen was also a very famous violinist, who suffered a dreadful accident at the height of her career. She survived but never played again. All trace of the violin was lost during the Second World War. We've always been convinced that it was destroyed during the London air raids. Obviously we were mistaken."

"Did this Helen Carter have any children?"

"Yes, but they were killed together with her and her husband during the war, in an attack off the coast of Sumatra."

"What's my connection with the violin supposed to be?" Lilly realized immediately that she had spoken her question out loud. "Um . . . I mean, I don't have any connection with Sumatra," she added, a little embarrassed. "My mother and grandmother are from Hamburg. Neither of them ever said anything about a violin."

A thought was forming on the edge of her mind. Until now she had always thought of the violin in connection with herself. But what if Peter . . .

"Well, I'm afraid you'll have to follow the violin's story back through its history if you want to find that out," Thornton said, driving out her speculation for the moment. "Perhaps it came into someone's hands during the war. Perhaps they saved it from the ship on which Helen and her family were sailing. The name Rodenbach doesn't happen to feature anywhere in your family tree? That was the family name of Helen's husband."

Lilly shook her head. "No, not that I know of." She suddenly remembered the copy of the music in her bag. "There was something else in the violin case."

She took out the copy and handed the page to Thornton. He had no sooner looked at it than he took a step back and sank down on the edge of a nearby desk as if he suddenly felt faint.

"'The Moonlit Garden.'" His voice was little more than a whisper.

"Is it possible that Rose Gallway composed it? Or perhaps this Helen Carter."

Thornton said nothing for a few seconds, but his eyes drank in one note after the other, as had Ellen's. Perhaps he now had the melody in his head.

"If this composition really was by one of those two women, it would be a sensation," he said finally, looking up from the music.

"The piece sounds quite exotic, so if you're saying that Rose Gallway was from Sumatra . . ."

"You've heard it?"

"My friend played it last night on the rose violin."

Thornton took a deep breath. "I'd love to do that, too." He considered briefly, then said, "How about a deal, Mrs. Kaiser?"

"A deal?"

"Yes. I'll help you with your investigation if you allow me to play your violin just once."

Lilly raised her eyebrows in surprise. "But your appointment calendar is full, and—"

"And I'm interested in finding out something about one of our former pupils," he completed her sentence for her. "There are gaping holes in the biographies of both Rose Gallway and Helen Carter. And then there's this composition. As yet we don't know that either of these women also composed music. But if they did, experts would be delighted to hear of it. And I would have contributed to shedding some light on the puzzle."

"Do you think it's possible?"

"If we dig around a little in the past, we're bound to come up with something."

"All right, then, Mr. Thornton, if it's not too much trouble," Lilly replied, causing her new partner to smile and offer her his hand.

"Call me Gabriel."

"Only if you call me Lilly."

"I think I can manage that. And I can assure you that it thrills me to be working on this project. We're not going to give up until we know how this violin found its way to you. And which of those two women composed this piece. Oh yes, may I take a copy of the music?"

Lilly nodded with a smile, wondering what the piece would sound like when he played it.

***

That evening Dean was out. After Ellen and Lilly had eaten with the children, they settled down to enjoy a bottle of French red wine that Ellen had brought back with her from a trip to Paris.

Enfolded by the warmth from the open fire and pleasantly relaxed by the wine, Lilly reported in minute detail on all that Gabriel had told her. The whole situation still seemed unreal to her, but she was now forming a plan in her mind, with stages she could aim for one by one.

"You made the right decision in accepting his help," Ellen said, staring pensively into her wineglass. "If anyone can find out who composed 'The Moonlit Garden,' it's Thornton. But it sounds like there are serious gaps in the records."

"There must be some information somewhere," Lilly replied.

"Yes, and you never know, perhaps this Rose has descendants. Perhaps you're even one of them?"

Lilly shook her head. "No, I can't be. Look at me, red haired and freckled. This Rose had jet-black hair and milk-white skin. And I haven't the slightest musical talent. You'd be more likely to be a descendant of one of them. You've got dark hair, and you play the violin."

"Nonsense," Ellen replied drily. "The old man came to you, not to me, so it must be something to do with your family."

"Or perhaps there's a connection with Peter." Lilly saw Ellen looking at her uneasily. "It's a possibility, isn't it? The elderly man could have been looking for him, found out he'd died, so came to me. I was his wife, and so . . ."

Lilly felt a pressure in her breast weighing her down. She suddenly wondered how well she had actually known her husband. Did the mystery lie not in her family but in his?

"Did you get hold of Sunny?" Ellen asked, clearly trying to divert their attention from Peter. On the way home, Lilly had told her about the video surveillance camera. Ellen finished her wine but kept the glass in her hand, as if reading something from the dregs.

"No, not yet. I'm afraid I'll have to leave it till tomorrow now. But if she succeeds in playing through the video and finding the right spot, I can show it to my mother. Perhaps she'll recognize the man. And if she doesn't know him . . ."

It occurred to Lilly that at least two years had gone by since she had been in touch with her parents-in-law, although they had always gotten along well. Perhaps not well enough to continue their relationship now that Peter was no longer alive.

"Then that only leaves Per and Anke." Not only had Ellen guessed her thoughts, but she clearly also remembered the two of them.

Lilly nodded. "Yes, Per and Anke. Who knows what they'd have to say if I suddenly turned up on their doorstep and told them this story."

"They liked you, Lilly—you know that. Perhaps they still do. They probably understand that you can't always be coming over for Sunday afternoon coffee. Peter's life came to an end, but not yours."

"Yes, and you can't imagine how often I've wished it could have been the other way around." Lilly sighed deeply, and the two sat in silence for a few minutes.

"Did Thornton say what he wants to do next? Did you exchange phone numbers and e-mail addresses?" Ellen resumed eventually.

Lilly nodded. "Yes, we did, but I'm sure it will be a while before he finds anything out. Can I use your computer to check my e-mails? If I'd known it was all going to turn out like this, I'd have brought my laptop."

"Of course. You don't even need to ask. My office door is always open to you. Jessie and Norma would be hanging around in front of the screen all the time if they didn't have to be in school."

"You mean that?"

"Jessie and Norma or you using the computer?"

"Computer."

"Of course—what's it there for? Feel free to use it. Write up everything you find out. And perhaps you should warn Sunny that you might have to stay here a bit longer than you intended. I'm not going to let you go, anyway, until I know whose workshop that violin came from and how it came into your hands. At least we've got Thornton on board now. Having access to his archives is priceless."

"Why haven't you ever been in touch with him before?" Lilly asked, her thoughts returning to his face with those dark eyes. He really was incredibly attractive! She was glad that she would still be involved with him, but on the other hand the prospect made her nervous, even though she feared she was not his type.

"There's never been any reason for our two companies to come into contact—that's all. He researches sheet music and former pupils; I examine and restore musical instruments and determine their value. They're connected, certainly, but our aims are quite different. The academic aspects of my activities are secondary. But Thornton is an academic through and through, and if he ever does get his hands on an instrument that needs dating, he has his own people."

Ellen smiled at her and laid an arm around her shoulders like she used to do when they played together in the attic. "It's so lovely to have you here and to be doing something together."

"Wherever this quest leads us," Lilly said a little skeptically. "Thornton said that both Rose Gallway and Helen Carter had a connection with Sumatra. Have you ever considered going on vacation there?"

"Never in my wildest dreams!" Ellen replied. Lilly knew that since her institute had become so successful, she rarely traveled. "But to be honest, I'd have nothing against a trip."

"What about your business?"

"I'm in charge of my own business, aren't I? I could simply write off the trip as research expenses." They looked at one another, laughing.

9

Padang, 1902

Welkom, the governor's residence, lay outside Padang near the Barisan Mountains. The white building nestled like a precious pearl in a lush green tapestry of paddy fields and palm groves. The Dutch-colonial style was a little different from the English, but the architecture was pleasing to Paul's eyes. The columns to either side of the entrance were graceful, and numerous tall windows reflected the rosy evening sky. The terraced layout and a staircase of shallow steps made the sloping grounds easy for visitors to explore.

It was even more beautiful than Paul had been led to believe from his father's and other travelers' accounts. The parkland he and Maggie drove through in their coach looked a little Caribbean with its palms and mango trees, and as they drew near, Paul could make out jasmine bushes, orchids, frangipani, and other shrubs that he had not been able to distinguish from farther away. All the flowers gave the air a wonderful scent, permeated with a hint of cinnamon. There must be some cinnamon trees growing in the governor's garden.

As if van Swieten had arranged for nature to put on a special display for this evening, a pink haze drifted down from the mountains, beyond which the pale face of the moon was still tinged with the last of the sunlight. Ghostly cries reached them from afar—monkeys, various species of which lived in the area in large numbers.

Paul was dying to get a once-in-a-lifetime glimpse of the wild anthropoid apes called *orang hutan*—man of the forest—in Malay in their natural habitat. The London Zoo had recently obtained a few more pairs, but they were deprived of all dignity and nobility behind bars. They may have been fine as a fairground attraction to frighten a gullible public, but Paul wanted to see them in all their glory, something he could only do here.

But Maggie seemed somehow intimidated by the strange calls. She didn't complain, but he could tell from her expression that the exotic natural world scared rather than delighted her. Had she no eye for the beauty of this region?

"Maggie, darling." Paul tried to lift her spirits by pointing out a particularly beautiful frangipani tree in full bloom, a specimen that must have been growing for many decades. A couple of black-and-white plumed birds with huge yellow beaks flitted about in its branches. "Just look at that tree! Wouldn't it be lovely to have something like that in our garden in England?"

The sight of the pink blooms with their yellow eyes finally succeeded in bringing a smile to Maggie's face.

"You're right, it's really beautiful. I wonder if the governor would give us a cutting?"

"I'm sure he would if we asked. This tree would make a real showpiece for our orangery. And who knows, perhaps he might even give us one of those birds. Did you know they're called hornbills?"

"Because of their huge beaks?"

His wife finally seemed to be relaxing a little.

"That's right, because they have a horn on their beaks. If we had a specimen like that, we'd be the envy of all London society with their boring parrots."

Maggie nodded her agreement and laid her head on Paul's shoulder. Her good cheer faded a little. "How long do you think we'll have to stay here?"

"As long as necessary."

"And how long is necessary?"

"We'll grace this wonderful land with our presence until I've reached agreement with the sugar plantation owner about my investment."

Without giving Maggie the chance to protest, Paul leaned over and gave her a kiss on the cheek. The touch of his lips brought a flush to her porcelain skin.

"But Paul, that's . . ."

"Not seemly?" Paul smiled broadly and kissed her again on the other cheek. "We're married. Why shouldn't it be seemly? I doubt anyone would think anything of it if I dared to kiss you on the lips in public—after all, I'm your husband now!"

Maggie suddenly resembled a summer apple that had been bathed in sunlight. Paul saw that several people had gathered on the broad flight of steps and refrained from kissing her again.

At the front door they were greeted by a dark-haired servant in traditional Batak garb. He was wearing the characteristic dark, patterned scarf bound around his head like a turban. He bowed to Paul and Maggie and gestured for them to follow him.

More guests were standing in the entrance hall. The huge, magnificently decorated room was alive with snatches of German, English, and Dutch, and Paul even caught a few words of French here and there. From the corner of his eye, he watched Maggie studying the other women. Some of them were very young and, to judge by their dresses, quite wealthy.

Paul was glad he had persuaded Maggie to take that walk into the city. He knew she had a tendency to feel inferior if she saw that a woman was better dressed than she was. The peach-colored silk dress made for her in three days by the Chinese dressmaker was easily equal to any of the others. Maggie held her head appropriately high with pride as she noticed one or two envious glances.

It was not long before the governor noticed the newcomers. Piet van Swieten was a tall man with a broad face, gray strands flecking his blond hair, and a white goatee. His shining eyes were as blue as the sky over Padang harbor, and his laugh boomed throughout the room.

Arms spread wide in welcome, he approached Paul and Maggie, calling out in slightly accented English: "My dear friends! I'm delighted to welcome you here!"

"Mijnheer van Swieten, the pleasure is all mine," Paul replied in Dutch. "May I introduce my wife, Lady Margaret Havenden?"

"I'm delighted to make your acquaintance, my lady." The Dutchman bowed elegantly and kissed her hand. "And I hope very much that my soirée will live up to your expectations of a cultural event. Out here, more or less in the middle of nowhere, one could say that the rules are quite different from those in Europe. The lack of certain things that are taken for granted in the Old World forces one to improvise."

"Have you invited any Balinese dancers?" Paul asked.

Van Swieten laughed. "Your father must have told you about them. No, on this occasion we have a different kind of artistic delight. She's a daughter of this country, but one who has been making the headlines recently, which makes me very proud. And you should be, too, Paul, as she's a half compatriot of yours."

"A half-caste?" Maggie blurted out.

"If you want to call it that . . . In any case, these . . . *half-castes* are an important mainstay of this country, no less hardworking and dedicated than anyone else here."

Paul detected that van Swieten sounded a little offended. He knew only too well that the Dutch regarded mixed marriages somewhat differently than the English. Their aim was more to keep the state and, above all, trade running smoothly. In order to do so, they needed the natives just as much as their descendants, even those born from mixed marriages.

"Please excuse Lady Margaret; she meant no harm by it. In the English colonies, marriages between white people and the natives are quite rare. And of course it doesn't mean that she has any doubt about the talents of your guest."

Van Swieten's expression softened, returning to its easy cheerfulness. "If that's the case, I'm sure you'll be delighted. But before we go any further, I'd like to introduce you to my wife and daughter. They're dying to meet you."

The governor led them deeper into the room. Curious looks from other guests followed them as they walked. Van Swieten's wife, whom Paul recognized from a photo, was in conversation with a rather stout elderly woman. The girl at her side was so similar in appearance that she must be her daughter.

"Geertruida, darling, come and greet Horace's son and his good lady."

The governor's wife, who was a good ten years younger than van Swieten, and who cut a fine figure in her dark blue dress, excused herself from the other women and gestured for the girl to come with her.

"This is my wife, Geertruida, and this is my daughter, Veerle." Van Swieten puffed out his chest with pride. "She will be getting married in two months."

The young woman, who looked about eighteen or nineteen, smiled shyly as the governor's wife extended her hand to Paul. He bent to kiss her hand, then introduced Maggie.

"Lady Margaret and I were married four months ago, shortly before my father died," Paul said, noticing as Maggie pressed her lips together in dismay. She never said it out loud, but he knew that she considered his father's death so soon after their marriage to be a bad omen.

"I was very sorry to hear about your father," van Swieten said sadly. "But it's clear that God arranges everything in the world in such a way that it keeps turning. You will be a worthy successor to Lord Havenden."

A moment's stiff silence fell between them before van Swieten remarked: "It's a pity you didn't celebrate your wedding here. If I were young again and wanted to marry, I know I would elope with Geertruida and take my marriage vows in Padang."

The governor's wife gave him a glance of disapproval. "Piet, you shouldn't talk like that. You know a wedding needs a lot of preparation. Even workers wouldn't dare to simply elope if they still have family."

"Workers may not dare, but the aristocracy can surely allow themselves to!" the governor replied, but his wife shook her head.

"You shouldn't talk like that in front of your daughter. She's not going to elope, anyway, are you, Veerle?"

The barely concealed threat in her voice made Paul smile. Geertruida van Swieten clearly held a tight rein on her family.

Seeming to find the atmosphere a little strained, the governor said, "Very well, I have to leave you for the time being, but I hope we'll have an opportunity to talk for longer later. Geertruida, can you please take care of our guests?"

"With the greatest of pleasure!" The governor's wife smiled at Maggie and Paul and led them over to the ladies with whom she had been speaking before. They were met by some admiring glances, and Paul looked at his wife with pride. Yes, she made a wonderful Lady Havenden. And perhaps she was even developing a kind of love for this country—the country that possibly held a future source of income for them.

***

The feel of the soft powder puff on her skin and the delicate scent that wafted from it had a calming effect on Rose. She had powdered her nose at least three times, an unnecessary action. She was surprised at herself—why was she feeling such stage fright? During the previous months, when she had been fêted as a rising star of the music world, she had played in front of far larger audiences than the one here.

But now here she was, in this room adorned with white furniture that had been given over to her as her dressing room, feeling as she had the first time she played for Mrs. Faraday. No, even worse, before her first concert at the conservatory, prior to which Mrs. Faraday had threatened she would smash her violin to pieces if she didn't play well. The threat had made her tremble like a leaf as she sat on her stool, since her unusual violin with its rose on the back had been her only possession back then—a possession given to her by her father, moreover, which made it all the more special.

But all had gone well, and she still had her violin. So there really was no reason for her to feel anxious. She was on safe ground with Vivaldi, as the piece was brilliant. Of course it felt a little strange to be playing *Winter* from *The Four Seasons* in Sumatra, but Mrs. Faraday had always been of the opinion that music was a language that was understood anywhere in the world.

Still, she was somewhat on edge. Was she anxious because the concert here was such an intimate occasion? Because she was in a private house? Or because the audience could hear the slightest mistake? Not that she had made very many recently. Her agent had praised her last concert to the high heavens, as had the press. But how quickly a reputation could be damaged! Women especially were scrutinized. All it would take would be for one of the governor's friends to have contacts in the music world, and the word would spread like wildfire if she played disastrously.

A knock at the door tore her from her thoughts. She expected Mai to appear, to fuss over her hair one more time, but the visitor she called in was Sean Carmichael, her agent.

"You look enchanting, my child!" he said with a light clap of his hands. "Like an angel waiting to charm humanity with her music and lead them to the path of righteousness."

"Don't exaggerate," Rose said calmly. If there was one thing that remained constant in their relationship, it was Carmichael's pre-performance flattery. The first few times it had done Rose a world of good, but she now knew that he would flatter her even if she looked disheveled and ugly—the main thing was that she brought money into the coffers. The higher the amount, the more excessive the flattery would be the next time.

"But I'm not exaggerating." Sean spread his arms, looking as if butter wouldn't melt in his mouth. "You look truly delightful. The governor and his guests will be captivated."

"What kind of man is the governor?" Rose asked, since on her arrival she had been informed that the man of the house was momentarily absent. A servant had led Rose and Mai to their assigned room and a little later brought her some lemonade and a few dainty cakes.

"At first glance he seems a little . . . shall we say unrefined. The Dutch have a completely different manner from the English."

"I know the ways of the Dutch here," Rose said. "And I don't dislike them."

"No, no, no, I wasn't implying that van Swieten was unpleasant." Sean raised his hands dismissively, then came up behind her. "I know you're from this region, and you have a lot to thank your Dutch teachers for. I only wanted to warn you about the governor's manner. He's the kind that wouldn't think twice about pinching young ladies' backsides."

"Sean!" Rose was appalled, but he merely laughed.

"Calm down, Rose! All that matters here is that you play well. The governor chooses his friends carefully—and to judge from the number and size of coaches outside, they're all influential people. I'll put my feelers out on your behalf; I'd be surprised if we didn't get an appearance in New York out of it at some stage."

Rose smiled at her reflection. Sean might indulge in exaggerated flattery, but he knew full well what she wanted. And to date he had always kept his promises.

"You'd like that, wouldn't you?" he said with a smile. "But now you should be getting ready. It won't be long before the guests want to hear you."

The words were hardly out of his mouth when Mai burst into the dressing room. She froze when she caught sight of Sean but then closed the door behind her.

"The governor's servant has told me you're due to play in a quarter of an hour. I'd better touch up your hair again."

"You'd do better to bring your mistress her violin and let her practice a little to soothe her nerves," Carmichael said as he vanished with a laugh from the dressing room.

"Don't listen to him," Rose said, seeing that Mai was uncertain what to do. "I can play no matter what, but I really could do with you seeing to my hair again. I look like a mop!"

As Mai picked up the brush and stroked it carefully through her long, black hair, Rose closed her eyes. The piece appeared before her note by note, and she imagined the accompaniment that she would not have tonight, but which she carried with her in her soul, and considered the places where she could best add ornaments to the melody. In this way she allayed her nerves, and when the knock finally came to say that she was due on, she arose in quiet anticipation.

***

Paul could not remember how many hands he had shaken. He was amazed to find how many men had known his father. Maggie had been spirited away by the governor's wife, who wanted to introduce her to a few of her friends. Seeing that she was content, Paul had let her go and was now paying for it by enduring a constant stream of questions about the former Lord Havenden.

"I'm really sorry that Horace departed this life so soon," said Mijnheer Bonstraa, the owner of a sugar plantation to the north of Padang. His father had spoken of him a few times. He had a good head for business—and an incredible way with the ladies. The woman who had been on his arm before he came over to Paul was a native, a good twenty years younger than he was, and stunningly beautiful. Bonstraa himself was very handsome for his age. He must have broken a few female hearts in his day.

"Many thanks for your condolences, Mijnheer Bonstraa."

"He really was a good man. So different from some of the Englishmen I've known. Please don't take me the wrong way, but your fellow countrymen can sometimes be difficult."

"Oh, there are plenty of younger people these days with refreshing attitudes and ideas. I assume we'll be seeing some changes in England over the next few years."

Paul had to smile as he spoke. Half Dutch himself, he knew what Bonstraa meant. His mother was full of joie de vivre, a woman who made friends easily and had even accepted Maggie's rather reserved mother with no preconceptions.

"You have a very pretty wife, Lord Havenden," Bonstraa said, trying to find Maggie in the crowd. "That's her over there, isn't it?"

Paul nodded. "We were married a few months ago, only a few weeks before Father died. I'm pleased that he was there, at least, even though his health was already quite bad by then."

"Poor Horace. He's left you with quite a legacy, but I'm sure you'll be a complete credit to him." Bonstraa extended his hand and touched Paul's arm almost paternally. "So, are you going to introduce me to your wife? As your father may have told you, I'm a great admirer of feminine beauty."

Paul had no chance to find Maggie and introduce her to his father's friend, as the sound of a small bell ringing brought the guests to silence.

"Ladies and gentlemen, I'm delighted to be able to present a very special guest to you," began van Swieten, who had positioned himself in the middle of the hall. "Some of you may have expected me to invite some Balinese dancers as I did on the last occasion, but it is not my intention to indulge in tedious repetition. As luck would have it, an outstanding daughter of our country is currently spending some time in her homeland, and so I'm able to offer you a very special cultural treat tonight. Miss Rose Gallway is a rising star of the musical firmament, currently enjoying great success with her violin all over the world. I consider it a great honor that she accepted my invitation to play for you tonight."

With a sweeping hand gesture he beckoned the violinist in. All the guests craned their necks; Paul could not see her immediately.

"This girl really is something special," Bonstraa murmured as he applauded. "Have you heard of her?"

Paul shook his head. He had not had much time for the arts—since his father had been unwell, he'd had to take care of the property and the estates. Every now and then he had to be seen at social occasions, but that was not enough for him to know which musicians were causing a sensation. The crowd parted and, with the proud bearing of a queen, a young woman with a cascade of black hair entered the room. She wore a ruched blouse and full black skirt, its gathered train bobbing delightfully at every step. In her left hand she held a distinctive red-grained violin, the bow in her right. She took up her position next to a black piano, looked around at her audience with a smile, and tucked the violin under her chin.

For a moment the room was so still that the proverbial pin could have been heard to drop. Then the first note rang out, clear as crystal, and Paul could do nothing else but gaze at this woman, who seemed to melt into the music and forget about the world around her.

***

As ever when a concert was going well, Rose felt as if her bow had developed a remarkable life of its own and was guiding her hand, instead of being moved by her. The notes were clear and precise, the tempo perfect, and when Rose closed her eyes, she could see malevolently sparkling icicles and wide fields covered by a delicate-looking but thick blanket of snow. A shudder ran through her body as though she were actually standing in the winter wind and watching the sun disappear behind a fir-lined horizon, the darkness following as swiftly as if the sun were sweeping a cloak behind it.

Before she went to England, she'd had no idea of what a European winter would be like—what frost would feel like, or the sensation of snowflakes being blown into her face. Winter on Sumatra was the season of rains. She remembered all too clearly the huge puddles she'd had to circumnavigate on her way to school while trying to shelter from the rain beneath a hat made of palm leaves. But despite the heavy downpours, it was warm and the air as humid as the cloud of steam above a pan of soup.

She had soon learned that it rained a lot in England, too—but this rain was not warm like the Sumatran rain that left the mountains steaming in its wake. The London rain was icy cold and the fog impenetrable, hostile. Until she became acclimatized, even in summer, Rose often shivered in her room, her hands wrapped around her arms for warmth. When winter came, a very harsh winter even for the English climate, she had discovered a wonder—frozen water. Although the cold affected her more than the other girls at the conservatory, she had spent hours admiring the glinting of sunlight on ice or allowing snow to melt in her hand until her skin was red and numb.

She could see the white crystals in her mind's eye now, and she felt the cold on her fingertips and the icy breath of the wind on her face. All these sensations carried her along as she played, and she regretted the performance coming to its end.

Only then did she become aware of her heavy breathing, the thumping of her heart, and the pressure of the violin beneath her chin. It was as if she had left her body while playing and was now slowly returning to it.

She looked around, a little dazed, and her lips formed a smile of satisfaction as she saw the audience staring at her, speechless. Had she awoken in them all the emotions she herself had felt? She would never know, and there may well have been people there who were not affected by the music, but that moment of pure silence before the applause broke out was immensely satisfying.

The applause—shot through with cries of "Bravo!"—was a little more delayed than usual, but these people had probably not been prepared for her playing.

Rose curtsied, as was expected from a grateful artist, before straightening up again. In that moment her eyes met those of a young man whom she had not noticed before. His hair was a golden color, and his eyes were as blue as the sea when it reflected a clear summer sky.

She had seen many fair-skinned, blond people in her life—her teacher had been a flaxen blonde, which had fascinated her as a little girl. But she had never seen anyone who radiated as much sunshine as he did.

As the calls for an encore grew, she came back to herself and turned her gaze away. She acknowledged her audience's request with a nod, and a little later *Spring* was resonating through the ballroom.

After the piece came to an end, a stocky man approached her and shook her hand somewhat roughly. From the description she'd heard of his behavior and a few remarks Mai had let drop in the dressing room, Rose concluded that this must be van Swieten. Heavens, this man really was one of those who would pinch a girl's backside—Carmichael had not been exaggerating there.

Practiced at maintaining polite reserve, Rose allowed his enthusiasm and his compliments to wash over her with lowered eyes and, as Mrs. Faraday had drummed into her, thanked him with a few calm, select words, although everything in her was crying out to run from the room, rejoicing in the simple delight of knowing she had played like never before in her life. No one needed to tell her that; she simply knew it.

The attention of the governor drew other men toward them. They approached, smiling broadly or looking her over like they would a horse at a market, while their wives hung back at a distance with sour expressions. Rose was used to this exchange, but it was never pleasant. This time, though, there was one of them she would have liked to get to know a little better.

Rose searched in vain for the sunshine man. Had he not liked her recital? Was he one of those unfeeling ones, as she thought of them? Or was he too reserved to throng around her shamelessly like the others?

In the face of the increasing number of admirers crowding around her, Rose's only way out was to flee. Under the pretext of needing to retire to her dressing room because she was feeling a little unwell, she made her excuses, although she had no intention of returning to Mai, and quite possibly Carmichael, in that room.

Her dressing room had given her a good view of the garden, and she wondered now if it would be the best place to go and cool down, to reflect on her performance. She hurried past the guests, ignoring the sharp looks she got from some of the older women, and finally reached the door. There she met a serving girl carrying a bowl of fruit.

"Excuse me, how can I get out to the garden?" she asked in Malay, causing the girl to stare at her wide eyed. Rose knew that her origins on her mother's side were scarcely visible—with her pale skin she looked like a European to the local people. The girl was even more surprised when she heard her speaking her native language fluently.

"I mean, how can I get out without having to face the crowds again?" Rose added with a conspiratorial smile that the girl found no less bewildering than her knowledge of the language. But she showed her the way willingly, sending her down the corridor toward the kitchen. The warm smell of cooking that met her made her stomach rumble. When another serving girl approached, carrying a tray of pastries, she quickly grabbed one and disappeared through a small back door, through which she had glimpsed treetops in the moonlight.

The warm wind that enfolded her outdoors drew a sigh of pleasure from her. The humid air was filled with the familiar smell of frangipani, orchids, and jasmine. Between the towering palms that grew on the estate was a deep yellow, waxing crescent moon. The light that spilled from the windows of the house illuminated the occasional branch of gleaming flowers against the darkness.

After devouring the pastry, Rose walked on and allowed the impressions of the garden, its sweet scents and its night-muted colors, to gradually penetrate her senses.

The farther she went from the house, the clearer she could hear the sounds of the natural world all around her. Rustling could be heard in the bushes, and every now and again a nocturnal bird flew up with a rapid beating of wings. In the distance, monkeys were calling into the night. The warm wind blew through the trees, the melody of her homeland that she had not heard for so long.

As the gravel crunched beneath her feet, she wondered if it were possible to capture all these impressions in a piece of music. Vivaldi had succeeded in portraying spring birdsong, summer drowsiness, the whirling of autumn leaves, and the crackling ice of winter in sound, so why shouldn't she create something similar? All she needed was time and a place in which to sink into the notes in her head, undisturbed by people.

She finally stopped on a small terrace that offered a view toward the sea and the city of Padang. The water was a narrow, dark strip, the moonlight not yet bright enough to sprinkle the waves with silver.

Beacons shone out to guide ships on their way, and light could be seen from scattered houses, looking from a distance like glowworms that had alighted in the bushes.

Rose had never seen her own country from such a perspective. Only once during her childhood had she left Padang, to visit her grandmother who lived far inland. Rose only had hazy memories of the visit—her grandmother's wrinkled face and the magnificent garden that had seemed like the stuff of fairy tales. Apart from these few snapshots, everything else had faded into oblivion.

She still recalled, however, that the garden had been terraced and that when she had stood on the top level, she could look out over the whole village.

"You look as though you're enjoying the view."

Rose whirled round. At first she couldn't make out the man approaching her along the narrow path. But as he came nearer, moonlight fell on his face, and she could see now that it was the Englishman she had seen on the edge of the crowd—the sunshine man. Without her knowing why, her heart began to thump wildly.

"Yes, it's wonderful. It reminds me . . ." Rose stopped. No, she didn't want to tell him that. The memory of her grandmother's garden, which she had only seen once as a child and then embellished over the years in her imagination, belonged to her and no one else.

Anyway, what was he doing here?

"What does it remind you of?" he asked, apparently undeterred. He came to a stop, almost as if he thought her an apparition that might vanish if he came too close.

"Of a place I knew as a child. It's not important now. What brings you out into the garden?"

"I was looking for you."

"Looking for me?"

"I didn't have an opportunity to speak to you earlier—and I also got the impression you didn't feel comfortable among your circle of admirers."

Rose felt blood rush to her cheeks and was glad that this man probably couldn't see it in the moonlight. "I'm a musician, not an actress. They may feel comfortable as objects of admiration, but I feel at my best when I'm immersed in my music."

"That was obvious from watching you play. Vivaldi is one of my mother's favorite composers. And who doesn't know *The Four Seasons*?"

"They're my favorite pieces, *Winter* and *Spring*. But aren't you going to tell me who it is I'm talking to?"

"Oh, forgive me, I didn't mean to be impolite." The Englishman looked a little embarrassed as he gave a brief bow. "I'm Paul Havenden. Lord Paul Havenden, to be precise, but I still haven't really got used to my title."

"It's my pleasure." Rose extended her hand, which he took gently in his and kissed lightly.

"Now that the formalities are over, we can continue to talk about music. You said you like Vivaldi?"

"Actually, I like any well-composed music that I can play on my violin," Rose said with a smile. "After Vivaldi, Tchaikovsky is my favorite composer. And we mustn't forget Mozart. Which composers do you admire?"

Havenden smiled a little awkwardly. "I'm afraid you will think me a philistine. I love music, but I don't have much idea about it. Vivaldi I know. Mozart, too, but that's probably it. I had to take charge of our estate in England at an early age, which didn't leave much time for my cultural development. But I can take pleasure in some things that the common man doesn't have the privilege of experiencing—like hearing you play."

"If the common man has enough money to pay for a ticket, he can go to a music hall and listen to me play. The arts are no longer reserved exclusively for the upper classes."

The Englishman gave her a wide smile. "I admit defeat. And I promise from the bottom of my heart that I'll pay more attention to the arts."

Rose knew he wouldn't. As soon as he was back in England, he would once again be bound by his obligations and soon forget this concert. "So what brings you here, Lord Havenden?"

"Business," he replied steadily. "Mijnheer van Swieten would like to offer me a share in a sugarcane plantation to the north of the city. It's run by an acquaintance of his who would have nothing against an Englishman getting involved. He's an old friend of my late father's. And you? Are you on tour here?"

Rose nodded. "My agent has gotten it into his head that, before we break into the New World, I should spend some time entertaining the crowned heads of Asia—and of course the whites who live here. I've already been to Siam, Burma, China, and Japan, and now I'm here."

"You've probably seen more than I have in my whole life." Havenden laughed harshly. "Up to now I've had to live off my father's stories."

"You've never left England before this?" she asked.

Rose couldn't imagine it. Apart from the occasional winter snows, what was so attractive about England? When her tour was over, she intended to settle in Paris—unless she had been invited to America by then.

"Yes, of course I have," Havenden replied. "I've traveled through Europe, to Germany, Italy, France, and Spain. But this is my first visit to a country outside Europe."

"And how do you like it?"

"It's marvelous! What else would I be likely to say to a daughter of this country?" He looked deep into her eyes, almost too deep for Rose's liking. Perplexed, she took a step back.

"The truth," she replied, more brusquely than she had intended.

"The truth is that I really do think this country is wonderful. My father had a number of friends here and used to go into raptures about the green jungles and the exotic flowers. And the beauty of the women, although you can imagine that didn't go down too well with my mother." After a short laugh at his own joke, he continued. "When I arrived, my expectations were very high, of course, but I wasn't disappointed. And if all goes well, I'll soon have a share in a sugar plantation. I'm hoping that will mean I can visit this country more often."

They looked at one another for a moment; then they heard a voice calling, "Paul?"

Havenden started, as if he had been torn abruptly from a dream. Rose looked at him with raised eyebrows.

"My . . . fiancée," he said quickly, and bent to kiss her hand. "It was a pleasure to meet you, Miss Gallway."

"The pleasure was all mine," she replied and watched as he turned and walked toward the voice of the woman who had called for him again.

Without knowing why, Rose was somehow sad to see him go. He may not have had much of an idea about music, but there was something about him she found really interesting. When she turned back to look at the view, the crescent moon had detached itself from the palm trees and was now making its way toward the darkly forested mountain.

"The young man was clearly taken by you."

Rose whirled around. One of Carmichael's more unpleasant habits was to appear behind her suddenly out of the blue, after listening in on her in secret.

"What are you doing? Why are you creeping around after me like a thief?"

"I'm not creeping around! I simply didn't want to interrupt your conversation."

Blood shot to Rose's cheeks. How much of their conversation had he overheard? Not that Havenden had gotten too personal, but she nevertheless felt as if Carmichael had been watching something intimate.

"He was only telling me how much he admired me, nothing more. Anyway, he's engaged." Why did she feel the need to add that? And why did it give her such a strange burning feeling in her stomach?

"I've been talking to van Swieten," Carmichael said, finally getting to the point of why he had approached her. "He's more than delighted with you—and more than disappointed that you're not being seen at the party. He would really like to continue his conversation with you."

The way Carmichael's eyes sparked as he spoke revealed that her agent meant every word. Artists were hired to perform, and they were usually expected to retire discreetly after their appearance.

"You know that I'm only involved in occasions like this for as long as I'm playing. I'm not particularly keen on being ogled like a side of beef at a market. Anyway, it's not the done thing to impose yourself on a host simply because you've been hired by him."

"So your Englishman wasn't ogling you?"

"That's completely different." Rose found it difficult to suppress the annoyance welling up inside her. Why was it any of Carmichael's business? She had spoken to the man; that was all. She'd be leaving in the morning.

"Very well, as you wish. In any case, I've got some good news for you, even if you insist on staying away from the company. Van Swieten wanted me to ask you if you'd like to stay on in Padang for a while—as a famous daughter of the city—to play a few concerts he'd like to organize for you."

"I don't need a patron for a few appearances."

"Don't you?" Carmichael raised his eyebrows. "You have to admit that it would be very nice to be able to play concerts without having to worry about audience numbers."

"As if we have a problem with our audience figures," Rose said, and sniffed scornfully, wondering if her agent had had a drop too much to drink. "The concert in Surabaja was sold out."

"It was indeed, and let's hope this lucky streak lasts. But it wouldn't do any harm to count an influential man like the governor among your acquaintances—even your friends. He may govern this island, but that's not to say he doesn't also have contacts in Europe."

"We don't have any difficulty getting engagements in Europe, either."

"But there may come a time when that's not the case. Everyone sees you as the rising star at the moment, but at some point you'll reach your zenith. And then we need to ensure that you shine for as long as possible, that you don't immediately fall from the sky. Arrogance never achieved anything, and it's all the more damaging to look a gift horse in the mouth—even when you're on your way to the top. Anyway, I think it would be a good idea to remain here for a while and accept van Swieten's offer. If I remember rightly, your parents live here. You could visit them between your engagements."

Rose had considered this and intended to visit her mother before she departed the next day. She had not had time before now, since they had arrived very late. And if she stayed, it might then be possible to see Paul Havenden again . . .

"All right," she said. "We'll stay here for a while, and I'll play the concerts."

Carmichael gave her a broad smile. "You won't regret it. I must ask you now to come with me and give van Swieten the good news yourself. He'll be delighted!"

As they returned from the garden, Rose was again subject to the penetrating gazes of the guests. Van Swieten was waiting for her, surrounded by men.

"Ah, here comes our musical sensation!" he called, handing his glass to a servant who had appeared silently beside him. "I thought you'd made your escape."

She had, but now Rose fixed him with a winning smile. "I'm sorry if I gave you that impression," she replied in Dutch. "After my concerts I'm always in turmoil and need a few moments to get a grip on myself and reflect on my playing." She could tell from the men's expressions that none of them really knew what she meant. "You have a truly wonderful garden, Mijnheer van Swieten."

"Now you're embarrassing me." He laughed. "I don't think it's a particularly fine example, and it's in urgent need of attention. You must have seen many far more beautiful gardens in England."

"I have to disagree—your garden can hold its own against any English garden, not least because it's not as dull here, and you can enjoy the flowers all year round."

Van Swieten's gaze rested on her for a moment; then he offered her his arm and led her out onto the terrace. "You have an extraordinary musical talent, and you're a daughter of my country. I therefore feel an obligation to give you my support. I'll be welcoming a large number of foreign visitors in the coming weeks, some of them very influential men from Europe, Asia, and America. If these people hear you play, they're bound to be enraptured and make sure your reputation is spread throughout the world."

"Mr. Carmichael and I are already working on that."

"But it would make your task so much easier! You know the musical world better than I do, so I don't need to tell you that there are times when it's not only about talent and ability but also about connections and being in the right place at the right time. I've followed your career since the day I heard that a young woman from Padang was causing a stir in the concert halls. Some people may take me for uncouth, but if there's anything I love unconditionally, it's my family and music. Your playing fascinates me, and on the basis of what I've heard about you, I believe I should offer you some support."

Where was this leading? Rose could not shake off the impression that his patronage would come with a condition—one that she might not want to accept.

"As I've already told Mr. Carmichael, I would like you to play ten concerts here in Padang before you continue your tour. Your agent assures me this would be possible."

Ten concerts! Carmichael had spoken of a few, but she had never thought it would be as many as ten. Would her tour schedule allow it?

"It's probably possible," Rose replied, her thoughts on one thing alone. America! How long had she dreamed of playing in New York? Would there be someone among these visitors who could get her there? And at what price?

"And what do you want from me in return?" she asked a little uneasily.

Van Swieten looked at her for a moment, then smiled. "Not what you may be thinking. No, I'll admit, there's only one thing I want in return. I want to make sure you achieve the greatest possible fame and tell everyone where you came from so the whole world learns of the existence of our beautiful island. And consider me a fatherly friend, nothing more."

Rose was ashamed to think that anything else had crossed her mind. For as long as she had been appearing on stage, certain men had always attempted to make immoral propositions under the guise of offering support. Clearly this Dutchman was an exception.

"I promise I will," she said. Van Swieten extended his hand to her.

When they returned to the hall, she saw that Paul Havenden was standing nearby. The graceful woman on his arm was obviously the fiancée he had spoken of, and she was giving him quite a look.

Get him out of your head, she told herself as she hurried over to Carmichael, who must have been burning to hear what she had to report about her conversation with the governor.

10

London, 2011

"Extracting the video shouldn't be a problem," Sunny said. Guided by Lilly over the telephone, she had taken down the camera and removed the memory card. "But there's hours of video there. You ought to think about deleting sections from time to time."

"Can you fast-forward through it? I only need one section, when that man appeared with the violin case."

Lilly had given Sunny a brief account of what it was all about. Of course Sunny's imagination had run wild, and she had come to the conclusion that this instrument was "hot" and that the old man wanted to get rid of it under some flimsy pretext.

"So why do you need it if you don't think the violin was stolen?"

Lilly sighed. She should have known that Sunny would probe.

"I want to ask my mother if she knows the man. It's a family matter. But you may as well not ask, because I'm not going to say any more about it. You wouldn't tell me your complete family history, would you?"

"Oh, well, there's not much to tell there. A typical middle-class family, that's all. You should see the way they look at me whenever I get a new tattoo."

"They must have gotten used to the way you look."

"Maybe they have, but I can assure you that every new tat is another shock for them. Anyway, I'll have a look at that video. It's completely dead here in the shop, sorry."

Lilly shrugged. "That's fine. I wouldn't have expected anything else. Can you e-mail the footage over when you've got it?"

"I'll try. Otherwise I'll burn it onto a CD."

"And make sure you reset the camera when you've finished. I don't want to be robbed while nothing's being recorded."

Sunny sniffed as if she doubted that anyone would want to snatch their antiques. "Don't worry, Lilly, I've got it covered. And if anyone comes here wanting to rob me, I'll—"

"Hopefully you won't bash them over the head with anything!"

"No, call the police, of course."

"Good girl." Lilly took a quick breath, then continued, "Would you have anything against looking after the shop for another two weeks perhaps? My friend thinks the identification of my violin could take a while yet. I'll double the amount we agreed on and give you a little bonus on top."

"No problem. My study leave lasts until April—I can stay here for that long."

"I won't need that much time. You've got to have some of your vacation to yourself. Otherwise your tattoo studio will be reporting you missing."

"No, no worries, I'm in touch with them on Facebook; they're not missing me. And I really enjoy running your shop. You know what? Yesterday an old lady nearly bought something!"

"So it's not completely dead?"

"No, people do come in occasionally."

"Good, that eases my mind. Don't forget the video, will you?"

"I'm on it now. Later, Lilly."

"Take care, Sunny."

Since Ellen had offered her computer, Lilly went into the study and booted up the machine. She was secretly hoping for a message from Gabriel, but her common sense told her it was impossible. He had a full schedule, and the fact that he had agreed to see her the previous day had been pure luck.

She was a little disappointed all the same to see that, although her in-box was full, apart from ads and spam there was only a message from her father, asking how she was and telling her briefly about a sailing trip he wanted to make with members of his club.

Lilly toyed with the idea of using this communication as a way of asking about the old man, but something held her back. I need the video, she thought. It will be better to show them the man instead of disturbing them with a set of stories.

Lilly merely wrote that she had come to London to spend a few days with her friend and would be in touch as soon as she was back home.

Not long after she sent the e-mail, the house phone rang. Was someone trying to reach Ellen? Or was it Sunny calling back? A look at the display told her it was not Sunny; it was a London number.

"This is Lilly Kaiser," she said as she answered.

She was surprised to hear a sharp woman's voice. That dragon of a secretary, she thought.

"Mrs. Kaiser? Just a moment, I'm putting you through to Mr. Thornton."

Lilly pressed her hand to her mouth to stop herself from shouting for joy. He was calling her! Her heart was suddenly beating wildly.

"Mrs. Kaiser?" the secretary asked, clearly expecting a response.

"Yes, I'm here. Please put me through."

There was no reply—just annoying hold music, though Lilly didn't have to endure it for long.

"Hello, Lilly." Gabriel sounded in a good mood. "I hope you can spare me a moment."

"Of course I can. Where are you?" Lilly heard a soft echo in the background, just like something she'd heard when they were down in the archive.

"I'm here among a stack of ancient wax cylinders and shellac disks," Gabriel said mysteriously. "And guess what I've found."

"A recording of Rose Gallway?"

"Yes, of the first concert she gave, in Cremona on June 12, 1895. Rose was just fifteen then, if the records are correct. Mrs. Faraday had obviously taken her star pupil to the city of the violin."

"Have you listened to the recording?"

"No, not yet. The cylinders are very delicate, and this is one that's particularly at risk. It may turn out that we can only play it once, so I've asked our technician to make a digital recording of it at the same time."

"Oh, of course . . ." Lilly bit her lip. She wanted to ask if she could be there when it was played back. What must it have sounded like when Rose played her violin?

"The reason I'm calling is to ask you if you wanted to listen to the recording with me—provided you've got the time."

Lilly gasped. "Of course I've got the time." What else would I be doing, she thought.

Gabriel laughed. "Excellent. I'd really love you to be there when we play it back."

"When do you intend to start?" Lilly glanced at the clock. Twenty past ten.

"Whenever you can get here."

"Right away, then?" Lilly's heart was pounding. She would have liked to call Ellen so that she could listen to the recording, too, but then she remembered what she had said the evening before about her institute not having much to do with Gabriel Thornton's school.

"If you're here in less than ten minutes, I'll have to pass, but I think we'll be ready to begin in half an hour. So you're coming?"

***

Lilly spent the whole of the taxi ride sitting on the backseat on tenterhooks. The traffic was fairly heavy that morning, slowing to a standstill again and again. Time, on the other hand, marched on, indifferent to Lilly's eagerness. She looked at her watch with a sigh. The half hour had already passed. Gabriel had promised to wait for her, but she hated to be late.

The taxi was forced to wait for another five minutes before continuing on its hesitant way. Lilly was about to give in to the urge to ask the driver to find a way around when she saw the school appear before them. At last!

"I'm sorry it took so long," the driver said as she handed over the fare. "The city's always hellish around noon."

"It's fine," Lilly replied politely, although she'd been about to lose her cool a few minutes before.

The warm notes of stringed instruments followed her through the corridors as she made for Gabriel's office. His secretary was no more welcoming than the first time, but she knew why Lilly was there and allowed her in to see her boss without objection.

Gabriel appeared to have been waiting for her and jumped up from his seat as soon as she entered. His sleeve was rumpled as if he'd just looked at his watch.

"Lilly, you're here at last! I was about to send out a search party."

"I'm so sorry. The traffic was particularly bad today," Lilly replied. "I hope you haven't begun yet."

"No, of course not. Come this way."

Gabriel led her down a long corridor. They stopped in front of a door through which muffled sounds could be heard.

"Our sound laboratory," he said as they entered.

Waiting for them at one of the workbenches was a man of around forty in jeans and a gray shirt with rolled-up sleeves. He was surrounded by a range of equipment and several other people who appeared to be technicians.

"Bob? This is the lady we've all been waiting for," Gabriel said, turning to Lilly. "Lilly, this is Bob Henderson, a true genius when it comes to computers and wax cylinders."

"He's exaggerating wildly," Henderson said as he offered her his hand. "I do what I have to do."

His modesty brought a smile to Lilly's lips.

"Good, we can start now," Henderson said, turning to his test apparatus.

As Lilly was trying to figure out how it worked, she noticed a narrow wax-covered cylinder fitted in place.

"We're fortunate that this wax cylinder—the one with the recording of Rose Gallway—is one of the more modern types," Henderson said.

He pressed a button, and the cylinder began to revolve slowly. There was an initial rush of white noise that was almost deafening, causing Lilly to worry that the recording would be irretrievable. But then the first note broke through, and the computer settings modified it so it could be heard more clearly.

Lilly smiled broadly as she heard the first phrases of *The Four Seasons* penetrate the insistent crackling. She recognized *Spring* immediately, as the Vivaldi was one of the few classical pieces she listened to regularly; she could even hum along to it.

The violinist was a virtuoso. Now Lilly knew what Ellen had meant the day before—this interpretation had soul. Even someone who had only a passing interest in classical music could hear it. The violinist's fingers seemed to fly over the fingerboard. Lilly was unable to analyze the ornamentation she used in her playing, but she was fascinated by the way she could produce the notes so rapidly and skillfully.

The recording was brief, reaching only the April storms of *Spring* before it came to an end. A rapt silence followed—even the technicians involved in testing the apparatus had paused in their work to listen. After a while, Gabriel shook his head, clearly stunned.

"No wonder the world was fascinated by her. I'd say this is one of the best violinists in the whole world. What do you think, Bob?"

"I'd say only Paganini played better," the technician replied, also clearly very moved by this snippet of music.

"How about you, Lilly?"

Gabriel's penetrating gaze rested on her in a way she found unsettlingly pleasant.

"It—it's—it was wonderful!" She was embarrassed by her stammering attempt at words, but Gabriel nodded with a smile before turning back to Henderson.

"I'm sure we can let Mrs. Kaiser have a copy of the recording, can't we?"

"Of course, but it will take a moment. Can you wait?"

"Mrs. Kaiser wanted to collect a few documents on Helen Carter anyway," Gabriel replied for her.

Lilly looked at him in amazement. Did she want to do that? Gabriel's search in the basement must have been a real success.

"That's fine, then," Henderson said. "I'll bring it to you in your office, Mr. Thornton."

"Thanks very much, Bob."

Gabriel led Lilly out of the sound lab.

"So, you've got some documents about Helen Carter for me?" she asked as they moved away from the door.

Gabriel nodded meaningfully. "It was a remarkable stroke of luck. Like the recording you just heard, we found it in the box of hopeless cases."

"The box of what?"

"It's where we put all the unplayable cylinders and records," he said with a grin.

"Why don't you just throw them away?"

"You don't throw away history!" he said in mock indignation. "We even hold on to the cylinders that can't be read with the equipment we have at the time. New processes are being discovered all the time, enabling us to coax their old sounds from more and more of them. The box of hopeless cases is more like a box in which all the items that *appear* hopeless are stored away safe and sound. Like that cylinder of Rose Gallway's recording. What a find!"

Down in the archive, Lilly saw that Gabriel had laid out a few documents on a desk.

"So these are the documents relating to Helen Carter?"

"Yes, that's right. I told you that she and her family were killed in an attack on their ship off the coast of Sumatra. I looked her up in Mrs. Faraday's old record books and tried to find out a little about her parents."

"Wasn't Sumatra once Dutch?" Lilly dimly recalled some stick puppets she had once been offered by a Dutchman. The puppets were very finely made, real miniature masterpieces, but she had been unable to imagine selling them in the center of Berlin. She had no idea what eventually became of them, but the Dutchman had told her they had come to him from his father, who had once owned a plantation on Sumatra, and that they were used for shadow plays.

"It wasn't only the Dutch who lived on Sumatra. There were other settlers there, too—German, French, and English. Emily Faraday kept a detailed record of her pupils, with notes on their origins and family. She was very active and followed the paths of her star pupils all over the world, even in far-flung places like Sumatra, since she believed that the most beautiful flowers can grow in hidden places. Rose Gallway's mother was from Sumatra, although her father was English. Helen Carter was the daughter of James and Ivy Carter. Mr. Carter ran a branch of an English trading company in Padang and was a friend of Piet van Swieten, the island's governor at the time."

"Could Rose Gallway and Helen Carter have known one another, do you think? Perhaps Rose gave Helen violin lessons!"

"It's possible, but we've got no evidence of it."

"But how else would Helen have come by the rose violin?"

"Perhaps Rose was attacked, and the thieves sold her violin after covering up its origin."

"What a dreadful thought."

"But not impossible. How else would Rose have been parted from her priceless violin?"

Lilly stored the information away in her mind, though as yet she had no idea what to do with it.

"So you really have no idea where Rose Gallway could have gone?"

"No. The violin alone could tell us that, but unfortunately it only gives us sounds, not words."

Gabriel searched briefly in the pile on the desk and produced a sheet of paper.

"I've summarized the most important information about Helen and Rose here. Unfortunately these facts, study notes, and teachers' reports don't give us any insight into whether either of them had any ambitions to compose. I'd bet that the real 'moonlit garden' is somewhere on Sumatra—and one of these women had something to do with it."

Lilly gave him a searching look. "Have you played the piece yet?"

The smile that flitted across his face gave her the answer before he could speak.

"Of course I have. And, if you like, I'd be glad to play you my interpretation."

"I'm all ears."

Gabriel laughed. "I don't have my violin here. And I'd like to practice a bit."

"OK. When do you think you'll be ready?"

"When you bring me the rose violin. To be honest, I was hoping you'd have it with you today."

"I'm sorry. Ellen's still examining it."

Thornton gave her a wink. "Well, that gives me a bit more time to practice."

Back in Thornton's office they waited for Henderson to bring them the recording, safely burned onto a CD. Gabriel had also made copies for her of all he had found concerning Rose Gallway and Helen Carter.

"I think you owe me something for all these favors." He gave her an impertinent smile as he waggled the jewel case containing the CD in front of his face.

"What did you have in mind?" Lilly asked.

"I was wondering about some kind of personal recompense."

Lilly went hot and cold. She thought of Gabriel as a respectable man, but these words sounded anything but. Or was that just her imagination?

"And . . . what would that be?" she asked a little uncertainly.

"How about we have dinner together sometime? You'd be paying, of course."

A sigh of relief escaped her. "Yes, of course. That would be the least I could do, wouldn't it? OK, then, I'm inviting you for a meal. But you'll have to tell me which are the best restaurants in London, since I don't know my way around too well—I need to make sure the recompense is a worthy one, don't I?"

"I'll mark down my preferences in a diners' guide and let you have it. Can I still get hold of you at Ellen Morris's?"

"Yes." Lilly felt her cheeks glowing. For a moment she and Gabriel regarded one another in silence; then she gave an embarrassed laugh. "Thanks once again."

"It's my pleasure. I really hope you manage to find something out about our Rose and her violin. I think you deserve to."

As Lilly nodded, she heard the hoot of the taxi waiting outside.

11

"The test results on the varnish are back," Ellen called out cheerfully as she entered the living room, where Lilly sat on the sofa, surrounded by a pile of papers.

Playing back Rose's CD recording on continuous repeat, Lilly had spread out everything Thornton had given her on the coffee table and had added some information she had printed out from the Internet. There was a lot of material on Sumatra, and Lilly had to exercise a degree of self-discipline not to get too drawn in to the wonderful images of dense palm jungles, pink skies, and delicious-looking food.

"That's wonderful!" she replied, putting the cap on the pen she had been using to mark the places she thought most important in the articles. "What did the lab find?"

Ellen glanced at the papers around Lilly. "Well, you've had a productive day, haven't you?"

"Extremely. Thornton called and invited me to the music school—to listen to a recording of Rose Gallway!"

Ellen raised her eyebrows. "Wow! So what's it like?"

"Wonderful!" Lilly reached for the CD player remote control. Soon the slightly distorted sounds of *Spring* were filling the living room.

"The recording was on a wax cylinder, and you can't imagine the complicated procedures involved in making a decent sound recording. But tell me, what have you got on the varnish?"

Ellen stood stock-still for a moment as if struck, obviously moved by Rose's playing, too.

"That's incredible! Where——"

"Thornton found the cylinder in a box. Apparently the recording was made in Cremona."

"It makes my laboratory results pale by comparison."

Ellen laid the envelope in her hand on a chair and sat down next to Lilly.

"Why?"

"Because all these test results say is that the violin originates from the early eighteenth century and that it was probably made in Cremona. And that our violin is no Stradivari."

"But that's great!" Lilly cleared her throat. "I mean about the date. It may be a pity that it's not a Stradivari, but I'm not really too worried about who the maker was."

"I feel a bit differently; I *am* interested in that aspect. But the results are only mundane theory. You've got a recording of Rose—from Cremona! A real clue! Does Thornton realize what treasures he's got there?"

"He does indeed, and he's proud of it, too."

Ellen shook her head pensively, then smiled broadly. "Tell me about the recording. And where's all this paperwork from?"

"Some of it's from your printer, some from Thornton himself. He also told me a few facts about Helen. I'm in the middle of sifting through it all."

They were interrupted by a ringtone from Ellen's purse. She took out her cell phone and called up the message that had just arrived.

"Oh, shit!" she said as she read the text.

"What's up?"

"Something's happened on Dean's building site. Some wall collapsed and started a fire."

Lilly gasped in shock. "But he's OK, isn't he?"

"Yes, thank goodness, but he'll have to stay there until at least midnight." She snapped her cell phone shut and then smiled. "I have an idea. Go and change into your new dress. Let's eat out tonight! We've got to celebrate our new find, or our luck might run out."

"What about the girls?"

"We'll take them with us, of course." Ellen slapped Lilly's thigh. "Now, off you go and make yourself beautiful while I tell them."

Lilly shook her head. How wonderful it is not to be alone, she thought as she rose and hurried into the guest room.

The restaurant Ellen had chosen was very elegant, but fortunately not too exalted. As they walked in, a few eyebrows were raised.

"Maybe they think we're a lesbian couple with children," Ellen whispered playfully.

"What's lesbian?" Norma asked immediately.

"When two women are married to each other," Jessie explained.

"But Aunt Lilly isn't married to Mum," Norma retorted.

"I should learn to hold my tongue," Ellen murmured. "My girls have inherited my good hearing."

They were shown to a table by an elegant maître d', and a waiter introduced himself. He shook out their napkins on their laps, handed them the wine list, and told them that the meal would be preceded by a small amuse-bouche to prepare their palates.

Lilly felt a little unnerved. She had never been to a restaurant of such refinement. Ellen's daughters, on the other hand, seemed more used to it.

"Tell me if I do anything wrong, won't you?" Lilly said, turning to Jessie at her side.

"Of course!" she said, visibly delighted to be able to help an adult.

As a tasting course to attune their palates to the individual delights of the eight-course menu was passed around, they chatted about Ellen's day at the institute and the treasures in Thornton's basement archive.

"Now that we know that Rose played there, what about a little trip to Italy?" Ellen said suddenly. "Follow in the footsteps of our little genius . . ."

"I have nothing against it," Lilly replied, amazed to think how she would have hesitated before the violin arrived on the scene. "I've managed to clear myself two more free weeks."

"Is Sunny doing all right in the shop?"

"Great! She's not bringing in a fortune, but at least no one's stolen anything. And she's got some peace and quiet to get on with her studies."

"How many tattoos has she got now?"

"I have no idea. You'd have to be married to her to count them all. And I doubt you've got a shot there, since she's got her heart set on a tattoo artist for a husband."

Ellen laughed out loud, perhaps a little too loudly for the couple at the next table, who gave them astonished looks. Ellen ignored them.

"What did she say about the video?"

"She's going to extract it and save it. When I'm back, I'll show it to Mama, and if it means nothing to her, I'll give Peter's parents a call. If the violin is somehow connected to their family, they might want it."

"You can't give that baby away so easily!" Ellen said indignantly.

"But it doesn't belong to me."

"What gives you the idea it doesn't belong to you? You were Peter's wife! If your in-laws have the slightest decency, and I'm assuming they do, they'll press the violin straight back into your hands. I imagine it would be a waste of time even to try and force it on them."

They paused as the dessert was served. The miniature work of art made up of a chocolate mousse, a crème caramel, cream, and a selection of fruits was so beautifully arranged that Lilly hardly dared disturb it with the silver spoon. But when she did, she was rewarded with a wonderful taste that beat all she had eaten so far.

"My goodness, if this dessert were a man, I'd be asking him for his phone number right now," she murmured quietly enough for the waiter not to hear. Gabriel immediately sprang into her mind, and she wondered which restaurant to bring him to.

**

That night, the aroma of the delicious dessert and thoughts of Gabriel Thornton haunted Lilly's thoughts for a long time. As she gazed out the window at the moon playing hide-and-seek among scattered clouds, she tried to imagine the music, but she didn't want to play the CD at that moment. As her inner ear failed to conjure it up, she thought instead of Gabriel's face, which had been so close earlier in the day.

She knew that his friendly manner probably meant nothing more than the fact that they were working on a project together and that they would probably go their separate ways when it was finished.

But she still enjoyed picturing his eyes, the dimples in his cheeks, his generous mouth with lightly pouting lips. The way his hair fell forward as he leaned over the recording equipment. She could somehow see it all more clearly now, and the image stirred something inside her. The excitement of the activities in the sound lab had hidden the feeling, so she hadn't noticed it at the time. But she felt it now, and a pleasant warmth spread through her. She also felt, for the first time in ages, the need to feel a man's skin against her body.

Gabriel's skin.

As she sank into sleep, cushioned in these thoughts, she heard footsteps outside her door. They were so faint that she thought it must be one of the girls. Did they want to take her dress?

There was a sudden knock.

"Lilly?" Ellen whispered softly.

"Yes?"

"Can I come in?"

Lilly sat up. Had something happened? She hadn't heard a car coming back.

"Yes, of course, come in. Is something up with Dean?"

"No, don't worry." Ellen sat down on the edge of Lilly's bed like she had when they were children. "I just can't stop thinking about Cremona. I know someone there who may be able to help us find Rose."

"But we've got Thornton," Lilly said, once again feeling that pleasurable pull in the pit of her stomach.

"So we have, and I don't mean to cast doubt on his knowledge, but several pairs of eyes see more than one, and perhaps my acquaintance can find out something about her in Italy. Perhaps she turned up there again after she disappeared."

Lilly shook her head, but Ellen's fervent enthusiasm was not to be dampened.

"We really should follow every lead. And even if she was only in Cremona as a girl, that's plenty. Don't you want to see the city she visited? Maybe it'll help us find out what made her tick."

And what's that all got to do with me? Lilly wondered, but something held her back from voicing her doubts out loud.

"What would you say to leaving this weekend?" Ellen said suddenly.

Lilly gasped in surprise. "What about Dean's building site? And the children?"

"Norma and Jessie can manage quite well without their mummy, and Dean's assured me it'll all be sorted out by the weekend, and he'll be free to look after them."

"When did he say that?"

"Earlier, on the phone. He called briefly and said it wasn't as bad as they'd feared. He'll be back home tomorrow, and then we can begin the preparations."

Lilly felt increasingly overtaken by events. She had hoped to see Gabriel again tomorrow, but how could she pass up the opportunity to see Cremona?

"When do you intend to go?" she asked, and was rewarded by a broad smile from Ellen.

"I'll see when the best flights are. Perhaps we can get a last-minute deal on an early-morning flight," Ellen said.

"OK, you look into it. I'll transfer the money over to you as soon as I can."

"Fine, let's do it. We'll have ourselves a lovely weekend and maybe find something out about Rose in the bargain." She stood and left the room.

The thought of traveling to Italy gave Lilly butterflies of excitement. If only they could take Gabriel with them . . .

Gabriel! She felt a sudden urge to tell him about the trip. After all, he may have a date in mind for our meal, she thought, but knew only too well that this wasn't the only reason. She wanted to tell him about the plan because he was somehow important to her—even if that fact was a bit bewildering.

After Ellen left to start her packing, Lilly got up, threw her robe on, and crept up to the study. She switched on the light, booted up the computer, and opened her e-mail.

Dear Gabriel,

I'm writing in case you've already planned a date for our dinner.

My friend has persuaded me to go on a sudden trip to Cremona, on the trail of Rose and our violin. You'll probably find this a bit of a surprise, but perhaps she left more behind her there—maybe more than a recording. I hope you understand and aren't annoyed with me.

As soon as I'm back, I'll let you know. And then we'll have our meal, promise.

Kind regards,

Lilly

Lilly reread the message before sending it. Did it sound too impersonal? Should she have included something more? Something to give him a little insight into her soul? She was about to add something but held back. No, that was fine; it was enough—enough to show him that she was serious about the dinner. Enough not to sound ridiculous. She pressed "Send." She felt strangely light and at the same time peculiarly tense. It was unlikely that he would see the message that night, but she enjoyed imagining him sitting at his computer and opening her e-mail. I hope he's not annoyed with me, she thought a little anxiously.

But before she could turn off the computer, an e-mail arrived with a soft ping. It was from Gabriel's office address. Was he still working? With shaking hands, she opened the e-mail window and read.

Dear Lilly,

I'm ashamed to say that I still don't have a date in mind. However, I do have a surprise for you, but as you're going away for a few days, I think it would be a good idea to keep it back until after you return from Cremona. I've been there once and found the city so captivating that I was only a hair's breadth away from staying there. To make sure that doesn't happen to you, and to make sure you come back to me, I'll say just this:

I've uncovered a small piece of news that throws a whole new light on Rose Gallway.

I hope you have a lovely time in Cremona and look forward to hearing about anything you unearth. I send you my best wishes and warmest thoughts.

Yours,

Gabriel Thornton

Lilly leaned back in the office chair with a smile. What had he discovered? Or was it really all just a trick to entice her back from Cremona? No, she couldn't imagine Gabriel doing such a thing. If he said he had something, then he had something. Lilly was far more interested in the fact that he'd said she should come back to him than the news itself. He could have worded it more generally, but as she read the message over and over again, the words *to me* jumped out at her.

Before she could read it yet again, the door opened and Ellen entered. Her eyebrows shot up in amazement.

"Oh, I didn't know you were up here!"

"I just contacted Gabriel to let him know I'd be gone a few days in case he found something new," Lilly explained as she closed the e-mail.

"Good. So let's have a look when the next flight's leaving. Dean just got back. If you're looking for him, just follow the smell of smoke." Ellen had an affectionate look on her face. "I'm so glad that he's OK."

"Me too." Lilly kissed her friend's temple and returned to her bedroom before memories of Peter could creep back in and spoil her lovely evening.

12

Padang, 1902

That afternoon Rose finally found the time to visit her parents.

She had not seen them since she had been sent to England, but she had never lost the yearning for the house by the harbor and the people on the street outside it. And for her mother and father, whose differences had been apparent to her even as a child. Her father was English—a tall, stocky man with broad hands, blue eyes, and hair as light as the sun. Her mother was a native of Sumatra, dainty, with thick, black hair and delicate almond-shaped eyes, which Rose had inherited. As a child she had sometimes noticed how her father was envied for his beautiful wife, and that had made her feel proud.

As she hurried through the streets of Padang, past market stalls selling fruit, coconuts, and rice, she thought again of the Englishman who had spoken to her during the governor's reception. Since those few minutes spent with him in the garden, she had visualized his face again and again—his sea-blue eyes, his golden-blond hair. The strange confusion she had felt the previous day had since grown—never before had she found a man so attractive, although she had been courted by plenty.

"Don't be afraid, lady, monkey do nothing," an old man declared in broken English.

Do I really look that white? Rose wondered. She replied in Malay: "I'm not afraid. But keep a good hold on him, or he'll vanish up a palm tree, and then you'll have to chase him."

The man stared at her wide eyed, surprised into silence. Rose turned with a smile and continued on her way.

The salty breeze that blew through the city's streets gradually became stronger and fresher. Her parents' house was near a few warehouses on the seafront. Her father managed the buildings for a major trading company. The house was not built on stilts like the natives' houses on Sumatra but in the Dutch style—with thick stone walls whose white-wash was marked with ever more cracks and dark patches.

Rose had often overheard the other girls at school saying how foolish it was. If ever there was a flood—and they occurred frequently on the island—it risked being destroyed. But that had not happened yet.

Rose noticed with delight that it was still standing and had not changed much. The window frames must have been recently painted, as the blue color was unfamiliar to her. The roof shingles were covered with a little more moss, but otherwise things were as they had always been.

Her heart thumping with anticipation, she walked up to the front door. Would Father be there?

She knew that her mother only ever left the house in the evenings—usually to talk to the neighbors—since she was always busy during the day, even though she and her husband had lived alone for some time.

As Rose entered, she heard voices, which she didn't understand at first. They were talking rapidly in her mother Adit's language, so fast that Rose could hardly translate a word in her head. It had been so long since she had heard the language!

Her mother had always used it when they were alone together, but since leaving home, Rose had almost always spoken Dutch and English, with the correct use of the latter being drummed into her mercilessly by Mrs. Kavanagh, the English teacher at the conservatory.

After a while, however, she tuned in and understood more or less what the voice that wasn't her mother's was saying.

"I was against you going away from the start. It's against *adat* for a woman to move away to her husband's house."

Adat. What was that again? Rose thought for a moment before recalling. Her mother had explained that before Islam had gained a foothold here, adat, the code of customs and conventions, had governed the life of the community. From birth to death, from building a house to cultivating rice—everything was controlled by adat.

"But I've explained to you a hundred times," her mother said with a sigh. "I decided to live here with him. You've left me in peace for so long, yet now that I'm almost an old woman, you're back and starting all over again."

What did she mean? Rose couldn't remember ever having seen this old woman. She leaned forward slightly in an attempt to catch sight of the visitor's face. She was brown as a nut, and the wrinkles on her cheeks looked like a deep-cut river delta. She must have been over eighty.

"It's your duty to take up your place with us," the old woman said more angrily. "It's prescribed by adat. Who would we be without our elders? You know it brings great honor."

"Honor I don't want! I want to stay with my husband; I want to see him every day, not merely to be visited by him. As far as I'm concerned, you can pass the honor and all that goes with it to someone else. I have a sister, after all."

Rose frowned in confusion. Her mother was to be granted some honor? Honor she didn't want?

Of course she knew her mother was from the north and had previously lived with her people, but she had never told her anything more.

A floorboard suddenly creaked beneath her shoe.

"Is someone there?" her mother asked.

Rose couldn't stay concealed any longer.

"Mother?" she said as she pushed aside the curtain that divided the back room from the kitchen.

At first the dainty woman, whose hair now had a few strands of silver, stared at her as if she had seen a ghost.

"Rose!" she cried out. She jumped up and rushed over to her daughter, the old woman who had been talking to her all but forgotten now.

Rose was now a good head taller than Adit, but that didn't prevent her mother from placing her hands on her face and gently drawing her down.

"You're back! My Rose has come back to me!"

Rose should have shown her respect by kissing her brow, but her mother gave her no chance, hugging her to her breast with amazing strength and bursting into tears. Rose was no better. She felt a lump in her throat until she finally managed to relieve it with a sob. They stood there for a while, holding one another, offering mutual consolation. Neither of them paid any heed to the old woman, but she eventually drew their attention back to herself by clearing her throat.

Rose now bowed to her, as was fitting, and at once felt as if she were twelve years old again, in the time shortly before her departure to England. The old woman accepted her gesture without a hint of emotion.

"So this is your daughter," she said in a tone Rose could not interpret. "Does she know where her origins lie?"

Her mother gave the old woman a look of warning. "She knows, but she has decided on a different life. A life away from the island. A modern life."

Rose looked between the two women in amazement. What was it she was supposed to know? She had no memory of any conversation with her mother in which they had spoken of her origins. Or of any honors and obligations, or eerie old women in strange dress.

The old woman sniffed disdainfully. "A person's life is not always a matter of their own choosing. That applies to you, and also to her. If I were in your shoes, I'd not leave it too long before informing her of the obligations she will have one day. If you don't, it's possible that your child will suffer bad luck and drag her whole family down with her." She turned to go.

Rose stared after her. What a peculiar woman! Why was she threatening her with bad luck?

Once the woman had disappeared through the curtain, Rose looked at her mother, who was rooted to the spot, her mouth moving weakly but no sound emerging.

"Who on earth was that woman, Mother?" Rose asked once she had recovered slightly from her astonishment.

"An old acquaintance," her mother replied a little absently. She appeared to bring herself back to reality. "I'm so pleased to see you again, my child. You didn't let me know you were coming."

"Everything happened so quickly—I received an invitation from the governor to play at a reception. And now I'm here."

"I'm glad. It's lovely that you haven't forgotten your parents amidst all this. You're famous now."

"I'm just a simple musician, Mother, you know that. Did you get my letters and parcels?"

"Every one, and I've kept them all safe. So often I wished I could write back to you, but as you travel so much, it would be impossible for my letters to reach you."

Rose had sorely missed receiving mail from her mother. She had written to Rose more often when she was at the conservatory, but it had become impossible now that she was in a different place every day, and though she could send messages and letters, she was unable to receive them.

"My tour will be over in six months," Rose said. "Then I'll insist to my agent that I be given some time to come and stay with you for longer."

"You should make better use of your time and allow a young man to court you," her mother said, laughing as she went over to the stove to boil water for tea.

"I don't think that's very likely," Rose replied. "When I'm on tour, I only rarely meet any men I like. They're mostly old and lecherous— not the sort of person I'd like to settle down and start a family with. Besides . . ." She hesitated briefly, since she knew how much her mother wanted grandchildren.

"Besides, your heart belongs to your music." Her mother finished her sentence for her. "That's always been the case, ever since you were little."

Before Rose could say anything more, her mother came over and took her hand in her soft, gentle fingers.

"Don't worry, Rose, I know what it feels like to have a dream. My dream was to free myself from all my family obligations. I . . ." She lowered her head, then shook it. "Perhaps she's right. Perhaps I should tell you about it."

"Tell me what?"

Her mother sighed deeply, then, without replying, went over to the stove and picked up the kettle, which was now boiling. After making the tea, she set two cups down on the table. Rose watched her. Had her movements always been so slow? Had she always been so faltering? No, Rose didn't think so. There had been something about the old woman that had shaken her badly.

"Mother?" she prompted gently.

"Yes, my child, I haven't forgotten. I'm only trying to find the right words. I really didn't want you to be burdened with this knowledge."

"What knowledge?" Rose didn't know where she was heading. What did her origins have to do with anything?

After pouring them each a cup of tea, her mother sat down and folded her hands on the table as if she were about to pray.

"Perhaps you don't remember that visit to your grandmother all those years ago," she began. Rose noticed her voice had a tremor in it.

"I remember the garden," she answered honestly. "And a little of my grandmother. But it is only a faint memory."

"You were three at the time. I can understand that the garden made more of an impression on you. It's always held a certain magic. It's also obvious that you didn't pay attention to the conversation between the adults."

However hard Rose tried, she could not recall any of the conversation between her mother and grandmother.

"Perhaps your memory's also wrong on another count: I went there alone with you. Your father wasn't there."

Rose shook her head. "I don't remember that."

"But that was how it was. I went up there alone with you because your grandmother summoned me to talk to her. Of course I didn't know what it was about. I hadn't seen her since I came to Padang with Roger. She called me to her to remind me of my obligations. At the time I was obedient enough to go to her. That afternoon ended in an argument, though. While you were enjoying the delights of the garden, many angry words were spoken between me and my mother."

As her own mother spoke, a long-suppressed detail found its way into Rose's memory. She saw a house with a magnificent roof adorned with pointed gables. It had been a palace to her then! Over the years, her imagination had added a golden roof, fine stone walls, towers, and huge windows to the building until it bore no resemblance to the real house. But now, strangely, she saw it as it had really been, with six peaks that looked like crescent moons stacked one above the other. Crescent moons of brown shingles, and in place of the stone walls she saw carvings on a red background, and window frames painted green and red.

But the memory was only fleeting. As Adit continued, the image faded from her mind.

"I'm sure you don't remember that I grabbed you by the arm and dragged you back with me to the carriage. Your father was waiting a long way out of the village because he was not allowed to cross the boundary."

Rose honestly couldn't remember but nodded to avoid complication. "And what does that mean for me now?"

"That one day you too will receive a visit from them. They'll try and persuade you to move to the family home to be the mistress over our people's rice paddies. It may not seem such a bad prospect at first glance. But if, by then, you have a husband, you'll be forced to leave him and live with your people. At best, he would be allowed to visit you, but the rest of the time he would have to live with his own people. That's why I've decided to go against adat—and therefore sacrificed my inheritance." She was looking Rose directly in the eye. "You have to know that your father means everything to me. Some people marry because their parents arranged it for them. I married him because from the moment I saw him, I knew there was no one else for me. I couldn't bear to be separated from him a moment longer than necessary. Now, you could say I'm separated from him when he goes to work, but that's not the same thing at all, because I know he'll be coming back to me. If I were to give in to the old woman's request, I'd have to leave all this behind and move to the family home. There was good reason for me to leave the village when I did. I didn't want to live without Roger."

Her mother reached across the table and took Rose's hand in hers, which was icy cold. "You're still too young to grasp the meaning of true love, but I'm telling you, when you do fall in love, every moment you're separated from that person will cause you great pain. For me, it's a pain I couldn't bear. Can you understand?"

Rose understood. And her mother was wrong to assume that she had no idea of love. True, she had not yet found a man to love in the same way as her mother loved her father, but what she felt for him was just like Rose's love for her music—and Rose had no intention of giving that up for adat.

Rose spent the rest of the afternoon helping her mother with the housework, something that had long become foreign to her. Immersing herself in the activities she had carried out as a child gave her a lovely warm feeling.

When her father arrived home that evening, he stopped in the doorway and dropped his bag in amazement.

"Rose?"

Roger Gallway was still a very imposing figure, even though time had turned his formerly blond hair completely white.

Rose used to believe her father was a very important man because he was in charge of the Dutch merchants' goods. Now she knew that he was only an employee, but he was as important to her as ever, in part since she had his work and goodwill to thank for her excellent education and her chance to go to England to further her talent.

The sight of his blue eyes and dimpled cheeks filled Rose with the same warmth she had felt on seeing her mother. She went over to him and embraced him in the hope that he would emerge from his trance. It worked, for he encircled her with his arms and pressed her to his chest. Rose soon felt one of his tears fall onto her cheek.

As her mother prepared the traditional *makanan*, a complementary array of dishes for which Padang was famed far and wide, Rose had to give him a full account of all that had happened to her recently. Of course her father had read all her letters several times, but he still managed to coax from her a few more details that she had left out or possibly considered unimportant.

As she spoke, Rose managed for a while to avoid thinking about the number of appearances that lay before her and the demands Carmichael placed on her—and above all, the fact that she would have to perform under the patronage of the governor for the next ten concerts.

"Where will your tour take you next?" her father asked as the delicious smell of the food filled her nostrils.

"I'll be staying on Sumatra for a few weeks. The governor would like me to play on various occasions."

"A great honor!" her father acknowledged. "If you like, you can come back here to stay with us. Your mother would love that."

Rose reddened. "I'm afraid that won't be possible. I have my dresser and my agent with me, and in any case, the performances are all in the evenings, so it will be the early hours before I finish." The look of sadness that crossed her father's face caused her to add, "But as long as my practicing allows, I'll visit you every day, I promise."

That did not appear to cheer Roger Gallway at all. He said nothing, but Rose knew full well that his brooding gaze signified nothing other than disappointment.

"Darling, leave her alone," her mother said as she came to the table. "She's not a little girl anymore, as you can see. She's a grown woman, and if she marries, she certainly won't be coming back to live with us."

"But she's not married yet."

"It'll happen one day. Until then, enjoy the fact that she's here."

Rose had no idea why, but she suddenly had a mental image of Paul Havenden. She shook the thought away and turned her attention to her bowl of rice, seasoning it with a sharp sauce and adding a few shrimps.

During the night, Rose found sleep elusive. Not that she would ever feel afraid in her childhood bedroom. On the contrary, the familiar feeling that had returned to her the moment she stepped over the threshold drove all tiredness from her and brought new images flooding back from her memory.

As long as she could remember, music had been her life. Many of the girls in Mrs. Faraday's school had been compelled by their parents to learn the violin, whereas Rose had considered it a loss if she was unable to play for a single day. With horror she remembered the terrifying time, hardly three months after her arrival in London, when she had fallen ill with scarlet fever and been forced to lie in a darkened room, scarcely a sound reaching her ears, because they were worried she would lose her sight and hearing. Those silent weeks had been the worst of her life but had also taught her to play melodies in her head without actually hearing them.

Her thoughts only rarely turned to men. She had many admirers, but she could not imagine a husband by her side. The Englishman was the first to awaken any passion in her, but even with him, she was not sure whether she would ever give up her talent to become his wife.

Ultimately she convinced herself that any such thoughts were madness in any case. Havenden is engaged, she told herself. He will never marry me. He was merely being friendly, nothing more. I'll probably never see him again.

***

The next morning, after taking her leave of her parents and promising it would not be years before they saw each other again, Rose made her way to the hotel. She was sure that Carmichael would be out of his mind with worry—if he lost her, he would lose his income, and he would never allow that.

The night before, Rose had finally managed to sleep, only to be haunted by a jumble of confused dreams. She blamed her mother's stories but did not hold it against her. It was hard to believe that someone from her people had appeared and demanded that she should give up her life to become the headwoman of her clan.

Rose knew that she would not yield to such a request, either. She wanted to see the world, not stagnate in some jungle village. She wanted a career, and to hell with the demands of some village elder!

"Miss Gallway, what a coincidence!" came a voice from behind her. Rose turned to see Paul Havenden crossing the street toward her.

"Lord Havenden," she replied a little hesitantly, her heart suddenly thumping wildly.

"To what do I owe the honor of seeing you wandering through the city so early in the morning? Are you going to the cockfight too?"

Rose raised her eyebrows. "Surely you're not going to see that dreadful spectacle?"

"I'm told it's meant to be very entertaining."

"Were you also told that the cocks fight to the death?"

"That's what usually happens in cockfights, isn't it?"

Rose pouted in disapproval. "It's barbaric! It may be a tradition in my country, but it's not something to be recommended to tourists."

"So what's your opinion of poultry being used for soup?" Havenden's eyes gleamed playfully. He seemed to enjoy arguing with her. "That may also be barbaric, but yesterday I was served a delicious local chicken dish."

"That's completely different."

"But the outcome's the same—the hens die. I'm sure the losing cock would taste very good in a soup."

Rose frowned. Her delight in seeing Havenden again had faded somewhat. The Englishman seemed to sense it, and he relented a little. "So what would you suggest I do instead?"

"I'm not sure I have any suggestions to make to you," Rose replied aloofly, but regretted it immediately.

"But you're advising me against going to the cockfight?"

"I didn't advise you against it. I merely remarked that those fights are barbaric," she said in a slightly milder tone.

Paul laughed, and although Rose's defenses were up, she could not help laughing with him.

"You'd be better off going to watch a shadow play, a *wayang kulit*," she said. "When I was a child, those puppeteers were everywhere. Though the plays are very long, and I never succeeded in watching one to the end, since my parents always came to drag me away and tuck me in bed."

Paul thought it over for a moment, then offered Rose his arm. "How about we go and find one of these puppeteers together?"

Rose looked at him in bewilderment before shaking her head. "I'm afraid I'll have to decline, as the shows are put on at night. Have you never seen a shadow play in England?"

She clearly remembered going to one of the cinematograph theaters in which shadow plays were also performed. That was also where she had seen, for the first time in her life, one of the moving pictures that had so fascinated her.

"I'm afraid I have no idea about it. But I could tell you quite a bit about horse breeding, if you like."

"Another time, perhaps," Rose replied, since she felt that Havenden was using it as an excuse to spend more time with her.

"Why not make that 'another time' tonight? How about accompanying me to the shadow puppet show?"

"I think your fiancée should be the one to accompany you. Good day, Lord Havenden."

Rose's heart was pounding as she turned.

"Miss Gallway, wait!" he called after her, but she refused to stop or look back, afraid that if she did, she might change her mind.

***

As Paul returned to the hotel, the image of Rose Gallway's radiant beauty shone in his mind's eye. What was the matter with him? He was a businessman, he had a wife, and if all went well, he would soon have a share in a successful plantation. But he felt as if there was something missing, something he could not put his finger on. Why was he being drawn to this woman so? Why had he denied Maggie to her, telling her she was his fiancée? It was not as if he was such a great music lover.

The fact that she had practically run from him only went to show that she did not care for him as much as he had assumed she did. Yet everything inside him was compelling him to see her again, to hear her play again.

"How were things in the city?" Maggie's voice cut through his thoughts. "Did you reach agreement with your attorney?"

Paul could hear the impatience in his wife's voice all too well as she reclined on her chaise longue, reaching for a piece of fruit from a nearby bowl. She was probably hoping they could be away from here as soon as possible, and her attitude was beginning to annoy Paul.

"Mijnheer Dankers is a really nice man, but we're still nowhere near reaching an agreement. I have to see the plantation first."

Paul saw the look of dismay in Maggie's eyes. He knew her fears and said, "Don't worry, you can stay here in the safety of the hotel. Though I'm sure the ladies in London would be bursting with jealousy to hear about your adventures in the jungle."

"I'm sorry, but I have no intention of becoming a second Marianne North and spending my time pressing flowers between sheets of newspaper."

Paul was a little surprised that Maggie had even heard of the natural scientist who had included Southeast Asia in her travels. Paul's father had met her once on a crossing and said what a brilliant example of a woman she was.

"Well, as I said, I'm not forcing you to go," he replied, and found himself wondering if Rose Gallway was so prickly.

"Thank you," Maggie retorted listlessly, fanning herself once again.

Paul stood by her in silence for a moment without really knowing what to do. His business obligations were finished for the day, and he was dying to go out for a ride or a walk. His wife looked as if she had taken root on her chaise longue.

"Someone told me that a really fascinating shadow play is being put on tonight," he began finally, hoping that Maggie would show some enthusiasm for a bit of culture. "Would you fancy seeing it?"

Maggie sat up. Red patches had appeared on her cheeks as if she had a fever. She did not, but rather was reacting to the island heat— even the ceiling fan didn't seem to cool her enough.

"Shadow play?"

"Yes, a puppeteer moves cutout puppets on sticks. It's a local tradition." The brief spark of interest that had flared across his wife's face faded immediately.

"That would mean going down into the city. Among all those . . . people."

"Yes." Paul sat down on the stool by the chaise longue and took her hand. "Darling, what's the matter with you? I got the impression at the governor's reception that you had a brilliant time."

"I did. But I'm still worn out from it, and I'm simply not in the mood for going out tonight."

"In the mood? But you're twenty-one! At that age women are usually in the mood for anything!"

"Most women my age don't have to suffer this heat."

Paul sighed. He couldn't rid himself of the feeling that Maggie not only was afraid of this country but seemed to despise it, even loathe it. There seemed to be no point in trying to persuade her to like it—she had already made her mind up.

"As you will. I'll go alone then," he said defiantly, and withdrew to the bedroom. The chances of Maggie relenting were slim, but perhaps she would reconsider.

***

That evening, as Rose was settling down for the evening, Mai appeared in her room in a state of agitation. She had a small envelope in her hand.

144

"There's a gentleman downstairs who gave me this letter for you," she said breathlessly.

Another message from the governor? Rose took the note, went over to the desk, and slit open the envelope with a silver letter opener.

Dear Miss Gallway,

I have managed to find one of the shadow puppeteers you told me about. Would you do me the honor of accompanying me to see the show? Today? Now?

Yours,
Paul Havenden

Every single word sent a spark through her veins. She felt her cheeks and brow began to glow as if with a fever. Such persistence! Had she not made it clear enough that she was not interested in spending an evening with him?

"What did the man who gave you the letter look like?" she asked.

"Oh, he is very good-looking. I think I got a glimpse of him at the governor's residence when I was in the kitchen. I don't know his name, but he's still waiting downstairs."

"He's waiting downstairs?" Rose looked at her, aghast. Havenden had not sent a servant? What was she to do now?

"Yes, he told me I should bring him your answer, miss."

Under the bemused gaze of her servant, who knew none of the details of the situation, Rose began to pace up and down in agitation. She would like nothing better than to go with Havenden to watch the shadow play. But would that be right? She read the letter again. It did not sound as though his fiancée would be with them. She couldn't go out for the evening with a man who had promised marriage to another!

She knew she should give the letter back to Mai and tell her to send him away, but something stopped her. Would it really matter if she went with him? After all, it was a harmless outing to watch the shadow play. Afterward they would go their separate ways, and everything would continue as before.

As Mai ran down to tell him that her mistress would accept his invitation, Rose went over to the clothes trunk that was her constant companion on tour. Mai was responsible for keeping her wardrobe in order at all times, and although the dresses were all very tasteful, Rose now doubted she had anything appropriate. Surely these concert dresses all looked too conservative.

She finally picked out a pink one with a tucked and frilled bodice, tight sleeves, and a very close-fitting long skirt. It might look a little like an evening dress, but it wasn't too pompous for an evening stroll through the city.

She was going to walk with Lord Havenden through Padang at night! It still sounded outrageous to her, but before she could reconsider, she whisked her dressing gown from her shoulders and slipped into the dress.

Mai returned after five minutes to take care of her hair. Her face was glowing as if Havenden had used those few moments to tell her some embarrassing tales.

"He's such a lovely man," she enthused. "What blue eyes he has!"

"Don't talk so much. Concentrate on getting my hair right," Rose said, taking her place in front of the dressing table mirror. Mai picked up the brush obediently but continued her chatter. Rose hardly heard a word of it, since her thoughts had leapt forward to the puppeteer's stall, where the lamps had probably already been lit and the delicately crafted puppets were being checked over.

Those works of art had been such a source of amazement to her as a child. A specific type of puppet was traditionally assigned to each character. The rajahs and princesses, the good girls and honest wise men and women always had slim bodies with long, narrow noses. The puppets for the evil characters were often plump with bulbous noses and, in the case of demons, hideously long teeth, which protruded from their distorted mouths in an embodiment of terror.

Did today's puppeteers still act out the legends of her childhood?

When she was finally ready, Rose felt a little like Cinderella in the fairy tale she had first heard a long time ago in the conservatory. Although it was forbidden, Rose had often slipped secretly into the kitchen to watch the women at work, every now and then sneaking an illicit mince pie or scone. These visits to the cooks were usually associated with stories, especially on the evenings when Laura was working. As Rose sat by the fire, she would listen to the tales that were so different from the legends she knew from home. Her Dutch teachers had also told her stories and fairy tales from their homeland, but her favorite was Cinderella, who had to toil for her stepsisters but finally got her prince with the help of her fairy godmother. Rose had always particularly loved the part where Cinderella entered the ballroom in her wonderful dress, and had wished that one day she, too, could wear such magnificent clothes.

Now she left her room with her heart thumping, wondering whether Paul Havenden, admittedly not a prince, but a lord nevertheless, would see in her a princess whom he wanted to whisk off on his white horse to his castle.

No, she warned herself. Don't be so silly. It would only break your heart when he returned to England and left you in a country on the other side of the world.

As she reached the staircase, she saw him waiting by the hotel reception desk below. Instead of settling himself in one of the leather armchairs, he was pacing up and down restlessly in a way that Rose found touching. Previously, he had betrayed no hint of uncertainty, but now he looked for all the world like a groom waiting for his bride. His dark suit and blood-red ascot suited him perfectly, accentuating the golden shimmer in his hair. He stopped his restless twisting of the walking stick in his hand to pull out his pocket watch and snap it shut again.

Rose decided not to keep him waiting any longer. She pressed her hand to her stomach and tried to breathe away the fluttering inside. Since nothing helped, she set her foot on the first step and called to mind Mrs. Faraday's advice on coping with stage fright. "Once you start playing, it will disappear of its own accord—you'll see."

The sound of her footsteps caused Havenden to turn. As he caught sight of her, a smile leapt to his face.

"Miss Gallway, there you are!" he called out. "I was afraid you might have changed your mind."

"I always stand by my word—though a lady does need a little time to get ready."

Havenden appraised her furtively before saying, "I can't imagine any situation in which you wouldn't look beautiful."

"Perhaps I should remind you that your fiancée wouldn't consider such flattery entirely appropriate."

Havenden's expression darkened, his lips pressed together as if he were suppressing a comment.

"Forgive me, I . . ." began Rose, who had a feeling she had somehow offended him.

"No, it's fine, and you're right, my fiancée certainly wouldn't like it. But I like you, and I can't do anything about that." He offered her his arm. "Shall we go? I'm worried that by the time we reach the puppet theater the show will already have begun."

In the light of numerous lamps and torches, the city looked like a scene from *The Thousand and One Nights*. The colonial facades seemed to fade into the background, giving prominence to the traditional local buildings. Exotic scents filled the alleyways as the delightful aromas of the food stalls drove out the smells of the harbor and the dirt.

Even at this late hour, merchants were offering their wares for sale. Their calls competed with the singing of the street musicians and the sounds of drums, *angklungs*, *sulings*, and *ouds*. Colorfully dressed young women were performing traditional dances by torchlight.

Although she had often experienced these magical scenes in her childhood, Rose felt as if she were walking through a long-forgotten wonderland. She usually only left her hotel rooms for her performances, the rest of her time being spent on preparing herself. At best, Carmichael might take her out after a successful concert, but they never lingered for long enough to see much of the places they visited.

That would also have been the case here had they not received the governor's generous offer. Indeed, she would not even have found the time to visit her parents. This made her feel even more grateful to van Swieten than she had the day before.

"You didn't tell me what a wonderful place your home city is," said Havenden, who seemed just as enchanted by the magic of Padang as she was. These were the first words he had spoken since leaving the hotel.

"I'm afraid I'd forgotten," she replied. "I've been traveling for months, and before that I spent several years in England."

"Do you have relatives there? Your name sounds English."

"My father's an Englishman. He's a warehouse supervisor for the Dutch. I was in England to study at Mrs. Faraday's conservatory, though I'm sure the name will mean nothing to you."

"It most certainly does mean something to me! Mrs. Faraday is still one of Trinity College's main competitors, though, of course, the latter only takes male students while the conservatory's pupils are all girls. My father often gave Mrs. Faraday financial support as an anonymous donor."

"Then it seems your family contributed to my education, and I thank you." Rose gave him a mischievous smile.

"As I know now what excellent musicians Mrs. Faraday produces, I'll certainly be continuing the tradition. Or do you need a sponsor or patron personally?"

"I find it a little strange that you're offering me such a thing when you've said yourself that you're not a particularly great music lover."

"That was before I met you. There's something about your playing that can turn the worst ignoramus into an ardent admirer of the art. Take me, for example."

"Then I hope to be able to inspire you to feel the same way about this unique form of theater." Rose pointed to a stall ahead of them. "There's the stage."

In fact, the structure could hardly be called a stage. Over a low wooden platform whose purpose was to ensure that all the members of the audience could see, a canvas sheet was suspended between two poles. The sheet was illuminated from behind by numerous lamps that projected silhouettes onto the fabric.

When they arrived, the play was already in progress. On the screen, Rose saw the silhouette of a number of bamboo canes and the finely detailed figure of a young woman, who was approaching the stylized forest with a knife in her hand. The puppet's movements were accompanied by the sounds of a gamelan.

A broad smile came involuntarily to Rose's lips, as there was no mistaking one of the legends her mother used to tell her. She glanced to her side and saw that Havenden was frowning in confusion. He couldn't understand a word, of course, so she decided to help him out.

"This is the legend of the Forgotten Girl," Rose explained in a whisper so as not to disturb the other spectators, most of whom were locals. "She's the youngest of seven sisters, and is always being forgotten. She doesn't get a husband, and instead has to work hard for her coldhearted sisters—without payment, naturally. But one day, a kindly fisherman gives the girl a small fish with golden scales. The girl keeps the fish, but the evil sisters soon come after her and try to talk her into giving the fish away. When the girl refuses, the sisters kill it."

"What a horrid story," Paul murmured in fascination. "In England that kind of thing would scare the life out of the children."

"But there's more." Rose glanced at the screen, where the Forgotten Girl was holding the glass bowl that contained the little fish. She marveled at how intricately made all the puppets were. "As she's looking for her fish, her sisters jeer at her and throw the fish's head at her feet."

Havenden snorted, but Rose nudged him sharply to stop him from commenting.

"The girl picks up the fish head, buries it in the forest, and cries bitterly. And look, out of the ground grows a tree with golden leaves and golden fruit. It glitters so brightly that a rajah—you'd say a king— who is riding past notices the Forgotten Girl. He makes her his wife, and they plant the sapling in the castle garden. Years later, there is a severe drought in the country. The evil sisters' buffalo starve and die of thirst, and soon the sisters have nothing left to eat or drink. They go to the rajah's castle, where they meet their sister, and they beg her to help them."

"I'm sure she won't be keen to do that after all the mean things they've put her through," Havenden said, clearly drawn into the story.

"You'd be right to think so—in fact, she shows her sisters the door and reminds them of how they used to torment her. But then the golden tree begins to sing, asking the Forgotten Girl to forget the suffering her sisters caused her and to have mercy on them. And so she lets her sisters share in her wealth. This shames the sisters so much that they shed tears of genuine regret and beg her for forgiveness."

Rose noticed how close she had moved to Havenden, and she took a step to the side and looked straight ahead toward the stage, where the story of the Forgotten Girl was playing out to the accompaniment of music and song.

Havenden seemed incapable of saying anything. He stared, spellbound, at the silhouettes, trying to make out which part of the story they had reached. It was not until the story approached its end and the little tree began to speak through the sound of the gamelan that he stirred.

"That's truly a moving story. My father would have loved it."

"What about you?"

"I loved it, too. I almost regret . . ." He paused, apparently struggling with the decision whether or not to say more.

"What do you regret?" Rose asked.

"Nothing. It's nothing," he replied, although it was obvious that he was thinking something. Rose decided not to press him. She was here to spend a nice evening with him at the shadow theater, nothing more.

As the puppeteer was carefully packing away his puppets in a chest, Rose noticed a stall nearby that was giving out a wonderful smell.

"Wait here; I'll get us something to eat," she said. Before Havenden could reply, she had hurried away. When was the last time she had eaten *klepon*? The rice balls filled with palm sugar and rolled in dried coconut had been a childhood favorite of hers. Her mother had always bought her some whenever they had gone to a shadow play.

The owner of the small stall had his hands full with preparing more of the fresh delicacies. A long line of patrons stretched before it, most people holding the hands of children. No one went to the wayang without buying something to eat. The traders knew it and set up their stalls all around the stage.

She returned to Havenden, carrying two bags cleverly woven from palm leaves, just in time for the gamelan to announce the start of the next piece.

"They're green!" he said in surprise as Rose handed him a bag.

"What do you mean? The palm leaves? Of course they're green!" Rose smiled playfully.

"No, the balls. I've never seen such green candy, only in shockingly expensive confectioners' in London."

"It's the juice of *pandan* leaves that causes it," Rose explained as she took one of the little balls in her fingers. "They use it to color the mixture. They also add rice flour and sweet potatoes. Try them—they're good."

Rose took a bite, and the sweetness of the palm sugar filling flooded into her mouth. Havenden looked on skeptically but eventually gave in. At first he frowned slightly, but then his features relaxed and began to light up.

"Mmm, that's really good."

"You think so?"

"Yes, really. I ought to take the recipe back home and sell these little cakes in London."

"Do you think Londoners' palates are ready for them?" Rose said playfully, popping another into her mouth.

"Londoners are always looking for something new. You know the English cuisine; it's not particularly imaginative, so they need an injection of foreign influence."

"Perhaps you should invest in a klepon stall instead of a sugar plantation," Rose replied with amusement.

"Perhaps I will," Havenden said, chewing. He delved for another little ball as the next fairy tale began—this one about the princess and the egg.

***

As they returned to the hotel shortly before daybreak, Rose felt as light as if she were one with the mist that drifted onshore at that time of day. The evening with Havenden had shown her that there was more to life than playing the violin, that there were things that felt thoroughly good and desires that had nothing to do with music, but with love and passion. She wanted to experience hundreds of evenings like this one, with Paul by her side.

With a blissful smile she opened the door to her room—only to jump with shock the very next moment. It was only with difficulty that she stopped herself from crying out when she saw Carmichael sitting on the sofa.

"What are you doing here?" she snapped as she closed the door.

"I wanted to talk about the concerts van Swieten has arranged for you. Mai let me in."

Stupid girl, Rose thought angrily as she pulled her hatpins from her hair.

"Where have you been?" Carmichael asked, his voice deliberately calm—a sign that he was seething inside.

"Out," Rose replied. She had no intention of explaining anything to him, especially not Paul. The evening had been far too enjoyable to spoil by discussing it with Carmichael.

"That's the second time. I couldn't get hold of you yesterday, either." Carmichael frowned, eyeing her suspiciously.

"I went to visit my parents and stayed the night there."

"You could have had the courtesy to tell me. At least send me a message."

"I'm tired," Rose said wearily. "Let's talk later. I don't feel like arguing with you now."

"Very well, as you wish." He rose and strolled toward the door as if nothing mattered to him. Before opening the door and leaving, he turned back to her. "You've been seeing that Havenden, haven't you? Mai told me."

Rose was too surprised to reply. She tried to think of an excuse but was not quick enough. She wouldn't put it past Carmichael to follow her to see for himself.

"You have to get that fellow out of your head," he snapped, striding angrily toward her and forcing her to take a few steps back. "Do you realize what's at stake? You're one of the best violinists in the world! If you let yourself get distracted, if you let him lead you astray, you'll ruin everything!"

"Who says he's going to lead me astray? How on earth did you come to that conclusion?" She threw her hat furiously onto the bed. She'd have quite a lot to say to Mai when she saw her.

"I saw the way he was staring at you during the reception. And you've been out with him tonight! What's it supposed to mean?"

"It means that, among everything else, I have a normal life, and I won't be dictated to like a little child about where I can and can't go!"

Carmichael snorted scornfully. "You think you have a normal life? You're an artist—you should be glad you don't have a normal life! Under any other circumstances you'd be married by now, and pregnant, perhaps even expecting your second brat. Don't go longing for a normal life; just think yourself lucky that you'll never have one! And if I catch Havenden trying to distract you again, I'll personally break his bones!"

With these words he stormed to the door, tore it open, and vanished.

Rose stared after him, stunned. What was all that about? He didn't usually care about her admirers—why now?

With a sigh, she sank down on the sofa, which was still warm where Carmichael had been sitting. Tears crept into her eyes, but as they threatened to blur her vision, she sprang up.

I'll show him, she thought. I'll prove to him that I don't have to forgo the pleasures of a normal life. You'll see, Sean Carmichael!

13

Cremona, 2011

A gray winter sky loomed above the city as the train drew into the station. Lilly and Ellen rose from their seats and took their belongings down from the luggage rack.

Lilly carefully clasped her violin case under her arm. She was still unsure whether it had been a good idea to bring the instrument with her. A few days ago it would probably not have caused her any concern, but now she knew that the violin was valuable—though it might not be worth a fortune, it had sentimental value, especially for Gabriel. If the violin were lost, it would probably be lost for many decades—and with it the mystery of Rose Gallway.

Ellen had insisted that it would be better for her acquaintance in Cremona, Enrico di Trevi, to be able to see the original rather than photos. While they were still at Heathrow, Ellen had managed to contact him, and he had invited the two women to his home near the Palazzo Trecchi and promised to help them in their search for Rose Gallway.

During the flight to Milan, they had formulated a plan of how they could get the most benefit from the weekend and find out as much as possible about the violinist.

"Maybe there are some old newspaper articles," Ellen had speculated cheerfully. "Enrico can translate them for us. If I know him, he'd do anything to see this violin with his own eyes."

As the train came to a standstill, they pushed their way to the door among the crowd of other passengers. Snatches of Italian swirled around Lilly, reminding her of a vacation with Peter. They had still been students and had backpacked their way around Tuscany without understanding a word of Italian.

She still couldn't speak the language, and the thoughts of Peter caused a bittersweet tug in her breast. She quickly pushed the feelings to one side. Now was not the time. Perhaps she could allow herself to sink into her memories later that evening, but now they had to make sure that they found Ellen's friend.

As they crossed the concourse, Lilly could see that Cremona Station was something special. It was more than a hundred years old, and its high arched windows filled it with light. She could easily imagine passengers from the olden days hurrying across the gleaming stone floor—women in sweeping crinoline skirts and beribboned hats, men in tailored frock coats. Girls in starched calico dresses playing with boys in short pants. Among them, newsboys in flat caps cried out the latest headlines from some local rag at the tops of their voices.

The image faded as they left the station and crossed the forecourt, which seemed rather bleak under overcast skies but must be a wonderful sight in spring and summer. Cars hooted nearby; scooters rattled past. There was a taxi stand close by, but before going over to it, Lilly turned once again to take another look at the station, its yellow paintwork the only splash of color in the gray winter scene. With its arches, the building reminded her of a small palace.

"Come on, Lilly, there's a taxi free at the back!" Ellen called over to her. As she turned, she saw that Ellen was already striding over to the vehicle.

The house in which Enrico di Trevi lived must have once been the residence of a nobleman, or at least a very wealthy man, as it was only slightly less magnificent than the neighboring palazzo. The facade fronting onto the street was very decorative, with a number of balconies and carved figures, including two stone atlantes that supported the slightly overhanging roof. At first glance, the bull's-eye panes in the windows looked like originals from a bygone age, but the panes were too clear and the lead too new.

Lilly guessed that the house had been built in the seventeenth century. A crack, possibly the result of an earthquake, worked its way up the left-hand side of the wall. Otherwise the building was in good condition, suggesting a place where she could revel in history.

Lilly had assumed that Ellen's acquaintance would be elderly, similar to Ben Cavendish, so she was surprised when an attractive man in his midforties opened the door. He was wearing jeans and a black shirt that set off his lightly tanned skin to amazing effect. His jet-black hair was longish, and his eyes shone like two silver coins.

"*Buongiorno*, Ellen!" he said heartily, embracing her friend so warmly that Lilly had the initial impression that she was watching a pair of lovers who had been separated for a long time. "You're as fast as the wind!"

He spoke excellent German.

"You can thank the Italian railways for that," Ellen replied before turning to Lilly. "This is my friend I told you about, Lilly Kaiser. Lilly, this is my friend Enrico."

"Pleased to meet you."

Enrico replied by kissing her hand—the last thing Lilly would have expected. "The pleasure is all mine. Why didn't you tell me you have such a pretty friend?"

"Probably because I haven't had the chance to talk to you about her." Ellen winked at Lilly. "But perhaps I should warn her what a ladies' man you are."

"Are you suggesting that I'm lying?"

"I didn't mean anything of the sort."

Before Lilly had time to think, Enrico laid an arm around her shoulders. "And what do you think? Is a man not entitled to tell a beautiful woman that she's beautiful?"

"Um . . ."

"Oh, Enrico, you haven't changed." Ellen tugged him away. Lilly's heart was thumping, and she was worried that her cheeks must be as red as tomatoes. Her face flushed as if she were still a teenager!

"I should have warned you that Enrico is a born charmer," Ellen said.

He stood aside and indicated for them to enter the house, giving Lilly a mischievous wink. In contrast to its exterior, the interior of the house was thoroughly modern, dotted with a few pieces of antique furniture that looked as though they had been in place for centuries, adopted by each new owner in succession. She was impressed and disturbed in equal measure by a huge modern painting of a bull that had just run onto the blade of a torero, bright red flecks of blood spattering its stylized form. The picture hung just above the snow-white sofa to which Enrico now led them.

"Coffee for the ladies?" he asked, hurrying over to the kitchen counter on one side of the huge living room that reminded Lilly of a modern loft apartment.

"Thank you, that would be lovely," Ellen said, answering for them both.

A short time later, Enrico had conjured up three espressos from an ultramodern coffee machine and placed the cups on the small coffee table in front of them.

"I see you've brought the violin with you," he said, turning to Lilly as he sat down in a nearby leather armchair. "May I take a look at it?"

There was no refusing the winning smile he gave her, and Lilly handed him the violin case.

Enrico snapped open the catches and lifted the lid. His eyes widened.

"This is clearly a Cremonese violin."

"An investigation of the varnish indicated that it was made between the middle and the end of the eighteenth century. Turn it over," Ellen said.

Enrico did so immediately and gasped as if he'd seen a ghost.

"The rose violin!" he burst out.

Ellen gave a deep sigh. "I wonder how it is that everyone in the world seems to know about this violin except me."

"How could you not know about it?" Enrico said with mock outrage. "Rose Gallway's violin."

The sound of the name sent sparks through Lilly's veins.

"Do you know anything about Rose?" she asked.

"Not an awful lot, except that she was one of the best violinists of her time. The Italians were crazy about her." He looked at the violin again, and an affectionate smile crossed his face. "As they were about its second owner."

"Helen Carter."

Enrico nodded. "Yes, Helen. Helen and Rose. And now you're its owner, Lilly. Perhaps we can expect similar musical wonders from you?"

"Oh no!" Lilly raised her hands in denial. "No, no, I don't play. I was merely given the violin. I don't have an ounce of musical talent."

Enrico's penetrating gaze was making her feel nervous. She secretly wished that Gabriel had come with them. If he had, she was sure Enrico would not be giving her such bewildering looks.

"Really? You have such a lovely voice. I get the impression you'd make an excellent singer."

"My skills are more with antiques," Lilly said in an attempt to steer the conversation to familiar territory. "For example, I could tell you the value of that little cupboard over there."

"Really?" Enrico gave her a broad smile.

"Can you tell us about Rose and Helen?" Ellen interjected. Lilly was not sorry in the slightest, as she found Enrico somehow unsettling. "Do you happen to know where our lovely Miss Gallway got to?"

"Well, no one knows for certain . . ." Enrico spread his hands, a little at a loss. "There were rumors that she had perhaps come to Italy, but so far no one has been able to prove it."

"What do people in Italy know about her?"

"That she was a child prodigy who grew into a beautiful young woman who caused a huge stir in the concert halls here." Enrico smiled enigmatically before looking down at his watch. "I have an idea. Why don't we visit the violin museum? They have a few old newspapers there, too. Perhaps they'll let us take a look even though it's the weekend."

"Do you think there may be some information about Rose there?" Lilly asked, feeling a glow of anticipation light up her face.

"They may keep a few clippings. There were detailed concert reviews in some of the gazettes—with fierce criticism of some unfortunate artists. We'll have to burrow through some huge stacks of paper."

"I doubt that will be necessary," Lilly said quickly, taking the CD she had brought with her from her bag. "I have a copy of a recording that was made of Rose here in Cremona."

"On June 12, 1895," Enrico said as he read the label on the disk. "That's brilliant! Where did you get this recording?"

"From the Faraday School of Music. They're researching the life of Rose Gallway there."

"You must play it for me tonight, but for now we'd better get going."

"Good idea." Ellen gestured toward the hallway in which they had deposited their bags. "First I think we should make a detour to the hotel and leave our bags."

"Hotel?" retorted Enrico. "Out of the question! You're staying with me!"

"But we—"

"Don't try telling me you don't want to cause me any trouble." He waved an arm expansively. "Just look at this palazzo, how huge and empty it is. Do you think I'm going to pass up an opportunity to surround myself with real people instead of ghosts?"

Lilly looked at Ellen, who seemed undecided.

"What do you think?" Ellen asked finally.

"Yes, what do you think, Lilly?" Enrico insisted with an engaging smile. "Are you really going to leave me here alone with all these ghosts?"

"Is this place really haunted?" she replied with a laugh.

"And some! If you stay, I'll give you a personal introduction. So?"

Lilly couldn't help returning his smile, but for some reason she would have preferred that he leave them in peace. Did she have a guilty conscience over Gabriel? Strangely, it was not Peter who sprang to mind at that moment.

"OK, since you're not going to leave us alone until we accept—yes, we'll stay," Ellen said before Lilly could reply. "Just let me call the hotel and let them know about the rooms, and then we can be on our way."

"There's no need for you to use your cell phone; use mine in my study. It won't cost as much."

"Yes, Daddy," Ellen joked. She obviously knew where Enrico's study was, since she vanished into the hallway and headed straight up the stairs.

"How old is your palazzo?" Lilly gazed around the room, which, despite its modern interior, still had the air of a museum.

"Oh, I think it dates back around four hundred years. Isn't it magnificent?" Enrico said enthusiastically, with a theatrical gesture.

"It is indeed."

"So you're interested in old structures like these?"

"Yes, very. It goes with my profession. I couldn't begin to say how much the building's worth, but some of the pieces you have here would bring in a real fortune."

Enrico smiled broadly. "It's a good thing I don't give a damn about money."

At that moment Ellen drifted in.

"I have to warn you—I wouldn't let yourself be seen near the Visconti Hotel if I were you. I blamed you personally for the fact we've had to cancel the rooms."

"You didn't," Enrico said self-confidently. "Well, even if you did, the people at the Visconti won't hold it against me. I have friends there." He winked. "Come on, let's go."

The violin museum was in the Palazzo Comunale, a two-story thirteenth-century building with massive arches and high windows on the edge of the Piazza del Comune. Directly opposite was the cathedral and the adjacent Torrazzo, the famous tower with a view over the whole city.

The square looked magical in the afternoon light. Lilly could vividly imagine how it must have looked in medieval times, the faithful streaming into the church, or standing outside the city hall talking to friends or business partners.

The museum itself was typically Baroque, with its gray-and-white marble, chandeliers, and cream-colored Empire chairs. Lilly and Ellen walked past the exhibits, gazing in amazement, while Enrico tried to get them access to the documents he had promised. They tried to catch a few snippets of what he was saying to the museum attendant. Although neither of them spoke Italian, they gathered that the man from the museum was far from enthusiastic. Eventually and reluctantly he decided to grant them access to the archive. The conversation eventually came to an end, and Enrico returned.

"We're in luck," he declared. "They'll let us look through a few newspapers, but we have to hurry, since they're not open for much longer."

Enrico led them to the museum attendant and introduced them before they left the exhibition hall and entered the archive, where not only collections were stored but also files and thick leather folders holding newspapers and magazines. A copier hummed softly in the corner.

"I've asked to see the newspapers for the week around June 12, 1895, first," Enrico said, indicating the two thick leather volumes on the table and switching on the reading lamp. "It's possible that the event was announced in advance. It must have been important because a recording was made, which was rare in those days."

As Lilly opened the first tome, she saw a slightly yellowed title page crowded with pictures. She was interested to note that the majority were drawings, not photos. But she had no more idea of the headlines than Ellen did.

"I think we'll have to hand the search over to you," she said to Enrico. "This is all Greek to us."

"That's why I'm here, isn't it?"

Enrico leafed rapidly through the large-format pages, finally stopping at a certain place.

"There's something here," he announced, turning the binder around. "Look at this picture."

Lilly's gaze fell on a rather awkward-looking girl who must have been fourteen or fifteen. She was holding her violin in her hand, turned so that the rose on the back was visible. Later, in the conservatory, Rose had stood in the same pose, although by then she had blossomed into a pretty young woman.

At the young Rose's side stood an older woman in a severe black dress. Her slightly graying hair was crimped at the temples in accordance with the fashion of the times. A metal-mounted onyx brooch could be seen at the collar of her dress. The elderly woman, who Lilly assumed must be Mrs. Faraday, had one hand on Rose's shoulder, and the other clutched a small notebook. While Rose looked friendly and somewhat unsure of herself, Mrs. Faraday's face radiated a coldness that commanded respect from Lilly more than a hundred years after the picture had been taken.

"According to the text, it seems that all the local dignitaries wanted to be seen at the concert. I'm sure some of them would have been more interested in the recording than the performance, but an appearance by Rose Gallway must have been very important even then."

Without her knowing why, the picture worked a remarkable magic on Lilly, as if she were being given the opportunity to see Rose through a window. Had she suffered under her strict teacher? Or did Mrs. Faraday look fiercer than she actually was? Had she filled her notebook with all of Rose's mistakes? Or did it have a particular purpose?

"Could I please have a copy of this?" she asked, finding it hard to tear her eyes away.

"I should think so. I'll translate the text of the article for you so that it will give you more to go on."

"Do you have time for that?"

"Of course," Enrico replied, the insolent smile flaring up on his face again. "If not for you, for whom?"

They looked through the papers for a while longer, and Enrico found some more useful material. There was another photo, this time of the concert, and a drawing of the performance on another page. This one showed Rose concentrating hard on the movement of her bow, looking lost to the world around her.

"The reviews were all excellent. It seems they were enchanted by the shy child prodigy," Enrico said. "But I'm afraid we're not going to find much insight into her later life here."

"Is it known whether Rose played in Italy again?"

"It's possible. I'm no expert on Rose Gallway, but there must be more to discover. I can't say how long it will take. You've only got tomorrow, so I think you should ring whoever it is you know at the Faraday School of Music and get his advice so I can help you better."

A smile sprang to Lilly's face, and she noticed Ellen was also smiling.

"I'll do that," she promised.

"You can also use my landline to keep your cell phone charges down."

"Isn't that a bit much to offer?" Lilly said, feeling a little uneasy. She got the sense that Enrico's favors would cost her something in return.

His hand cut through the air and waved away her concerns. "Nonsense. We're on the trail of a mystery woman—I'm not going to worry about a euro or two!"

Before she could say any more, the attendant appeared and reminded them that the museum was about to close. Enrico persuaded the archivist, who was about to go home, to agree that they could return the next day, even though it would be Sunday, to look through some more newspapers.

Outside the Palazzo Comunale they were met by a deafening peal of bells, which caused the pigeons that had settled on the square to flutter up in fright.

Once the racket stopped, Enrico said, "How about I invite you to dinner? We could continue our tales about Rose and Helen."

Neither Lilly nor Ellen had anything against the idea.

After a lovely dinner in Enrico's favorite trattoria and an evening stroll through the old town, Lilly was feeling pleasantly tired. Since Enrico's palazzo had several guest bedrooms, she had her own room, complete with a seventeenth-century wardrobe, a richly carved *cassone*, and a four-poster bed with heavy silk drapes that radiated a subtle scent of lavender. Lilly wondered who might have slept in that bed in earlier times.

Before settling down beneath the heavy covers, she went over to the window again to enjoy the lovely view of the old town, now lit by streetlamps. She sat down in the broad recess and watched the few passersby who were still out at that time of night. She thought of Peter—he would have liked it here.

But his image in her mind was soon displaced by the face of Gabriel Thornton. Oh my God, Lilly thought, I'd almost forgotten him! She looked at the clock by the bed. Would Gabriel still be up at half past ten? Would it be better to leave the call until the next day?

After deliberating briefly, she reached for her cell phone before remembering that Enrico had offered the use of his landline. She wasn't sure if she wanted to accept the offer—did she want to sit downstairs in the living room talking to Gabriel? She decided against it. Although they were very unlikely to talk about anything personal, she didn't want to be overheard. She took a deep breath and dialed Gabriel's number. There was a crackling on the line, and then he answered.

"Thornton."

"Gabriel . . . I . . . I hope I'm not disturbing you."

"Lilly!"

Did he sound horrified? Lilly turned hot and then cold. Perhaps she should have waited until the morning.

"I know it's late," she began. "I . . . I could call back tomorrow."

"No, tell me what's up now—you've got me on the line, after all. Has something happened?"

He sounded worried, which made Lilly feel even worse.

"No, everything's fine. It's just that . . . we've found some pictures of Rose. In a newspaper. One shows her and Mrs. Faraday—at least I assume it's her."

"That's wonderful! When was the picture taken?"

Her brief remark had clearly been enough to kindle his enthusiasm.

"On the day the recording was made."

"Brilliant! As far as I know, I don't have that one in my files. Some documents were destroyed in the war. That's an excellent find."

"Really?" Lilly's heart was pounding. Why? She had only told him that she had found the photo.

"A really excellent find. Could you bring me a copy, please?"

"I will. Signor di Trevi is going to translate the text for us."

"Di Trevi?"

"Ellen's acquaintance. We're staying in his palazzo, and he managed to persuade the people at the museum to let us go back tomorrow and look at some more newspapers. There were a few reviews of the concert, and we might discover more about Rose."

Lilly had to stop herself. You can't keep on chattering away, or he'll think you've had a caffeine overdose.

"That all sounds amazing!" Gabriel replied. "But I get a feeling that's not the only reason you're calling me."

"No, I . . ." Lilly hesitated as it dawned on her how he might have meant it. She forced herself to stay calm. "I wanted to ask you if Rose may have given any other concerts in Italy, and if so, when. That would make it easier for us to find the newspapers in which they were reported. They're bound in pretty thick volumes, and it could take weeks . . ." Lilly paused when she got the feeling Gabriel was smiling into the phone.

"That shouldn't be a problem," he replied, and she did hear the hint of a smile in his voice. "But I'm at home at the moment."

"Oh, I'm sorry. I didn't mean to disturb you."

"No need to apologize—you can call me anytime. Well, almost anytime. I don't usually answer during meetings or lessons."

"Of course."

Lilly wondered why she felt so damned unsure of herself. Gabriel was so friendly; there was no need.

"Do you have access to a computer in the palazzo? Or is there a house ghost who'll deliver e-mails?"

"I think so. I mean that there's a computer. I haven't seen the ghost yet." Lilly giggled as she imagined a ghostly butler handing her a print-out of an e-mail on a silver tray.

"OK, I'll e-mail you the files tomorrow morning. Of course, the information's not complete. At some stage Mrs. Faraday lost sight of her protégée, but I'll send you all I have."

"Thank you; that's very kind."

"Anytime, Lilly." The way he said her name filled her with the kind of warmth she had not felt since she was with Peter. And yet it was completely different.

"Well, then . . . good night . . . Gabriel."

"Good night, Lilly. And remember to come back from Cremona. I'm looking forward to talking to you again."

He hung up. Lilly held the phone to her ear for a moment longer, even though the conversation had ended. Her heart was still thumping and seemed as if it would never stop. She had felt the same way when she met Peter, and she had probably been just as nervous. It had all been such a long time ago . . . Suppressing a brief tinge of sadness, she set the phone down by the bed. Shortly before she went to sleep, she realized that she was smiling.

Later she dreamt she was in a dressing room like the ones she rec-ognized from the old films. A large mirror dominated the room, and on the door of an antiquated wardrobe trunk hung a dressing gown and two dresses—the clothes of an adult woman.

Lilly was all the more surprised to hear a child laughing in a corner of the room. Turning toward it, she found herself looking into the face of a girl of around seven or eight who bore a slight resemblance to Helen Carter—at least, she had the same thick, black hair.

"Are you looking for something?" the child asked, clearly not shy.

Lilly didn't know what to say at first. "I—I" she stammered, but then the words flowed back to her. "I'm looking for Rose."

"I'm Helen," the child said with a giggle.

"But you're a child!"

"Weren't you one once?" the girl retorted, and hopped up to a table on which a violin case lay.

"Yes, I was. But . . ."

What should she say? She didn't know.

The girl ran her hand over the violin. The violin! Perhaps she should ask about the violin.

"Where did you get the violin?" she heard her dream voice saying.

"I was given it," little Helen replied.

"By whom?"

"By a woman."

"And what was this woman called?"

The girl only laughed in reply. Had Mrs. Faraday given the girl the violin? It was likely. Lilly wanted to ask the child, who bore a spooky resemblance to Helen, what had become of her, but the girl was now opening the case. The violin looked much newer in the dream than it did now. As Helen ran her fingers over it, a false note sounded, as if it were out of tune.

"The solution to the mystery is hidden in 'The Moonlit Garden,'" the girl whispered once the harsh note had faded.

Lilly looked into the child's eyes and noticed that they were an unusual golden brown, as if a beam of light were shining onto the irises.

"What do you mean?" she asked, but the girl was not interested in answering her questions.

"Look, I can do magic!" she cried out. Laughter filled the room before she vanished into thin air.

As Lilly awoke, she realized that the moon had vanished from her window. A scooter rattled past along the street. She could still see the dream image before her eyes. Little Helen had told her that the solution to the mystery lay in "The Moonlit Garden." Her mind scrambled to make sense of the visions. The dream had only come to her because she had seen the photo the day before, and it had imprinted itself on her mind, she told herself. But what if the solution to the mystery really was to be found in the sheet of music?

Lilly felt like getting up to look, but she was overcome by a wave of fatigue. She sank back to sleep, this time without dreaming.

14

The next morning, Lilly considered what to do next. Her residual tiredness had been driven away by a strange restlessness. She went to the table where the violin case lay and took out the sheet of music from the lining.

She recalled what Dean had said—was there a code somehow concealed in the music?

If there was, it was one she was unable to unravel, since the piece was purely instrumental, with no text that could be readily interpreted. She gave up with a sigh, placed the page on the desk, and went for a shower. Together with the warm water, a shower of questions rained down on her. Perhaps Ellen and Enrico might be able to detect something in the notes of the beautiful sheet music . . .

Still unsettled, she turned off the water and dried her hair before wrapping herself in one of Enrico's fluffy bath towels She loved the feel of it against her, especially since the washing machine at home had a tendency to stiffen her own, turning them into something akin to cardboard.

The scent of coffee wafted down the corridor, enticing her into the kitchen. She found Ellen there, sitting at a long wooden table, her hands wrapped around a red coffee mug. She looked a little lost sitting at the oversized piece of furniture. Did Enrico really have occasion to entertain so many guests that such a table was needed to seat them all?

"Hey, there you are!" Ellen greeted her. "I was beginning to think you weren't coming down today."

"I called Gabriel yesterday evening," Lilly admitted, causing her friend to raise her eyebrows.

"Now that's what I call bold! Dragging a man from his sleep like that."

"He wasn't asleep. At least, he didn't sound as if he was."

The memory of the telephone conversation brought a smile to Lilly's face, momentarily pushing the questions about the sheet music into the background.

"Well, I'm sure he was wide awake the moment he heard you," Ellen said, taking a sip from her mug. "My goodness, this is almost as good as the coffee Terence makes."

"Where's your friend?" Lilly asked, glancing around the room. The kitchen looked like the kind of place that would be ideal for filming a celebrity-chef show.

"Enrico's gone to town to fetch us some breakfast. But don't get your expectations up—the Italians don't usually eat much in the mornings." Ellen rose and made for the expensive coffee machine. "I'll swap you a cappuccino for an account of your phone conversation with Gabriel."

"Deal," Lilly replied over the humming and slurping of the machine. "But I'm not sure the details of the call are as exciting as you think. It won't be news to you that Gabriel hasn't refused to help me."

"Just as I thought—I'd have bet the contents of my wardrobe on it."

Ellen set the coffee cup in front of her and sat back down. Lilly blew into the foamed milk and sipped cautiously.

"What do you think?"

"Delicious." Lilly drank again, then put the cup down. "Gabriel's going to e-mail me the concert dates. And then . . . I had another dream."

"A dirty dream involving Gabriel?" Ellen's eyes lit up mischievously.

"No, not that. I dreamt of Helen. Helen as a very small girl. She told me that the solution to the mystery would be found in 'The Moonlit Garden.' Do you remember what Dean said? That business about the code?"

"Do you really think the melody contains a hidden message?"

"Could it be possible? I've never been fully familiar with music notation, but you are."

"I am, but I've never been approached by MI6 with an offer I can't refuse. I wouldn't recognize a code if it were right there under my nose. It was only a dream, Lilly. Information your brain was processing."

"You're right. But what if it's true anyway? Perhaps the composer was clever enough to hide a message in the notes."

Lilly had brought the sheet music down with her and now spread it out on the table. To her, the notes looked like small birds' footprints. There was no obvious message, no code. Ellen would certainly see them with different eyes, but after staring at the page for a while, she shook her head.

"A piece of music. All I see is a piece of music, nothing else. And I'm married to a man whose greatest hero is James Bond."

Before Lilly could reply, the door opened.

"I see you're both awake and pretty as the morning sunshine," Enrico said cheerfully as he bustled into the kitchen and set down a basket containing two paper bags carrying the smell of a bakery, and a large jar of jelly.

Lilly stopped herself from rolling her eyes, satisfying herself with glancing at Ellen, who betrayed no reaction.

"Hey, ladies, what's up with you?" Enrico asked, clearly expecting a response to his greeting.

"Nothing. We've just got something on our minds," Ellen replied as she sipped her coffee. "Lilly had a confusing dream, and now we're wondering whether it's possible to conceal a code in sheet music."

She pointed to the page in front of Lilly.

"What kind of code?"

"A code that Rose, or maybe Helen, might have wanted to pass down into the future," Lilly said, turning the page so that he could see the composition. "A secret, perhaps. Possibly even the whereabouts or fate of Rose."

Enrico considered for a moment before shrugging.

"I wouldn't rule it out. In earlier times people were said to have been very inventive when it came to encoding messages. I'm not the right person to answer queries like that, but I do have a friend, a historian, who's interested in medieval espionage. Rose obviously lived in much more recent times and had nothing to do with the Borgias, but he might be able to give you some answers."

Ellen smiled at Lilly. "We're gradually getting so deeply in debt to you that we'll never be able to repay you in a lifetime."

"You don't have to," Enrico countered, this time without a hint of his usual suggestiveness. "If there really is a code concealed in this piece of music, it'll be a sensation. Now, have a good breakfast—the archive awaits us. While you're eating, I'll try phoning my friend. Perhaps he can help."

***

All morning Lilly was unable to get the dream out of her mind. Was it really possible that there was a hidden message among the notes? She was a little annoyed with herself for not having paid more attention during her music lessons. But even if she had, would she have been in a position to detect a code? Probably not. And it wasn't even certain that there *was* a secret message. It was a dream, Lilly, just a dream, she told herself repeatedly. But something urged her not to let it go.

Enrico had been unable to get hold of his friend. He had left him a message, and Lilly now felt as if she were on hot coals, her mind full of Helen's girlish voice haunting her with its laughter.

"Well, your Mr. Thornton has been a great help," Enrico remarked. They were back in the museum, waiting for the newspapers he had requested to be brought to them. "I'm only surprised that he hasn't turned up here himself to look for the articles."

"He has a school to manage and can't always take the time off to inquire about the school's former students," Lilly said, somewhat surprised at the intensity of her tone. After all, Enrico's words hadn't sounded all that critical.

"I'm sorry—I meant no offense to your friend. I was just a bit surprised."

"No, forgive me. I'm just a bit on edge because of Rose," Lilly replied, her embarrassment earning her an amused look from Ellen. "And I must admit, I'm a bit nervous about the sheet music."

"Pietro will be in touch soon," Enrico said confidently. "He's probably been taken off somewhere by his wife. She's very keen to make sure they spend the little spare time they get together. He's probably strolling through the park with her, enjoying the lovely weather, and pining for his cell phone. He's not allowed to switch it on when they go for their walks."

Strolling through the park. Lilly smiled sadly as she repeated the words in her head. She used to stroll through the park with Peter on Sundays, when time allowed. When the first magnolias were in bloom, they always went out together, at least when the sun shone. Would she ever enjoy walks like that again? She could imagine doing so with Gabriel, but would that ever happen?

"Look here!" Enrico's voice tore her out of her thoughts. "Rose at eighteen. Perhaps the last time that cranky old lady accompanied her."

The photo, which dominated the center of the newspaper page, showed Rose looking similar to the way she had when Lilly first saw her among Thornton's documents. Mrs. Faraday looked older, and Lilly could see a man in the background. Rose's lover? That was Lilly's first thought, but then she shook her head. The strict music teacher surely would not have allowed that. But why was he in the picture? It looked as though he had slipped in at the last minute.

"Does the article say anything about who this man is?" Lilly pointed to the picture.

Enrico's eyes skimmed the newsprint; then he shook his head. "The guy makes me think of football fans," he said, causing Ellen to laugh.

"Football?"

"Yes. You know, those fans who pop up and shove their faces or fingers into the picture when their idol is being interviewed?"

"Do you really think people did that kind of thing in those days?" Lilly asked, although she suspected he was right. Yes, it looked as though he had wanted to push his way into the picture.

"People haven't really changed that much over the last century," Enrico said with a laugh. "There were brazen, pushy people back then, too. Perhaps this man was an ardent admirer of Rose."

A shrill ringing suddenly interrupted the silence that had fallen. Enrico delved into his pocket as the young museum attendant who was keeping an eye on them frowned in disapproval. The conversation was short and to the point. As Enrico hung up, his eyes were shining mysteriously.

"That was Pietro, the strolling historian. He listened to my message, and he's now asking for a copy of the music. He'd like to look at it."

Lilly gave a soft whoop of joy. "So it's possible?"

"According to Pietro, yes. But you should also be prepared for the possibility that there's nothing there. My friend can't find a code that doesn't exist."

"But he's going to try."

"You can be sure he'll look at it closely. And if there's the slightest hint of a secret, he'll find it, guaranteed."

"Then we should get it to him as soon as possible," Ellen said. "Does he live nearby?"

"No, in Rome. We'll have to send it to him. If you can get a letter ready by this evening, I'll post it tomorrow."

"Do you still always send everything by mail?" Ellen asked in surprise. "Doesn't your friend have an e-mail address?"

"Of course, but I don't have a scanner. You know I only have the essentials when it comes to technology." He turned back to Lilly. "Have you brought the page with you? We should copy it here. I don't have a photocopier, either."

Lilly nodded and handed him the sheet of music.

***

In return for all that Enrico had done for them, Lilly and Ellen offered to cook him a meal that evening.

"German food? Are you sure?" he joked, his expression one of feigned dismay. "I don't think I have any bratwurst or sauerkraut in my fridge."

"Those eternal clichés!" Ellen said with a roll of her eyes. "You're an Italian, not an American. You should know us better than that."

"And we're not intending to serve you up knuckle of pork," Lilly added with a laugh. She was almost beginning to feel sorry that they were leaving the next day. Despite her initial impression of him as a sweet-talker, Enrico had turned out to be a friendly, helpful man. And she loved Cremona. It was a pity that they had not had the opportunity to visit the violin makers' workshops. If she came again, she would make sure she did.

Despite Enrico's fears, Lilly and Ellen conjured up a very passable pasta dish, which they polished off during a cozy evening around the long kitchen table. Enrico then insisted on showing them around the palazzo, including the rooms that were closed off because he didn't use them. After some gruesome stories about murdered counts, unfaithful poisoners, and the ghost of a midwife who had been killed by a countess after a stillbirth, they returned to the living room.

"What do you plan to do next?" Enrico asked as they enjoyed a glass of red wine from the palazzo's wine cellar. "The newspaper clippings aren't really going to help you explain why you were given the violin."

"But at least I've discovered some more about Rose," Lilly said. "Anyway, we haven't heard the analysis of the music yet. Maybe it will tell us more than we think." As soon as they'd arrived home, Lilly had put the copy of the music in an envelope. Now it was a matter of waiting.

"What if it doesn't?" Enrico pried.

"Then we'll try and find some new clues. In the meantime, maybe I'll be able to discover the identity of the mystery man who brought me the violin. Surely he'd be able to tell me how he came to the conclusion that I'm entitled to it."

"If he doesn't keep eluding you," Enrico reminded her. "He obviously had his reasons for not telling you anything. Why should he have changed his mind if you see him again?"

"I've got to try, at least. I don't want to keep something that doesn't belong to me."

"Oh, maybe it does belong to you. Sometimes there's no knowing the complicated paths followed by people—or things. The violin must have belonged to someone after Helen Carter—as far as I know, she was unable to play after she suffered an accident. Perhaps she sold it to one of your forebears."

Lilly was about to protest that this was out of the question, but Enrico added quickly, "You'll find out—and I'd be delighted if you would let me know once you've solved the mystery."

"I certainly will," Lilly promised, gazing into the wine in her glass.

When she finally slipped between the heavy sheets of her bed, her head was filled with a whirl of scents and words. As all concrete thoughts slipped into the background, she gave in to a pleasant drowsiness and allowed herself to sink into sleep.

15

Padang, 1902

The concert at the Grand Hotel—attended by all the big names among Padang's plantation owners—was a huge success. As Rose immersed herself in the melodies, she knew she had never played better. It must be due to the fact that she had noticed Paul in the audience. Catching sight of him made her feel incredibly light—all the more so as she realized he was not accompanied by his fiancée.

Full of satisfaction, she had drawn her bow across the strings and played until a flow of images enfolded her and whisked her away from the concert hall. Yes, that night she had played for Paul, for him alone. What was even more satisfying was that Sean Carmichael's concerns were unfounded. Her growing feelings for Paul—whether or not they were reciprocated—inspired her to play better.

As she left the stage amidst the cheering of the audience, she threw her agent a withering glance. Since the incident following her return from the wayang, they had hardly exchanged a word. Anything that passed between them was in the form of notes, delivered by Mai, who had been disciplined for telling Carmichael about her evening with

Paul. She should have punished her with silence, too, but she needed the girl. Mai cried for half an hour following the slap Rose had given her, and that seemed like punishment enough.

As Rose swept back into her dressing room, she felt as if she were walking on air. This time she would have no hesitation in mingling with the guests, as perhaps it would mean a chance to exchange a few words with Paul.

However, she wanted to change out of her stage clothes first.

"Mai, fetch me the blue dress with the lace trim. And be quick about it!"

The Chinese girl obeyed in silence. Since Rose's punishment, she limited herself to saying only the bare essentials in an attempt not to anger her mistress further. Rose was a little touched by this, since she had done the same every time she had failed to please Mrs. Faraday. The vitriolic torrent of words that flowed from her teacher's red-lipsticked mouth had not been soon forgotten.

Since everything had gone so well and fate appeared to be on her side with the presence of Paul, she decided to show a little leniency. She had no desire to be the malicious dragon Mrs. Faraday was. When Mai brought her the dress, she gave her an encouraging smile, which the girl returned uncertainly.

"Would you like a little free time this evening?" she asked as Mai began to unfasten the dress Rose was wearing.

"But, miss, you need me," she replied cautiously, as if she suspected a trick that might lead to a further slap.

"Of course I need you, but I do think you should have a few hours to yourself. I'll be mingling with the guests after this. If you like, you don't need to be back until later tonight. There must be a few things you'd like to see in Padang."

Mai gaped for a moment, unable to say a word.

"Do you really mean that, miss?" she ventured eventually.

"That's what I said, wasn't it? But if you prefer, you can go back to the hotel and wash my underwear. It's up to you."

"No, no . . . I mean, I'd love a little free time, if you don't mind."

"Go to the wayang. The stories they enact there are wonderful. And you might meet some of your own people there to talk to."

"Thank you very much, miss." Mai gave a brief bow. "I won't be back late, and I won't cause you any more trouble."

"Good. Now help me into this dress and do my hair. When you've finished, you're free to go."

Rose left the dressing room half an hour later. A few of the guests had tried to visit her before the show, but Mai had determinedly sent them away, explaining that Miss Gallway would soon be appearing among them.

As she walked down the corridor to the assembly room in her best blue dress, Rose's heart was thumping. Would she manage to speak to Paul?

As soon as the assembled company noticed her arrival, they broke out in applause. Van Swieten approached her, kissed her hand, and led her into the middle of the room. She only gave half an ear to his brief speech, as her eyes were searching the crowd for Paul. She couldn't find him. Had he left already? She was overcome by panic. If he was not there to talk to her, she would be at the mercy of the other men. She knew their questions all too well—they were always the same. The women talked only very rarely to her, since they regarded her as little better than a woman who earned her money by selling her body.

Of course the men thronged around Rose, showering her with compliments. Since she was unable to find Paul, she looked for Carmichael, but he was nowhere to be seen in the crowd, either.

Suddenly, as the forest of black frock coats and suits opened before her, she caught sight of Paul's blond mop of hair. She couldn't simply break free from the others and run to him—that would certainly have caused tongues to wag—but just then, as if he had heard her silent call for help, Paul looked up and came toward her. It was a while before he could press through to her, but his presence alone gave Rose the strength to bear the questions and the remarks and to reply with good humor.

Paul finally succeeded in extricating her from the crowd on the pretext that he wanted to introduce her to his fiancée. The others did not seem to have noticed that she wasn't there.

"You don't know how grateful I am to you!" Rose whispered as they vanished into a seldom-used corridor that led to the library.

"I take it you're as unenthusiastic as ever about conversation with your admirers," Paul said with amusement as Rose took out a handkerchief and used it to fan herself.

"If only it were a conversation! These men always ask me whether I'm spoken for, what it feels like to go out on stage, and whether, as a woman, I feel the need for a protector."

"It looks as though the last one is definitely the case," Paul said with a grin.

"Of course it isn't! I was born in this city, and I went away to London to study when I was still a child. I don't need anyone to look after me—unless it's someone to protect me from men who would like to take me as their lover or recommend their sons to me for that purpose."

Rose felt herself blushing with these words. She had not intended to speak so openly with Paul, but he seemed not to take offense.

"Well, there's no doubt you're a modern woman. I'm sure many of the ladies here would be delighted to have one of these well-heeled plantation owners as a protector."

"But these ladies are also satisfied with growing old on a plantation. That would never be enough for me, I'm afraid. I need music and I need the stage."

"And the applause?"

"What artist doesn't?"

"And yet you shun the admiration after a concert."

"As I've said, it has nothing to do with my art."

Paul looked at her for a long moment.

"Would you permit me to take a closer look at your violin?" he asked, which confused Rose a little, as none of her admirers had ever asked to see the instrument. Or was Paul perhaps expecting her to invite him to her dressing room? For a moment she regretted her pleasure at his presence, then told herself that Paul was not like the others—and if he turned out to be, she would have no hesitation in speaking her mind to him.

"Of course, but I'll have to fetch it from the dressing room."

"It would be a great pleasure," Paul replied, stepping back to let her past.

Rose smiled briefly—she had not misjudged him after all. "Very well. I'll be right back."

"I'll be waiting."

As she entered the dressing room, she saw that Mai had already left, but not without first tidying the room. Rose smiled to herself. The girl really was trying not to anger her again. Her hands were shaking as she picked up the violin case. She was even a little jealous that Paul was interested in the violin, but in truth, she and the violin belonged together.

Rose felt a little like a thief as she slipped into the corridor after a furtive glance up and down. Paul was waiting for her, leaning casually against the wall. Fortunately no one had discovered them, and their absence did not yet seem to have been noticed.

Rose set the violin case down on a small table in front of a vase of flowers. Against the background noise of the ballroom, she opened the lid and carefully removed the violin.

"This is a truly beautiful instrument," Paul said after looking at it in awe. "Where did you get it? It must be very old."

Rose gazed at the violin dreamily before touching it gently with her fingertips.

"My father gave it to me. He bought it from a Chinese merchant."

"A Chinese merchant?"

"Yes. Amazing, isn't it? I once saw a Stradivari in London. It looked a bit like this violin. I'm sure it wasn't made in China. And then there's the rose."

"The rose is really unusual on an instrument like this."

As Rose started to turn the violin over, Paul's hand moved forward and lightly stroked her fingers. Rose paused for a moment and looked up at him. The way Paul was staring at her unsettled her slightly, and at the same time triggered an unfamiliar feeling in her breast.

"I . . . I ought to be going," she said as she laid her violin back in its case.

At once she felt silly, and as though she was acting extremely improperly. Paul was engaged to be married. She couldn't . . .

"Wait."

Paul encircled her wrist with his warm hand.

Rose looked at him, bewildered. The feeling she had at his touch, the burning longing in her chest, was something she had only felt before when she gave herself up to her music.

"Please let me go," she said softly, although everything inside her was crying out to feel more of him than just his hand.

"I'd like to see you again, Rose," he said, almost pleading. "Please, will you accompany me to the plantation? That way we'd have a chance to get a few hours to ourselves."

"But what about your fiancée?"

For a moment, Paul looked taken aback. Then he replied, "Maggie is terrified of nature; she'd never come with me. But you are fearless, and I can't imagine anything nicer than spending some time with you. Please."

His hand pressed harder on hers. And Rose's confusion grew.

"I can't," she said.

She could hear how weak her voice sounded and feel her heart demanding to be alone with him. It's only one day, she told herself. What could happen? I'll go with him, look around the plantation, and then we'll return. In a few days I'll be off to India, and after that we'll never set eyes on each other again.

Then there were the rules of etiquette drummed into her by Mrs. Faraday, according to which she should on no account get involved with any of her admirers. And people here would certainly not approve of her having any kind of entanglement. Her behavior would reflect on the governor, who was giving her such generous support.

But it's only a trip out into the jungle, her heart insisted. There are bound to be other people present. And perhaps you may even be able to help with your local knowledge.

"Please, Rose," Paul begged. "I promise you won't regret it. And who else could guide me through the wilderness of your homeland?"

"I'm sure there are plenty of suitable guides who would be happy to offer you their services."

"You're right, but my Malay isn't particularly good."

"The guides also speak very good Dutch and English."

Paul tucked her fingers between his warm palms.

"Rose. Please grant me my wish. You led me into the world of the traditional puppet theater; now I'd like to lead you into the jungle. It's only a ride out, nothing more. And you'd get a chance to enjoy yourself on the plantation—I've heard they also have extensive gardens there."

He was so close to her now, and the way he looked at her was so insistent that Rose had no alternative. "All right, I'll come with you. But I still have a few concerts to play this week."

"Just tell me when would suit you, and I'll make my plans accordingly. But you have to promise me that if there's the slightest sign that a tiger's about to jump out, you'll lead me to safety."

"I hardly believe there are any tigers about to jump out. They're very shy, and although I spent quite a bit of my childhood running around the jungle, usually in defiance of my father, I never saw one. I'd be in no position to warn you."

"Then I'll take care of our safety."

Their faces were by now so close to one another that it would only have taken the slightest movement for them to kiss. Rose suddenly sensed someone looking at them and drew back. As she turned, she caught sight of a man she didn't know watching them, looking a little out of sorts.

"I really should be going now," Rose said. She picked up the violin case and disappeared in the direction of the dressing room.

***

That evening, as Paul returned to his hotel, he felt deeply confused. He still had Rose's scent in his nostrils and still believed he could feel her hand in his. Even though he knew he shouldn't, he was beginning to feel that his marriage to Maggie had been a mistake. How could feelings like his for Rose arise in so short a time? Were the tropics perhaps affecting his mind? Was the heat disturbing him? No, he was sure that Rose would have attracted his attention in London, too. Especially there, he thought, as she would have stood out like an orchid in the grass among the gray streets and stiff conventions.

Should he claim this flower for himself? The mere mention of divorce would probably cause a huge scandal. Not even his tolerant mother would understand that, let alone Maggie and his parents-in-law. He would become an outcast in London, with no one who valued their reputation having anything to do with him.

Feeling hot, Paul tore his tie from his neck and flung it down on the sofa, which was empty, since Maggie had already gone to bed. She would have accompanied him to the concert, but he had told her that he wanted to meet some investors and she would only get bored. She had believed him and stayed back at the hotel, leaving him free to go.

He was a little ashamed that he had lied to her—and also for the fact that he had come to feel a certain dislike for her when he saw her lying there on the sofa. She would probably be back to her animated self the minute they set foot on the ship bound for home.

Paul slumped down heavily on the sofa. What should he do now? Carry on as before, curb his ever-growing passion, and return home with Maggie? Or follow his heart? Win Rose for himself, get a divorce, and live happily with his new wife. It all sounded so easy . . .

But what if she didn't want the same thing? He sensed that she was attracted to him, but was that enough for her to accept his proposal? Or would it be better to wait until he was actually divorced? Did he really want to get divorced? He had never before been afflicted by such a dilemma.

His head was aching. He rose and went to the bathroom, ran some water into a bowl, and plunged his head into it. The water was not as cold as he needed, but he felt his veins contracting and the pain diminishing a little.

"Aren't you feeling well?"

Maggie was suddenly behind him, causing him to jerk up in shock. She had thrown her dressing gown over her nightdress, and her hair flowed loose over her shoulders. To see her standing there like that would once have filled him with a deep desire—but now he felt nothing. And, even worse, his thoughts strayed to Rose as he wondered what she would look like in this situation.

"It was all a bit much," he explained, reaching for a towel and rubbing his hair dry. He narrowed his eyes to drive away the image of Rose.

"It's all because of this dreadful heat and this dreadful country," Maggie muttered as she took hold of his arm. "We ought to leave here as soon as possible. When do you intend to view the plantation?"

Once again, Maggie's words incited a deep loathing within him. This country—she blamed this country for everything! Why couldn't she see how wonderful it was here? Why was she so determined to return to the gray cold of England? If it were up to him, he would move and come here to live—in the warmth, in the country Rose came from. He could be so much happier here than in a cold place with a wife who was always complaining.

How he would have liked to tell her all this to her face, but as his father had taught him, he kept a tight rein on his feelings and closed them off from Maggie. He didn't brush away her arm as he longed to do, and he didn't show his annoyance at her negativity. He played the devoted husband, as was expected of him.

"I'm sorry, but you'll have to put up with being here for a few more days. My attorney is meeting with the plantation owner and arranging an appointment to view it. As soon as I know the time, I'll find a guide and set off to see Mijnheer van den Broock."

There was no need for her to know that the appointment depended on Rose alone and that his attorney and the plantation owner were merely waiting for his word.

"Well, I sincerely hope that the appointment will be soon. I want to be able to spend some time with you again without being scorched by the sun."

With these words she led him into the bedroom. Paul let her have her way, but once Maggie had gone back to sleep beside him, he continued to stare at the ceiling, trying to master his thoughts, which constantly returned to Rose.

***

Despite all Mai's promises not to upset her, Rose no longer trusted her not to give anything away to Carmichael, so she decided to deliver the message containing her concert dates to Paul in person. Of course she knew about his fiancée and that she therefore couldn't simply turn up at his room. But she was sure the hotel porter would have nothing against her buying his silence. She dressed in a plain brown dress and checked in the mirror that she looked like an everyday housewife, one of the many residents of Sumatra who were half English and half native.

After stowing the discreet envelope, which bore nothing but Paul's name, in her skirt pocket, she left the room. Mai had gone to see one of the dressmakers in the city, as Rose's dress had suffered a slight mishap when she undressed the evening before. Rose had instructed Mai to wait until the dressmaker had repaired the split seam, giving her enough time to reach Paul undetected.

It had not been difficult to find out in which hotel he was staying—the city had one hotel that the English preferred and recommended to one another. She had even heard the name on frequent occasions while at Mrs. Faraday's in London. The Newcastle Hotel was by the harbor, one of the few that had an English name. Her own hotel, the Batang, stood right in the city center and was run by local people. Carmichael had also wanted to stay at the Newcastle, but there had been no vacancies, and Rose had actually been pleased that she could spend some time in the heart of the city, her old home.

Having made sure that Carmichael wasn't loitering in the vicinity of the hotel—he must be either in his room or out on some business or other—Rose went out through the glass doors and threaded her way through the stream of passersby. Many of them were locals, the women carrying either children bound to their bodies in pouches, or baskets of rice, sweet potatoes, or fruit. The Dutch, most of them wearing suits or frock coats, were engaged in lively conversations, their wives chatting with their neighbors. Rose was still familiar enough with the streets of her hometown to know all the shortcuts. Since she did not have to pay too much attention to her clothes, she hurried along narrow alleyways. The smell of spices and garbage filled her nose as she jumped over a rivulet of water someone had tipped out onto the street and flicked the hem of her skirt against a small dog who had settled down comfortably on a street corner.

And there it was before her. The hotel was one of the grandest in the whole of Padang. Its white facade would not have looked out of place in London and was punctuated by balconies, on some of which men in light-colored clothing stood watching the world go by, or women in wide-brimmed hats sat whiling away the time until lunch.

The local people, who knew how keen the English were on taking souvenirs back with them, had laid out cloths on the sidewalks and dotted them with jewelry, decorated boxes, pictures, and carved figures. A few people, Europeans judging by their appearance, lingered before them, while the passing locals did not even spare them a second glance.

Rose took the letter from her skirt pocket and strode up to the hotel doors, which were a masterpiece of carved timber and glass.

The interior of the hotel was like those in London and Paris and, apart from the Sundanese bellboys, there was very little to suggest that they were actually in Sumatra. The crystals and lamps of the magnificent chandeliers were reflected in the polished marble floor, the middle of which was covered by red carpets. The aroma of coffee and tea hung in the air, but there was no trace of the spicy smell that pervaded the corridors of her own hotel.

Giving every appearance of being nothing but a messenger, a servant of some anonymous mistress, Rose handed the letter to the red-liveried porter.

"Can you please give this to Lord Havenden—to him alone and no one else."

She emphasized her words with a bill, which she pushed discreetly across the reception desk. The porter gave her a questioning look but nodded as the money disappeared beneath his hand. He tucked the letter carefully into a drawer; Rose thanked him and turned to go.

Outside, one of the English browsers, who had clearly been persuaded to buy some jewelry, turned and smiled at Rose. She returned his smile noncommittally and hurried on.

At that moment she saw Paul, who had also paused before one of the merchants' displays. The woman on his arm was without doubt his fiancée. She was wearing a cream-colored dress that looked like it had come from a Paris fashion house, and her face was flushed with the heat. In the hand that was not tucked into Paul's arm she held a delicate white parasol. That won't offer you much relief from the heat, Rose thought somewhat maliciously. Once she was back in England, her skin would either be as brown as a nut or ruined by sunburn.

Yet she felt a pang of jealousy to see the way Maggie leaned affectionately on his arm and whispered something in his ear. Paul didn't seem unhappy with this woman—in fact, he only had eyes for her. He didn't once look at the street scene or notice Rose.

And if he did, would he acknowledge me? Would he come over to me, introduce her to me, talk to me? Or would he walk past as if I were any other woman? Is he only interested in my fame?

Carmichael's words came back into her mind, and she was angry with herself for letting them. A normal life . . . All she wanted was a life at the side of a man who loved her. Could Paul be that man? She didn't know. At that moment she began to doubt, and her doubts were soon so strong that she felt like running into the hotel and taking back her message. If she failed to get in touch with him, if she simply forgot him . . . But he was bound to find another excuse to be seen by her. And then she knew she wouldn't have the willpower to send him away.

As she was still wrestling with her doubts, the couple moved on. The Englishwoman's parasol blocked Paul's view of the street, preventing him from noticing Rose. In any case, it was too late now for her to return to the hotel. If she did, he would see her, and she didn't want to make a spectacle of herself in front of him and his fiancée. She continued on her way and turned into the next side street, away from the spell of the sight of him. Things were now in his hands. If he changed his mind, she would drive him from her mind.

As she came to the street where her hotel stood, she saw Mai nearby, talking to an elderly Chinese woman. There was no reason for her to be afraid of her own servant, but nevertheless Rose felt butterflies in her stomach as she hurried across the street, hoping that Mai wouldn't see her.

It was similar to the time in London when she had secretly ventured out into the city by night with a few other girls, even though they had been warned of the dangers posed by the riffraff roaming the streets. As they walked, they had told each other wild tales of Jack the Ripper, who had terrorized the neighborhood years ago but had never been caught, and they had delighted in the creepy feelings aroused by the light of the gas lamps. Their feelings had intensified when they returned and crept down the corridor that led past Mrs. Faraday's bedroom. They had managed not to wake her—and now, back in her hotel, Rose realized that Mai had not seen her either. With a smile of relief she turned to climb the stairs, ignoring the porter's look of amazement as she charged up.

***

"Oh, look at those darling little elephants!" Maggie cried out, pointing to the carved figures spread out at the feet of a tanned boy in traditional dress.

Paul looked at her with amazement. She was like a different person today. The heat was still wearing her down, but she had not complained once during their walk through the city. She had not objected when Paul had suggested stopping to watch the fishermen hauling their nets from the sea, even though she must have feared getting sand in her shoes and a film of salt on her lips. Was she getting used to this place? Or did she instinctively sense his dissatisfaction, his inner conflict that had increased since his night with Rose?

"Yes, aren't they lovely?" he replied as he tried to conceal his unease. "Would you like one?"

Maggie nodded, and Paul bought the small, smooth figure with fine lines carved into its back.

"It looks a little Indian," he said as he passed it to her.

"I hope it will bring us luck," Maggie said as she stroked the surface with gloved fingers.

"Elephants always do." Paul kissed her temple lightly and led her to the hotel entrance.

"Sir, there's a message for you," the porter said as soon as he saw them come in, handing him a small envelope. At first Paul was baffled, but as he took the letter, he recognized the handwriting and was hardly able to stop himself from smiling.

"What's that?" asked Maggie, who had noticed him slipping it quickly into his pocket.

"Nothing special. Only a message about the plantation."

Maggie's expression darkened again as if she had forgotten until that moment why they were there.

Paul tried to ignore it as he led her toward the staircase. Not a single word passed Maggie's lips until they were in their room.

"Do you really have to buy that plantation?" she asked after removing her hat.

Paul raised his eyebrows in surprise.

"What do you mean? That's why we made this journey. And in any case, I'm not buying the plantation. I'm acquiring a share."

"Even a share will mean you'll have to keep coming back here, won't it?"

"Of course. I have to keep an eye on my business interests. And the owner will expect me to be involved. What else are partners for?"

Maggie pressed her lips together. However relaxed she had been before, she had now changed completely. It was as though a storm had rolled in to drive away her happiness. Did she suspect . . . No, that was impossible. The evening he went to the puppet show with Rose she had gone to bed early, and she was still asleep when he got back. In any case, there was no way she would creep around the streets of a foreign city alone, spying on him.

"What's the matter, Maggie?" he asked in an attempt to pacify her, although his heart was thumping, and he wondered again if it had been a good idea to make her his wife. His mother had always supported his father in all he did, but he couldn't be certain his own wife would do the same. If something like the investment in a plantation, and the income it represented, could cause an argument between the two of them, how would it be with any other matters that arose?

"I just don't want to be here a moment longer!" she burst out angrily. "I hate this country! I hate this heat! I hate these people! Have you seen the children? You can't get rid of them. They hover around like bluebottles. And then there's that dreadful stink everywhere! I want to get away from here—that's all there is to it!"

This outburst came as such a surprise to Paul that he was momentarily unable to reply. Her eyes gleamed with fury in a way that did not belong to the Maggie he knew. When had this incredible rage taken hold of her?

What she had just said rendered him speechless, but the anger in him soon boiled up like a pan of milk forgotten on the hot plate.

"This country that you hate so much has made my family wealthy! And I don't see why I should forgo the chance of establishing a successful business here! The only mistake I've made about Sumatra is believing that you would support me. I should have left you at home, in the gray fog of London. That would have suited you better, and I'd have been spared your constant childish whining!"

Maggie stared at him as if he'd slapped her; then her face crumpled and she burst into tears. She might have hoped this would soften him, but Paul made no move to comfort her. On the contrary, he felt that all his accusations were confirmed. In many respects Maggie was still a child, and behaved as one. He almost expected her to stamp her foot when she didn't get what she wanted. No, he didn't want a wife like that. He needed a strong woman, one who would stand behind him in his enterprises.

Paul let her stand there for a moment longer before realizing that he would have to do something if he didn't want to listen to her complaints all afternoon.

"Forgive me. I didn't mean to be so heavy-handed," he said, and approached her to take her in his arms. As if she were waiting for this move, she leaned on him, and he stroked her hair, trying to ignore the tears soaking into his shirt. But his thoughts were constantly drawn to the letter in his pocket, and how long he would have to wait for an opportunity to open and read it.

When Maggie finally disappeared into the bathroom to wash the tears from her face, he seized his moment. He tore the envelope open and felt a pang of disappointment as he saw nothing but a row of figures on the page. A secret code? He would have found it appropriate, but then it occurred to him what they really meant: the dates of Rose's concerts. She was free on the days in between them, and as it turned out, there were three days, shortly before his departure, on which she could accompany him.

Against a background noise of water splashing into the bath, he sat down at the bureau to compose a reply. Maggie might hate this country, but Rose didn't. He couldn't imagine a better companion than her. She would make the journey a pleasure, telling him stories and possibly even casting him in a more sympathetic light in the plantation owner's eyes—none of which he could expect from Maggie. He fixed a date and then wrote another message to the plantation owner, who had given him free rein to arrange the appointment.

***

On the day they were to set out, Rose was incredibly nervous. Neither Mai nor Carmichael knew where she was going. She had explained her absence with the excuse that she was traveling inland with her mother to visit her grandmother during the three days' grace period before she had to prepare for the next concert. She was still unsure of her feelings for Paul Havenden. The reply he had sent her consisted of more than mere figures; in fact, it had been written with feeling.

Although it had been nearly a week ago, she could not rid herself of the mental image of Paul with his fiancée. What if he was only playing with her? Or was it the beautiful Englishwoman he was deceiving? What did he really feel in his heart?

She had not seen him since at her concerts; either he had been otherwise engaged on business or had to look after his fiancée.

"Miss, begging your pardon, but you wanted to leave at seven."

Mai, looking rather sleepy, tore her from her thoughts. Rose had not returned from her concert until after midnight. She was due to give only one more, the day before she set off for India. And then, during the crossing, Rose would have to try not to think about Paul on his way back to England and the fact that she might never see him again.

"Yes, you're right. I should be going," Rose said. Dressed in her most elegant green riding habit, she picked up the carpetbag filled with everything she would need on the trip. She had to smile as she felt the weight of the bag. As a child, when she had traveled through the jungle with her mother, she had needed a fraction of all these things. And even now, she could manage in the wilderness with just a few provisions. But she had Paul with her, and there would probably be a guide and others accompanying them. She had to appear as civilized as possible, as it was actually anything other than moral to travel in the company of a man without a chaperone.

"Take care of my things, and look through my dresses," she instructed Mai, to ensure she didn't waste time daydreaming. "If you find any stains or damage, make sure that they're all seen to by the time I return. I'll be checking!"

"Yes, miss, I'll make sure that everything's in good shape."

Rose nodded. After betraying her to Carmichael, her servant had given her no other grounds for displeasure.

"Very well. Take care of yourself, behave properly, and keep Mr. Carmichael happy so he doesn't start getting ideas about coming after me and fetching me back for a last-minute engagement in some bar."

"I'll do that, miss," Mai replied, smiling. "And you look after yourself in that wild jungle."

"It's not as wild as you think. If you keep to the tracks my people have followed for many years, there'll be no risk of being eaten by tigers." Rose was surprised at herself. Since when had she thought of the inhabitants of Sumatra as her people? "And the men of the forest wouldn't harm anyone."

"Men of the forest?" Mai's eyes widened in surprise.

"Orang hutans, as they're called in the local language. Large apes who were once taken for people. I'll tell you about them when I get back."

With that, Rose took her leave and left the room. She had hoped that Carmichael would have forgotten to come and say good-bye, but there he was, coming toward her down the corridor.

"Have a good trip," he said. They were the first words spoken between them since their argument. She had even let him know she was going in writing, and when they met, she barely had a word of greeting for him. "Look after yourself. Especially your hands. Without them . . ."

"I'm worthless. I know," Rose replied, a little indignant. "Don't worry. This is my homeland—I know my way around. I'll be back in two days."

As she moved to go past him, his hand shot out and stopped her. Carmichael's eyes bored into hers.

"How long are you going to sulk? Wasn't I right that you're not an ordinary woman? You should hear how full of praise people are for your concerts! Many of them are comparing you to an angel. And when this region's newspapers finally catch up, I can show you the reviews. They're going to be better than ever before."

Rose extricated herself from his grip. She was flattered to hear that she was well received by the people here, but it also confirmed that romance, or even love, did her nothing but good.

"Then perhaps you should apologize to me," she replied coolly. "Or save it until I return. I've done nothing wrong—my playing is as brilliant as ever, so the scene you made with me was completely unjustified. And now, if you'll excuse me, I don't want to keep my mother waiting."

With that she turned, and without looking back at Carmichael, she knew he would be staring after her with a sour expression.

In case her agent was unable to resist spying on her, Rose had made detailed arrangements with Paul. She was to go to the harbor so that anyone following her would get the impression that she was heading for her parents' house. Shortly before she got there, she would turn off into a small alleyway, where he would be waiting for her.

Rose's heart was thumping as she stepped around the puddles. There had been a heavy rain shower the previous night, which had done nothing to freshen the air. Mist was now clinging to the mountain slopes like cotton wadding draped over green velvet.

She paused shortly before reaching the alleyway. Her hands were clammy with anticipation, and her cheeks felt flushed. If anything happens to us on this trip, it won't only be Carmichael who curses me to high heaven, she thought. She shook her head, pushed these thoughts aside, and strode determinedly on. She heard horses snorting, and as she rounded the corner, she saw three of them. A brown-skinned local man was holding two of them by the reins, and Paul was stroking the mane of the third.

"Ah, here you are!" he called out as he caught sight of Rose. "I was beginning to think you'd changed your mind."

"Why should I?" Rose replied, then greeted her fellow countryman in Malay. "You must be waiting for someone else?"

"No, why?" Paul gave her a broad grin. "My attorney, Mijnheer Dankers, has ridden on ahead. He wanted to talk to my future business partner. Prepare the ground, if you like."

"Isn't the plantation owner keen on going into business with you?"

"Yes, of course, but the plantation I'd like to invest in isn't doing too badly, and we can't rule out the possibility of him finding another partner. For example, if I were to be unpleasant to the owner, the transaction certainly wouldn't come off."

Rose had to accept that the world of men was still a mystery to her. She sometimes found it absurd to listen to Carmichael's reports of how arrangements came to be made, but she told herself she was an artist, someone who had no need to understand business.

"So you've got to make sure you're nice to him," she replied, causing Paul to laugh.

"Your delightful company will play a part in that. Everything else will be dealt with by my attorney. All I need to do then is to smile and make a few intelligent remarks."

"Do you really think that I can influence the plantation owner?"

Paul's eyes met hers, and she was struck dumb. It was not the look of a man who saw her as a mere traveling companion he was taking along to make a good impression on a potential business partner. That look promised something completely different.

All Mrs. Faraday's warnings about moral behavior flooded back into her mind. It was not seemly for a young woman to ride out into the wilderness with a man. A chaperone or at the very least a servant would be essential. Yet here she was with a man whom she found incredibly attractive, accompanied only by a guide who would certainly do nothing to safeguard her virtue.

But did she want to safeguard her virtue? She was not the spoiled daughter of an aristocratic family. And she considered herself to be clever enough to avoid a scandal. Why shouldn't she give in to what her heart desired?

"So, you're not waiting for anyone else?" Rose looked around. She suddenly felt an overwhelming urge to leave the city, since she never knew what Carmichael might be doing.

"No, we can get going. I hope this isn't the first time you've been on horseback."

Rose shook her head. "My father taught me to ride. I may be a bit rusty, but once I'm in the saddle, I'm sure it'll soon come back to me."

Once they had left the city behind, Rose felt a deep sense of relief. Until then she had been afraid that Carmichael would appear, realize what was happening, and drag her from the horse. But it hadn't happened, and now she was surrounded by the magnificent greenery of the jungle with its birdsong and monkey calls.

"It doesn't seem to worry you, being here in the great outdoors," Paul remarked as he steered his horse to walk beside hers. Their guide rode on a little ahead, but Rose knew full well that there was little danger lurking beside these tracks. The tigers were deeper into the jungle. Only older animals who were too frail to hunt ventured close to human settlements. Snakes and spiders were scared off by the hoofbeats, and the peaceable orang hutans posed as little danger to the travelers as the numerous types of small monkeys. A sharp-eyed observer could see any number of magnificent birds and butterflies.

"Of course I'm not worried. This is my home," she replied with a laugh. "Believe me, I'd be more afraid to ride through certain areas of London. Out here there's nothing that could put us at risk."

A smile flitted across Paul's face. "Good old London isn't as bad as you make out, but I know what you mean. It's paradise here. The more I see of your island, the more I come to the conclusion that this must have been the Garden of Eden."

"I'm sure there are others who come here and think the same. Nevertheless, I've seen a lot of beautiful places."

"But none to compare with your home island, I imagine?" Paul gave her a searching look.

Rose realized there was no point in denying it.

"No, hardly anywhere comes close to Sumatra." She smiled. "Do you intend to come here often?"

"After all I've seen, yes. I find the island really inspiring, and it's good for my health to be away from the cold and damp for a while. Of course, I have to take care of my business interests in England, too, but I can imagine spending a few months a year here—perhaps spend the winter here, when England is at its most cheerless."

"And what does your fiancée have to say about that?" As she saw Paul's expression darken, Rose regretted asking.

"Ah yes, Maggie." He paused, giving the impression he regretted his answer before he had spoken it aloud. "She has a very low opinion of this country. I feel as if I have to say that every day to people I deal with." He shook his head. "To be honest, I'm no longer sure whether Maggie is the right woman . . ." He hesitated, and to judge by his expression, he must have been having dark thoughts. "I mean, I don't know whether I . . . want to marry her."

Rose gasped with shock. "You can't say something like that!"

"Yes, I'm saying it," he replied forcefully, as if trying to convince himself of the words. "I'm saying it because that's how I feel! If I can come to an agreement with this plantation owner, I'll have to spend time here regularly. A lot of time, and I don't want to spend it alone. I need a woman who's willing to travel with me, who's prepared to venture into the unknown. I don't need a woman who's afraid of monkeys or the local people, even though there's nothing to fear."

Rose looked at him, deeply shaken. She had not expected him to be so open. Part of her was delighted, but mostly she was shocked. Had her secret wish for everything to turn out in her favor really been so strong? But what if it threatened to come true? Would she be prepared to marry Paul? Or at least become his lover? Would she be prepared to give up her music for him? Certainly not the latter, but Paul would be sure to understand that.

They rode on in silence until the sun sank gradually to the horizon and the air became thick with mist. The guide finally rode up to them and reported in broken Dutch that the plantation was nearby.

"Did you hear that?" Paul turned to Rose with a smile. "We'll soon find out whether the plantation is a worthwhile investment or a drain on resources."

The plantation house looked a little weathered, but it glowed like a pearl amidst all the surrounding greenery. The owner had two dogs to keep guard over his property. Rose recognized them from a distance as bloodhounds, since some of the wealthy gentlemen in London had acquired similar animals to protect their land and property.

The high black iron gates, each with a finely wrought rosette at its center, looked forbidding, as did the tall hedge that rose up on either side of the gateposts and screened the property from prying eyes. Why these safety precautions? Rose wondered. Out here no one would dream of robbing them, and wild animals would find their way in whatever the barriers. The dogs would not stand a chance against a tiger.

A bell rang out over the grounds to announce their presence, and a furious barking started up as the two muscular black dogs hurled themselves against the gates with such force that the horses jumped back in fright.

"Well, if the man of the house hasn't heard the bell, the dogs certainly have," Paul remarked.

Only a few moments later two men walked down the path toward them. One of them, a tall, strong-looking guy who reminded Rose of a game warden, carried two leashes, which he used at lightning speed to restrain the raging beasts. He snapped at them sharply and gave the leashes a couple of short, sharp tugs. The dogs yammered briefly before settling down submissively at his feet.

"Spiked collars," Paul whispered, correctly interpreting the question in her eyes.

The second man then opened the gates. He was clearly not the owner of the plantation but the butler of the house.

"Welcome, Mijnheer Havenden," he said, turning to Rose inquisitively.

"This is my fiancée, Maggie Warden," Paul said, shocking Rose into silence.

"Mijnheer van den Broock and Mijnheer Dankers are expecting you. Please, will you follow me? Anders will take care of the horses; they'll be in the best possible hands with him."

The servant, who had so much and yet so little in common with an English butler, turned to go. Only then did Rose dare to throw Paul an indignant glance. What did he mean by simply introducing her as his fiancée? The two men they were about to meet must know what Paul's fiancée looked like. She would have liked to haul him over the coals then and there, but she held back. If it all blew up in his face and the men started to ask questions, it would be interesting to see how he talked his way out of it.

Full of fear and resentment, Rose hardly noticed the wonderful garden. It was only as they reached the steps leading up to the house that she became aware of a sea of flowers. The plantation owner had little regard for the traditional English garden, allowing everything to grow rampant, similar to the methods of her mother's ancestors. As they climbed the steps, she saw beyond the house, almost hidden by all the greenery, the planters' and harvesters' sheds. Behind them, terraced fields of sugarcane stretched into the distance.

"At first sight it's not at all bad here, is it, darling?" Paul asked with a shameless grin.

Rose made no reply. The real Maggie probably wouldn't have responded any differently, she thought as the servant led them through the entrance hall into a kind of reception room with timber paneling almost hidden behind an array of paintings. By now, Rose felt fit to burst, but she put on a pleasant face until the servant finally left the room.

"What did you mean by that?" she hissed angrily at Paul. "Your attorney must know I'm not your fiancée!"

"My attorney doesn't care about such things, and in any case, he hasn't seen Maggie once."

"Have you been planning this the whole time?"

A mischievous smile flitted across his face.

"No, it occurred to me on the spur of the moment. And it does save us a lot of explanation. Otherwise everyone would want to know who you are, the nature of our relationship, and so on. As my fiancée you'll be accepted as you are and can enjoy your anonymity."

"But it's the height of impertinence!"

"Oh, come on, Rose. I'm sure you've got nothing against a bit of harmless fun. See it as that and enjoy it. It's only for two days. Anyway, I'm sure our host will envy me such an enchanting woman, and it will make him a bit more kindly disposed toward me when it comes to discussing the conditions."

An enchanting woman? Under other circumstances she might have enjoyed hearing it, but right then his remark made her furious. Was Paul laughing at her expense? And if the whole thing was meant to be a bit of fun, why had he not included her from the start?

Before Rose could start up with a new tirade, the door opened again, and the servant reappeared accompanied by two men. One was of medium height and somewhat stocky build with dark hair and a long beard, while the other was tall and blond and dressed in simple but stylish clothes that identified him as the plantation owner. Paul threw Rose another pleading look before offering the blond man his hand.

"Mijnheer van den Broock, it's a pleasure to meet you in person. This is my fiancée, Maggie Warden, who is completely delighted by your wonderful estate."

Suppressing her resentment, Rose managed a smile. She noticed that the man scrutinized her closely, probably noting the hint of the exotic in her appearance, but as she didn't want to cause trouble for Paul, she said: "I'm delighted to meet you. Paul has been talking about nothing but the plantation for days."

Van den Broock, who did not look like a man with much of a sense of humor, laughed. "Ah well, we'll soon see how long his enthusiasm lasts. My plantation is doing well but could be more profitable if I had a reliable partner."

"I believe you, and I'm sure that Paul is the right man for the business."

Had she gone too far? Again she noticed van den Broock staring at her skeptically.

"You speak outstanding Dutch. May I ask where an Englishwoman learned to speak it like that?" he asked eventually.

Rose had not even noticed that she had replied in the plantation owner's own language. Now she realized that in playing the part of the real Maggie Warden she should have acted as if she didn't understand him. Her pulse began to race.

"I learned it from my mother," she replied, which was not actually a lie. She lowered her gaze, feigning shyness but in reality in an attempt to conceal her anger with Paul. "She learned the language as a child."

"Remarkable. I'm glad that I'm in company where I don't have to inflict my poor English on anyone. Now, shall we move to the dining room? My cook is a real miracle worker, though I fear I don't value his wonderful creations as much as they deserve. But I make it up to him by regularly inviting guests to dine with me, thus allowing him to show off his talents to the full."

The meal the cook conjured up for them consisted mainly of local specialties, some of which were sharply spiced. Van den Broock seemed to be as used to this cuisine as Rose was, but Paul was clearly having problems with the hotness. The sight of him reaching for his water glass, his eyes streaming, too proud to admit that it was too much for him, made up a little for the game in which she was an unwilling accomplice. The food brought heat to her own cheeks, but her mother's cooking was sometimes even hotter than that of the plantation owner's cook.

After dinner, van den Broock drew them into a seemingly endless conversation about sugar production. He was extremely knowledgeable about the climate, animals, and species of Sumatra as well as being thoroughly versed in the region's political circumstances. Paul responded with anecdotes about his estate back home, about horse breeding and arable farming, which appeared to be a favorite topic of both men.

Rose was pleased that the plantation owner only rarely spoke to her. The questions he did ask revolved mostly around London, which van den Broock had never seen. This meant that Rose could answer effortlessly, although she had to take great care not to lapse into anecdotes about Mrs. Faraday's conservatory. Once, when the talk turned to her interests, she almost gave herself away by enthusing about Vivaldi's works. Paul immediately made light of it, remarking that she was a more than competent violinist, whereupon the plantation owner naturally asked for a sample. Fortunately his violin was a really basic instrument, and she ensured her playing was deliberately lackluster so that no one noticed this woman was actually one of the best violinists in the world.

Paul found this highly amusing, and after she finished, gave her a conspiratorial wink so that Rose found it impossible to stay angry with him. Yes, it really was amusing to mislead the plantation owner like that. Rose played along, and the rest of the evening was enjoyed by them all.

***

When she finally lay in her bed, she looked pensively out the window, watching the bats and night birds that flitted past every now and then.

That evening she'd had a small taste of what it would be like to be Paul's fiancée. She had enjoyed being acknowledged by the men without once having to show what she was capable of. Yet she had also noticed that in their eyes she was nothing more than an appendage of Paul's. Onstage and afterward all eyes were on her, and no one who heard her play ever doubted her talents. By Paul's side she had felt downright worthless—or was that merely because of the new identity he had imposed on her? She still felt a little resentful toward him because of it. Where would the harm have been in introducing her as an acquaintance? Van den Broock did not give the impression of being a great music lover, but she could have contributed a lot more to the conversation than she was able to under the circumstances.

Yet, however annoyed she felt with Paul, she enjoyed being close to him. Even if he was a dreadful rogue, she nevertheless wanted to make sure he got his share in the plantation. On the way back—provided the attorney, who had been very reserved the whole time, did not ride with them—she would tell him exactly what she thought.

The next morning she was woken by Paul at the crack of dawn, since van den Broock had promised to show them around the sugar plantation. At first she had no idea where she was, but when she saw Paul, who had simply let himself into her room after knocking, she jumped up.

"What are you doing here?" she cried out in alarm, pulling the sheet up to her chin.

"Good morning, Rose. Please excuse my coming in unannounced like this. Yesterday I . . . I had a flash of inspiration. I couldn't stop thinking about it, and I think I should make the most of my opportunity."

He paused briefly and took a deep breath to calm himself.

"Couldn't it have waited till later?" Rose asked in amazement, feeling a little nervous as Paul seemed completely out of sorts.

To her huge astonishment he suddenly knelt down by the bed.

"Rose, will you be my wife?"

Rose's eyes widened in shock, and she flinched back as if he had handed her a hideous bug.

"You've lost your mind."

"Not at all. I'm completely serious. Could you ever envisage becoming my wife? Living by my side, here, on Sumatra?"

"You're forgetting that my profession requires me to travel the world. And I have absolutely no intention of giving up my violin and my concerts."

"You wouldn't have to. We'd merely have a main residence here. You'd go on your tours and, if you allowed it, I'd accompany you. And if ever your agent allows you a break from creating world history, you'll be here with me, and we can go on long trips exploring the jungle, or whatever else you want."

Rose shook her head. "You're forgetting your fiancée."

"Engagements can be broken off."

Now Rose was convinced that Paul really had lost his mind. Perhaps it would be better to leave right now and let Paul explain why his "fiancée" had made such a quick exit. She edged back and, keeping the sheet drawn tightly around her, finally stood.

"I don't know what's moved you to make me such an offer so early in the morning, but I'm sure you must be having another joke at my expense."

"I'm not joking at all!" Paul said, looking taken aback as he moved away from the bed.

"That's even worse! Don't you realize what the consequences would be? What a scandal it would cause?"

"I don't care! I've been turning it over and over in my mind all night. I only know that it feels right. That it's the right thing to do."

Rose shook her head. Her heart was thumping wildly. She had also toyed with thoughts of what it would be like to be his wife, but she had never in her wildest dreams thought that he might be contemplating it seriously. And she was still convinced that the heat was affecting his reasoning. How else could he have come upon the idea of wanting to dissolve his engagement?

"I shouldn't have come with you," she said eventually, unsure whether it was disappointment stirring in her breast, or something else. "Please leave me now. I must get dressed. Whatever else happens, I have to play out this farce for a while longer."

Paul looked at her steadily. His expression was one of disappointment mixed with longing. Could he perhaps be serious? But even if he was, it was completely crazy!

"All right," he said finally. He sighed and lowered his eyes in perplexity. "Please forgive me. I thought . . ."

Rose was all too eager to know what he thought, but before she could summon the courage to ask him, he turned and left the room.

***

With a huge knot in her stomach, Rose appeared in the dining room, where the cook had prepared a wonderful breakfast for them. The three men were already engaged in lively conversation. They stood as she approached.

"I hope you slept well, Miss Warden," the plantation owner said in English, which was indeed less than good.

"I slept very well, thank you," Rose replied, trying to keep any trace of an accent from her voice as she believed van den Broock was still testing her.

As she sat down, she glanced at Paul, who was taking his seat like the others. But he stared into his teacup as if he had found something extremely interesting in there. Rose could see the disappointment in his features. Feeling confused, she looked into her own teacup, where clouds of milk were blooming in the tea, which a Sundanese servant had silently poured for her. Had she just lost an opportunity?

When Paul had left her room, she had believed she had done the right thing, but now she doubted herself, and this doubt spoiled her appetite and kept her silent.

She did not brighten up until they set out to view the plantation.

"I hope the walk won't be too strenuous for you, Miss Warden," van den Broock remarked as they strode across the courtyard to the accompaniment of the bloodhounds' barking.

She wanted to reply that she had walked a lot farther than a mere tour of a Sumatran plantation, but fortunately she knew how to hold her tongue.

"I like to take long walks. You've no need to worry about me."

The plantation owner laughed. "I really believe you're marrying the right woman, Lord Havenden. We need this kind of spirit on Sumatra."

Paul just nodded, still refusing to look at her. Fortunately, van den Broock appeared not to be concerned by the lack of any display of affection between them. He paused for a word with the burly manager who had so effortlessly tamed the bloodhounds on the previous day, and then he asked Paul, Rose, and the attorney to follow him.

The plantation was spread over a number of terraces and looked like a piece of paradise. The cries of monkeys reached them from the distance, and colorful birds flew by over their heads. Rose was reminded a little of her visit to her grandmother all those years ago, but she soon realized that van den Broock had no real intention of creating a garden here. As was the way with the Dutch plantation owners, all the land was put to practical use and managed to bring in the maximum profits.

The sugarcane grew particularly well here. On one side of the plantation the green shoots pushed their way toward the sky, while at the other end the long, sturdy canes with their sharp-bladed leaves were being cut down. The men who worked here almost all wore light-colored, wide-legged pants and simple cotton shirts, a few of them working bare-chested. Their heads were bound by bandanas to soak up the sweat. They skillfully stacked and bundled up the harvested sugarcanes and carried them down to the sheds for further processing.

Van den Broock did not follow the workers but led his visitors farther upward. His plantation did not extend the full way up the mountainside, but the highest terraces offered an amazing view of the landscape, which looked like a green sea with waves breaking over the edge of the plantation.

"There have been times, especially in the early days, when I wondered if I could succeed. My father established the plantation, but he didn't live long enough to see it come to fruition."

"Then its success must have been thanks to you," Paul replied.

"Well, I worked hard at least," van den Broock replied with apparent modesty, although Rose could hear the pride in his voice. "But now I've reached a point where I can't take it any further alone. I need a strong partner, one who will help me expand."

"I hope I can live up to your expectations."

"You should think hard about it. Owning a plantation can be very demanding. It's likely that you'll have to spend many months of the year here on Sumatra. You should ask yourself whether your future wife and family will accept that."

Paul looked at Rose, who lowered her eyes uneasily. But why? It was not up to her whether he could enter into this business. She was not to be his wife, but this Maggie! This Maggie, who had no feelings for Sumatra and who clearly longed for nothing more than to leave. She found this thought strangely worrying. Not because of the island but because of Paul. And because of her own feelings. She had never been in love, and so she had no idea how it felt. But the burning in her breast could fit the description.

They eventually turned away from the cultivated area and followed a small party carrying sugarcanes down to the sheds, from which a loud rattling could be heard.

It was mainly women who worked in the bamboo buildings, pushing the sugarcane into a huge press, whose grinding gear was driven by a steam engine via a broad belt. The clattering and chugging drowned out all other sounds, and even van den Broock's remarks could hardly be heard.

Rose watched in fascination as the machine drew the sugarcane into its depths and ground it up. If an arm was pulled in between the iron teeth, there would be no hope of rescue. But the women worked extremely cautiously, with routine and precision in movements that they had obviously repeated endless times.

The thick, golden-brown juice flowed along a bamboo channel into a vessel that, once full, one of the women would take over to an open fire. There it would be boiled and the viscous syrup poured into molds.

"This is our gold," van den Broock claimed, holding a cooled lump up for them to see. "No one can say how long the gold mines will continue to yield. But the riches here will never dry up, as long as we have this fertile soil beneath our feet."

As van den Broock went on at length about the amazing opportunities offered by the sugar trade, Rose noticed that the women who worked here kept looking over at their master a little fearfully before quickly averting their eyes. Some of them looked quite thin beneath their clothes. Did the plantation owner not care for them properly?

During her childhood Rose had occasionally heard tales of how some plantation owners arbitrarily seduced, beat, and exploited their workers. In the city they had hardly been aware of it. Obviously the native workers in the harbor had labored hard, but no one ever saw the Dutch openly treating their workers badly. Her father took care to ensure that the people who worked for him had enough to eat and could provide for their families.

But now Rose had a queasy feeling in her stomach. After all, she, too, was half native. Even if that was not obvious from her appearance, she suddenly felt ashamed to be standing there with van den Broock, watching these women with their large, fearful eyes. She rarely had misgivings about the Dutch being the masters of this country, as they had been here since long before she was born. But at that moment, she thought it unjust that the master of the plantation had these women laboring for him—and clearly didn't pay them well, judging by their skinny bodies and hollow cheeks.

Then one of the women looked right at her. Her eyes were as dark as the fertile soil of the plantation, and Rose noticed that she had a scar on her cheek. It looked like the result of a blow with a switch. Had van den Broock done that? The woman's eyes burned into her soul.

"Miss Warden? Are you coming?"

A voice pulled her from her thoughts. Without her realizing, the men were already at the door. She looked once more at the woman, who had returned to the heaps of sugarcane, before turning away with a numb feeling in the pit of her stomach.

After being in the sheds, which were filled with a heavy, sweet scent, the air outside seemed fresh and sharp. A low rumble sounded from the mountains. The sky had been clouded over the whole time. Was rain now on its way? Rose felt a strange desire to stand outside beneath a shower, in the hope that the rain would clear her mind and wash away her confusion. But even if the storm came, she couldn't simply run out and welcome the water with open arms. Rose Gallway might be able to do so in an unobserved moment, but Maggie Warden would certainly never consider behaving in such a way.

"We should be making our way back. The rain comes in very quickly around here, and we wouldn't want the lady to get soaked from head to toe." With these words van den Broock trudged ahead, leading them back along a narrow, almost concealed path.

No sooner had they returned to the house than Rose was drawn back into her thoughts and the memory of that morning's conversation. Paul had decided to take up the investment in the plantation, and with van den Broock's agreement, the two of them sat down together with the attorney to discuss all the details of the transaction.

As neither the "fiancée" nor any other woman was allowed to be present at the meeting, Rose sat by her bedroom window, from which she could look out over the garden. Surprisingly, there were European fruit trees here, which must have been planted by van den Broock or his forebears. They were flourishing but looked a little out of place, as if they belonged in a garden in England or France.

Paul's question had felt just as inappropriate. To become his wife might open a lot of doors, but it would also close a lot. Above all, though, was the fact that she yearned for him. She couldn't imagine anything better than living with him. Before him, she had not had any such feelings toward a man. And she couldn't imagine another man ever having such an effect on her again.

In between her thoughts of Paul she was again plagued by her guilty conscience about the workers. Would anything change if Paul became a shareholder? Perhaps she should advise him against taking it on. But could she do that? She was not his fiancée; she was not someone who could tell him to do anything. Perhaps that would change if she accepted his proposal. If she became his wife, she would be able to not only satisfy her personal desires, but at some stage perhaps also do something for the women here. She surprised herself with it all—until then her head had been filled only with music, and she had never concerned herself with wider issues. But the women's looks had opened a door in her heart, and suddenly Paul's proposal did not seem such a bad, inappropriate idea.

**

That night, she found that she couldn't stay in bed for long. All that had happened plagued her to such an extent that she rose and began to pace restlessly up and down. What was the right thing to do? It still seemed completely absurd that Paul had proposed marriage to her, but was that not what she had secretly dreamed of? Had he somehow sensed her wishes?

Rose rested her forehead against the window and smiled softly, imagining Paul's face as he asked her to play his fiancée. Was it not the case that lovers behaved completely irrationally? Mrs. Faraday had always warned her against losing her heart, because with it she would also lose her head. She didn't have the feeling that she had lost her head, but if her former teacher was right, Paul was showing strong signs of being in love. What more could she wish for? Paul returned her feelings. And if she looked at it rationally, she had also acted stupidly in secretly coming away with him. As sheet lightning flashed outside her window and raindrops pattered on the panes, she came to a decision: she had to speak to Paul!

She quickly threw on her dressing gown and tiptoed to his room. Paul was lying in bed, breathing peacefully, but jumped up when he sensed her presence.

"Rose!" he cried out in surprise. "What are you doing in my room?"

"I . . . I couldn't sleep," she confessed, fiddling in embarrassment with the edge of her dressing gown. "I wanted to ask you something."

"What was it?"

"Do you . . . do you really mean it?"

Paul looked at her sleepily. He still seemed as if he couldn't believe his eyes or thought he was still dreaming.

"What do you mean?" he asked drowsily. But he seemed to quickly realize, after seeing the hint of disappointment on her face. "Of course I mean it! Do you want me?"

Rose saw the eyes of the worker woman before her eyes. And she felt her heart thumping, felt the longing burn through her body. Your dream could come true, a voice in the back of her mind whispered. Don't let this chance slip away . . .

"Yes," Rose answered firmly, ignoring her inner voice that warned her against taking his proposal seriously—there were so many potential obstacles in the way of them marrying. "But it would mean so much trouble for you. You would have to break off your engagement, and your mother . . ."

A shadow flitted across Paul's face but only briefly before a smile drove it away.

"Don't worry about that. My mother will like you—she really will."

"But I'm not from a noble family. I've seen how some aristocrats see musicians as good-for-nothings."

"But not a violinist who's played for royalty! If the governor of Sumatra invites you to play here, that makes you anything other than a good-for-nothing. I'll make that clear to my mother if she brings it up. But she's a kind-hearted woman, and even if she does get worked up, she'll calm down eventually. I promise you, when I introduce you to her, she'll be charm itself."

Rose nodded. At that moment she was prepared to believe anything he said.

"And what about Maggie?" she objected. "I imagine she'll be the one hit hardest by disappointment."

"Maggie deserves a different husband, believe me. I'm far too adventurous. I found that out here in Sumatra. While I'm interested in everything I can find, she's even wary of the local people. It would be better if she married someone else, a man who would stay with her in London, who would take her out and introduce her to his friends while ensuring that she has plenty of female company to keep her occupied with inconsequential conversation about fashion and servants. And it would be far better for me to have a wife who loves adventure, who's not afraid of the jungle, and who's adaptable enough to slip effortlessly into the role of my fiancée even when she isn't."

He reached for her hand and held it tight. Rose's heart was still beating wildly. Now she had no doubt about his sincerity.

"But the crucial question is, do you love me?" he asked, his eyes fixed on hers. "I love you, and I'm prepared to deal with any adversities if I know you'll be waiting for me here."

Rose searched her heart. Did she love him?

"Oh yes, I love you!" she replied. "I've probably loved you since the moment we met in van Swieten's garden."

Paul pulled her to him and kissed her. "Then let me worry about the rest. I'll separate from Maggie, and when I return, we'll get married."

His lips met hers again, awakening a wild, unfamiliar longing in her. Although she knew it was wrong, that it went against everything Mrs. Faraday had drummed into her, and that she should know better, should leave the room, she allowed his lips to slip from her mouth, wander down her throat, and pause on her shoulder.

"Oh, Rose," he breathed, a shudder running through his body.

For a moment he was still, gazing at her, exploring the feel of her skin with his hands. His movements set her body alight, aroused something deep inside. She felt an all-consuming longing that came over her occasionally at night without her knowing how to get relief. But now she knew. Paul's warmth, the scent of his skin, were the answer.

Her heartbeat thundered in her ears, and when he finally drew her down onto the bed, she didn't resist. Breathing heavily, Paul drew her nightdress up above her thighs and pulled down his pajama bottoms. Rose couldn't see him, but when he gently penetrated her, she felt it. It took her breath away. The pain only lasted a few moments before giving way to renewed desire.

"I love you, Rose," he gasped as he sank down on her and began to move carefully. Rose wrapped her arms around him and tried to shut out the reproachful voice of Mrs. Faraday calling her a whore.

She was doing what she wanted, and it felt right. He was the man she loved. She wanted to belong to him forever. And at that moment she didn't care about anything she had heard about supposed morals. She wanted him, his scent, his kisses, and the weight of his body on hers. Her hands traced the muscles beneath his firm skin, the hair at the nape of his neck.

And when Paul came, something exploded inside her and drove out all doubts and all thoughts of reproach.

16

London, 2011

As Lilly and Ellen left the airport, they were met by cold, wet weather. When they left Cremona it had been at its most beautiful, the sun shining down on the station and accompanying them all the way to the airport in Milan.

"We should have stayed in Italy," Ellen grumbled, using her free hand to draw her woolen coat more tightly around her body. Her attempt was in vain: the stiff fabric resisted, and the wind dragged one end of her scarf out from the collar. Ellen narrowed her eyes and turned her head aside. It did no good. She finally stopped, parked her suitcase, and straightened herself out. "It's a pity that duty calls, or I'd ask Dean whether we could move to Italy for the winter months in the future."

"And what would become of your violins then?" Lilly asked with a laugh. She also felt the damp cold, but she was warm inside, looking forward to seeing Gabriel again. What would he have to say about the pictures and the newspaper articles?

Enrico had translated two of them already and had promised to e-mail the rest later. As soon as she had all the texts, she would try to make an appointment with Gabriel. Or should she perhaps contact him sooner, to invite him to the promised dinner?

As they waited in a line for a taxi, Lilly imagined their meeting, and her thoughts soon drifted in another direction. She saw herself walking among the magnolia flowers of a park in spring with Gabriel, talking about Rose and Helen.

"Hey, you're miles away!" Ellen nudged her friend. Lilly had been so immersed in her daydream that she had not noticed they were at the head of the taxi line. The driver loaded up their luggage as they took their seats in the back.

"A penny for your thoughts," Ellen said, but before Lilly could reply, the driver had gotten in.

"Where to, ladies?" he asked.

Ellen gave him the address, and then he turned up the heat and the radio. Indian dance music blared from the speakers so loudly that he could hardly hear the operator on the two-way radio.

As he entered the flow of London traffic, Lilly stared in fascination at the figure of Ganesha hanging from the mirror, which danced every time the car changed direction. It looked so funny that it must raise a smile from even the most grumpy passengers in this taxi. The driver soon began to talk to them, his accent so thick that Lilly struggled to understand. Ellen seemed used to it, though, and she chatted cheerfully with him as if she had just met an old friend.

After an hour and a few small traffic jams, they were back at Ellen's house. When they opened the doors to get out, the Indian beats thumped through the neighborhood, scaring a few crows, who cawed loudly in competition with the music. Ellen paid the driver, and he zoomed away.

"You still haven't answered my question," she remarked as she tapped in the entrance code and the gates snapped open.

"Which one?" Lilly asked, maneuvering her suitcase through the gate.

"What you were thinking about before Shah Rukh Khan introduced us to his favorite music."

"Who's Shah Rukh Khan?"

"Indian actor, very famous. Don't change the subject. You were thinking about *him*, weren't you? Gabriel Thornton."

Lilly felt color rush to her cheeks.

"I knew it!" Ellen winked. "Was it dirty?"

"No, what makes you think that? I like him, that's all. And if you like someone, you're entitled to think about them, aren't you?"

"Of course." Ellen smiled enigmatically.

"What about this Enrico?" Lilly tried to steer the conversation away from Gabriel, since she was reluctant to speculate about things that might never happen. "I got the impression you two know each other well. Is there anything you haven't been telling me?"

Ellen laughed and shook her head. "No. At least not what you're thinking. I could never be unfaithful to Dean. Though I have to admit that when Enrico and I met in connection with a job, he was quite interested in me. I never took any notice, though, and somewhere along the line we became friends. That's all. Anyway, I got the impression he was more interested in you. Why weren't you a bit more forthcoming with him?"

"Forthcoming?" Lilly frowned. "What do you mean? You think I should have performed a striptease or what?"

"No, but you must have noticed he was flirting with you. Why didn't you play along with it? It could have been fun."

"Because . . ." Lilly hesitated. She knew the reason full well but had no desire to return to the subject.

"Gabriel Thornton, am I right? He's why."

"I'll answer that one when I know the answer myself," Lilly replied, although she sensed her friend was right. Her feelings for Gabriel went beyond mere attraction, but she had no intention of revealing that to Ellen. Who knows whether he actually wants me, she thought. And she felt another twinge of guilty conscience about Peter. Let's wait and see, she told herself. I'd just like to see him again first.

Apart from the low roar of the wind in the treetops, all was quiet. Ellen breathed deeply, then smiled to herself.

"To be totally honest, I wouldn't like to spend the whole winter in Italy. There's no nicer place than home, don't you think?"

"You're right," Lilly replied, although she wasn't sure she was really looking forward to returning to Berlin. It would take her away from Gabriel and the chance to get to know him better.

"How about cooking together again this evening?" she asked, taking her friend's arm as they dragged their suitcases up the path.

"I'd be happy to. Dean will be delighted to hear that someone else is trying to read a code in the music."

They had begun to unpack their things when the telephone rang. Assuming it was a business call for Ellen, Lilly didn't take any notice and continued what she was doing until she heard footsteps come to a stop outside her door. Ellen knocked and entered. She gave Lilly a meaningful smile as she whispered, "For you!"

Lilly gasped as she took the telephone.

"So, you're back?" Gabriel Thornton asked.

"As you can hear."

Lilly looked at Ellen, who headed out of the room. She glanced around briefly, grinned at Lilly, and pulled the door closed behind her.

"I hope you were able to use the information I gave you," Gabriel was saying.

"Yes, thanks! It was a great help! We found a few articles I believe you don't have."

"I told you, didn't I, that we lost a lot of material during the Second World War? I'm sure that the things you've found will be a valuable addition."

Lilly hesitated a moment before saying, "I had a strange dream in Cremona."

"About me, perhaps?" Gabriel laughed.

"No, about Helen. When she was a child . . . Do you believe there could be a code contained in the sheet music?"

"A code?"

"Well, it was only a dream, but maybe my subconscious was trying to tell me something. There must be a reason why this particular piece of music was tucked into the case lining. In my dream, little Helen said the solution to the mystery was to be found in 'The Moonlit Garden.'"

Silence followed. Was Gabriel still there? Could he be laughing at her? Her stomach tightened. Maybe she would have been better off saying nothing about it.

"Gabriel?" she asked hesitantly.

"Yes, I'm still here. I'm just thinking."

"It's pretty improbable, isn't it?"

"I wouldn't say that. Secret messages have been concealed in pieces of music before. There may be something like that in 'The Moonlit Garden.' If there is, then one of the two women, Rose or Helen, was a real genius. That is, if she composed it herself."

"Ellen's acquaintance has a friend who knows about codes. He may be able to bring something to light. If you . . ."

"I'm afraid I don't know anything about codes, nor do I have any friends in the secret service, but I'll nevertheless take a closer look at that music. Perhaps the secret only reveals itself if you look at it for long enough."

Lilly smiled at her reflection in the window. Gabriel was a wonderful man.

"Thank you," she said softly.

"There's no need to thank me. We're both in this together, after all."

"We are, but you could still have thought I was going mad. Who believes in dreams these days?"

"You! And if I'm honest, I do, too. What would life be without dreams and mysteries?"

"So, what news do you have?" Lilly leaned her cheek against the windowpane to cool it.

"Well, I think that's something we should talk about face-to-face."

"OK. When can you spare the time?"

"How about tomorrow noon? We could sit down in the cafeteria again and be amazed at the cook's culinary creations."

"If that's convenient, then it's fine by me," Lilly said happily.

"And you can tell me what else you did in Cremona. I'm dying to hear your view of the city."

"I'll do my best to describe it."

"Good. I'm looking forward to seeing you tomorrow."

After saying good-bye, Lilly hung up and sat for a moment on the edge of the bed. It felt so good to hear Gabriel's voice! And she was looking forward so much to seeing him again. Not only because of the apparent mystery that he had discovered but also because she missed him.

"You should invite him here," Ellen said when Lilly returned the phone to her. It was almost as if she could read the content of the conversation Lilly had just had on her face.

"What?" she asked.

"For dinner. A discussion between experts."

"But . . . we've just arranged to meet for lunch. In the cafeteria."

"But I'd like to be there if you're exchanging information. Change the arrangements."

"I can't."

"Why not? Surely you know how to use a telephone."

"Of course I do, but I can't just invite him here."

Ellen tipped her head to one side and gave her a penetrating look.

"Hm, that's strange. I don't think you're particularly unsociable. It seems to me that you like Gabriel more than you're letting on. So much more that I could almost believe you don't want to share him with me."

"What gives you that idea?"

"Because whenever you're taken with a man, you get rosy cheeks like one of those cutesy Hummel figurines."

Lilly bit her lip guiltily. "All right, I admit, I think he's nice. But it doesn't mean anything."

"It doesn't mean anything?" Ellen folded her arms. "Lilly Kaiser thinks a man is nice. How often does that happen? When was the last time you thought someone was *nice* and you blushed up to your ears?"

"You're crazy," Lilly countered, but her friend was right. Before Gabriel she had not been interested in any man. She rarely even noticed them when they looked at her on the street. And the male customers in her shop were either married, insufferable, or far too old for her.

"Yes, I may be, but nevertheless, call him up and invite him here."

"You really don't mind?"

"Who was it that suggested the idea?"

"OK, if you insist."

Lilly was reluctant to let Ellen see the way she reacted to Gabriel's voice, so she took the phone with her out of the room. With a thumping heart and trembling fingers she dialed the number and carefully ran through the right words to change the arrangement they had made earlier.

It was not Gabriel who answered but his secretary. Lilly was shocked into hanging up, but then asked herself why. After all, she hadn't intended to have a romantic conversation with him. I'll try again later, she told herself, and returned to her unpacking.

Half an hour later, Lilly was sorting through her documents when the telephone rang. Without hesitating, Lilly answered the phone and was about to hurry from the room to take it to Ellen, since the call was bound to be for her. But then she froze.

"I thought it must have been you," Gabriel began without preliminaries. Lilly's ears began to glow again.

"What was?" she asked, although she knew she was very bad at concealing guilt. His secretary had probably told him about the strange call, and he must have known from the number who was too cowardly to speak to the dragon.

"That call. Did you just want to hear my voice again, or was there another reason?"

"You obviously have a rather high opinion of yourself, Gabriel," she retorted, unable to suppress a grin. "But yes, there's a reason."

"One that you didn't want to share with my secretary?"

"Yes." Lilly took a deep breath and continued, "I'd like to cancel our lunch and invite you to dinner here instead. To my friend Ellen's house."

"Ellen Morris's? Wow, that's explosive! You could easily have passed the invitation on through my secretary."

"Well, I've told you now."

"And your friend agrees?"

"She's involved in the research," Lilly replied. "And she's got nothing against getting to know you—on the contrary."

"Good. Just tell me when to come."

"When suits you?"

"That's up to you—you're the hostess. Anyway, I don't know how much longer you're going to be in England, so firstly, we shouldn't waste any time, and secondly, I'm entirely in your hands. If necessary, I can get Eva to change a few appointments."

"How about tomorrow?" she asked.

His reply came like a shot: "Perfect!"

"Eight o'clock?"

"Perfect!"

"Tuxedo and bow tie?"

"What?"

"Just testing whether you were listening and not just saying any old thing." Lilly laughed.

"I'm listening. And I'll wear anything you'd like to see me in, but I can't consider this the meal you promised to invite me to."

Lilly turned red as she remembered the promised dinner. A meal at home with her and Ellen certainly didn't count. "Um . . . no, of course not. This is just a little . . . opportunity to exchange information."

"Fine, see you tomorrow." She could hear that Gabriel was smiling.

"See you tomorrow," she replied with a grin, and hung up.

"So?" Ellen asked as she appeared in the living room. Her friend could obviously tell with whom she had just been speaking.

"He's coming tomorrow at eight. With his latest findings."

Ellen clapped her hands in delight. "That's excellent! In the meantime I've had an idea about what to cook."

"Do you have the time?" Lilly asked skeptically. "You do have to go back to the institute. And what about Dean?"

"Don't worry, I've thought of everything. There'll be plenty of work waiting for me after I've allowed myself this little break, but it's not a problem. And Dean won't mind—it's been ages since we've had anyone over for dinner, and it'll be a nice distraction from all the stress on the building site."

"Then let's order in. Pizza? Gabriel eats in the cafeteria. He'll have nothing against it."

Ellen shook her head vehemently. "Out of the question! If someone comes for a meal at my house, they don't get served pizza. I give them a proper meal! I'd be a laughingstock if I couldn't manage that."

Before Lilly could say a word more, the door opened. Jessie and Norma were back from school. With cries of delight they fell on Ellen and kissed her; then they hugged Lilly and began firing off a barrage of questions about Cremona.

17

In low spirits, Rose looked out the window, regretting a little that she was not staying in the hotel by the sea. If that were the case, she could at least have seen the ship on which Paul was sailing away.

His promise burned inside her, as did the memory of the passionate embraces that night on the plantation.

"I'll be back," he had said and kissed her ardently. "Just let me sort out my affairs at home."

Would he keep to his word? Or had he forgotten her as soon as he was out on the ocean? No, Paul was not like that. She might not know much about him, but that was one thing she was sure of.

Rose turned back to her suitcase, which stood open in the middle of the room. It was actually Mai's job to sort it out, but she had forgotten one of the dresses at the dressmaker's and had gone to fetch it. Rose had just begun to pack a few small items of lingerie when Mai burst through the door, completely distraught.

"What's the matter?" Rose asked in amazement.

"Mr. Carmichael wants you to come immediately, miss," her dresser said, gasping.

"Go where?"

She hoped he hadn't arranged another appearance for her. All she wanted was to get away from here, away from the unbearable wait for Paul's return. She had to distract herself, see the world. That was the only way she could bear the time until she was back in his arms.

"To the harbor. There's been an accident."

Mai pressed her hands to her mouth as if she had already said too much. Rose stared at her for a moment, then shot over to her like a bird of prey and gripped her by the shoulders.

"What's happened?" Rose cried, terrified that the accident could have involved Paul. Paul, who had perhaps changed his mind and returned. Mai stared at her in dismay. She didn't answer, and Rose shook her without thinking. "Tell me, what's happened?"

"Your father, miss," Mai finally managed to say.

Rose released her and stepped back, then stumbled to the door.

***

With her hair streaming behind her, not caring that her clothes were awry and her makeup smudged, Rose hurried through the streets of Padang. Mai had followed her for a time, but Rose had lost her servant somewhere on the way. It was better that way, as Rose didn't need her help right then.

Her heartbeat drowning out all the noise around her, she tried to convince herself that it couldn't be so bad, that as soon as she turned the corner, she would see her father coming toward her, laughing at her for worrying.

Once at the harbor, she was immediately faced with a crowd that had gathered around an overturned crane. Harbor workers were trying to reach the scene of the accident with ropes and other equipment.

"Let me through!" Rose yelled in agitation, in her own language and in Dutch. The people she knew stepped back immediately. Rose tried to ignore their horrified looks. Where was her father? The fact that she had been summoned meant he must be injured, but surely he had only received a few scratches. Nothing bad ever happened to a man like Roger Gallway . . .

She reached the crane and saw that a number of men were busy trying to lift the heavy structure. It had fallen onto the street, crushing some chests and a small timber house beneath its weight. She heard shouts and whimpering. A few women in the crowd were crying. An unpleasant smell rose slowly from the ground.

Rose stared at the crane as if it were a monster. She forbade herself from finishing the thought that had sprung into her mind like a tiger. Nothing serious has happened to him, she tried to tell herself. He'll be back on his feet in no time.

She was so absorbed in looking at the crane that she did not notice the man who was striding over to her until he was right beside her. Dr. Bruns, who had often helped her family, took her by the arm. Rose felt sick as she saw the blood on his arms and sleeves.

"Please don't go any closer, Rose," he said, using her first name since he had known her since childhood and had never been able to accustom himself to calling her Mejuffrouw Gallway. "Your father is buried beneath the crane along with a couple of workers."

"But you must be able to save him!" she burst out. There was a roaring in her ears, and she had difficulty understanding what the doctor was saying. "You can, can't you, Doctor?"

Bruns's face, already pale, turned even whiter as he lowered his head uneasily.

"Unfortunately there's nothing more we can do for him."

Rose stepped back in horror. Her mouth opened but no cry came, even though everything inside her was crying out, It's not true! It can't be true!

"I want to see him!" she managed to say eventually. "Perhaps there's been a mistake; perhaps it's not him."

"Rose," the doctor said slowly, in the same voice he had used to persuade her to take medicine against a fever that had laid her low as a child. "I'm sorry, but there's no doubt that it's your father. And I don't think it's a good idea for you to see him right now."

The quiet emphasis of his words wore down Rose's defenses. Her mind still refused to believe it—but Bruns was not the kind of man who would lie to her in a situation like this.

"You'd best go to your mother's house. I wanted to send someone, but it would be better if you were there to look after her yourself."

Rose nodded numbly and turned.

"I'll come over to see you this evening. We should be finished here by then," he called after her, but she hardly heard.

In a daze, and feeling slightly dizzy as if she were trying to walk the deck of a rolling ship, she made her way through the crowd. This time, she had no need to ask to be let through; the shocked expression on her face was enough to make people draw back. Every now and then someone touched her arm, probably people she knew, but Rose paid no attention to faces. She did not even notice when she had left the throng behind her.

"Miss Gallway!" called a woman's voice. For the first time, Rose stopped and looked up. Mai had caught up with her but did not dare to approach to within more than a couple of yards.

"Go back to the hotel, Mai," Rose heard herself say. "I don't need you at the moment."

"But, Miss Gallway, I . . ."

"Can you do what I say for once without arguing?" Rose hissed and closed her eyes in agitation. She felt tears rolling down her cheeks. The last thing she needed was a talkative girl who had not the slightest idea how she was feeling. Mai withdrew in shock.

"Yes, miss. I'm going, miss," she said and whirled around.

Rose did not watch her go but continued on her way to her parents' house. Pain raged in her, together with fear of her mother's reaction. For a moment she tried to persuade herself that the doctor was mistaken. That her father was waiting for her at home, ready to take her in his arms and comfort her.

As she entered the front door, her mother rushed toward her. Her eyes widened in shock when she saw her daughter's expression.

"What's happened?" she asked as she caught hold of Rose's arms. Her hands were cold and clammy, and her lips were trembling. Had she any idea what had happened? Rose was at first unable to speak a word. You've got to tell her, she said to herself. Now, say something! But her mouth would not obey.

Only after a long silence did she manage a single word. "Father."

She said nothing more. That was all Adit needed. With a dreadful wail she threw herself into her daughter's arms and both of them burst into tears.

***

The following days swept past Rose like a school of fish past a sea anemone. She got up in the mornings and saw to her mother, who was unable to leave her bed, unable even to bear the light of day. People came by occasionally—the pastor, the undertaker, neighbors. Rose talked to them all, though afterward she could not recall a word she had said.

Her grief for her father made her long all the more for Paul. When would she see him again? When would she be able to feel his arms around her? When could she allow herself to be comforted by him? When would he be there to take away all the dreadful pain that was raging inside her?

Each day finally came to an end without her having done a thing, not once touching the violin that Mai had brought for her the day after the accident.

Rose had never wondered whether she could bring herself to play a requiem for someone beloved at a funeral. But as she knew how much her father had liked to listen to her play, the task had fallen to her now. She asked Carmichael to make the necessary arrangements and bring the music she needed to practice.

She had only played Mozart's *Requiem* once in her life, yet she remembered every single note. She had to summon all her strength to set the bow to the strings by her father's graveside. Her hands were shaking, and the thought that she would never see her father again made her knees weak until she almost collapsed.

As the first melancholy notes rang out over the cemetery, the pain became a little more bearable. Rose allowed herself to be carried away by the melody and ignored the tears that flowed down her cheeks. Her father's soul should ascend to Heaven accompanied by beautiful music, she thought. When she finished playing, she stepped back, head bowed. She did not look at the other mourners, but she could sense they were moved. Even the pastor was unable to find the words at first. The melody echoed in the silence for a few moments before the funeral continued.

On their way back from the cemetery, Rose and her mother were very quiet. Adit felt that it was unseemly to arrange a funeral reception, so she had simply thanked those present and withdrawn.

Rose did not know whether people understood her mother's decision, and at that moment she did not care. She kept asking herself whether her presumptuousness in seeking her own happiness was at the root of it all. But what could she have done to prevent her father from being struck down by a falling crane? She had not been down at the harbor; she had no idea . . .

The two women sat down at the kitchen table, and although they looked at one another, they were each lost in their own thoughts. At that moment Rose wished Paul were still here, that she could have the chance to talk to him, to lean against his breast. But her beloved was far away, and she was sitting here. Darkness crept over the house, and the bustle of the street outside faded to stillness.

More days of lethargy followed. Rose spent most of the time sitting by the window and trying to catch a melody in her head that she could never quite hear.

***

Carmichael managed to be patient with her for two weeks, but at the start of the third week he appeared at the Gallways' house. When she saw him at the door, Rose felt like hiding away or running out the back door, but she knew that would be childish. And she also knew there was no avoiding what Carmichael was going to ask. The tour should continue, to India and then on to Australia. Rose had all the dates in her head and knew that he had already cancelled three appearances. Cancelling more would not do. But could she simply step out onto the stage as if nothing had happened? Could she play?

As Carmichael knocked for the second time, she stared at her hands. They appeared not to have changed since playing the *Requiem* at the cemetery, but Rose nevertheless doubted that she could play as well as before the accident. The music came not only from her hands but from her soul, and this was now doubly wounded. She couldn't simply act as if nothing had happened.

"Aren't you going to answer the door, child?" her mother asked suddenly. The persistent knocking had roused her from her bed, and she was standing, pale and wretched looking, in the kitchen. "I know you can't stay here forever. Your life is calling you, Rose."

"But what about you?" Rose asked helplessly, hoping that Carmichael would go away. But he remained where he was, listening. He must have heard their voices from the start.

"I'll be fine, Rose. It will be hard for me, and I don't know how I'm going to live without your father, but imagine how it would have been if you hadn't happened to be here but were at the other end of the world. The news probably wouldn't have reached you until weeks later, and you wouldn't have been here for weeks more."

"But—"

"Now go and open the door—otherwise he'll beat a hole in it. At least hear what he's got to say. Then you can make your decision."

Rose nodded, and as her mother withdrew back into her room, she smoothed her dress and went to the door.

"Rose, thank God!" cried Carmichael, who had obviously been worrying. "I thought . . ."

"Don't worry, no one here is seriously ill or threatening suicide," she replied harshly, stepping aside to let him pass. "Come in. I assume you want to speak to me."

Carmichael studied her quickly before walking past her.

"How are you and your mother?" he asked as he stood, somewhat at a loss, in the kitchen.

Rose suppressed a cynical answer, saying merely "As you'd expect."

"Very well," he replied, looking in embarrassment at his shoes.

"Sit down," Rose said, making her way slowly to the kitchen table.

Had her body always felt this heavy? Over the last few days she had felt distanced from everything, but Carmichael's visit seemed to bring her back to reality.

"You must have come to tell me that I should prepare to continue the tour."

Carmichael looked at her, first with surprise and then with apparent relief, as if she had saved him from broaching the subject himself.

"You know we're behind on our schedule. Of course it's understandable in your situation, and no one understands that better than I do—I, too, lost my father in an accident—but the promoters won't wait forever. And if we disappoint a whole country, it will have a bad effect on your reputation."

Rose knew that, but her doubts were stronger than her fear of losing her reputation. She thought, not for the first time, that she was responsible for supporting her mother—especially financially, as it was by no means definite that the owner of the crane would be able to pay her a pension or damages.

"When would the next feasible date be?" she asked, again drawing a surprised look from Carmichael.

"Um . . . as far as I know . . . Delhi . . . yes, that's it, Delhi . . . on the seventeenth."

Of course Rose already had the date in her head. It was not the first time she would be playing in India. She had been in Delhi shortly after her first major performance, at the invitation of an earl who had seen her in London. She had been fascinated by the colorful city with its wonderful palaces. Perhaps playing there would distract her a little.

"All right, we'll go to Delhi," she decided suddenly, even though she didn't know whether she could resume her previous repertoire. "Have everything packed and tell me when we depart. I'll stay with my mother until then. She needs me."

Carmichael nodded and got to his feet. "Give her my condolences, will you?"

Rose nodded and went with him to the door.

Once he had gone, Rose went to her parents' bedroom. Contrary to her expectation, her mother had not lain down again but was sitting on a wicker chair by the window, from which she could see the sea between two houses.

"You're going on tour again, aren't you?" she asked without looking around.

"Yes, Mother. I'm not doing it because the music is more important to me than you, but to ensure I'm able to support you."

At first her mother, who had doubtless overheard the conversation, said nothing.

"Even if you did put the music before me, I wouldn't hold it against you," she said eventually. She stood heavily, as if she had lived through eighty-five years rather than forty-five.

"But, Mother, I . . ."

"It's fine, my love. Your father was so proud of you, and it would be a great shame for you to stay here and watch your fame fade away. Go on tour with a clear conscience. Play. Play well for your father, who will probably be watching you from Heaven." She came up close to Rose and took her face between her hands. "You're something very special, Rose. Promise me that you'll always take good care of yourself, because your father will live on in you and your children."

"Nothing's going to happen to me, don't worry," Rose replied bravely. "I've come through life well so far."

"You have indeed, but now that you're all that's left to me, take particular care of yourself, won't you?"

This request seemed a little strange to Rose, but she nodded, took her mother's hands, and pressed them to her own brow.

"Do you think the old woman . . . ," she began hesitantly after straightening up. "Do you think she's cursed us, after you refused . . ."

Adit shook her head. "No, my child, that woman has no power to curse us. If that were the case, if it were my fault that your father is dead, I would have ended my life immediately. Perhaps it was fate trying to warn me by sending the old woman, but a different decision couldn't have saved your father. Some things in life are predetermined. Now, clearly, I should take up the inheritance of my people. One day you'll be the one faced with this decision. As long as I live, I'll prevent them from coming to you. But when I'm dead, you'll be the next headwoman. When that time comes, you'll have to decide what's important to you."

Rose looked at her pensively. She had already made one decision. As soon as Paul returned, she would go with him. She had no intention of telling her mother that, though, not when she had just lost her husband.

"I will," she said simply.

She took her mother's hands again, and as she pressed them to her cheek, she sent out a silent wish that Paul would come back soon.

18

London, 2011

Lilly shifted around nervously on the sofa. She felt as if a heap of dynamite were about to explode beneath her.

She was beginning to regret agreeing to Ellen's suggestion. At first it had seemed an excellent idea, but now she was afraid that Ellen would be able to see the confusion Gabriel caused within her. The fact that she was behaving like a schoolgirl was the perfect evidence.

Ellen grinned at her. "You seem to be really looking forward to Gabriel's visit."

"Me?" Lilly froze, as if caught red-handed.

"You're fidgeting around on that sofa as if you had ants in your pants. I haven't seen you so excited since Markus Hansen took you to the prom."

"Don't be silly!"

If she were honest, she felt as on edge as on the day of her first date with Peter, but since the date had been preceded by absolute chaos, Ellen had not noticed the extent of her excitement. And anyway, that was different.

"I'm just looking forward to hearing what he's found," Lilly said.

"Yes, he's probably discovered the perfume Rose Gallway always used."

"Don't be mean!" Lilly dug her elbow into Ellen's ribs.

"I'm not. I'm just saying it's likely we'll have more to report to him than he has to tell us."

"Let's just wait and see."

The sound of a car engine brought their discussion to an end.

"There he is!" Lilly jumped up from the sofa and was about to hurry to the door, but Ellen held her back.

"Wait a minute. Let him get out of the car first!"

Lilly stopped, smoothed her dress down, and hopped from one foot to the other.

"Actually, you should be the one who opens the door, shouldn't you? You're the hostess, after all."

"I am, but he's coming on your account. Why don't we both go? We're a team, aren't we?"

The bell rang, and it took all Lilly's self-control not to run to the door. At a leisurely pace, as if they were only waiting for some distant acquaintance, they went into the hall. Lilly stood back to let Ellen answer the door.

"Good evening, Mr. Thornton."

"Please, call me Gabriel."

"I hope you found your way here all right."

Thornton smiled broadly at them both. "It wasn't totally straightforward, to tell you the truth, but I've made it." He handed them a small bunch of flowers. "Just a token of thanks for allowing me to take up your time this evening."

"Come in, Gabriel."

Gabriel gave Lilly a brief wink, and she responded with a wide smile as he was shown into the living room.

Ellen had planned everything meticulously. She had prepared nibbles and a nonalcoholic cocktail as an aperitif, followed by pasta Milanese with the obligatory veal escalope—they had agreed to serve something Italian in honor of their visit to Cremona—and an excellent tiramisu, for which Lilly had immediately demanded the recipe.

Jessie and Norma had been given a pizza and as a special treat were allowed to eat it in their rooms, which they were delighted about. The music they were playing was not too loud, though it was audible enough to drift down to the living room, but Ellen didn't mind.

Unfortunately Dean had been unable to get home in time, since the building site was still placing great demands on him, but he had promised to join them later, not least because he wanted to know what Gabriel thought of the supposed code in the sheet music.

As they ate, Lilly and Ellen took turns telling him of their experiences. Gabriel listened keenly and looked with interest at the copies of the newspaper articles.

"You've found a real treasure there," he said as he picked up the copy with the photo of a young Rose next to Mrs. Faraday. "I don't know this photo, actually, and the same goes for the other articles. Mrs. Faraday probably had the editions of the newspapers sent to her, but a lot was destroyed in the war. Because of the air raids, some chests containing archive material were put into safe storage—material that never turned up again after the war. We assume that it was destroyed or that it's moldering away in some attic."

"So what else do you know about Rose?" Lilly asked. "You promised us some new information."

Gabriel gave a broad grin and raised his hands. "Fine, fine, I surrender. No need to get the torture instruments out."

"We never intended to go that far," Ellen replied. "But you've just vastly improved your chances of dessert."

"It can't get any better than this wonderful main course, but as an inquisitive man I'm looking forward to it." He straightened up in his seat and looked as if he were delving into his memory. "Before you went to Cremona, I had another good look through our archive but didn't find much new there. As you know, Rose Gallway was a particularly interesting former student of ours. The information we have about her had already been collected and archived by my predecessors. But they missed one thing. Perhaps it didn't seem particularly important to them, but when I was looking through the files, it hit me like a bolt of lightning."

"What did you find?"

"Our music school used to have a boardinghouse where pupils who weren't from London lived. At a certain time of year, Mrs. Faraday would travel far and wide, investigating talented young people recommended to her by music teachers. The boardinghouse was run by one Miss Patrick, about whom little is known apart from her dates of birth and death. But she was an avid collector of information and documents relating to her charges. The moment Mrs. Faraday decided to bring a girl to her establishment, Miss Patrick entered the scene and made an entry in her house journal.

"These house journals—there was one for each year group—contained reports on the conduct of the pupils, although only major disciplinary incidents were recorded. But there were also lists of things that were acquired—and their dates of origin. As soon as a new pupil arrived, she wrote down everything she knew about the girl. Rose must have given her a fairly detailed report, as there's a lot on her page."

"So why didn't your predecessors take any notice of it?" Ellen asked after taking a sip of wine.

"Because they believed these journals were nothing more than yearbooks full of cost accounts and edifying stories that Miss Patrick had noted down. But not only did they fail to see that these edifying stories mainly came from the girls themselves, they also didn't notice the beautifully presented fact sheets among all the petty details."

"Well, don't keep us in suspense—what was it you found?"

Gabriel took a small envelope from his pocket, which Lilly guessed contained a couple of copies. He didn't take them out, but replied, "We already knew that Rose Gallway came from Sumatra, and we also knew her date of birth, May 9, 1880. But there's quite a sensational fact about her parents." Now he took one of the copies from the envelope. "Her mother's forename was Adit, and she was from the village of Magek, while her father was an Englishman."

"You can't really tell that from her appearance," Lilly said with a nod. "She looks more Italian or Spanish."

"Her eyes are a bit exotic," Ellen said, tapping the copy of the photo of Rose as a very young girl. "It's particularly obvious in this picture."

Gabriel nodded. "You're right, but Europeans sometimes have almond-shaped eyes and deep black hair. The photos don't give the slightest hint that her mother was a Minangkabau, whose tribe lived around the center of the island."

Lilly raised her eyebrows. Ellen put her espresso cup down.

"Who are the Minangkabau?" asked Lilly, who was hearing the word for the first time.

"A traditional Sumatran tribe who live their lives according to the adat, a set of rules governing the society, in which the women were in charge."

"A matriarchy," Ellen remarked. Gabriel nodded.

"That's right. Of course, it's Islamic there, and only men are allowed to study the Koran, but property is inherited through the female line. Every family has a headwoman who is honored by all her descendants. The eldest daughter is chosen to take over the leadership of the clan, while her sisters either swell the family ranks or establish a new clan."

He unfolded the sheet of paper and handed it to Lilly, and in doing so seemed to deliberately brush his hand against hers. How soft his skin felt, and how strong his fingers! It was the hand of a musician, but also the hand of a practical man.

Somewhat perplexed, Lilly turned her attention to the photocopy. It contained no background information on the Minangkabau, but Rose must have stated with pride that her mother belonged to the tribe. And there was more—the fact that she had lived in Padang and had gone to school there, where she had caught the attention of her Dutch music teacher, who insisted that she have violin lessons.

"Let me guess!" Ellen said as she looked at it. "Rose's mother was a servant for an Englishman who got her pregnant."

Gabriel gave a short laugh. "Ellen, where did you get such a bad impression of nineteenth-century men?"

"Well, isn't that the usual cliché? Whenever the English colonial overlords employed native staff, they brought children into the world with some of the women."

Gabriel still wore a look of amusement. "Yes, that may be the usual cliché, stoked by plenty of novels and films, and I don't doubt that it did happen. But it looks like things were rather different here."

Gabriel fell silent and looked between the two women, his gaze finally resting on Lilly. She could tell her cheeks had begun to glow with excitement, and she felt butterflies in her stomach.

"In fact, it seems that Rose Gallway had perfectly respectable origins. Her father was a warehouse supervisor in Padang, an Englishman, and he married Adit in the proper way. The amazing thing is that she lived with her husband. I've been doing a bit of research on the Minangkabau. It seems that their customary practice is for women to remain in their mother's house and have a kind of long-distance marriage with their husbands, who, in the eyes of their families, belong to their own mothers. Any children who are born belong to her house, not his."

"So Rose's mother broke with tradition."

"You could say that. It doesn't necessarily mean things stayed that way, though. The Minangkabau are a very traditional people—perhaps she changed her mind and went back to them. I think that's our

starting point. All trace of Rose vanished on Sumatra. Once her career began to decline, she traveled back there without explaining to anyone what her intentions were. I assume that her visit was something to do with her parents. Perhaps there are still traces of her and her family in Padang and Magek. As property is inherited down the maternal line, her name should be known—even if there are no church records, the Minangkabau might have kept records of their forebears. Or at least oral histories."

"Then there's nothing else we can do but travel to Indonesia," Ellen remarked, although her expression suggested that she wasn't serious.

"That would be one possibility," Gabriel agreed. "The other would be to request documents from there. There are some very good music schools in Indonesia that might be prepared to help me."

Lilly sat there as if turned to stone. She felt that it would not be enough merely to request documents from Indonesia. She had to follow in Rose's footsteps. She had to go to Sumatra!

"So, that story must have earned me at least a portion of dessert—what do you think, ladies?"

A little later, after polishing off the tiramisu and settling down in the armchairs around the hearth, they resumed their conversation about the rose violin and its owner.

"Have you found anything new about Helen Carter?" Lilly asked, suppressing her thoughts about how she would get to Indonesia.

"Of course I looked for her in the house journals, too, but the good Miss Patrick had died by then, and her successor was a little less detailed in her bookkeeping. The new arrivals were still noted, but the entry about Helen didn't tell us much new. Her parents were James and Ivy Carter from Padang, she was born on December 12, 1902, and the old Mrs. Faraday, who was still traveling widely at eighty-three to inspect talented youngsters, became aware of her because people were enthusing about this new prodigy. Helen is said to have taught herself most of her skills, as was often the case with musical geniuses like that.

After the earthquake in 1910, her name crops up fairly frequently, until she was finally visited by Mrs. Faraday. She must have been invited to come and study with her, because in 1911 Helen Carter entered the conservatory as one of the youngest pupils ever admitted. Mrs. Faraday took personal charge of her in the early years but then had to hand over Helen's lessons to her teachers when she suffered a stroke. She cared for Helen until her death in 1916 and made her the star she was in 1919 and 1920—the start of the Roaring Twenties."

"And then the accident happened."

"Yes, the accident in which she was hit by a bus and the world was deprived of a star. Helen survived but never played again, as her left hand was mutilated."

"That must have been terrible," Ellen murmured, looking at her own hands. "If music is your passion . . . When I was a child, I sometimes wished something would happen to my hands. After an initial enthusiasm for playing the violin, I lost interest, but my parents insisted I continue. I did, for their sakes, but Lilly will confirm to you how much it got on my nerves."

"Oh yes," Lilly interjected before Ellen continued.

"But I can imagine what it would feel like to have given my heart and soul to it. To suffer an injury that prevented me from following my calling would have been dreadful—comparable to my institute burning down."

"You can get insurance against it these days," Gabriel said. "I know a number of professional musicians who have insured their hands for substantial sums of money—higher than their lives. But there was nothing of the sort in those days. And I don't believe that a passionate musician could ever be compensated with money for losing the ability to play. Their financial security would be ensured, but what's that compared to passion?"

"Could that be why Helen married, because she had no choice and would have been ruined otherwise?" Ellen asked.

"No, I don't think so. She would have chosen a man with her heart. There's no indication that she had any financial motive in marrying."

"Then at least she found love," Ellen murmured gratefully.

For a few minutes they were silent, each lost in their own thoughts.

Gabriel finally turned to Lilly. "Don't forget, you promised me that I could play your violin. Have my stories at least earned me the right to hold it in my hands?"

Lilly blushed. She should have shown him the violin before now—how impolite of her!

"Of course. I'll just go and fetch it."

As she jumped up, she felt Gabriel's eyes between her shoulder blades. Back with the violin case, she carefully lifted the instrument from the red lining and handed it to Gabriel. He turned it over, full of awe, looked briefly at the rose, and then turned it back to study the front.

"Rose Gallway's violin. I would never have believed I'd have the pleasure of holding it in my hands. Sometimes miracles do happen."

"And you really have no idea how the violin came into Helen Carter's hands when it had belonged to Rose Gallway?" Ellen asked pensively.

"We think Rose must have sold or pawned it. Or perhaps it was stolen from her. It's possible that Rose could have been the victim of a burglary—that would explain the violin's disappearance."

"But was there no one to keep an eye on it? Even then musicians had such things as managers or agents."

"True, and in Rose's case we know who that agent was. His name was Sean Carmichael, and he was quite a go-getter. He saw the potential in Rose at an early stage. Unfortunately her decline hit him quite hard; perhaps he even dropped her. We're still looking into that, and now that you've brought it up, I'll make it my next priority to look into his story."

With that he set the violin under his chin. Lilly was about to ask if he felt like playing "The Moonlit Garden," but he had already begun.

She realized with surprise that he was playing the very piece. He had clearly learned it thoroughly.

Overcome, she closed her eyes and tried to imagine herself in a garden—a garden with wild flowers, trees with low-hanging garlands of leaves, thick bushes in which small animals were concealed. Above the scene hung a moon that made all the colors seem pale but stole nothing of the beauty from the place.

The vision remained for a few minutes until Gabriel finished playing. He slowly lowered the bow and looked at the violin in wonder.

"It's no surprise that people used to say Helen Carter was a descendant of Paganini. If I can get a sound like that from the violin with my modest abilities, what would it have sounded like in the hands of a genius like her? Or Rose Gallway, whose talents were perhaps even greater?"

Before Lilly could protest, they heard a car approaching, and a little later Dean appeared in the living room.

"I'm sorry I'm so late," he said with a sigh. "That building site's driving me crazy."

"Dean, this is Gabriel Thornton." Ellen introduced him to their guest. "And I think we've got a couple of stories left over for you."

***

It was not until long after midnight that Gabriel took his leave. Lilly led him outside.

"That was a really lovely evening," he began with a shy smile, his hands shoved in his pockets. "Your friend and her husband are very nice."

"They're wonderful people. I've got a lot to thank them for. They've always been there for me, especially after my husband died."

Gabriel seemed to remember. "Yes, you told me about that on the plane. It's good to have people you can rely on. I wish I'd had such good friends to fall back on after my separation from Diana."

"Your wife?"

Gabriel nodded, and for a moment he looked so vulnerable that she longed to take him in her arms, but she held herself back. She sensed that he liked her, but that still didn't give her the right to throw herself around his neck.

"I'm sorry," she said, unable to think of anything better.

"There's no need to be. Diana and I weren't meant for each other—it's as simple as that. And my mind was so much on my job that I neglected my friends. I got what I deserved. But you make mistakes in life in order to learn from them, don't you?"

He smiled at her and then took something from his pocket.

"I've got something for you here," he said softly.

Lilly saw that it was the second photocopy, the one that he had not removed from the envelope earlier. It was a transcript of a legend bearing the title "The Forgotten Girl."

"Our good Miss Patrick must have picked up this story from Rose. It's a well-known Indonesian legend as far as I can tell—it appears in a few collections. Unfortunately we have no evidence that Rose composed 'The Moonlit Garden,' but this shows the influences on her during her childhood. I read that the legends are told through the medium of shadow puppet shows in Indonesia. Perhaps she used to watch them when she was young."

"Maybe. Thank you."

"You're welcome. You know that if I find anything else I'll let you have it."

"When will we see each other again?"

Gabriel gave her a wide smile. "You still owe me dinner, don't you? This evening was very nice, but I consider it more of a business meeting."

"What kind of dinner are you thinking of?"

"It should be more of a private affair, don't you agree?"

Lilly blushed. When had she last had a meal in private with a man?

"I hope I haven't shocked you," Gabriel added, noticing her hesitation.

"No, not at all. And . . . you're right, perhaps we should do that."

"Only if it's what you really want. I want you to know that I'm not helping you merely because I want to go out with you. You'd get my help anyway, but I thought—"

"Friday," Lilly burst out. "Are you free then?"

Gabriel raised his eyebrows in surprise. "Yes, of course. And if I find there's something else on my calendar, I'll cancel it. You're one for snap decisions, aren't you?"

"Well, I don't know how much longer I'll be here. And who knows, perhaps . . ."

"Perhaps we'll enjoy it so much we'll want to do it again."

"It's possible, isn't it?"

"It's possible." Gabriel looked at her intently, then leaned forward and kissed her cheek. "Good night, Lilly."

"Good night, Gabriel. Safe journey home."

"No worries. I don't want to miss that dinner." He went over to his car and climbed in with a wave.

19

Padang, 1910

Helen loved to hide. When she sat beneath the bushes behind the house, certain that no one could find her, she would tell herself the wildest stories—stories of princes and rajahs, of demons and wonderful princesses. Sometimes she would hide from her mother, sometimes also from Miss Hadeland, her Dutch music teacher.

"Helen!" came her mother's voice from the house, but the girl ignored her.

She ran farther around the house, toward the garden gate, where the thick shrubbery hid the garden from the street. There was a particular spot where the branches had formed a kind of sheltering dome, which was a wonderful hiding place for Helen.

Normally she was alone when she came here—until her mother found her—but this time she saw outside the garden gate a tall, dark-haired lady wearing a pretty, dark blue dress. She was looking expectantly along the path, as if waiting for someone. She had clearly not yet seen Helen. The girl thought for a moment. Should she speak to the lady? Her mother didn't like her to talk to strangers, but did that apply to someone who looked perfectly harmless? She finally plucked up courage and came out from behind the high stone gateposts.

"Hello," she said to the lady, who stepped back in surprise, looking at Helen with wide eyes. Since when had a small girl been able to frighten a grown woman?

"Who are you, then?" Helen asked, and smiled in the hope that the stranger would look a little less scared.

"I . . ." the lady began, still looking rather afraid.

"You must have a name," Helen insisted, wondering whether or not to ask the lady in. The cook would by now have prepared the scones they always had for afternoon tea. Served with cream, they were simply delicious, and this lady would be sure to like them.

"Yes, I have a name," the lady said, a little more confidently. She crouched down in front of Helen, who now saw that there were tears in her eyes.

"Why are you crying?" she asked, reaching out her hand to the lady. How pretty she was! She had never seen such a beautiful lady. Even her mama wasn't as beautiful as this.

"I'm crying because I'm so happy to see you," the lady said. She closed her eyes as the girl touched her cheek. Helen felt the lady begin to tremble. A tear ran over her fingertips.

"But you shouldn't be crying if you're happy." Helen withdrew her hand and stared in amazement at the tears that looked like dewdrops.

"Sometimes people cry when they're happy, too," the lady replied. She pulled a handkerchief from her sleeve and dabbed it beneath her eyes. Then she gazed at Helen wistfully for a while.

"You have a wonderful garden here," she said then, pointing over Helen's shoulder. "Do you know what all those flowers are called?"

Helen shook her head. "No, not all of them. But I know what roses are, and fangi . . . fragi . . ."

"Frangipani," the lady suggested helpfully.

"Yes, that's it—frangi . . . pani." If Helen spoke slowly, she could master the word. "And orchids and jasmine."

The lady laughed briefly. "You do know a lot of flowers! The most important ones, I'd say."

"But we have lots more," Helen replied. "Would you like to see them?"

"Later, perhaps."

The lady jumped as she heard Helen's mother calling.

"I think I ought to go now," she said and tucked the handkerchief back into her sleeve. Her voice sounded suddenly softer, as if she meant to whisper.

"Will you come to visit me again?" Helen asked, listening to her mother approaching.

"Yes, I'll visit you," the stranger promised. "But please don't tell your mother. She mustn't know I was here."

"Why not?"

"Because it's a secret."

"A secret?"

"Yes, a secret. And if you keep it to yourself, I'll bring you something lovely next time."

"What?" Helen asked, but the lady glanced over her shoulder and saw Helen's mother striding toward the gate.

"You'll see. I'll be back soon." With that she turned and hurried away.

A moment later her mother appeared behind her. "Helen, there you are! I've been calling you all this time!"

Helen knew, but she could hardly tell her mother that she had not wanted to answer.

"Who was that woman you were talking to?" Helen's mother asked as she craned her neck in an attempt to see her. But the lady had already disappeared.

"I don't know," Helen answered, sensing that she shouldn't tell her mother any more if she wanted to find out what the present was that the lady would bring her.

"What did she want from you?"

Helen bit her bottom lip. What should she say? She wouldn't dream of lying to her mother, but she mustn't betray that pretty, mysterious lady, who might be a princess or a good fairy.

"She said that we have a beautiful garden."

It seemed the right thing to say, since the lady had indeed praised the garden. Helen's mother smiled and swung her up into her arms.

"Ah well, I hope you were polite enough to thank her."

Helen nodded again. "Yes, I did, and I also asked if she wanted to come in, but she didn't. Then she said good-bye."

Ivy Carter pressed a kiss to her daughter's brow as the worry lines between her eyebrows deepened, which always made her look thoughtful or cross.

"Have I done something wrong?" asked Helen, who knew this expression only too well. It was the same one her mother wore when Helen had been naughty.

"No, you've done nothing wrong, my darling," her mother replied. "It was very polite of you to ask her in, but you should always tell me first. You never can tell what people are like."

"But she was really friendly!" Helen said with raised eyebrows.

Her mother sighed and looked sad for a moment.

"Very well. Now come in. The scones are ready, and I'm sure you're dying to try one."

Helen nodded eagerly and skipped behind her mother into the house.

***

That night, Helen lay awake for a long time, watching the shadows play on her bedroom ceiling. The outlines of the windows and the trees swaying in the wind from the sea used to seem eerie to her, but now she knew they were only trees, not demons.

That discovery had left her a little disappointed, as she loved fairy tales. She had especially liked the shadow puppet play that her father had taken her to recently. Together with her friend Antje Zwaneweg she had talked for days about the beautiful, sometimes creepy puppets that had moved so wonderfully behind the illuminated screen.

From then on, when she looked at the shadows on her bedroom ceiling, which had previously scared her deliciously, she knew that the trees really were only trees. And the shadows flitting by were night birds out looking for food.

But now she had a real secret! Would the mystery lady come back tomorrow? She had said "soon," but Helen knew that wasn't a precise time. When she told her mother she would have her room tidy soon, it usually took at least a day or two before she had finished. How long would it be until the mystery lady returned?

***

The next morning, sitting with her mother in the classroom, where she was supposed to be practicing her letters, all Helen could think about was when the mystery lady would come. She was afraid that she might appear by the fence when Helen was not there. If she did, maybe she would think Helen didn't want to keep her promise.

She felt like running outside that very moment and looking for her, but she knew her mother would not allow her out until she had finished her rows of letters.

"Helen, are you listening to me?"

The girl jumped. She had heard her mother saying something, but she had taken no notice of the words.

"Helen, what's the matter with you today?" her mother asked with concern, setting her book to one side. "Your thoughts are miles away."

Ashamed, Helen looked down at the desk in front of her. What should she say? She didn't enjoy her lessons with Miss Hadeland, but she liked learning with her mother, because she had promised Helen that one day she would send her to a really nice school, one where she could read lots of books and play music.

Getting no reply from Helen, her mother came over to her, crouched in front of her, and gently stroked a lock of hair from her face.

"Are you tired, darling? Did you sleep badly?"

Helen found it simplest to nod, although in fact she hadn't slept much. But she couldn't, no, she *shouldn't* admit that she was so absent-minded because she could only think about when the lady would appear with her present. If only she had named a day and a time!

For now, her mother let it be and continued with the lesson, but without demanding too much participation from her daughter. Helen knew, however, that things couldn't carry on for much longer like this. How could she distract herself from thoughts of the beautiful mystery lady?

During the days that followed, Helen would run down to the gate whenever her mother was not there, to keep an eye out for her mysterious visitor. Of course she was not alone in the house—there were the cook and the maid, but when the mistress of the house was away, they just sat together in the kitchen, chatting over a cup of tea.

Helen was all the more pleased now that no one was interested in her and they all assumed she was up in her room doing her homework like a good girl.

Thoughts of the mystery lady and her promised gift filled Helen's mind from the moment she opened her eyes in the morning. At breakfast she toyed listlessly with her porridge, and she was unable to concentrate during her lessons. Her gaze wandered again and again to the window, and her thoughts kept turning to the gift the lady wanted to give her. What would it be? A bracelet? A bouquet of flowers? No, there was no need to make a great secret of either of those. Perhaps it was a wooden box containing a precious jewel? Or something much more exciting, like a book of spells or a talking doll?

As she stood at the gate and waited, she went through all the things she knew of, and as she ran out of familiar items, she invented new ones.

She never allowed herself to be disheartened by the idea that she was waiting in vain. When her mother fetched her from the gate with a look of bemusement and asked her why she was standing there, she quickly thought of a suitable answer before saying she'd be back there the next day.

One day she had a music lesson with Miss Hadeland. Helen called her Miss, even though she was Dutch, as she found it difficult to get her tongue around the Dutch word for *Miss*. Miss Hadeland didn't seem to mind, so long as Helen practiced the piano regularly.

Recently Miss Hadeland had become a little dissatisfied with her. Once, Helen had overheard her saying to her mother: "She doesn't seem to be making any progress. The child plays, but she doesn't seem to be enjoying it."

"That may well be the case," her mother had replied. "Would it be an idea for her to try playing a different instrument?"

"The piano is one of the easiest instruments to master, especially for women! If she can't master that, how can she be expected to learn another instrument?"

"Give her a little time; she's only seven. Her hands are still growing. She'll get more dexterous as she gets older."

"Mozart could play whole sonatas when he was only six!"

"Our Helen is no child prodigy, and nor should she be! I only want her to have a good ear for music and to get pleasure from playing. Be a little more lenient with her."

But Miss Hadeland was not lenient with her. As if possessed with the idea of making a child prodigy out of her, like Mozart, whose compositions Helen had to play, she urged her pupil ever onward. She often rapped her knuckles, once so badly that Helen ran to her mother in tears.

Her mother had given the teacher a piece of her mind, and since then the blows had not been so hard or so frequent, but the words she used to plague Helen made up for it.

So it was on that special day.

"Even a camel walking over the keyboard wouldn't sound as clumsy as your fingers!" she shouted, pacing up and down in front of Helen with clicking heels. "It hurts my ears to have to listen to it. Come on, play that passage again!"

Helen, who had already had enough of playing the passage and who was by now thoroughly nervous, put her hands to the keys and began to play the hated passage again. She thought that this time it was better than before.

Then it happened. The switch whipped across her fingers before Helen saw it coming. She withdrew her hand in shock, and a dreadful discord filled the room.

This time she'd had enough! She jumped up, stamped her foot, and cried out, "I'm not playing anymore!"

Before Miss Hadeland's anger could reach her, she ran out. Panic caused her heart to thunder in her breast. With one ear she listened behind her, assuming the piano teacher would follow her. She heard nothing, but perhaps it would take Miss Hadeland a moment to get over the surprise.

Full of rage and a little fear, Helen ran back to the bushes where she waited every day for the lady. At that moment she was not thinking of her but rather was wishing every disease under the sun on her piano teacher. The bubonic plague Antje had told her about came to mind.

As she reached the bush with its colorful flowers, Helen came to a sudden standstill.

The mystery lady had appeared like a ghost before her. She stood by the gatepost, as still as if she had been turned to stone by a magic spell. When she saw Helen, a smile crossed her face.

"You're here again," she said softly.

Helen suddenly forgot the pain in her hand. All these days she had been waiting and now, on a day when Miss Hadeland had been so stupid, this lady had appeared like a good fairy, as if to comfort her after what had happened. Helen moved closer to the gate. The lady stretched out her hand, which felt pleasantly cool against the angry flush on her cheeks. It was then that Helen saw she was holding a long case in her other hand.

"I've been here every day, hoping you'd come back," Helen said, managing with difficulty to keep back her tears of joy.

"I'm sorry I made you wait. I . . . I haven't been too well," she replied. "And there was something I had to do. But I'm here now, and I've brought you your present."

The lady pushed the black case between the railings of the gate.

"What's in it?" the girl asked in fascination.

"Something very special. A violin."

The girl's eyes widened. "A violin? For me?"

"Yes. If you want it, it's your violin. If you take it, you should learn to play it. I've heard you're learning to play the piano."

"How do you know that?" the girl asked. The lady smiled gently.

"I know a lot about you, Helen. And that's why I'm giving you the violin. It used to be mine, but I can't play anymore."

"Why not? Have you forgotten how to do it?"

Helen may not have particularly liked her music lessons, but she could never have forgotten the movements Miss Hadeland had drummed into her.

"No, there's another reason." The lady looked at the girl briefly before asking, "You have a strong heart, don't you?"

"Of course I have," Helen said, although she didn't really know how the strength of a heart was measured. If it was a matter of how fast it could beat, at that moment she had the strongest heart in the world.

"Good. Then you'll be able to play the violin for a very long time."

"But how will I learn how to play it? Can you show me?"

"What's wrong with the woman who teaches you piano?"

"She doesn't like the violin," Helen replied. "I don't even know whether she can play one. All she does is tinkle away on our piano and hit me with a stick on my fingers when I make mistakes."

"She hits you?" the lady asked in shock.

"Only when I do something wrong. I don't do that often."

The lady pressed her lips together, then reached through the gate for the girl's hand and looked at the welts. Then she stroked the back of her hand gently. Again it looked as though tears were gleaming in her eyes.

"She has no right to hit you! You'd better tell your mother if it happens again. She can scold you when you do something wrong, but she should never hit you."

"Oh, it's not so bad," Helen said, trying to reassure the mystery lady, who she sensed really cared about her. "It's a bit of a nuisance, but I can still play. And in my head I call her a silly cow."

The lady laughed briefly—or was it a sob? Helen couldn't quite tell.

"Anyway, I've told Mama, and she had a word with her. And today I simply ran away."

"Take good care of your hands, won't you?" the lady said now, still holding Helen's hand firmly. "And please will you promise me something?"

Helen nodded eagerly. For a gift like this she would have promised almost anything, especially to this lady.

"Promise me that one day you'll become a truly wonderful musician. A violinist, all right? Provided you come to grips with the instrument."

"I promise," Helen replied, but then she realized it was a bit rash. "But first I have to learn to play it."

The lady looked past her, toward the house. Was someone coming? Helen looked around, too, and saw nothing.

"I can teach you a little about how to play it. But we need a place where we can't be seen by people on the street or by your mother or your music teacher. I'll show you how to hold it and sing you the notes the instrument would make. Do you think you can learn in that way?"

"But how should I practice?" Helen asked in amazement, since she'd never heard of that way of practicing before.

The lady looked toward the house again, but this time not to check whether anyone was coming.

"The house where you live is a really big one. Maybe you can find a room. I'm sure your mother goes out on errands during the day, doesn't she?"

"Yes, she always goes out for two or three hours in the afternoons. You could even come in."

The lady shook her head. "No, I can't do that. If your mother saw me, she wouldn't be pleased that I was there. Anyway, this is supposed to be our secret, isn't it? Do you like secrets?"

Helen nodded. Yes, she liked secrets, even though she had found out that keeping them was difficult.

"So where should we meet?" she asked.

"You tell me. I assume you're not allowed to leave here alone?"

Helen thought about it. Where could she hide away with her new friend and learn to play the violin? Then she had an idea. She had only been to the place once, because it was not their property but their neighbors'. It was a garden that had grown wild. She called up a small pavilion into her mind's eye. That was the place to go with the mystery lady.

"I know of a place, but I'll have to show you. It's not so easy to find."

"Is it in your garden?" The lady looked as if she wasn't too pleased about that.

"No, outside it. Follow this fence until you come to a hedge. We'll meet there."

Helen darted through the bushes. She made her way straight to the gap between the fence and the hedge, through which the other, neglected grounds could be reached.

Helen peered through the gap, and since her friend was taking some time to reach it, she glanced up toward the white timber house with its paint peeling off in large flakes. Did anyone still live there? The windows looked like sad eyes. Maybe the house felt lonely without anyone to live in it.

Helen heard a rustling behind her and turned. The lady appeared, a little out of breath, as if she had been running. But she couldn't have been, or she would have been quicker.

"So this is your secret place," she said as she dabbed at her brow with a handkerchief. Helen noticed that the lady's lips were as blue as the bilberries she had seen in one of her picture books.

"Is everything all right?" she asked, concerned, as she had never seen a person with blue lips.

"Yes, I'm fine now," the lady said, but in the same tone of voice her mother used to say she was all right when she had a headache.

"Do you like it here?"

The lady looked at the house. "It seems a bit spooky. Aren't you frightened?"

"This isn't the place. Come on, I'll show you."

She took the lady by the hand and led her through the long grass that grew so high it almost concealed her. Although the grass blocked her view a little, it didn't take her long to find the pavilion, which looked no more cheerful than the house. But perhaps someone visiting regularly would bring it back to life.

"There it is!" Helen said, pointing happily at the building, its sides clad with thin clapboard.

"Do you really think it's safe here?"

"Yes, not even Mama has ever found me here. If we don't make too much noise, no one will notice we're here."

"Very well, then we'll meet here. Shall we say every Tuesday and Thursday afternoon? I'll wait here until you come, all right?"

"All right."

"And take good care of the violin. Hide it away so that no one can find it."

Helen nodded eagerly.

"You're a good girl." The lady stroked her cheek affectionately. "But you should be getting back to the house now."

"You really will come back?"

"I promise. And this time I won't keep you waiting so long. Thursday is in two days' time. I'll be here then."

Helen hugged the violin case to her in delight, then took her leave of her friend and ran with a light heart back to the house. She didn't go in by the front door in case Miss Hadeland was waiting there. Instead, she hurried through the tradesman's entrance, then up the stairs to her bedroom, where with a thumping heart she hid the violin under her bed.

As she left her room, she thought perhaps she should look around for a place where she could practice in secret. She had always been a little afraid of the attic, but maybe the violin could protect her, and she could drive away the ghosts that haunted the top floor with her music.

But before she reached the attic stairs, she heard footsteps behind her.

"Where have you been, Helen?" her mother asked reproachfully as she caught sight of her daughter. "And why are you hiding up here? You're supposed to be having a music lesson!"

Helen held up her hand, showing her mother the fresh welts, and said with the utmost conviction: "I never, ever, ever want to play the piano again!"

20

London, 2011

With a sigh, Lilly checked her e-mail in-box. Still no message from Enrico or his friend. She had been hoping so much that she would hear whether there was any news about the sheet music, which might provide a key to her dream of Helen. And something else was bothering her.

Since Gabriel's visit, the idea that she should perhaps fly to Sumatra had not left her. She felt that the solution to the puzzle lay on the island. But would she dare to make such a journey alone? She had not traveled far afield since Peter's death. But something had changed in her, something connected with the violin, Rose, and Helen, and also Gabriel.

She had spent the whole morning looking for a reasonably priced trip, but the results were disheartening. The price of a flight to Sumatra alone was horrendous. Her antiques business might cover her bills, but she had nothing left over to afford a trip to Padang to follow the trail of the two violinists. Did this mean her search had come to an end?

The sound of the telephone startled her out of her thoughts. She wasn't expecting a call, but she hurried down the stairs and picked up.

"Lilly?" asked a man's voice she knew all too well. There was a lot of noise behind him, as if he was standing on a busy street.

"Gabriel, to what do I owe this honor?" she quipped. Was he unable to wait for their dinner date? The morning after his visit he had sent her a few suggestions of London restaurants.

"I'm afraid I have some bad news for you," he said a little hesitantly. "I've had a call from Diana, my ex-wife, you remember?"

"Yes," Lilly replied. "Has something happened?"

"You could say that. I've got to go and see her, look after her. I'll tell you more when we meet. I'm on the way there now, but to my deep regret I'm afraid I can't even name another day for our date yet. I can't make it on Friday in any case."

Lilly swallowed. Her delight at hearing Gabriel collapsed into a heavy lump in her stomach.

"OK," she said, and although she tried not to, she couldn't help sounding offended.

"I'm really sorry, Lilly, but I promise you we'll have that dinner. It'll happen—better late than never, hey?"

Lilly forced a laugh. "Yes, I guess so."

"Good. I'll be in touch when I'm back in London, all right?"

A lump in her throat prevented her from answering. She would have liked to know when that would be.

As if he had read her thoughts, he added, "It could be in a day's time or a week, but I'll be back, I promise."

"OK," Lilly replied, and felt like hanging up, but she heard herself saying, "Look after yourself, Gabriel."

"You too. See you soon, Lilly."

And he was gone.

Lilly stood numbly by the telephone table for a moment. He's going to see his ex, she kept thinking, and although it probably meant nothing, disappointment spread through her. She had looked forward so much to their evening, and now . . .

Don't be so childish, she told herself. You turned him down yourself last time.

She put the telephone back in the cradle and went upstairs. Perhaps she could still find a way of getting to Sumatra. If she busied herself with the search, then she wouldn't have to think about Gabriel at his ex-wife's—and the idea that Diana might be more important to him than she was.

***

"What are you looking for?" Ellen asked as she leaned lightly on Lilly's shoulder and looked at the screen. It was now the afternoon and Lilly was still searching for a special offer. And she still had not succeeded in coming to grips with her disappointment at Gabriel's cancellation.

"A lottery win," she murmured.

"And you're hoping to find one in Padang? Do they have a special lottery there or what?"

"No, I need it to get to Indonesia. But the whole idea's probably crazy anyway."

Ellen was quiet for a moment before carefully turning the office chair around and forcing Lilly to look her in the eye.

"What's the matter?"

Lilly pressed her lips together and looked at her knees.

"Gabriel called."

"And?"

"We were going to go out to dinner on Friday, but he's cancelled."

Ellen shook her head incredulously. "Did he give you a reason?"

"He said there were some family matters he had to see to."

"Oh. Well, these things happen."

"It's to do with his ex-wife."

There was another pause.

"His ex-wife?"

"Yes, Diana. He said she'd asked him for help, and he had to go and look after her."

A smile flitted across Ellen's face. "You're jealous."

"Don't be silly, why should I be jealous?" Lilly said defensively, trying not to reveal that Ellen had hit the mark. "We're friends, nothing more."

"Really? The looks he was giving you when he was here led me to believe he was interested."

"I didn't notice," Lilly claimed, a little put out.

"Oh, Lilly!" Ellen threw her arms around her. "You don't fool me. You're afraid he might rekindle a flame with his ex, aren't you? You don't know anything about the reasons why they separated. They could have had an amicable separation and still be friends. Don't give up before you know what's behind it all. He hasn't cancelled your date but just postponed it, am I right?"

Lilly nodded. "Yes, he said it was only a postponement, but he hasn't given me another date."

"Who knows what's happened? Just wait and let him get back to you. I wouldn't worry about it if I were you. We'd be better off having a look to see if there's a way of getting you to Padang."

They sat at the computer until the evening looking for a suitable travel offer, but nothing affordable came to light. Lilly felt her mood growing worse, and even Ellen's attempts to cheer her up with jokes about travel agents did nothing to help. She wasn't going to have her date with Gabriel, and she would probably never get to Sumatra. The mystery of the two violinists would remain unsolved forever, and she could keep asking until she was old and gray what hidden family secret could explain why she was now the owner of a famous violin.

She was very quiet during dinner and couldn't say whether it was because she couldn't afford the trip to Indonesia or because she kept thinking of Gabriel, who had gone to see the woman he was once married to. The fact that she didn't know more about Gabriel and his past was driving her mad. Was Ellen right that they were still friends? Was there still anything between them? Was she making a fool of herself to hope for more from him? A dinner for two was a long way from them getting together.

All these questions finally followed her to bed, causing a restless, completely muddled dream about Indonesian temples and landscapes in which she was running after Gabriel but never caught up with him.

***

Two days later, during which she had continued to wait in vain for a message from Italy, Lilly found an envelope next to her coffee cup. She had overslept. Ellen was already on her way to work, the girls had long since left the house, and she had even missed Dean that morning. Was this the letter she had waited for?

The sight of *Lilly* on it in Ellen's lovely, sweeping handwriting left her in no doubt that it was for her.

Ellen had sealed the envelope tightly, as if it contained secret state papers, so Lilly took her knife and carefully slit the top.

At first she saw nothing but thick, white paper. Lilly found that the white sheet was simply a brief letter folded around a second narrow, colorfully printed envelope. As Lilly turned it around, her face fell. She looked at the envelope in bewilderment for a moment, then placed it on the table and ran from the kitchen to fetch the phone.

It took her a while to get through; the phone in Ellen's office was incredibly busy that morning.

A man's voice finally answered. Terence, Ellen's secretary.

"What can I do for you?" he asked in a tone of voice fit to pacify the most irate caller.

Lilly asked for Ellen and was told that her friend was in a meeting at the moment but would call her back as soon as possible. Lilly felt like asking how long she would be, but she merely thanked him and hung up.

With a shake of her head, she stared at the two logos that adorned the envelope. One was a purple goat's head on a gray background, while the second had blue-and-turquoise lines arranged to form the head and wings of a flying eagle.

"Oh, Ellen, what are you doing?" Lilly murmured. She studied the words, reading them again and again, wondering if she had missed something.

When the telephone rang, she shot out her hand and picked it up before the first tone had finished.

"Ellen?" she asked before the caller had a chance to say anything.

"My goodness!" her friend's voice replied. "What's up?"

"That's what I want to ask you!" She looked again at the turquoise-and-blue emblem. "I have a message from you here."

"What do you say to that?" Ellen replied, and her grin could almost be heard.

"Don't you think this is a bit excessive? I'll never be able to repay it in all my life."

"It's only a gift voucher. And a suggestion of how you could use it, if you want."

"This is more than a voucher!"

Lilly could practically hear Ellen waving her concerns aside.

"I've gotten you two flight vouchers so that you only have to pay a quarter of the price. I could have paid for the whole trip but know you wouldn't accept that. After the conversation with Gabriel, I knew you had to go to Rose's homeland. So give me the pleasure—take the voucher and book the trip. Look at it as an early birthday present."

Lilly rubbed her thumb pensively over the logo of Garuda Airlines, an Indonesian airline. The goat belonged to Qatar Airways, the flight that would take her to Padang. All she had to do was book . . .

"Hello, Lilly, are you still there?" Ellen asked.

"Yes, I'm here. I'm still waiting for someone from *Candid Camera* to jump out and tell me it's all a joke."

"Lilly, we've known each other for more than half our lives. Have you ever known me to pull your leg?"

"No. But even so, this is too expensive, it's—"

"It's no problem for your rich friend. And you know I don't want anything from you in return. I simply want you to follow the trail of Rose and Helen. And for you to take charge of your own life again. By traveling alone you can prove to yourself—and Peter—that you can manage without him and do anything you want to. You have to break the spell that's been binding you. The violin was a sign, and I feel that it's changed something in you. So take the opportunity—you're ready to do it!"

Lilly was unable to say anything at first. Her friend was right; without a reason she would never have considered traveling to Indonesia alone, even if she could have afforded to. The violin had turned her life upside down. Or rather, Rose and Helen had.

"Let's talk about it this evening. Terence is pestering me," she heard Ellen saying. "But I'd advise you to book the flights before too long or they'll be gone. And should you decide to accept my gift, I'd suggest you use the time to find out all you can about Indonesia."

"All right. Thank you!" was all Lilly could say.

"Excellent. Love you!" And she hung up.

It took Lilly a while to get over the shock. Her surprise slowly gave way to a joy and a fear she had never felt before. She had never flown any farther than London without Peter. Before coming here to see Ellen, she had hardly left Berlin. And now she was going to the other side of the world? The thought gave her butterflies in her stomach, and her hands went cold.

She called the number of the travel agent that Ellen had given her and booked the flights that would take her to Padang in just two days' time.

By the afternoon she had grown used to the idea that the trip was actually going to happen. She was still a little uneasy about accepting such a generous gift from Ellen, but she also knew that it would do her good.

And she wanted to go to Indonesia! She wanted to find out what had happened to Rose, and she also wanted to discover more about the life of Helen Carter.

She suddenly thought of Gabriel and realized she wanted to call him to tell him of her unexpected trip. But could she do that? He had been at Diana's for a couple of days, and the fact that she was going away was hardly earth-shattering news. But it was important to her, and she felt a desperate need to tell him.

She scrabbled for his cell phone number and dialed. Gabriel answered after the third ring.

"Lilly, what a surprise! Are you missing me that badly?"

The humorous tone of his voice dispelled her brief doubt that she was calling at an inconvenient time.

"I wanted to tell you something. It's . . . something . . . Something's come up."

"I hope it's nothing unpleasant. Is everything OK with you? Has your acquaintance's friend from Rome been in touch?"

"No, it's not that. There's something else . . ." Lilly took a deep breath. If she told him now, there would be no going back. "I'm flying to Sumatra in two days."

Those words coming from her mouth sounded so unreal. Gabriel also seemed surprised, since he said nothing for a couple of moments.

"Congratulations!" he replied eventually, and Lilly was sure he had his impudent grin on his face again. "So we'll have to push back our dinner a little further still."

"I'm afraid so," Lilly replied, regretting it deeply. "But you must still be tied up with your . . . family matters."

"A bit, but it's not as bad as I thought. How come you're intending to go so soon?"

"Ellen says I should set off as soon as I can, while the trail is still fresh. Good old hunting wisdom."

"Have you any huntsmen in the family who can confirm that?"

Lilly giggled to herself. "No, of course not. But it's an incredible opportunity, and I think she's right when she says I should do this by myself to finally break free from the spell."

"What spell is that?"

Had she said too much? She hesitated a moment but decided it would be fine for Gabriel to know.

"After my husband's death I hardly went anywhere. I hid myself away, shut myself off in my own little world. The day I got the violin . . . something snapped. My view of the world shifted."

She paused briefly, listening for a reaction in the ether, but at the other end she heard only Gabriel's steady breathing.

"Anyway, my flight leaves in two days at ten in the morning. According to the schedule I'll be in Padang the following morning."

"That's good. I mean, that you're going. Not only for Rose and Helen but for you."

Did he sound a little disappointed? She felt like asking him whether he wanted to come with her—as head of the music school he must be able to afford it. But it wouldn't do.

"Even if you only manage to find a few pieces of the puzzle," he continued, "you'll have made the trip and broken the spell. Then you'll be free and you can find your way again. And apart from that, you'll have a whole lot to tell me—provided you don't forget about me completely."

"How could I?" Lilly replied with a smile.

"There must be a whole crowd of good-looking men in Indonesia who would turn your head."

"That may be the case, but I think . . ." She had almost told him that her head had been well and truly turned, but she stopped herself just in time. "I don't think I'm . . ."

She'd almost said the wrong thing again. Of course she didn't yet feel ready for a new relationship, but if she told him that, he might give up on any hopes he had in her.

"I think I understand what you mean," Gabriel replied, to which Lilly thought, I hope not! Please don't take it like that. "And I'll be waiting patiently until you get back. You haven't told me yet how long you intend to be away."

"Oh, it's only for a week."

"Really? I thought you were disappearing for at least a month."

"No, just a few days. But I hope it will be enough time to track them down. You don't happen to know anyone in Padang who could show me around a bit while I'm there?"

"No, unfortunately not. And even if I did, I should remind you that you've been told to carry this off by yourself. Even if it all comes off really badly, you'll still have a week to remember. And who knows what it will bring you."

***

Before Ellen came home from work, Lilly had already gained a little more self-confidence. She still felt as if she were in a dream, but when her friend sat down to dinner with her, wearing a broad smile, the last traces of doubt vanished, and she realized that in just two days she would be sitting on a plane bound for Jakarta.

"It's just a pity I can't take you with me," she said a little regretfully.

"Don't worry, Dean will keep my spirits up," Ellen replied with a shrug, looking affectionately at her husband, who for once had arrived home in good time for the evening meal.

"I don't doubt it, but . . ."

"It's your trip, Lilly." Ellen reached across the table and stroked her hand. "If it's as beautiful there as the pictures on the Internet promise, we can go back together for a vacation."

"Or I can take you there on a second honeymoon," Dean said.

"Did we have a proper honeymoon in the first place?" Ellen laughed.

"Of course. We went to Scotland, remember?"

"Oh my God," Ellen groaned.

Lilly suppressed a grin. She knew the story of the disastrous vacation well.

"You and me in a tent," Dean recalled. "You've got to admit it was romantic."

"It was romantic until the downpour. We froze our arses off."

Jessie and Norma giggled quietly. Probably no one at their school said that kind of thing.

"But then we found that castle."

"You mean the castle ruins!" Ellen gave her husband an affectionate smile. "But yes, it was romantic. As long as I had you with me it was romantic. And that's still the same to this day."

Lilly smiled, but she had a strange feeling inside. She thought again of Peter, but the pain was no longer so sharp. And when she imagined Gabriel taking her to Scotland sometime . . . It could rain and hail all it liked, and she wouldn't complain.

"Well? We're dying to hear what you've got to tell us," Dean said, tearing her from her thoughts.

"The woman at the travel agency said the hotel is very comfortable and quite old—perhaps Rose or Helen even stayed there," Ellen said. "There must be a few museums and an archive there, and you can make yourself understood well enough in English. Anyway, you're a grown woman, and the travel agent assured me that Indonesia is a fairly safe place. You'll be able to travel and carry on your searches, and if you don't find anything, just enjoy the exotic sights."

Lilly wasn't sure if she'd manage it all, but she'd see. She felt like she had once the grieving for Peter had reduced to a bearable level. The way ahead was unclear, and absolutely anything could happen. Then she had turned inward, had lost her courage and closed herself off to protect herself from being hurt by another loss. Now she would be daring to take a step or two outside herself, making herself vulnerable. But perhaps that was exactly what she needed.

"Will you bring us something back from Indonesia?" Norma burst out hopefully. From her sister's pleading expression she clearly felt the same way.

"Of course," Lilly replied. "They probably have some cool T-shirts there."

"Or jewelry," Jessie said.

"Now, now, young ladies, let's not get greedy," Ellen warned.

"It's fine," Lilly said. "If I see something suitable, I'll bring it back for you."

"Then I'd like something, too," Dean joined in with a laugh.

"Yes, a lucky elephant for your building sites. That's something you could really use right now."

Dean waved her away. "It's fine, don't worry, Lilly. Enjoy your flight and come back safely. That's all we ask."

21

Lilly wrung her hands in agitation as she waited for her bags to be checked in at the airport. She was going to Indonesia, flying to Sumatra! On her own! However much she was looking forward to the trip, at that moment she felt nervous and wished Ellen could have come with her. How would she find her way around a strange country? She didn't even speak the language. Don't be silly, she chided herself. If Gabriel could hear you, he'd die laughing at you.

Now she was wishing that she'd phoned him one more time the day before, but her preparations had not left her any time. Before she had realized, it was midnight, which left her just a few hours to toss and turn restlessly in bed.

In the morning she had found an e-mail from Sunny on Ellen's computer, saying that she couldn't send the video file by e-mail because it was too big.

The video! Lilly had almost forgotten it, but it made no sense to have it sent to London. Lilly wanted to watch it at home, when she would have the chance to visit her mother and ask her about it. She had replied that Sunny should keep the video safe until her return.

Now she was standing here, feeling as if she had swallowed a swarm of bees and wishing that she were already on her flight.

"Lilly!"

On hearing her name, her instinct was to look around, but she told herself there must be several Lillys around here, one of whom had probably forgotten something.

"Lilly!" the call came again.

This time she turned to see Gabriel waving energetically at her. What was he doing here? Wasn't he with his ex-wife? After all, he had said it would be for a while longer.

"For a moment there I was afraid you had a double," he said as he approached, clearly out of breath. "But that would have been a more rational explanation than a sudden loss of hearing on your part."

"What are you doing here?" she asked, amazed. "I thought you were at—"

"That's been sorted out. Diana's mother was in the hospital. I always got on well with the old lady."

"How is your . . ."

She almost said mother-in-law, but that wasn't exactly true, was it?

"My ex-mother-in-law is a lot better now. Diana was hit quite badly by it all, as her mother's been well until now. Since she knew how attached I am to Jolene, she told me about it, and as it seemed quite critical at first, I went to see her."

"So your relationship with your ex-wife . . ."

"Is on friendly terms." Gabriel finished her sentence for her. "Yes, we get on well again now. Not well enough to try again together—we're too different for that. But we talk and get in touch if anything out of the ordinary happens. Her new boyfriend is into sailing, a sport that has never really appealed to me."

Although Lilly hadn't asked for an explanation, she was glad that Gabriel had told her more than he had on the phone.

"So, after all that excitement, why are you here at the airport?" she asked.

"I wanted to see you." His smile bowled her over. "Since I'm going to have to do without you for a week. Apart from that, I have something here for you. I could have kept hold of it as the perfect bait to make sure you come back to me, but I think you should know about it now. It could shed a completely new light on your search."

Gabriel smiled at Lilly in anticipation, then handed her a letter. It was very tattered, as if it had been carried around for years. It was addressed to a Lord Paul Havenden at an estate near London.

"Where did you find this?" Lilly asked, using all her self-control to stop herself from tearing the envelope open immediately.

"Among the documents of Mr. Carmichael, our dear Rose's agent. I nosed around a bit and came across one of his descendants, who had a briefcase containing some of her grandfather's letters. When it became clear that Jolene would pull through, I made a small detour to visit the old lady. She had no desire to delve deeper into his past, but she had never had the heart to throw the briefcase away. When I called to see her, she gave me the documents without batting an eyelid. In fact, she looked relieved that I was taking some clutter off her hands."

"Or perhaps it was because she knew what the briefcase contained."

"Oh, I'm sure she knew! But as I said, I don't think she considered these letters to be of any value. As far as I know, the Havenden family no longer exists, so there's no danger of triggering a scandal."

"Scandal?" The paper in Lilly's hand suddenly felt warmer, which could only mean that all the heat had drained from her fingers.

Padang, March 27, 1910
My dear Paul,

You have probably long since forgotten me; in any case, that night on the plantation and your promise seem so distant to me that it could have been a lifetime ago.

You must be married by now, your plantation flourishing, and you probably have a brood of children. I'm sure you no longer think about our kisses and passionate embraces, but I can't forget you. Not because I still love you—no, I'm a stranger to such feelings now. Meeting you threw my life totally off course, making me wish sometimes that I had torn up the governor's invitation that took me to Welkom.

I'm writing to you now because that night bore fruit, a little girl. I can live with the guilt, and I have also succeeded in banishing you from my heart.

But I have recently been given a fatal diagnosis. Dr. Bruns is of the opinion that I only have a few months to live, a year at best. So I'm asking you again to care for your daughter because I am unable to. If you give your agreement to the bearer of this letter, he will tell you where you can find her.

If you don't wish to do that, you will never know her name.

Rose

After reading the words in an undertone, Lilly fell silent. She needed a while to take in what she had just read. Goose bumps ran over her skin. "Rose had a child?"

"A daughter, it seems."

"Why didn't anyone know about it?" Lilly looked in bewilderment at the handwritten page, which contained such disappointment and despair.

"Because our Mr. Carmichael could obviously keep a secret. And because he must have been aware of the scandal this letter would have caused if it had come to light. I charged one of my people at the school with finding out about the Havendens, and he unearthed something really interesting. According to him, Lord Havenden traveled to Sumatra with his wife, Maggie, to purchase a plantation. He must have met Rose sometime during that trip and got her pregnant."

Lilly shook her head in amazement. "This letter is incredible!"

"It is indeed. Rose was asking for help for her and Havenden's child because she was seriously ill. Another aspect we know nothing about, but which goes some way to explaining why she disappeared so suddenly. She must have died of the illness, which she doesn't go into detail about here."

"Why did Carmichael have the letter in his possession?"

A smile spread over Gabriel's face. "How about we talk about it over coffee? There's a bit of time until your flight, isn't there?"

Lilly had to smile, too. He had come all the way here to show her the letter, even though she was about to set off for Sumatra.

"Of course. We've got quite a while yet. I arrived too early."

"Excellent. Come on then. I know where we can get a coffee quickly and also have somewhere to talk."

Soon they sat, each with a mug of coffee, at a table in the airport's food court.

"So, what are your theories about it?" Lilly asked after taking a sip of the hellishly hot and hellishly insipid drink.

"Well . . ." Gabriel took a deep breath as if preparing himself for a long speech. "There are several possibilities. Firstly, Rose could have given Carmichael the letter and asked him to forward it. It's not out of the question that he tried to pass on the message, and Havenden either refused it or didn't even let Carmichael in."

"You don't think that would have been a bit mean? To get a woman pregnant and then simply leave her in the lurch?"

"Huh? It would be typical of an English aristocrat! But I've decided not to prejudge Havenden. The nobility of that time were trapped by their obligations, and that's often still the case today. The marriage could have been arranged. That's something that still happened often at the beginning of the last century. Perhaps he really did love Rose. And he might have wanted to do something for his daughter. Maybe he did. Whether or not that's the case, we can only find out if we know what this daughter was called."

"Why would Carmichael have kept the letter?"

"That's a good question. Havenden could have turned down Rose's request. Or Havenden could have agreed to the request, but he gave the letter back to make sure that no one found it who shouldn't."

"But if he did that, he would have made himself open to blackmail by Carmichael. If he was Rose's agent, he can't have had a very high opinion of the man who got his precious young star pregnant."

"Perhaps Carmichael did blackmail Havenden, who knows? The third possibility is that the agent withheld the letter, never handed it over at all."

"Why would he do something like that? After all, Rose was asking her former lover for help. I don't see anything wrong in Havenden having the chance to care for his daughter."

"You're right. Well, now I'm going to follow two directions—firstly, I'll pay Carmichael's descendants another visit and ask them if they'll dig into their family history a little. And secondly, I'll try and find the descendants of this Havenden. As you've read, he had a fiancée or a wife, and Rose's assumption that he had children with her could well prove to be true."

"The heirs will hardly be delighted to find out about an illegitimate child."

"Well, that depends. Illegitimate children have always been an occurrence in noble families. And it happened ages ago. If the child was born sometime between 1902 and 1909, he or she will certainly be dead by now."

"How do you get to those dates?"

"Rose's life is well documented up to 1902, and after that there are a few gaps, such as a six-month period when it isn't clear where she was. Perhaps that gap is mere coincidence, or perhaps it was when she gave birth to the child."

Lilly nodded. She had an idea. "Rose's child could have had children, too. And there could be grandchildren who have a legal claim to her inheritance. I don't know much about it, but I imagine a DNA test could still prove a family relationship. Those people would then be the rightful owners of the violin!"

"Whoa, slow down, Lilly. Think about it—there's someone else in our story: Helen. She was the violin's last owner. It's her descendants who would have a claim to it. But I stress *would*, as her family could have sold the violin just as Rose's did."

Lilly sighed. "You're right. So we're still a long way from finding out who the violin really belongs to."

"You'll have to carry on your detective work for a while longer. But first, enjoy your days in Sumatra—and use them well. While I continue to research among the people here, you see whether you can find any trace of Rose and her child. And at the same time you can also look out for anything about Helen Carter. I reckon there's still a lot more to discover about her."

"I will," Lilly promised, looking into his eyes.

A thought seemed to enter his head but remained unspoken.

"We'll keep in contact, OK?" he asked.

"Of course. I'll keep you updated."

"And I will you."

They looked at one another briefly; then Gabriel suddenly leaned forward and kissed her.

At first Lilly froze, but as he put his arms around her and drew her to him, she yielded. The touch of his lips sent a warm shiver down her spine.

"I hope I haven't lost the chance of you writing to me," he said softly as their lips parted.

Lilly stared at him in confusion, at first unable to reply.

"Of course not," she managed to say. "On the contrary."

Gabriel nodded with a smile. "OK, I believe we're a little closer now to our dinner together. As soon as you're back from Sumatra, I'll be taking you up on it, you understand?"

Lilly nodded. Her cheeks felt feverish, and she wanted to press her ice-cold hands against them. Gabriel held her tight and looked into her eyes for a moment more before they had to part.

***

During the flight to Dubai, Lilly couldn't get the letter out of her mind. Rose had a child by an English nobleman. What had become of the child? Had she vanished without a trace, like her mother? After Rose died, had the child been sent to an orphanage or a foster family?

Anything was possible, and Lilly decided to make a list of the places she needed to visit to look for information. As Rose was half English, it was possible that her child had been baptized. If there were any surviving church registers, the baptism would be in there. Gabriel had limited the period to between 1902 and 1909—the truth must lie somewhere between those dates. Looking through church records for an eight-year period would still mean a lot of work, and she wasn't sure she would be able to manage it in just a week.

They landed in Dubai at a quarter to seven. Lilly had two hours to rest a little before the plane took off for Jakarta. First she got something to eat, and then she strolled through the shops in the airport building, although she had no real desire to buy anything. She finally found a place in the terminal and settled down to watch the people who were hurrying through the airport.

She saw a very stout Arab man in a traditional djellaba accompanied by two women in burkas. She sometimes saw similarly dressed women in Berlin, but these burkas were richly embroidered, and the man who walked before them was clearly wealthy. A group of Arab businessmen were deep in a lively conversation accompanied by animated gestures. The Germans, on the other hand, stood stiffly when talking to one another. As well as the traditionally dressed Arabs, there were also many Asian and European tourists; most of them, like her, were only changing flights here.

A glance at her watch told her that only a few minutes had passed, and she got out her travel guide. The illustrations were wonderful and awoke memories in her. Memories of a travel fair she had visited with Peter. They had made travel plans for the future, for when he had more of a foothold in his job. At times like that she could not have imagined that it would never happen—at least not together.

"You haven't found anything to take your fancy in the duty-free shops then?" came a voice next to her.

Lilly almost dropped the guidebook in surprise. The man, who had sat down on the seat beside her, gave her a broad smile. His dark blond hair was graying a little at the temples, and his face was tanned. His words were colored by a distinct Dutch accent.

"No, I couldn't think of anything to buy there. I've got all I need in my luggage."

"Are you going to Padang, too?"

"Yes," Lilly replied, a little perplexed, and closed the guidebook. "How do you . . . ?"

The man pointed at the guidebook. "I'm good at guessing. I think I saw you on our plane. Qatar Airways, wasn't it?"

Lilly nodded, completely caught off guard.

The man seemed to be considering something for a moment before adding, "I'm Derk Verheugen, and you're the first German I've seen here since we landed."

"Really?" Lilly asked in amazement before it occurred to her that she ought to tell him her name.

"I swear it."

"Lilly Kaiser," she said by way of introduction.

"Pleased to meet you. I hope I'm not disturbing you. It's just that it's nice to find a kindred spirit. What takes you to Padang? Or is that a bit too personal?"

Lilly was taken aback, and a little afraid of him, since no one had ever been so forward with her. Besides, he wasn't her type, although his blue eyes looked friendly, and he didn't seem any more than ten years older than she was.

Perhaps he's a human trafficker, she thought uneasily. She was relieved to see that there were two airport police officers standing nearby, just in case, and hoped she would at least be free of him once they got on board the plane. "I'm on the trail of a violinist," she replied.

"Are you a concert promoter?"

Lilly shook her head. Perhaps he's not such a madman after all, she told herself, still careful to stay on guard.

"No, I'm researching a violinist who lived more than a hundred years ago. She vanished without a trace in Sumatra. And she had a child there, whom no one knows anything about."

"She probably met a rich plantation owner. There used to be a lot of them on the island."

"But that wouldn't be a reason for her to disappear! No, I believe there must have been something else. I'd like to find out what it was, and also why the violin she owned found its way into the hands of another violinist who was also born in Sumatra."

"It sounds very exciting. It almost makes me sorry I didn't study history."

"What do you do?" Lilly asked, realizing that her inhibitions were gradually receding. There was something about him that inspired trust, although it would show through more clearly if he weren't so direct.

"I'm a dentist."

"A dentist?" Lilly had expected all kinds of things, but not that.

"Don't worry, I've left my equipment at home," he joked. "I'm traveling for completely personal reasons and don't intend to be pulling any teeth. Unless you need it, that is."

"But I thought you didn't have your equipment with you."

"Oh, I'm sure something could be arranged." Verheugen laughed. "But you're right—I'm not planning anything like that. I'd rather be free to enjoy the beauty of the country."

At that moment the flight was called.

"I think we should be going," Verheugen said cheerfully. "Do you think the person sitting next to you would change seats?"

"I doubt it." Lilly smiled. "But there's no harm in trying."

Of course Lilly's neighbor didn't want to swap, and they had no better luck on the next flight. Lilly was unsure whether she should be happy or sad about that. The Dutchman had a good sense of humor, and she felt sure he had a store of interesting anecdotes, even though his manner was a bit too direct for her. She appreciated the quiet presence of the Indonesian businessman sitting next to her reading some local newspaper, and she concentrated on her guidebook.

Minangkabau Airport was largely destroyed in the tsunami of 2004 and subsequently rebuilt in the style of the island's traditional buildings, she read before craning her neck to look out the window. Her book had told her that the extensive palm groves of the island could be seen when arriving from the air, but today they lay beneath a thick blanket of fog. Only a few isolated green mountain peaks emerged from the white veil.

The guidebook also stated that the green carpet of palms had numerous gaps caused by felling and clearance by fire, but the government was making efforts toward reforestation. Perhaps it was a good thing that the forest was hidden by fog.

She got a brief glimpse of the airport before the plane was readied for landing. The building was designed in the traditional Minangkabau style, with its layered pointed gables resembling a series of recumbent crescent moons. It seemed fitting, as did the name of the airline she had changed to in Jakarta—Garuda, which was also the national symbol. Garuda was a part-bird and part-human divinity reputed to protect the people of Indonesia.

What would she find here? Was there still a "moonlit garden" waiting for her to discover it? Would she find out what had become of Rose Gallway and how the violin had come into the hands of Helen Carter?

Dr. Verheugen was waiting for her in the airport building. Lilly was still not entirely sure what to make of him, but her instincts told her that he was simply being helpful. Perhaps he needed a bit of company, too.

"Have you got all your things?" He indicated her suitcase.

"Yes, and now I need a good sleep."

"I can understand that, but you should leave it for as long as you can to help accustom yourself to the time difference. Or you could have a little nap and set your alarm to wake you in time for dinner."

"Are you a regular visitor to Sumatra?"

Verheugen smiled. "I think of the island as a kind of second home. I come here twice or sometimes three times a year."

Lilly stopped herself from widening her eyes in surprise. When she thought how much Ellen had paid to get her here!

"I hope you're staying at a good hotel," he said.

"The Batang Hotel," Lilly replied, opening her guide to the relevant page. "But I only know what it says here in my guide."

"The Batang is very good. It's run by an English couple. It was built by Dutchmen, as far as I know, and it's been used as a hotel for a long time. I've only heard good reports from anyone who's stayed there."

"Where are you staying?"

"With some people I know in the city. I'm glad you've chosen the Batang—it's not far from me, and if you like I can show you where to find the archive where the documents from colonial times are kept. Don't expect miracles, though. There have been a number of earthquakes since then, and some items may have been lost forever."

"You'd do that? I mean, show me the archive?"

"Yes, I'd be glad to, provided you don't think I'm being intrusive. I realize it's one of my bad habits to be a bit impulsive—if I hear of something I can help with, I feel compelled to do it. If you think I'm acting inappropriately, I'll happily step back, but I'd be pleased to assist. If you like, I can also act as interpreter. Many of the documents were produced in Dutch, and although the archivists speak English, of course, you'll get a lot further with Malay and Dutch."

"But won't I be inconveniencing you?" Lilly asked a little uncertainly. Apart from Ellen, she had rarely met anyone who was prepared to help her unconditionally, without her having to ask. "You must have plans of your own."

"The person I want to meet isn't arriving for another two days, so I've got some time for you. And it's not every day I meet someone who wants to dig around in the colonial history of Sumatra. I'd be pleased to be at your service if you'd like to tell me a bit more about these two women. I need some exciting stories to tell my patients when I'm back in Amsterdam."

As if it isn't exciting enough simply to be here, Lilly thought. She was glad that she hadn't ignored or rebuffed Verheugen.

"Great, I'll look forward to it. Thank you for your help. I'll be pleased to tell you something about the former owners of my violin."

"Great. Shall we meet tomorrow at ten outside your hotel? I'll only stay around for as long as you need me. If I'm getting to be a nuisance, you only have to say."

"OK," she replied and shook hands with him. Verheugen smiled, and they went outside to the waiting taxis.

22

Padang, 1910

Helen ran as if she were fleeing from a pack of wild dogs. Her mother had gone off on her daily rounds later than expected, and even the maid seemed reluctant to budge from Helen's side. But now she was finally free to run upstairs and fetch the violin case. Completely out of breath, she reached the hedge and paused a moment to recover before slipping across the neighboring garden to the pavilion.

With a thumping heart and the violin under her arm, she carefully opened the door and breathed a sigh of relief as the dusty light falling through the window illuminated the figure in the blue dress. Her lips had regained their color, and she looked very calm as she watched the girl enter. While waiting, she had been writing something down in a notebook, which she hastily put aside.

"There you are!" she said with delight, reaching out a hand to stroke Helen's cheek.

"I'm sorry I couldn't get away before," Helen said, eager to apologize for being a few minutes late.

"It's fine. This pavilion is nice, hidden from the sight of people on the street. And I'm certain now that no one lives in the house, so we won't be disturbed."

She took the violin case from Helen and opened it. As she gently ran her finger along the strings, a melancholy expression came to her face. It was as if she were looking at the picture of a friend who had died a long time ago. Helen had noticed the way her mother looked at the picture of her sister, who had been dead for several years. She always looked like that, and after a while she would turn away in embarrassment and wipe away a few tears with a handkerchief. But this lady wasn't crying as she carefully lifted the violin from the case.

"Have you tried holding it in position?" she asked. "Do you know how to hold it?"

Helen shook her head. "No, I didn't dare."

"But you must have looked at it?"

"Yes, of course!" Helen replied.

"What do you think of it?"

"It's wonderful!"

"Did you see the rose on the back?"

Helen nodded eagerly. As soon as her mother had left her alone, she had rushed to her room and taken a look at the violin. She had never seen anything so beautiful. When her fingertips touched the varnished wood, as gently as if it could disintegrate at her touch, she knew that this was the instrument she wanted to play.

"Good, then that's something I don't need to show you."

"Why does the violin have the rose on it? Did someone paint it on?"

"No, darling, the rose was burned into the wood by the person who made it. He wanted to make it especially pretty. Fortunately it doesn't affect the sound."

"Can you play it for me so I know what it sounds like?" Helen asked.

The lady hesitated before nodding. She tucked the violin beneath the left side of her chin and began to draw the bow across the strings. Although she tried not to play too loudly, the melody filled the pavilion. She hardly played for a minute before laying the bow down.

"I'm afraid that will have to be all for now."

Helen beamed at her. "That was beautiful! Will I be able to play like that one day?"

The lady gave her a broad smile. "I hope you'll be able to play a lot better than I do, but let's start by teaching you how to hold it."

She got Helen to position the violin exactly as she had, although she did not allow her to use the bow but made her hover it above the strings. It seemed difficult to Helen at first, but she kept trying until the lady was satisfied.

"What's happened with your music teacher?" she asked when she allowed Helen to take a short break—something that Miss Hadeland never did.

"Mama dismissed her for a while," Helen replied, not without a little malicious satisfaction. Miss Hadeland had looked really silly when her mother had reprimanded and suspended her for four weeks.

"Once you have given some serious thought to your teaching methods, we'll let you continue with the lessons," Ivy Carter had said as she sent the teacher on her way. "If you don't reconsider, we'll not only cease to employ you, but we'll spread the word that you strike your pupils. I find it hard to believe that another family would take you on in that case."

Miss Hadeland could have claimed that she had plenty of other work and did not need their money, but she said nothing, merely creeping meekly from the house. The sight of her leaving had caused Helen to clap her hands with pleasure. The hated piano lessons were over for the time being.

Before the lady could tell her any more, Helen was distracted by a movement. A huge, colorful butterfly was fluttering at the windowpane, clearly unable to see that a glass pane separated it from the outside world. When the lady noticed it, she smiled.

"Look, here's your first audience! But the butterfly will have to wait a while for your playing to be good enough to enjoy."

"Do you think butterflies can hear?"

"Why shouldn't they? I believe that even plants can hear. It's said that if they hear beautiful music they will grow better." The lady fell silent for a moment before adding, "Why do you think the jungle grows so well on this island? There's always music here somewhere in the evenings, and the monkeys have their songs, too."

"Is that true?"

The lady nodded. "Later, when you can play properly, you can try it out. But now we have to practice the fingering. I'll tell you where to put your fingers and sing you the note the violin would make. I hope my singing won't hurt your ears."

Helen laughed, and the lady showed her what it would sound like. The girl was struck by her fine singing voice. She was sure she could easily have been an opera singer.

The lesson flew by. Helen was annoyed that she had lost those precious minutes when she had not arrived on time. Her friend comforted her. "We'll see each other again on Tuesday. Try to play whenever you can. Even if your playing doesn't sound quite like mine, don't give up. One day you'll get there—you wait and see!"

Back in the house, Helen's cheeks felt flushed with excitement. Since she heard the sounds of the maid moving around, she quickly ran upstairs to prevent her from seeing the violin. She would have liked to practice, but a coach stopped outside the house and her mother got out.

She might have more luck the next afternoon. The lady was right—the sounds she made with the instrument could not be called playing, but if she practiced a little, the melodies would soon sound sweeter.

From then on Helen practiced everything the lady showed her on Tuesdays and Thursdays, but only when her mother was not at home.

The maid, who was supposed to be looking after her, had other things on her mind. She had recently begun to meet Jim, the neighbors' stable boy, in secret behind the stables. That meant that Helen had at least one extra hour every day—an hour in which she withdrew to the attic and played.

How different the tunes sounded when they came from the instrument! When she'd first started practicing, she only had the sound of the mystery lady's singing in her head, but now she heard the violin properly—and it was much louder than she had thought at first. She had no sheet music, so it was left to Helen to remember not only the fingering but also the lady's voice. She built up a small repertoire, which she would have loved to play for her friend, but during their lessons the lady still insisted on Helen playing silently or to the accompaniment of her soft voice.

But when she allowed Helen to rest, the mystery lady, whose name Helen still did not know, would make up for it by telling her wonderful fairy stories about girls with golden fish or a princess who slipped from an egg like a chick. Sometimes she brought Helen a few sweet treats. Helen's favorites were the green balls filled with palm sugar and coated in dried coconut.

"Make sure you don't eat too many," the lady warned her once when she gave her a whole bag full. "If your mother sees you aren't hungry, she'll suspect something, and that will put our secret in danger, and I won't be able to come anymore."

"Don't worry, I'll keep a few back," Helen assured her. Under no circumstances did she want to lose her lovely lessons with her friend, especially as she felt that she taught her far more than Miss Hadeland ever had. She sometimes found herself wishing that she could introduce her friend to her mother and have her as her real music teacher.

She suggested it once, and the mystery lady's expression darkened.

"You mustn't ever tell her about me." The lady's voice was as friendly as ever, but Helen felt she had almost crossed a boundary that would cause her to lose the lady's friendship.

"I promise I won't say anything," she replied quickly. "Honest. It would just be so lovely if you could be my proper music teacher. If you could hear what I sound like playing the violin."

"Maybe I will one day," the lady replied, but she looked so sad, as if she believed it would never happen.

***

A few weeks later, Helen's mother had a visit from some of her friends and neighbors. They met occasionally for afternoon coffee at each other's houses in turn. This time it was Ivy Carter's turn to host.

She spent the whole day before in the kitchen with the maid and the cook, baking cakes and grinding coffee beans. Since Helen was forbidden from nibbling at any of the cakes, which gave out a wonderful smell, she got the violin out from under her bed and practiced her fingering in silence, imagining the associated sounds.

Since the visit of the friends and neighbors fell on a Wednesday, she was still able to see her friend the day before, although she had to be so much more careful because her mother was not going out but spending the day baking in the kitchen. After making sure that no one was watching her, she ran to the hedge and soon afterward entered the pavilion. Once again she found the lady writing.

"What are you writing?" Helen asked, since, as usual, the lady quickly tucked the notebook away in her corset, which had begun to fit ever more loosely over the recent weeks.

"A diary," the lady replied. "I'm writing down everything that happens to me each day."

"Do you also write things about me?"

"Oh, I write a lot about you."

"Why?" Helen asked, wide eyed.

"Because I like you and enjoy being with you."

"Can I read it sometime?"

The lady smiled at her. Her lips were a little blue again, and she looked like Helen's mother did when she had one of her migraines.

"Perhaps. One day, certainly, because I'll give it to you. Then you can read about what you were like as a child. I've also written down all the stories I've told you. When you're grown up, you can tell them to your own children."

Helen liked the sound of that, even though she found it difficult to imagine how she would look as an adult woman. Maybe like her mother? Would she still be playing the violin then?

The next day Helen was unable to practice, as her mother's friends arrived for coffee and she not only was dressed in a frilly dress that scratched and pinched but was expected to sit still the whole time, on her best behavior and responding politely when the ladies remarked how big she had grown. Helen knew all too well that she had not grown big—she was still way too small for her own liking. And at seven years old she was well aware that it was a waste of time to be sitting there listening to all kinds of strange gossip instead of practicing up in the attic.

Helen sat by her mother's side on the sofa, suppressed the urge to swing her legs, and listened to a thoroughly boring conversation. The only consolation was that she could now try the delicious cakes her mother had baked.

"My goodness, Mevrouw Carter, who here plays such heavenly violin music?" asked one of the neighbors suddenly as she put down her coffee cup.

Her mother's perfectly plucked eyebrows shot up.

"Violin? You must have misheard, Mevrouw Hendriks. No one plays the violin in this house."

"Really?" the neighbor insisted, her eyes on Helen. "Until recently I'd always heard your daughter playing the piano. She hasn't changed her instrument then?"

Ivy looked at her daughter in confusion.

"Helen? Could you explain the meaning of this to us? Have we recently acquired a violin-playing ghost in the house?"

At first Helen did not reply. She was too busy feeling annoyed that her neighbor had such good ears. But how could she know that the violin could be heard so far afield? And that no secret could last forever?

Helen slowly got up from her chair. She ignored her mother's bewildered shaking of her head. She was not a woman to get worked up over nothing, and she was unlikely to follow her daughter. Because of the visit, the reprimand for Helen's behavior would not come until the other women had left. But Helen didn't care anyway.

"Helen? Where are you going?" her mother asked.

Helen walked resolutely forward, ignoring her mother. She left the parlor with its amazed occupants behind and had hardly crossed the hall before she began to run. She stormed up the stairs faster than any adult could have run after her. Her heart was racing madly. What should she do? Hide? Wait until her mother came up and wanted to know what was happening?

After slamming the door shut behind her, she leaned against it for several long moments, listening. Nothing happened. No footsteps on the stairs, no voice calling to her. Did her mother not mind what she had done? Or was she merely too shocked to do anything? Were her neighbors complaining about her behavior?

Helen had to do something. With a racing heart, she crawled under the bed and brought out the violin. She opened the lid of the case and ran the tip of her finger down one of the strings. Silently, she asked the instrument: What should I do?

The violin answered in its own way—with a soft tone that sounded like the wind sweeping around a corner of the house. Did this mean it was time to bring the secret out into the open? But what about the mystery lady? She had told her never to say anything to anyone. What should she do now that her neighbor had already heard her?

Since the violin had given away her secret, she couldn't be seen as the guilty one if she broke the promise. After a few minutes, she had made her decision, and it brought such a feeling of relief. Keeping a secret was very difficult, especially from people you loved. Helen closed the case again, took hold of the handle, and carried it out.

She heard an excited babble downstairs. The women were talking away at her mother, some saying that Helen was badly brought up, others merely curious as to what it was all about.

Silence fell as Helen entered the room. All eyes were on her, but no one said a word. After staring at her for a moment, their eyes wandered to the violin she was holding. Helen knew that if she wanted to keep it, she had to show them she could play—otherwise her mother would demand that she give the violin back, and there was no way she wanted to do that.

Slowly, ignoring the women's looks and her mother's questions, Helen put the case down on the floor, snapped open the lid, and picked up the violin. A murmur ran through the visitors.

"Ivy, what—" began one of the women who knew her mother a little better than the others.

But before she got an answer, Helen had tucked the violin under her chin and begun to play—feeling through the way she thought the notes sounded best. She played an old song that her mother had once sung to her when she was very little. The tune was very simple, but it was pretty. Helen had often wanted to play it on the piano, but Miss Hadeland had never allowed her to.

She finished her recital, and silence reigned. The notes had flown through the window, and Helen imagined them falling like dewdrops to the ground and helping the flowers to grow.

With a serious expression she packed the violin back into its case and waited for the opinion of her listeners. They were speechless. Helen wanted to ask whether Mrs. Hendriks had heard that song, but she had used up all the courage she had when she ran out and then brought the violin to light. Now she felt a little shrunken—so much had just been taken out of her.

After a while, Ivy rose. Her face was pale, but she didn't look angry. Instead, her eyes were shining with tears.

"That was wonderful, Helen," she said, going down on one knee before her. "Who taught you to play like that?"

Helen pressed her lips together. She had already given so much away. Could she now tell her mother about the lady—the lady who had shown her how to hold the violin, the lady who taught her where to place her fingers on the fingerboard to produce the best sound? How could she betray the trust of the lady who had taught her to play in silence so that she could practice even when her mother was at home?

"I taught myself," she said. "I practiced every day when you were out. Playing out loud."

"But why did you do it in secret?" her mother wanted to know. "And where did you get this beautiful violin?"

It had been obvious that the questions would come. Her mother knew full well that there was no such violin simply lying around in the attic. The piano on which Helen always practiced had belonged to her mother, but the violin . . .

No, she shouldn't say it; she shouldn't betray the mystery lady!

"Helen, please tell me," her mother asked in that gentle voice that Helen had never been able to resist.

The earth suddenly began to shake beneath her.

23

The next morning Lilly felt as though her head were filled with cotton. Thanks to the hotel's Wi-Fi, she had sent Ellen a short e-mail the previous evening to say she had arrived safely. She had also sent Gabriel a brief message. She hadn't received a reply from either of them, but she was reassured to know that these two people who were so important to her knew she was all right.

She had intended to follow Verheugen's advice, but she had been so tired that, despite hearing her alarm clock, she had ignored it. When she came to, it was three o'clock in the morning. She had been unable to go back to sleep, so she read her guidebook, making notes of places she wanted to visit.

In the solitude of the room she grew pensive. This was not going to be a relaxing vacation. She had too much to do, and the pressure to find something out was too great. Would she manage to discover any trace of the two violinists or how the violin was connected to her? It was now completely irrelevant whether the violin originated with her family or Peter's. And if nothing else, she had to overcome the reserve that she had wrapped herself in since Peter's death. Perhaps she would finally succeed in doing so and would be able to allow people to really reach her and to let someone into her heart without being afraid of losing them.

Gabriel, she thought, closing her eyes with a smile. Perhaps he was someone she would allow to get close to her. His kiss had been more than enjoyable, and it had given her the feeling that he would be there when she returned. Why should she keep him at a distance? He was a very attractive man with a soul she wanted to dive into and explore. Perhaps she should let herself go a bit more when she got back . . .

When the hands of her clock approached seven o'clock, she went outside onto the balcony to watch the morning come to life. There was already plenty of activity on the street below her—men on mopeds were moving boxes about, clearly on the way to the harbor, where they would find fishermen pulling in their heavy nets. There was a gradual swell of noise from the traffic on the streets, which, as in all large cities, was never really still, and the occasional shout rose above the hubbub. A truck struggled up the street and came to a standstill outside the hotel.

Lilly was a little envious of the guests on the other side of the building. The view from their rooms would be of the harbor and the old Dutch galleon moored in a narrow branch of the river. The hazy, pink morning sky must look wonderful over the water.

When the street noise became too much for her, she turned away and went to check her e-mails again. Ellen had not replied, and there was still no word from Gabriel. The sun might be rising here, but it was probably still evening in Europe.

After breakfast, a little before ten o'clock, she went downstairs to the hotel lobby. It wasn't really her style to be going around an unfamiliar city with a complete stranger, but Verheugen seemed to have no ulterior motive, merely wishing to help her in her search, even though she had told him very little so far. Was he really only being friendly and unusually helpful? Could it be that the Dutch were just more open than the Germans?

She had only been waiting for a few minutes when Verheugen emerged from one of the open-sided minibuses Lilly had seen on the way there. The sky-blue vehicle was adorned with an airbrushed portrait of a movie couple that reminded Lilly of a Bollywood advertisement.

She shouldered her bag and went to meet Verheugen, who was wearing a fresh white, lightly embroidered shirt and long khaki pants.

"Good morning. Did you sleep well?" he asked.

"Kind of," Lilly replied honestly. "I wanted to follow your advice, but I was too weak willed."

"Don't worry, a ride in one of the local taxi-vans will soon wake you up."

"What do you mean?" she asked nervously. His words certainly didn't imply safe driving.

"Enjoy the surprise! Life would be boring without a touch of risk, don't you think?"

As they left the hotel, they were met by a confusion of people and vehicles on the street. The hot, sultry air was filled with a mix of smells in which gasoline predominated.

Among the Minangkabau, Lilly also saw a number of Chinese, as well as a few Europeans and Indians. The local women wore colorful head scarves and long skirts, as in many Islamic countries. Some of them puttered past on mopeds. She saw the minaret of a mosque in the distance. Sheer fatigue meant she had failed to hear the call to prayer the previous evening, but it had reached her in the morning when she showered.

On one building she saw a long fabric banner painted with a fairly kitschy-looking pair of lovers.

"That's an ad for a movie," Verheugen explained.

"It looks like a Bollywood poster."

"People here have similarly romantic taste, but Indonesian movies can be very different. Sometimes you'll find imports from India here, and of course subtitled Western blockbusters."

What must it have looked like here a hundred years ago? Lilly imagined people traveling in coaches and rickshaws.

She thought of one of the websites she had found when browsing the Internet for information about the country and wondered if cockfights were still held, and whether the shadow puppeteers for which Indonesia was famous still put on their shows into the small hours of the morning.

On the streets, the motorbikes, cars, vans, and bicycles were interspersed with the distinctive open-sided minibuses, some of which had some inventive additions. The din of the various noisy engines was accompanied by horns and loud music. Lilly noticed that there were no lane markings, and apparently no rules about who drove where. She saw no sign of any pedestrian crossings.

Lilly's head, already groggy, was reeling from the noise level. She jumped when a strange signal rang out from a bright pink minibus that had stopped right in front of them. It was similar to the sky-blue Bollywood van but was adorned with a swirling tribal pattern and a rear spoiler.

"I think he's here to pick us up. Come on!" Verheugen asked the driver something and then beckoned for Lilly to get in.

As the speakers pounded out loud music, the driver performed a veritable slalom through the stream of traffic. There was no chance of conversation in this vehicle. The three women and two men who were also sitting in the open-sided van seemed to know this, as they sat in silence, fanning themselves listlessly with their newspapers.

Although she tried to press herself as hard as she could into her seat, at every bend Lilly feared she would be flung out through the open door. Every now and then the driver stopped with a screeching of brakes, and some passengers got out while others climbed in. Lilly saw that the passengers paid before getting on and assumed that Verheugen had paid her fare.

After ten minutes the hellish journey was over. The driver hooted his horn and came to a halt by the sidewalk. Verheugen gestured for her to get out.

"I hope you're not feeling unwell," he said, after the vehicle with its loud music had raced away. "You look a bit green around the gills."

"I'll be fine," Lilly replied, although her stomach felt quite queasy. Fortunately it only lasted a few moments once her feet were back on solid ground.

They walked a block farther before Verheugen announced, "Here we are."

He indicated a park in the center of which was a large structure that looked very similar to the airport building. The museum also had a traditional crescent-moon roof—or, as Lilly had read in her guidebook, a "buffalo horn roof." The locals called this architectural style *rumah gadang*, which meant something like "big house."

"That's the Adityawarman Museum, Padang's main museum," Verheugen said. "It houses mostly Minangkabau artifacts, but there are also many exhibits from the colonial era, and it has a good archive. All that remains from the Dutch period is kept here."

"Have you been here to look for something before?"

"A few years ago I was seeking information about a specific house, and someone suggested I look here."

"Did you find what you were looking for?"

"Yes, and I was amazed at all the things they have."

As they climbed the red-tiled steps and passed a modern tower, Lilly stared in fascination at the roof and its numerous curved gables. Verheugen followed her gaze.

"Do you know why the Minangkabau design their buildings like this?" he asked.

"It has something to do with buffalo, doesn't it?"

"Correct. Have you heard of the buffalo fight?"

Lilly shook her head. "No, my travel guide didn't cover that."

"You should contact the publisher and suggest an addition." Verheugen smiled. "In the dim and distant past, a warlord from Java threatened to attack the island. To prevent bloodshed, the two kings agreed to set buffalo against one another instead of their warriors. The Javanese found the largest buffalo they could, while the Minangkabau let a buffalo calf go hungry for a while and fixed a long iron spike to its muzzle."

"Oh, I can guess what happened," Lilly exclaimed. "The hungry little buffalo rushed up to the big one, thinking it was a cow it could suckle for milk."

"Exactly! That was how the little calf killed the big buffalo, and the Javanese had to leave the island."

"It seems a very sensible solution for those times. In our country I'm sure they would have laid into each other with cudgels and swords."

"The Minangkabau are in fact a hospitable people. It didn't cost the Dutch much effort to colonize Sumatra. Later, when the economic situation worsened, the Dutch caused some harm here, but I'll tell you more about that later."

Lilly agreed, since she was incredibly excited to see what the museum would hold. Would she find out here about the church registers and Rose's daughter?

"You'll only find a few really old buildings here on Sumatra," Verheugen was saying now as he perched his sunglasses in his thick hair.

"Because of the earthquakes?"

"Yes, the earthquakes and other disasters. It's a miracle that there are still some houses from the early twentieth century here—we have the good quality of the structures to thank for that. This museum was built in the 1970s. It looks good for its age, doesn't it?"

The fans inside the museum did their best to freshen the air a little. The display cases were filled with magnificent clothing and household objects from past centuries. There was even a bride's headdress, the traditional *sunting*. Lilly wondered whether a woman could actually wear this huge, elaborately worked creation made almost completely of solid gold without hurting her neck.

It was not long before her companion had found someone who knew about the archive. After a brief exchange of words, Verheugen beckoned for her to join them.

The woman he had been speaking to wore a sky-blue scarf over her hair and a dark blue suit with a long skirt. Lilly was surprised when she greeted her in English.

"I'm Iza Navis, and I'll be happy to help you."

"She's the deputy curator of the museum and knows where the treasures are kept," Verheugen added, causing the woman, who appeared to be in her late twenties, to look a little embarrassed.

"I'll certainly do my best to help you as much as I can," she said modestly. "So, what can I do for you?"

"I . . . I'm looking for some church registers from 1902 to 1909." Lilly began with the first thing that entered her head, earning a look of surprise.

"Church registers?"

"Something like registers of births." Verheugen jumped to Lilly's rescue.

"Oh, of course," the curator replied. "We have a few church registers, as you call them. They were a donation from the estate of a church that was damaged in an earthquake in the past. Not many visitors are interested in them; that's why we keep them locked away. But if you don't mind waiting a moment, I can let you into the reading room."

The room was small and rather plain, containing a few desks with reading lamps and a bookshelf with titles all in Malay. Lilly and Verheugen took a seat after the curator told them they would have to wait a moment.

"What do you want with church registers?" Verheugen asked, getting out and polishing his reading glasses.

"Shortly before I left, I discovered that the violinist, Rose, had a daughter. I'd like to see if the baby was registered and baptized."

"Indonesia was struck by a few earthquakes in the early twentieth century. It could be possible that the mother and child were both killed in an accident."

"Whatever happened, Rose asked the father to care for the girl. Either he never received the letter or simply didn't care."

"Or he did care and rescued the girl while keeping her origins secret?"

At that moment the door opened and a young man wheeled in a number of thick old books on a small trolley. As well as church registers, Iza Navis had added a few bound volumes of newspapers from the period and a few other books that at first glance did not seem to have much to do with what Lilly wanted to know. She intended to glance through them, though, as she might be surprised.

Looking through the church registers turned out to be a difficult job, since many of them had suffered a great deal of water damage and had not been expertly dried out. Although Lilly had little knowledge of book restoration, she hated to see the way the pages had been allowed to stick together. These were valuable documents of a bygone age, kept here for posterity but not restored.

"This doesn't look good," Verheugen remarked after a brief look. "Perhaps I should have brought my equipment after all—a scalpel and tweezers could perhaps be useful for separating the pages without tearing them."

They set to work all the same, making sure to take great care. At first they only looked through the church registers; then, once they had seen enough, they turned to the bound newspapers, which were in much better condition but largely written in Dutch.

"If you see a name or a picture that makes you think the article would be of interest to you, pass it over to me, and I'll translate it for you," Verheugen offered.

The smell of old paper and mildew surged up to them as they leafed through the pages. The individual newspapers were not particularly thick, with most editions consisting of eight pages, including a whole page of advertisements for household goods, soap, pomade, and men's garters.

Lilly skimmed the text in search of a name she recognized. She looked at the pictures, which were mainly very old photos of colonial-era Padang, with the occasional view of sugarcane and tobacco plantations. There were family portraits here and there, but Lilly found no mention of Rose Gallway.

"I might have something for you here," Verheugen said after a while. He turned the book around and pointed to a name in the midst of a page of text that was completely incomprehensible to her.

"Does your violinist spell her name like this?" Verheugen asked.

Lilly nodded and felt a spark of hope.

"Can you please read what it says?" she asked as she stared at the photo. It looked as if something had collapsed.

"'Last Monday there was a regrettable accident in the vicinity of the harbor. A badly secured crane fell onto a group of workers who were being given their instructions by their overseer, Mijnheer Gallway. Three men were killed, including Mijnheer Gallway, who leaves behind a wife and daughter, Rose, the famous violinist, who has just given a series of concerts in her hometown.'"

So Rose's father had been the victim of an accident! Lilly was stunned. How would things have been for Rose and her mother after that? After Peter's death she had felt as though someone had ripped her soul from her body.

"It must have been a dreadful time for them," she remarked in a hollow tone, trying not to think of her own past.

"It is for anyone who loses a loved one." Verheugen seemed to have had his own experiences, if the deep furrow above the bridge of his nose was anything to go by. "It looks as though you didn't know about it."

"No, nor does the head of the music school Rose Gallway attended."

"Well, it was a long time ago. This newspaper is from 1902. And it happened in another country. Why should he know?"

"You're right. He hasn't done any research in Sumatra yet."

Lilly looked at the article for a while, regretting that she did not understand Dutch.

"It says that Rose had recently given a few concerts," Verheugen said. "Perhaps there'll be something about those in some earlier papers."

They went back to leafing through the pages. Verheugen unearthed eleven more articles from his volume. As the newspapers had been bound in reverse sequence, Lilly looked at the extracts in reverse order.

The two pictures accompanying the first article were particularly beautiful. One showed Rose standing between the governor and a man in evening dress, smiling almost shyly into the camera. The second picture was taken on the rear terrace of the house, looking out over a rather unclear moonlit landscape. The black-and-white photo only gave a hint of what a wonderful view there must have been.

Lilly gazed at the pictures as Verheugen translated the article for her. It told of how Rose Gallway had been invited by the governor to play at the annual reception for the region's plantation owners. What would the reception have looked like? What colors would the ladies' dresses have been? It took her back to her childhood, before they had a color TV.

The next articles were mainly concert reviews, which praised Rose's music and her charisma to the high heavens—the whole of Padang seemed enchanted by her.

And then Verheugen produced a real gem from the volume.

"Can that be true?" Lilly asked, as she looked at the small portrait of a couple in the middle of the small article. The photo caption revealed who the man at Rose's side was.

"What do you mean?" Verheugen asked.

"This is Paul Havenden. Lord Paul Havenden."

The man's face was turned away from the camera, which disappointed Lilly—but at least she had seen the man whom Rose had taken as her lover and who had got her pregnant. She quickly noted this article for a copy, fiendishly excited by the picture.

"Ah, the father of the unknown child," Verheugen said with an indignant snort. "I can understand why the woman wrote him that letter. In her shoes I'd have read him the riot act!"

"Perhaps there's an explanation for his behavior."

Verheugen shook his head. "I doubt it. He got his lover pregnant and then disappeared—I'm convinced of it."

Lilly looked at the young man's elegantly proportioned face. His profile reminded her a bit of Gabriel. Had Paul Havenden acted maliciously? Had he forgotten Rose once he returned to England? Or had there been obligations he was unable to release himself from?

"We should find out the whole story before judging him," Lilly said, still delighted with her find. Gabriel will be thrilled, she thought.

By the time evening came, they had some more clippings about Rose's performances, a report on her wardrobe for the final concert, and another one about her father's fatal accident. The name of Gallway, unfortunately, did not appear in any of the church registers.

What did you expect? she asked herself. Did you think you would solve the whole mystery on the first day? Be satisfied that you have a picture of her with her lover. Gabriel's sure to be delighted!

It was highly likely that when the Dutch left the island they had taken a lot of documents with them. It might be better to try looking in Amsterdam for more about Rose Gallway's daughter. If there were any documents from colonial times, they were sure to be kept in a museum of colonial history.

"I'm very sorry that you haven't found much," the deputy curator said as they returned the documents.

"Oh, we've brought some things to light," Lilly replied with a smile. "We're very grateful to you for letting us see the newspapers."

"If you'd like to see some more documents from the Dutch period, you should go by the governor's former weekend residence."

"Weekend residence?" Lilly wondered aloud before realizing that must be the house with the terrace shown in the photo. The house in which Rose Gallway played!

"It's a modern expression, I know. I couldn't think of a better word. The governor worked here in Padang, of course, but he had a country house outside the city, where he received visitors. It survived the earthquakes reasonably well, but over the years no one purchased it. If it remains vacant, it will have to be demolished one day."

"Can that be done so easily?" Lilly asked.

"I'm afraid so. There is such a thing as a protected monument here, but if buildings are in too much of a state of disrepair, they're demolished eventually."

"Isn't it worth making a museum out of it?" Verheugen said, speaking Lilly's thoughts out loud.

"It's possible, but sadly the funds just aren't available for it. And in any case, some people here still have an uneasy relationship with the colonial times. The state organizations consider it a greater priority to research the Minangkabau culture and present that to the public." Her tone was slightly regretful, even though she likely was Minangkabau herself.

"What will we find in the weekend residence?" Lilly asked. "Do you keep uncatalogued items there?"

"You could say that. There are a few boxes out there that we still don't have room for here. There's a custodian who keeps an eye on the house and its contents. If you tell him I've sent you, he'll let you in."

"Thank you very much; that's very kind," Lilly said, trying not to grin like someone with an eye on stealing the family silver. The house where Rose had played! Possibly even the house where she had met Paul Havenden. Would she be able to sense their ghosts there? Even if the boxes only held damp and rotted junk, she was sure the journey would be worthwhile.

"So? Shall we go and see the governor's house?" Verheugen asked as they left the museum. Twilight was creeping in, and the air was noticeably more humid.

"Yes, we must. Perhaps I'll find the door to the terrace shown in the newspaper photo."

"I'm sure you will—provided the custodian or collapsed ceilings don't bar your way."

"I'll need to find someone to take me there."

"That someone's standing right in front of you," Verheugen said.

"Really?" Lilly raised her eyebrows doubtfully. "Haven't I taken up enough of your time?"

"I don't consider it wasted time, but rather time well spent. I'd be happy to go up there and see what we find. If you've got a guilty conscience about that, you could invite me for a meal today. What do you say to that?"

"Provided you tell me where we can go. I don't know my way around at all."

Lilly thought of Gabriel, hoping that their dinner would happen soon after she returned.

"There's a very good restaurant near your hotel, where you can get excellent *rendang*. Or even a whole *makanan Padang*."

"What's that?"

"You have to think of makanan Padang as a kind of buffet. You're served with a number of different bowls containing various kinds of strongly spiced fish, vegetables, and rice. You choose what you want and only pay for what you've eaten."

"Sounds interesting."

"It is, but in some restaurants you have to keep an eye on the price. You can't go wrong with rendang. It's made from beef, also very spicy and served with rice. I hope you've got a strong stomach."

"No problem." Lilly was not afraid of spicy food. With Peter she had been to almost every Indian and Thai restaurant in town and, unlike him, had proved to be well able to tolerate hot seasoning.

"Excellent. Can I suggest that I pick you up in an hour? We can reward ourselves for all our hard work and drive away the smell of musty paper."

***

The restaurant that Verheugen recommended was full of people, a marker of its quality as well as making it difficult to secure a table. There was nothing for the two of them to do but join the line of waiting diners.

"If we're lucky, it'll take less time than we think," Verheugen said, causing Lilly to wish she could share in his optimism. Nothing ever seemed to be a problem for him. If he had to wait, he simply spent the time people-watching or talking.

Lilly gradually felt as if some of this spirit was rubbing off on her. Back in Germany, when faced with a restaurant full to bursting, she would have turned on her heel and left. Yet she was now standing here with no intention of going back to the hotel. She drank in the scents and sounds, the voices and the colors. Some of the locals were dressed in traditional colorful sarongs, while others were wearing white shirts and pants. The women's heads were, without exception, covered by colorful scarves.

A table was finally free after around half an hour.

"Believe me—it's worth the wait," Verheugen said as they sank down onto the cushions arranged on wide rattan mats. Between them was a low table with a pretty marquetry top. The waiter appeared almost immediately with the menus, which were bound in thick leather. They were partly in Malay and partly in Dutch. Every now and then there was also an English translation, although these were rather bad.

"What does this mean?" Lilly asked, pointing to a line of the menu.

"That? Coffee from the cat!"

"Coffee from the cat?"

"The coffee beans are eaten by a particular breed of wild cat and then excreted. The beans, fermented in this way, are used to make a very expensive coffee. You could get a whole meal here for the price of a single cup."

"I'm not sure I'd want coffee that's been . . ." Lilly shuddered.

Verheugen laughed. "It's a delicacy! It's highly prized here, and the pricey beans are ordered by connoisseurs from all over the world."

"Beans that have been excreted by a wild cat?"

"I can see that we should stick to *tuak*."

"As long as that doesn't come from inside an animal."

"No, tuak is kind of an early stage of *arak*. It's obtained from the flowers of the sugar palm and has a very low alcohol content."

"It sounds fine."

"It certainly is. So let's have that."

He had already given a discreet sign to the waiter, who appeared at their table in a flash. Verheugen ordered while Lilly looked at him with admiration.

"I've got no idea what you're saying, but your Malay is clearly very good."

"If you have the kind of connections I do with this country, you want to be able to speak with the locals without reminding them of the tales their grandparents told about the Dutch. There are still some who don't have a particularly high opinion of us."

Lilly must have had a questioning expression since he added, "Indonesia has a rather checkered history. Have you heard of the VOC, perhaps?"

"You mean the East India Company?"

"Yes, an association of Dutch merchants and seafarers. It has a very long history and, at times, a bloody one. Some governors of Sumatra and Bali were so cruel that the royal family stepped in and ordered the VOC representatives to moderate their conduct. When the VOC broke up in 1799, the climate improved, and there were fewer acts of cruelty. But voices were gradually raised against the colonialists. In the 1920s an independence movement arose to fight for freedom from the Dutch. During the Second World War, Indonesia was briefly occupied by Japan, and colonial rule was finally ended."

"With all that knowledge you'd make a good historian."

"Perhaps I will one day, after I retire. Or I'll become a travel writer and report on my trips around Indonesia. By that time I don't think I'll want to return to the Netherlands."

From what she had seen so far of Sumatra, Lilly could understand it.

He spent the evening telling her about everyday life here as well as a little about his dental practice, although that did not seem as important to him as Indonesia. Lilly wondered whether the person he was intending to meet here was his wife. Verheugen was an attractive man with a good sense of humor. The way he spoke of Sumatra and its customs revealed that his connection with the country was based on more than merely his love for the countryside and the people. He must have some personal link. Although she told herself it was none of her business, she couldn't help feeling interested in what the woman he might be meeting here looked like. Was she a pretty local woman like Rose's mother no doubt was? After seeing the local women, Lilly had decided that Rose must have owed her famed beauty above all to her mother.

"I hope the food wasn't too hot," Verheugen said as they stepped out into the night air. Although it was still quite warm, Lilly shivered a little. She always did when she came out from a warm restaurant. "Some tourists find it rather too much the first time."

Lilly shrugged. She could still feel the tingle of the spices on her lips, but it hadn't troubled her.

"I love spicy food," she replied. "It's never troubled me, but when I think of Peter . . ."

"Your husband?"

Lilly lowered her head. A gray cloud settled over her good mood.

"He was, yes. He died a few years ago."

"I'm sorry. I can imagine how you felt. My life has also been full of loss. But since I got to know this country, I do believe it's getting better all the time. I can promise you that, simply by being here, you'll be a different woman when you go back. And that happiness will accompany you from now on."

Lilly thought for a while about these words as she lay on her bed beneath the cool of the air-conditioning system and the protection of a mosquito net. She felt a creeping suspicion—was Verheugen perhaps not merely being friendly but actually harboring hopes? Hopes that she could not fulfill . . . All at once she felt uncomfortable. She found Verheugen eccentric in a nice way, and the fact that he was so willing to help her embarrassed her a little, although she was very glad of it. But she could not imagine him as her partner. She wasn't even totally sure about Gabriel in that role—definitely not Verheugen. Was that really what he wanted? Ellen would say she was taking it all too seriously, that even in this day and age there were still people who were altruistic.

You shouldn't assume anything where he's concerned, she told herself. This Dutchman's really friendly, and you shouldn't do anything to upset him. But if he does start showing any signs of wanting more, you'll have to put him right.

She finally closed her eyes and looked inside herself. Was the change Verheugen had spoken of already under way? Would she only notice it once she was back at Ellen's house? No, she could feel it already. And as her thoughts wandered with anticipation to London and Gabriel, she sank into sleep.

24

Padang, 1910

With the violin case hugged tight to her chest, Helen crouched in the grass and stared apathetically at her shoes. After the earth began to shake, everything happened so quickly. The visitors had scattered like frightened hens, and Helen barely had time to put her violin in the case before her mother had grabbed her by the arm and dragged her outside. They were hardly out of the house when the tremors got stronger. Stones broke away from walls, tiles rained down on the lawn.

Her mother led Helen into the garden, to the place she had always found the most boring, as nothing other than grass grew there.

"Lie down!" her mother cried, stretching out on the ground. Helen did the same but kept her violin case close by her, not wanting anything to happen to it.

The earth shook beneath them for a moment with great force before suddenly stopping. A silence followed that was more profound than anything Helen had ever heard. Even the monkeys, whose calls could be heard in the city, were still. The sounds of the sea could no longer be heard, almost as if the earthquake had swallowed the water. Antje

Zwaneweg always claimed that earthquakes caused deep rifts to open up in the ground, which swallowed everything around them.

And now here she sat. Was this the punishment for betraying the mystery lady? Perhaps she really had been a magic fairy! But could her rage be so terrible when she had given her such a beautiful gift?

"Helen, Ivy!" She heard her father's voice. "Thank God nothing's happened to you."

Helen's mother, who had been as silent as her daughter the whole time, got to her feet. "James, you're here at last!"

Helen's father drew his wife into his arms and kissed her.

"I'm sorry I couldn't come any earlier. A number of houses in the city have collapsed. There are so many people dead."

"My God, that's awful! Do we know any of them?"

"I don't know yet, but I've heard that the victims were mostly natives and Dutch. Since my help was no longer needed, I ran straight back here to look for you."

He bent down to Helen. "Are you all right, little one?"

Helen nodded without raising her eyes. She kept her gaze fixed firmly on her shoes, hugging the violin case tightly. She sensed her father exchanging a look with her mother, and she knew how her mother could communicate with her husband without saying a single word.

"Where did you find that case?" Helen's father asked. He was about to reach down for it when her mother said, "It's pointless. She won't let go of it."

"Is it so important to you?" her father asked, his voice full of understanding. Helen nodded.

"She's had quite a shock with the earthquake," Ivy remarked. "And just before . . . Just before that she played us all something on the violin that's in that case."

Her father looked at Helen for a moment and then placed a hand gently under her chin. He looked into her amber eyes for a long moment before asking, "So you have a violin?"

"Yes," Helen answered truthfully before her tears began.

"Why are you crying?" Her father gently wiped the tears from her cheeks with his thumbs.

"I'm worried you'll take it away from me," she said.

"But why would we do that? Unless you know of a reason?"

Helen suspected what her father really wanted to know and shook her head.

"No, it belongs to me. I haven't stolen it."

"Who did you get it from? Or did you find it in the attic, perhaps?"

It would have been easy to answer yes to her father's last question, but Helen knew that would make her a liar. Like her mother, he knew what was in the attic.

"Where did you get it from?" her father asked again.

"I can't tell you."

Her father's eyebrows shot up. "Why not?"

"Because I promised."

Her father sighed. He was not a man to be easily annoyed, but he hated anyone concealing things from him.

Fear overtook Helen. Could she tell him the truth? Or would that cause something else dreadful to happen?

"Who did you make the promise to?" he asked, a hard, threatening edge creeping into his voice.

"I can't say." Helen looked pleadingly at her father. "Please, Daddy, don't make me say any more."

Now her father looked at her mother.

"She can play," her mother said. "She came down earlier and played us a tune."

"Perhaps Miss Hadeland . . ."

"I doubt it. She's so besotted with the piano. It seems as though our daughter has chosen herself another instrument." She gently stroked her child's head. "Some things can't be denied forever."

Helen didn't know what her mother meant by that, but she didn't give it a second thought. At that moment all she wanted was to keep her violin—even though the earthquake had happened, an earthquake she might have caused with her betrayal.

"Could I have a look at the violin?"

Helen pressed her lips together. Fresh tears ran from the corners of her eyes. Her thin arms were closed around the case like iron bars.

"You won't take it away from me, will you?" the little girl asked.

"I promise. I only want to look at it."

Helen trusted her father. She released her grip and set the case down before her. The sound of the locks snapping open seemed excessively loud, and as her father touched the violin, she shuddered as if he had suddenly touched her.

"What a beautiful violin," he murmured, carefully turning it in his hands. He saw the rose on the back and turned pale.

"Ivy . . ."

He was unable to say more than his wife's name. He showed her the violin, and her hand flew to her mouth in alarm. They were now communicating with their eyes, as they always did when Helen was not supposed to hear. She was sure they must be asking each other whether she had stolen it after all. She was arming herself mentally against the accusation when her father suddenly said out loud to her mother, "I think you're right. There are some things that can't remain hidden forever."

A second round of silent looks passed between them before he laid the instrument back in the case.

"Who was it that taught you to play the violin?"

"I taught myself."

Of course it was not the whole truth, but if she had revealed all, she would have betrayed the lady.

"You're a very special girl, Helen." Her father closed the case and took his daughter in his arms.

"What's going to happen with the violin now?" Helen felt like snatching the case back up into her arms.

"As long as no one asks for it back, you can keep it," her father replied after a moment's consideration. "But you'll understand that I'm going to ask around to see if a violin has been reported stolen anywhere. We don't want anyone to be sad because they're missing their instrument, do we?"

Helen nodded with a smile, since she knew that the mystery lady would not ask for the violin back.

After that, her mother frequently asked where the violin came from, but she never received an answer. Helen was sure that the earthquake had been a warning. If she revealed any more of her secret, something even worse might happen to them.

***

Once the mess left in the wake of the earthquake had been cleared up, her music lessons with Miss Hadeland were resumed. At first her teacher was less than pleased that Helen had abandoned the piano for the violin.

"The violin is an instrument for gypsies!" she complained to Helen's mother. "The piano is far more suitable for a young lady who wants to be thought well of in society."

"But you said yourself that Helen wasn't making any appreciable progress on the piano. She may have become bored by playing it, or"— she raised a hand to silence Miss Hadeland's protests—"or the piano simply isn't her instrument. Perhaps you should hear how she plays the violin. I'm sure you'll change your mind."

Helen, who had followed the conversation from a chair near the door, now stood as if her mother had given her an unspoken command.

Unhurriedly, she took the violin from the case, silently asking it not to cause another earthquake. All she really wanted to do was learn how to play. After all, that was what the lady had wanted her to do. To play.

As she positioned the bow on the strings, Miss Hadeland made a face. "Look at how she's holding the violin. You have to stand up straight when playing!"

"Let Helen try it her own way first," her mother said. Although her voice was calm, it carried an underlying threat that held the music teacher back from criticizing Helen further. She sat tight lipped, stiff in her high-backed chair, her expression indicating that she did not expect Helen to produce a single clear note from the violin.

Determined to show her that she could play perfectly well, Helen drew her bow decisively across the strings.

As the first notes resounded through the music room, she saw from the corner of her eye that Miss Hadeland's face was transformed. Her arrogant expression vanished, and her mouth gaped as if she were witnessing a miracle. It gave Helen the confidence to play well, and she immersed herself in the music, her heart seeming to beat in time to the rhythm of the piece.

When she had finished, she felt weightless. Breathlessly she set the violin down, the sweat cooling on her body. A wonderful clarity came to her mind, as if a fresh wind had blown in through the window to drive away the mustiness.

Silence reigned for a few minutes. Her mother looked expectantly back and forth between her daughter and the music teacher. Helen stared straight at Miss Hadeland. She didn't like what she saw.

"What's the matter, Miss Hadeland?" Helen asked fearfully. She thought she had played well. She was sure her friend would have been pleased with her. But the music teacher's eyes remained fixed for a long moment on the violin in her hand.

"Nothing, it's nothing," she finally managed to say. "It was a lovely performance."

"So, do you believe it would be worth teaching her?"

"Certainly," Miss Hadeland replied a little woodenly. "Of course she still has a lot to learn—in particular she has to get rid of this . . . unusual style, but I'm sure that she has more talent for it than the piano. It's not everyone who can master this art."

Ignoring her final sentence, Helen's mother immediately said, "Very well, then please teach her. We'll increase your pay a little, as I believe it will be worthwhile for Helen to master the instrument properly."

Miss Hadeland nodded, and her glance fell on the violin, which was now lying dormant on its velvet bed in the case. Helen saw a momentary envy flare up in her music teacher's eyes before she appeared to get her feelings under control.

"Thank you, Mrs. Carter. I'll do my best for her. Perhaps the world will soon be seeing a new child prodigy."

Helen did not believe that her talent was the stuff of prodigies. She found it much easier to play the violin than to bring forth complicated melodies on the piano, but she saw it all as the result of her meetings with her friend—the mystery lady whom she still had not seen again. Miss Hadeland, on the other hand, was a disciplinarian who did not really give the girl anything. Instead, she had her endlessly repeat any phrases she got wrong until her fingers felt completely numb from pressing on the strings.

Whenever Miss Hadeland seemed impossible to satisfy, Helen concentrated her thoughts on the mystery lady who had shown her so simply and kindly how to play. As often as time allowed, she went to the garden fence to look out for the lady, but she did not come. Had something happened to her in the earthquake?

Then again, she would tell herself, the lady might be angry with her because she had failed to keep the violin a secret. She would have liked to be able to explain that she had been unable to do anything else, but the lady seemed to have disappeared without a trace.

Her mother often came into the music room to see how her daughter was progressing. On those occasions Miss Hadeland would give her a slightly freer rein and was not so quick to criticize Helen when she made a mistake. In any case, her mother seemed to be very pleased with her playing.

"Helen says she taught herself to play," she whispered to the music teacher one time when she thought Helen was out of earshot. But Helen's sharp ears meant she could hear clearly what they were talking about.

"Of course that could be possible," Miss Hadeland replied. "Many great violinists were self-taught. And the way she plays means it's possible that she has developed her own technique. In any case, I'd be interested to know where she got the violin."

"She's staying stubbornly silent about it, however much I try to coax it out of her," her mother replied. "But some time ago she mentioned a mystery woman she met at the gate. Perhaps she was the one who gave her the violin. Perhaps it was a traveler who had no idea what to do with the instrument."

"That means the violin might be stolen."

Her mother may not have noticed the covetous gleam in her music teacher's eyes, but Helen saw it clearly. She hugged the instrument to her breast and silently swore that she would keep it safe and prevent anyone from laying a finger on it.

"No, I don't think so. And even if it was stolen, the crime didn't happen in this area. James has asked around all over the city, but no one has lost an instrument. Of course, most people are still preoccupied with the aftermath of the earthquake, but I'm sure they would have noticed a missing violin."

Helen noticed Miss Hadeland mulling these words over for a few moments, and again she felt a compulsion to hug the violin close and assure it that it would never fall into anyone's hands but her own.

25

Padang, 2011

"Do you want to drive or shall I?" Verheugen asked, gesturing toward the jeep. It looked like a former military vehicle, the camouflage paint-work peeling in a few places and specks of rust showing on the tailgate and doors. Lilly felt like remarking that this vehicle would never pass its safety inspection in Germany, but she didn't want to sound overly critical when Verheugen had been so generous with his help.

"I think you're probably more familiar with vehicles like this than I am."

"If you mean I have a lot of experience driving one of these, then you'd be right. I assure you they're easier to drive than you'd think. Why don't you have a go on the way back?"

He swung himself up into the driver's seat. Lilly looked skeptically at the jeep for a moment longer, but if her companion had confidence in it, why shouldn't she?

Verheugen turned the engine over a few times before it spluttered to life. "Well, at least the engine seems OK," he said, laughing. "Climb in. I promise I don't drive like the Padang taxi drivers!"

Lilly obeyed, and they were off.

As they threaded their way through the stream of traffic on the city streets, Lilly was glad she wasn't driving. Vehicles roared past them, and some cut them off, seemingly unconcerned about causing damage. Pedestrians spilled fearlessly from the sidewalks onto the street, taking their lives into their hands as they leisurely made their way across despite the speeding streams of traffic. Horns hooted loudly, and frequent curses were shouted out, but obstacles were soon cleared, and the whole fray continued unabated.

At last they reached the outskirts of Padang, where the houses had an air of poverty. Unlike in the city center, many of the houses here were built on stilts, in accordance with the Indonesian tradition. There were also a few crescent moon–style houses, but other architectural styles predominated.

After following the busy main road to the north for a while, Verheugen turned off onto a sandy track.

"Are you sure this is the right way?" Lilly shouted above the engine noise that seemed to have gotten louder.

Verheugen nodded. "I studied the map yesterday evening. We have to cross a stretch of bushland, but the way should be fairly clear. The house was in use until the 1950s, in any case. After that, it was simply forgotten. After the end of the colonial period the people here were not eager to research the history of their former overlords. There had been far too many dark incidents that seemed better forgotten. The Rawagede massacre on Java, for example."

"What happened there?"

"The Dutch wanted to win back their colonial possessions with a war. It led to this massacre. Around four hundred and thirty dead. Not the kind of thing to make them popular with the people. Interest in the colonial period is gradually beginning to grow again, as the museum showed us, but there's still a long way to go."

As they drove, Lilly noticed shadows flitting among the trees every now and then. There were numerous breeds of monkey on the island, but the animals she caught sight of disappeared so quickly that she was unable to identify them.

After they had driven for about an hour, a weathered red roof appeared among the palms. A little later they saw a dirty white wall showing through the leaves.

Verheugen parked the jeep in front of the entrance, which gave the impression that the house had long been abandoned. The custodian did not appear to take much care of the grounds but kept the grass outside the gate from growing too high.

As the engine noise died away, a strange silence fell over the place. Lilly heard the occasional rustling and twittering of birds.

She looked in fascination at the intricate wrought-iron gate, which hung a little crookedly on its hinges and was secured with a chain. Not a lot remained of its former magnificence. The high masonry gateposts were overgrown with moss. The garden had long been untouched by human hands, and the plants had grown exuberantly, obscuring the whole length of the fence. The drive leading up to the residence could still be made out, but tall blades of grass pushed their way through the flagstones. The edges were no longer straight lines but waves of green. The long branches of overhanging trees reached almost to the ground.

"Depressing, isn't it? You saw the old photo. This could once have been taken for an English country garden, but now it's increasingly turning into a jungle."

As the chain securing the gates was not padlocked, Verheugen quickly removed it and pushed one of the gates open. The shrill squeaking scared a few birds from the brush, and something on the ground scuttled off through rustling leaves—but there was no sign of the custodian.

"What if he's not here today?"

"Then he won't disturb us," Verheugen replied as he looked around.

Given its poor security, Lilly was amazed that the house had not been completely plundered. She was sure there would be no useable furniture inside, and even the stones from which it was built had some value and could easily have been sold.

As they approached the house, the custodian suddenly appeared from among the trees and called out to them. Verheugen understood and replied, causing the custodian's tense expression to relax.

"Does he not want us to look around here?" Lilly asked after the conversation had ended and the custodian ascended the stairs leading up to the house.

"He asked what we wanted here. I gave him the name of our friend from the museum, and he turned as meek as a lamb. He's going to unlock the house for us but declined to give us a guided tour."

"We don't need one of those anyway, do we?"

"The only thing we need here is a good pair of ears and a bit of luck."

"Why good ears?"

"Because I'm not sure how safe the floorboards are in there."

"Unsafe ceilings and rotten floors. Perhaps we should float through the door."

"Tell me when you've found out how to do that," Verheugen replied with a laugh.

The custodian opened the large front door, which must have welcomed streams of guests in its day. They were hit by a musty smell of old leaves, sand, and damp. The windows were boarded up, but badly, allowing a diffuse light to fall on the parquet that could hardly be seen beneath a thick layer of dirt. However, it was clear to see the route the custodian usually took through the house. The well-trodden path, with the parquet gleaming beneath as if it had actually been polished, led directly to a small door, behind which Lilly suspected there must be a toilet. They headed in. The custodian had told Verheugen that the boxes containing the documents were in the library, toward the rear of the house.

After crossing a spacious hallway, they reached the ballroom, its former glory only a faded memory. Lilly recalled the pictures in the newspaper and imagined she could see the elegant audience that Rose had played for—all the ladies' silk dresses, and the gems and feathers that adorned their hair. In 1902 the Charleston had not yet been invented, and many of those women would still have worn corsets. The men who gathered here to seal business relations or keep an eye on the competition would have worn high collars and tailcoats.

Rose would have stood among them with her magnificent wavy hair and her unusual violin. Lilly wondered again whether it was here that she had met Paul Havenden, if he had been one of the governor's guests when she played here. Had they fallen in love in this very place?

Lilly looked for the window through which the photo of the terrace had been taken, but she couldn't make it out because of the boards over the windows.

"I think I know where the library is," Verheugen said suddenly. "Follow me."

Lilly tore herself away from the tall windows and the richly carved beams that ran the length of the ballroom ceiling and walked after him.

As always happened when she had anything to do with old furnishings or houses, the antiques dealer in her awoke, but this time she found nothing to satisfy her. No one had forgotten a valuable marquetry cupboard in a corner; there was no bureau with drawers full of old love letters. The house seemed to have lost its inner life a long time ago; all that was left were shadows on the walls and floor to indicate where pictures, pieces of furniture, and carpets had once been.

And yet . . . there was something very special about this house. Some old houses left to rack and ruin looked so gloomy that they seemed frustrated to have been forgotten. But despite everything, this house radiated a certain warmth. Perhaps she was merely imagining it, but it seemed as though it was happy that someone had at last noticed it and that people were visiting again—just as they had when its former master had been alive.

"This must be the library."

Verheugen pointed to an open double door with flaking white paint. Behind it was a room that was big enough to have been a second ballroom. There was no longer any indication that this room had once been a place of learning and conversation. The bookshelves were gone. All that was left was a number of boxes lying around on the floor. The air was damp and musty, and Lilly would not have been surprised to see a fat tropical spider drop down from the ceiling.

"My goodness!" she said as she caught sight of the untidy piles of papers and books. The sides of the cardboard boxes had fallen prey to the dampness, and long cracks split their sides like gaping mouths. It was only a question of time before the boxes collapsed completely, and their contents were distributed across the filthy floor.

"It's such a shame that no one is interested in this house," Verheugen said. "I should speak to a few people back home, those who may have enough money to buy the building."

"Do you think the government here would just allow it?"

"I'm sure they would. And if a foundation were to buy it, all the better. Or it could be converted into a wonderful hotel. I'm amazed no one's considered the possibility."

"The people here must have other things to do than worry about the weekend residence of their former oppressor. Even if they don't see it like that, I'm sure they have more pressing problems."

"You're right again. Now then, let's have a look and see what treasures are hidden here."

"OK. I suggest you start on the right, and I'll take the left. We can work slowly toward each other."

Verheugen nodded and they set to work.

Lilly looked skeptically inside the first box. All it contained were a few bills from the 1940s. They were no use to anyone now—either the amounts due had long since been settled or forgotten, or the companies that had issued them no longer existed. On the bottom of the box Lilly felt a damp growth of mold that caused her to withdraw her hand quickly. Things did not look much better in the next box. Invoices, delivery notes, the remains of old schoolbooks with names on the covers that had faded to illegibility. A note in a child's handwriting that declared how much its owner hated algebra. Beneath this were a few more schoolbooks in Dutch. These might have been of interest to someone, but they were worthless to her.

"Have you found anything yet?" she asked Verheugen.

"No, it's all junk. It seems as though they forgot to burn it, and now people think it might be of value. What about you?"

"The same. Do you know anyone who might have a use for damp-stained old schoolbooks?"

"No. I suggest we leave them here."

"Good idea," Lilly agreed.

She was about to give up on the third box when she moved aside another moldy invoice to reveal a thick brown leather cover.

"It can't be!" she murmured, so softly that Verheugen had not heard. She pulled out the photo album. It was bound in thick tooled leather and felt fairly heavy—no wonder, as it contained a lot of photographs, both on paper and on thin plates.

Lilly opened it reverentially and found herself looking into the faces of the governor and his household. She saw his wife and daughter as well as all the servants. Maids with starched aprons and caps, a butler with a strict expression, a cook, and, to judge from their clothes, two domestic servants and two stable boys. She was struck by the fact that all the servants appeared to be locals, none of whom looked as though their master treated them badly.

The next few photos showed the interior of the house and the views from the windows. These included the terrace and the garden itself, which was a blend of native vegetation and Dutch horticulture. Lilly had to smile when she saw that there was even a bed containing beautiful tulips.

The following pictures were less interesting. Obviously the album was not so much a personal family album as a kind of photographic record of the history of the house. There were photos of a reception for a sultan, a number of extremely important-looking men who would probably have smoked cinnamon cigars with the governor, official events, and even a three-foot-high Christmas tree imported by who knew whom for the festive celebrations.

The next photo sent a shiver down Lilly's spine. The woman in the middle was none other than Rose Gallway. The picture was a variation of the one she had seen in the newspaper. It seemed that the governor—Lilly was sure he would have been the owner of this album—had asked for a copy of his own.

Unfortunately there was little of interest on the following pages. Rose appeared once more, again among a few people who clearly wanted to be seen with her. There were some more scenes involving important men, and after a while another picture of the whole household, in which the governor's daughter was this time accompanied by a husband and child.

As she leafed through, she noticed something beneath a semitransparent parchment-like interleaf, something thick that couldn't be a photo plate. She carefully lifted the interleaf and saw a thin black notebook pressed between the pages. It clearly didn't belong there, but over the years, during which the album had lain forgotten, it had become a part of it. Lilly carefully freed the little book and opened it.

Compressed between the photos, it had been protected from the damp. The paper looked in good condition and, although the ink had run a little, the words were still clearly legible.

The notebook was written in English, and Lilly's breath caught in her throat as she realized who the author was.

This diary is my atonement. Rose Gallway.

The words on the first page seared themselves into Lilly's eyes. Rose Gallway kept a diary! And she spoke of atonement! What could be concealed in it? And how did it get here? Had all the documents found after the departure of the Dutch colonial masters been stored here?

Lilly glanced furtively at Verheugen, who was busy rummaging through another box. She felt like showing him the little book immediately, but something held her back. It might seem ungrateful, but before she showed him this treasure, she wanted to read it herself, acquainting herself intimately with the woman who had once owned her violin.

Apart from that, how would he react if she told him she wanted to take it with her? These were archived documents, and she could be risking a serious penalty if she simply took it for herself. This little notebook would be a real sensation for Gabriel's music school.

While Verheugen was still immersed in his box, Lilly quickly stowed the notebook out of sight beneath her T-shirt. I'll decide what to do later, she thought. I want to read it first.

"Well, Lilly, have you found anything?" she heard suddenly. She started. Had he noticed her hiding the notebook away?

"You could say that," she replied uncertainly, picking up the album.

The notebook quickly reached her body temperature, and as she rose and crossed to the other side of the room, she hardly noticed it anymore.

"Do you think there'll be anything against me taking this with me?" she asked, handing the album to Verheugen.

He whistled in amazement. "Well, what a find! I'd be surprised if anyone wanted this, but it's an important document of the age."

That answered Lilly's question. "Then I'd better leave it here."

"I would if I were you, but I'm sure no one would have anything against you making copies of the photos to take away."

Lilly nodded. "Have you found anything interesting?"

"I've no idea whether there's anything of interest here. They all look like accounting records to me. It seems as though the governor only left behind those and a few newspapers and magazines."

"It looks like they're something for the people at the museum."

"True, but I think we should keep looking. Perhaps we'll still find a church register or something of the sort. You never know—there may be some passionate love letters lying around here." Verheugen winked. "I'm grateful to you for the opportunity to be here. This is the most exciting search I've ever undertaken."

"Are you sure?" she replied a little hesitantly. "You must have seen a lot of the world."

"I have indeed, but I've never been involved in research work like this. It's simply wonderful to be discovering a part of the history of my country. You must know that Sumatra is still of great interest to the Dutch. There are even museums dedicated to it. I visited one once, but it's another matter entirely to be in direct contact with the history like this." He gestured toward the box. "Anyway, it's great fun, and I'm delighted that I got talking to you at the airport."

Did he really mean that? Of course it was fun to be looking through the boxes, but wasn't he overreacting a bit? Probably not, Lilly thought. It's just his way.

"I'm also glad to have met you," she replied, smiling now. "I doubt I'd have gotten this far without you."

"Of course you would have!" Verheugen replied, but he seemed visibly pleased that she appreciated what he had done for her. "Let's see if we can find anything more before it gets dark. I don't think the electricity supply has reached here yet, and I'm sure the custodian will want to be finishing work."

Lilly agreed with a laugh and returned to her work. She was now consumed with impatience. Whatever else happened, that night she would have the chance to read about the guilt Rose wanted to atone for in her diary.

26

Padang, 1910

During the month following the earthquake, life in Padang slowly got back to normal. The sea murmured as it always had, the wind sang, and the cries of the monkeys resounded from the mountains down into the city.

The residents cleared the rubble and buried their dead. Some had been impossible to identify, and their graves were marked with a plain cross in the hope that at some stage someone who was missing them, or at least knew them, would make themselves known.

Helen practiced the violin with determination, never letting the instrument out of her sight. It was with her at mealtimes, during her lessons, and when she went to bed. Any moment when she found that she had nothing to do she would whisk out the violin and play songs that Miss Hadeland had not taught her—simple songs that sounded all the prettier for it. Sometimes Helen noticed her mother looking at her with concern, but she said nothing.

One day, her mother appeared in the music room. She was accompanied by a woman who looked ancient in Helen's eyes. Her snow-white hair was held in a bun, and her slender body was clothed in a black dress that made her look even thinner than she was. Her angular face looked as though life had worn away all its curves, and her nose stood out from her face like a bird's beak.

"Helen, I'd like to introduce Mrs. Faraday," her mother said. "She happens to be here in Padang to look at the pupils of Mejuffrouw Dalebreek. She has also heard of you and would like you to play something for her."

The woman gave Helen a piercing look. Helen dared not avert her gaze, but she was also unable to look directly into her eyes. Instead she concentrated on the gold-mounted gemstone that the elderly woman wore at the neck of her dress.

"Mrs. Faraday, I consider it a great honor . . ." began Miss Hadeland, but the elderly woman, without removing her eyes from the girl, raised a hand to silence her.

As Helen continued to stare at her brooch, the elderly woman approached her.

"How old are you, child?" she asked in a sharp voice reminiscent of a badly tuned violin. Her clawlike hand reached out to the girl's chin, and cold fingers touched her skin.

"Seven years old, madam," Helen replied as politely as she could, as she did not want to anger this birdlike old woman. She did not match Helen's image of a witch—she looked far too respectable for that—but it was impossible to tell what hidden depths lay beneath the facade.

"Seven years old. Just the right age. When they're too old, their fingers are already too stiff to learn the fingering properly."

Although she was speaking about her fingers, the woman's eyes continued to scrutinize Helen's face, a peculiar experience for the girl. Then the elderly woman said, "Play something for us. The most difficult piece you know."

Helen did not need to think for long. Unhurriedly, she took the violin from its stand and positioned it under her chin, noticing as she did so the elderly woman's attention turning to the instrument. She could not interpret the look that flamed in her eyes.

After a while Mrs. Faraday raised a hand, tearing Helen from her playing.

"You play very well, girl. And the sound of your violin is truly wonderful. Where did you get it?"

"It was a gift from an acquaintance," Helen's mother quickly replied for her. The elderly woman betrayed no reaction.

"You remind me very much of a girl who was once taught at my establishment. She was also very gifted and also had that way of playing. Someone has clearly tried to drive out your natural way of playing."

Her look, bordering on anger, fell on Miss Hadeland before her eyes returned to Helen. They were no friendlier than before, but at least without reproach.

"Yes, that girl was one of my best pupils. She may not always have been obedient, but great things could have become of her. Unfortunately she threw away her career and forgot all I ever taught her." She paused briefly, then reached out again to Helen's face. "Yes, I see a lot of her in you. Perhaps you're like her. This time I won't allow a great talent to be wasted."

Helen did not know why, but these words made her heart start thumping wildly. What did she mean by it?

"What do you think of going to England and learning to play the violin properly there? I run a music school in London, and I would like to have you as a pupil there. You know a certain amount, but I'm sure there's a lot more in you to be discovered. I don't know how much longer I have left in this world; perhaps this journey will be my last. I can't say what will happen next, but I'm certain that you'll never get an opportunity like this one again. So?"

Helen did not know what to say and stood wringing her hands in indecision. Her mother soon stepped in.

"I think that Helen is hardly able to grasp what a great honor this is."

"Talk to your daughter," Mrs. Faraday said. "And if necessary, make the decision for her. You should always keep it in the back of your mind that this girl could achieve great things in the world—provided she receives the right guidance."

"I'll talk to her," her mother replied as Helen glanced over to Miss Hadeland. She was looking a little bewildered, staring the whole time at the violin on its stand. She only came back to life once Mrs. Faraday made her farewells and, together with Helen's mother, she accompanied the elderly woman to the door.

Helen remained behind and as she carefully polished the violin with a soft cloth and placed it back in its case, she wondered what the elderly woman had meant. She should go to England to learn to play the violin? Did they play differently in England?

For the rest of the day Helen was unable to think clearly. The encounter with the elderly woman dominated her thoughts, and she began to wander restlessly through the garden. She kept close to the fence in the hope that the mystery lady might appear. Her friend was bound to be able to tell her what Mrs. Faraday meant!

But however much she examined the women who passed the garden of her parents' house, none of them looked as beautiful to her as the mystery lady who had given her the violin. With a sigh, Helen lowered herself to sit beneath a tree. What should she do now?

She looked over to the house, where her mother was still talking to Miss Hadeland. Did her music teacher perhaps not want her to go to England? *England.* It sounded so distant, and somehow so cold. It certainly wouldn't be as warm and sunny as here, but London also had a ring of adventure to it.

By the time evening came, she was fit to burst with excitement. She was scarcely able to eat a bite of supper for fear that her mother might have reached a decision she did not like. She shifted restlessly on her chair as her mother chatted with her father, apparently taking no notice of her. The conversation finally turned to Mrs. Faraday's visit, but her mother merely praised her for playing so well and told her husband that she wanted to talk to him about it later.

Helen was finally told to go to her room, which pleased her. Perhaps she should do as she had always done since she'd had the violin—consult it. After all, if she went to London it would have to accompany her.

She drew the case out from under her bed and flicked the lid open.

The next moment she started in fear.

Her violin had disappeared.

***

Helen cried continuously for hours as her mother tried in despair to comfort her. Helen's lips turned blue, and she seemed unaware of anything that was happening around her. She was grieving as if for a real person, and Ivy Carter could only hope that her husband could find out what had happened. There was no trace of it. After the violin had been found to be missing, he had gone immediately to Miss Hadeland's lodgings.

Ivy refused to believe that the music teacher would have stolen the violin, but who else could have done so? The elderly Mrs. Faraday? No, that was impossible; she could hardly have slipped back into the house unnoticed.

Helen finally cried herself dry, not because she was any less upset, but because her eyes, her whole body, could go on no longer. She fell into a strange paralysis, which her mother was unable to penetrate, even with scones and sweetened milk. With swollen, vacant eyes, she stared up at the ceiling for so long that her eyelids eventually grew heavy and sleep overcame her.

***

Helen found no peace, even in sleep. Terrible dreams afflicted her. The mystery lady appeared, her face pale and black shadows beneath her eyes, reproaching her for failing to take proper care of the violin. She remorselessly repeated her accusations, and her face became ever more frightening.

Helen awoke with a scream and found herself alone in her room. The door was ajar, and a beam of light fell into the room. Voices reached her from downstairs. One of them was her father's. He must have returned from his search.

"I've looked all over the city for that Hadeland—nothing," he said to Helen's mother. "She abandoned her room this afternoon and seems to have vanished without a trace. I've spoken to her landlady, but she could make no sense of her behavior."

"Did you tell her that she's stolen our daughter's violin?"

"I said we suspected as much. The landlady will tell me when she sees her again."

Her music teacher was supposed to have stolen it? Helen recalled the covetous looks, and her chest tightened. Miss Hadeland had sometimes treated her rather harshly, but Helen would never have believed that she would steal the most precious thing she possessed.

Distraught, she crept back into bed, feeling as though not only her eyes were burning but her whole body. What if she never got the violin back? How would she continue to play—and who would teach her? The elderly woman with the cold eyes perhaps? Trembling, she hid beneath the sheets and thought for a while about what had happened. I'm not to blame, she told herself. I didn't see her go anywhere near my violin case.

***

The next morning, when Ivy Carter entered her daughter's room, she found the girl semiconscious and running a fever. Shocked by her condition, she called her husband.

"It must be because of all the crying. She got so dreadfully upset," he said and hurried off to fetch the doctor.

They did not recount the whole story to him, merely saying that the girl had been crying a lot because she had lost a personal treasure.

"It's probably her nerves," the doctor pronounced as he took Helen's pulse. "Her heartbeat is strong, and I can't find any other symptoms of illness. I'll leave you some fever powder, and I recommend you apply a cold compress. And if at all possible, find or replace whatever the child has lost, as she's obviously very attached to it."

After the doctor left, James Carter paced up and down the dining room in agitation until his wife finally came back downstairs.

"How is she?" he asked. She shook her head.

"No better. I couldn't get her sufficiently awake to give her the fever medicine. Even the compress didn't rouse her from her sleep. I'll try again later."

"That damned woman!" James muttered angrily. "What on earth has gotten into her?"

"I'm sure the police will find Miss Hadeland."

"I'm not talking about her!" her husband snapped. "You know who I mean! She had no right to visit the child. Not after all that happened. And then the violin! Why in God's name did she come looking for Helen? And how did she find her? Does she intend to take her away from us? After all we've done?"

"I don't believe she will—otherwise I'm sure she'd have taken some steps toward it already. And who knows why she gave her that gift."

"She made our Helen promise not to say anything. Who knows what she's told her."

"I don't believe she's told her anything that calls our authority into question—otherwise Helen would have rebelled in some way a long time ago."

"So what's the meaning of this fever?"

"It's hardly likely to be a result of Helen seeing her. Helen adores that violin; she treats it almost like a person."

"That's unnatural in itself," James muttered in annoyance, but tears of worry gleamed in his eyes. "She shouldn't show such love for an object!"

"Do you know what Mrs. Faraday said?" Ivy asked without agreeing or disagreeing with his assertion. "That she was just like her. That she has the same talent. It would be a shame for it to be wasted, if . . ."

"I'm not sure, Ivy," James said, regaining a little composure. "If we can protect her from all this fuss, if we don't give her any more encouragement, we might be saving her all kinds of trouble."

"But we'd be depriving the world of something wonderful then. Mrs. Faraday may be a hardhearted woman, but I got a very clear impression that she knows what she's doing."

"So you think we should send her to England?"

Ivy could imagine the unspoken thoughts behind his words. If she went to England, she could be sought out by that . . . woman.

"I could go with her to begin with," she suggested. "I'd see to it that she was properly and safely accommodated and that all was well with her."

"And how long do you think it will be before she learns the truth? Mrs. Faraday's supposition is so damned close to the truth that if she just puts two and two together, she could lead Helen into total confusion."

Ivy tried to pacify her husband. "They're suppositions, nothing more. She'll never find any proof. Mijnheer van Swieten gave us his word of honor."

"I don't want to lose my little girl, Ivy," James said, taking his wife in his arms.

"You won't," she promised. "One day our daughter will be a very famous woman. The whole world will look up to her. We can't deprive her of this opportunity, whatever happened in the past. In any case, if Helen is in England, we'll be better placed to protect her from any further attempts to make contact with her."

James considered all these arguments and finally nodded.

"All right, perhaps it's for the best. But I ought to get Helen a new violin first. I'm afraid that the damned Hadeland woman has vanished with the instrument and has perhaps already traded it in."

Ivy kissed him gently on the lips. "I'm sure you'll find her a new instrument. I hope that will cheer her up a bit."

***

Meanwhile Helen was dreaming again, but this time not dreams full of anger and reproach. She was in a garden, most of which was veiled in mist. Occasional patches of color showed through the white fog—rhododendron, magnolia, frangipani flowers, and vivid orchids.

However much Helen looked around, she could not make out the beginning or the end of the garden. Someone had set her down in the middle and left her no instructions about where to go. She took a hesitant step forward and noticed that she was wearing her best white dress.

Could she have died? She had never seen a dead body before, but she knew from some of her friends who had lost family members that dead people were always made to look particularly beautiful before they were buried. It was probably because they took the clothes they were wearing up to Heaven with them, and the angels did not like to have to look at unsuitable clothing.

But if she were really dead, why did no angel come to fetch her?

"There you are," a soft voice said suddenly.

Helen whirled around and saw the mystery lady. She was wearing the same dress as she had when Helen saw her for the first time. She was still very beautiful, but now substantially paler than before. She reached out her hand.

"Would you like to walk a while with me?"

At first Helen was unsure whether she should be afraid and run away. But where to? The garden was all there was. She reached out her own hand to the lady, who led her a little way through the fog, until they finally stopped by a small stone seat.

"I'm sorry," Helen said before they sat down. Although the lady's expression was kindly, Helen feared she was about to experience something similar to her previous dream. "I don't know how the violin got lost. When I opened the case that evening it had simply gone."

"It's not your fault," the lady replied. "The person who stole it from you is sure to be found soon and punished."

"How do you know?"

"Because that's always the way. You can do something wrong, but you must know that it always comes to light. Guard against doing anything wrong, Helen."

The girl nodded eagerly, thoroughly relieved that the lady was not angry with her.

"Why are we here?" Helen asked as she looked around. The fog had still not cleared. It clung like cotton to the branches of the shrubs that surrounded them.

"I'd like you to promise me something," the lady replied.

"What kind of promise?"

"If you get your violin back, I'd like you to do everything you can to become a famous violinist. Will you promise me that?"

"Oh yes, I promise!" Helen said enthusiastically.

"You'll get it back—I promise you. But now I must go."

"Will we see each other again? My mother's considering whether she should send me to Mrs. Faraday's school in England."

"I don't know whether we'll meet again. But think on your promise, won't you? Play as well as you can."

"I will!" the girl replied.

The lady rose and slowly walked away.

"Farewell, Helen," she said, turning once more before she was swallowed by the drifting fog.

Helen remained on the stone seat for a while, looking at the place where the lady had disappeared. She was amazed at how peaceful their meeting had been. Would she really get her violin back? Before she could stand and look for a way out of the garden, she was enclosed by darkness, and she slept on dreamlessly.

***

Three days later, foresters found Imela Hadeland in a remote, impassable place. She was crushed and half buried beneath a horse that had not survived the fall. In her hurry to leave the city, she had chosen a route through the bush that even the native people avoided because of the danger of sliding down a steep slope. The fact that she was on horseback at all surprised people somewhat, since she had never come across as an experienced rider. She always preferred to travel by coach or ship, and if she had done so again this time, she would probably have gotten away. But her fear of being pursued because of the theft had been greater than her common sense.

Helen's parents were sure that her motive was greed—Imela Hadeland had clearly been in need of money and hoped to raise some funds by selling the violin. She had planned her deed skillfully. She had bought herself a little time by leaving behind the violin case, since the absence of the case would have been noticed before the loss of its contents.

Helen was shocked to hear that her music teacher had been found with a broken neck. Of course no one told her openly; the word was merely that Miss Hadeland had suffered an accident that she did not survive. But Helen heard her mother and father talking as they stood outside her door, assuming she was asleep.

No one spoke of the theft of the violin, either. The instrument had been found undamaged close to the corpse, and as there was still no one else who had claimed it, it was returned to Helen. It appeared one morning, as if by magic, on the chair by her bed, and the girl immediately recovered from her strange illness. The fever cleared up, and Helen was her old cheerful self within hours. And she played. She played fervently and for hours at a stretch, as if to recover the lost hours in a single day. She had made a promise to the mystery lady and intended to keep it.

Just a few days later, her parents called her into the parlor and asked her if she wanted to go to Mrs. Faraday's Music School in England. Helen was delighted. She had heard a few stories from London, the city from where her great-grandparents came, and was now burning with a desire to see the place for herself. The fact that her mother wanted to travel with her only made the decision even easier. She was worried about not seeing her father for such a long time, but she thought about what the lady had said. If she kept her promise now, if she did all that had been asked of her, then perhaps everything would be all right and stay that way.

27

In her hotel room that evening, with the impressions of the day still alight in her mind, Lilly took out the thin diary.

After leaving the governor's house without making any further noteworthy finds, they had driven back to Padang. Lilly was lost in thought during the journey. Should she write to Ellen and Gabriel today? Or would it be better to keep the news until she was back? After a little to-and-fro debate, she decided not to release the bombshell until she was back in London. After all, she still needed to examine her find properly herself.

Verheugen had offered to present the album to the museum and ensure that the photographs were copied. Lilly had thanked him and asked him to take her back to the hotel. There Verheugen took his leave of her, saying that he had to go meet someone at the airport that evening.

After taking a refreshing shower and eating a little fruit brought to her by a friendly chambermaid, she felt in the right mood to devote her attention to the notebook. Outside her window a magnificent sunset was spreading its colors over Padang. Oranges, reds, and violets blended to form a breathtaking veil as lights came on one after the other in the buildings, and the character of the street sounds gradually changed. The traffic was still swarming, but Lilly hardly noticed the blaring of the horns now, although she liked the scraps of music that occasionally drifted up to her. Was there a shadow play taking place somewhere in the city right then? Or a concert?

Ellen would certainly have insisted that she should go to see it, but this evening belonged to Rose Gallway.

With a feeling of awe, Lilly traced her finger over the cover of the little book before moving to the hotel bed, from where she had an excellent view of the sky.

"Well then, Rose," she murmured. "Tell me more."

***

This diary is my atonement. Rose Gallway

Perhaps it is too late to begin a diary, but I need to do this to get my thoughts in order.

Writing is an effort for me, but I want something of myself to live on. Something that might survive the passage of time, something that will explain to people in the future why I acted as I did.

Since the doctor gave me the diagnosis and I found out how little time I have left, I have been consumed by a single thought: making good my previous mistakes.

I have been reproaching myself for all those years. I may have avoided the major scandal, for which I was initially very grateful to Mijnheer van Swieten, but the price I paid was emptiness, loneliness. The loss of my talents. My decline. I hardly trusted anyone anymore; I was completely indifferent to men.

And now a man has appeared who gives me new hope. He is completely different from those who see in me only the beautiful woman whose image accompanies them in their dirty desires.

Cooper Swanson is one of the most unattractive men I know, and that in itself makes it possible for me to trust him. He only speaks as much as necessary but is an extremely good listener and gives you the feeling that his mind soaks up every detail like a sponge.

He is prepared to carry out my wish, although it will be difficult. Van Swieten has been dead for three years—are there really documents recording what was done back then? I doubt it. They will surely have done everything possible to remove all trace.

But I will begin at the beginning. At the crossroads of my life where, without knowing it, I chose the wrong path.

After my father was killed in the accident at the harbor, life changed for my mother and me. I prepared myself to continue my tour without any idea of whether or not I really had the strength to go through with it. My mother began to make her own preparations—to return to her home village of Magek. As a new warehouse supervisor had already been found and the house would only belong to her for a few more months, she sent a messenger to her village to inform the old woman who had come to find her that she would take up her place with her family in the village.

As we said our good-byes I wept bitter tears. During my travels it had always done me a lot of good to know that she was there, in the little house by the harbor. Now if I wanted to see her, I would have to travel deep into the jungle—impossible, given the schedule Carmichael had planned for me.

We parted one day before my ship was due to set sail, as an oxcart had already been sent from the village to collect her.

Once again she urged me to listen to my own heart whenever I was faced with a decision. Unaware of the situation that I was already in, I promised her I would, and watched the cart disappear into the jungle with tears in my eyes.

Full of pain and longing, full of reluctance and uncertainty, I finally went on board the *MS Flora* that was to take us to India.

During the crossing I began to feel strange. My moods swung like the ship on the sea. Sometimes up, sometimes down. Sometimes my dresser, Mai, would seem like the kindest person in the world to me. Sometimes I detested her deeply and drove her away when she came to fix my hair. I could imagine her talking about me to Carmichael. She thought me a raving madwoman. And Carmichael? No, I'm sure he didn't share her views. He had worked with artists before and knew how eccentric they could be.

In my case he believed that my condition was shaped by past events, and he indulged me. When I was raging, when I hit Mai, when I failed to show up, when I was in a bad mood, he said nothing. But I knew myself that something was happening within me, something that controlled me like a puppeteer moves a marionette, causing me to behave irrationally.

Otherwise how could I have turned into such a formidable dragon?

On our arrival in Delhi, with many miles still to travel overland, I felt awful. My legs were swollen as if I were afflicted by dropsy; I would sweat with the slightest exertion. And then there was the nausea.

At first I tried to hide it. I told myself it was because of the dreadful food on board the ship and during the journey. I was determined that Carmichael should not know what the matter was, as he would start in again with his reproaches and insistence that I should not abandon the tour. He would even have propped me up in the middle of a swoon, leaning me against a pillar and pressing the violin into my hands.

And so, once in Delhi, I secretly sought out a doctor, who gave me the revelation that shocked me to the core and which, from that moment on, removed my ability to play like I had before. It was as though something suddenly rose up inside me against the music that had previously been my source of wonder and fulfillment.

Even when practicing for the concert, I noticed that the images had gone. For as long as I could remember, images had always been inextricably linked with my music. Every piece triggered new ones. When I played, the weight of the world was lifted from me—I believed I was no longer standing on the stage. But now I only felt weighed down. Not even when I played at my father's graveside did I feel so heavy, so incapable.

The absence of the images, the absence of the high, made my fingers uncertain. I was suddenly afraid I could no longer do justice to the music. And fear hung over it all. Fear that I could no longer hide the secret I had been keeping. It made me even more uncertain, and my anger became my shield and my weapon, which I began to use to drive people away.

I still remember the day when my secret could no longer remain concealed. It was the day on which I had to admit that my passion for my music was about to expire.

"The concert was a disaster!" Carmichael cursed as he paced up and down in front of me in my hotel room. "What on earth was the matter with you? You played as if your head was somewhere else completely. If you allow yourself to repeat that performance, your career will be ruined!"

I made no reply. I stared past the music stand into empty space. The memory of the disastrous concert resonated inside me like the harsh note of a breaking string. Again and again I heard the passages, felt the refusal of my fingers, the weakness of my bowing hand.

I had played badly. So disastrously that the shock of it was clearly noticeable among the audience. Never before had anything similar happened to me!

And never before have I felt so small. I felt all those feelings that I had been concealing beneath my mercurial temper: sadness for my father, yearning for my mother, and the destructive longing for Paul. Since that guilty night at the plantation, I had been hoping every day to hear from him.

Of course I was fooling myself. How could he reach me in Delhi? I had left a message at the hotel where I had stayed the night, just in case he tried to contact me, but he was probably not yet even back in England.

There was something else to add to my state of uncertainty. Spiteful voices arose in my mind, voices whispering to me that he had merely been using me to satisfy his desire, to be able to add me to his collection of trophies from the tropics.

However much these voices babbled insistently, I refused to believe them.

Could the man who had stroked my back so tenderly, kissed my skin and my lips so passionately, really have lied to me?

No. Impossible. Paul may have been trapped by social convention, he may have been promised to another and not have found the strength to call off the engagement, but I was sure he was not a liar.

It fueled a remarkable defiance in me. As Carmichael continued his tirade, warning me how it would all turn out if I did not come to my senses, I took a deep breath and said, "I'm pregnant."

Carmichael sagged in shock against the door frame. I will never forget the expression on his face. No blow could have silenced him as effectively as those words.

"What did you say?" he asked in bewilderment.

"That I'm pregnant," I replied.

Carmichael let out a noise that sounded like air escaping from a balloon.

"Bloody hell! It was that Englishman, wasn't it? I'll wring his neck if I ever see him again! When did you . . . That evening when you were away?"

"That's nothing to do with you," I snapped at him.

Carmichael snorted like a bull in the bullring. "Do you know what this means?"

"That I'm going to have a baby."

"That you're about to destroy your whole damned career!" Carmichael slammed his hand down on the chest of drawers by the door so hard that I started in fright. "What do you think the concert promoters are going to say when a pregnant woman steps out onto the stage? Let alone the audiences? If you were married, it might be different, but as it is . . ."

I stared at him defiantly. What he was saying was true, but at that moment I felt superior to him. And I also felt a wicked delight in the fact that I had caused him such annoyance.

Of course it was bad for my career, since an angel was only given the role if she stayed pure and at least gave the appearance of living on nothing but light and air like a flower. Passions and desires of the flesh were not part of the image.

"You should go to see an abortionist."

These words lashed me like a whip. I should have known that a man like Carmichael was always ready with a counterattack.

"Have you lost your mind?" I said, stunned.

The doctor's pronouncement may have shocked me, but the last thing I would have thought of was to get rid of the baby. It was Paul's child, a little Lord or Lady Havenden. It was my assurance that he would come back to me.

"Not here, of course," Carmichael said, relenting a little while ignoring my reply. "We'll go to England. And once there, you can simply get rid of it."

"No," I replied icily. "Apart from the fact that I would be risking my own life, it would be sheer murder!"

I didn't mention the third reason—that I hoped I would soon be Lady Havenden—because if I had, I would only have earned myself Carmichael's scorn. It was enough that the voices in my head continuously plagued me with the notion that Paul's intentions could have been dishonorable.

Carmichael looked at me in anguish. "Rose, don't you understand? This could grow into a horrendous scandal. An illegitimate child! No one will allow you to play for them until you're married."

"We can keep it a secret," I suggested. "Granted, I wouldn't be able to play for a few months, but—"

"And where would we tell the audiences your child came from?"

"Do I have to justify myself to my audiences?" I muttered.

It turned my stomach to think of the people watching me as I played those false notes, glaring as if I had conjured up the devil.

"You're in the public eye, in the spotlight! You're not the kind of woman who can simply disappear for a few months to give birth to a baby. We have a schedule!"

"But what would be the problem with taking a six-month break?" I countered. "We've been touring for two years already. The public will understand."

Carmichael snorted again. "And in the meantime someone new will be raised up as the public's darling, won't they? No, I won't allow it."

"I refuse to have an abortion!" My voice rose shrilly. "If I were killed by some back-street abortionist, you'd have even less of me; I'd never play ever again. I intend to have this child. When I'm on tour, it can stay with my mother, and that's that!"

Carmichael ground his teeth. He was furious. Let him be! I knew what his reaction would be. He would simply leave. Turn on his heel and slam the door behind him. And so he did this time, too. The crash of the door in the frame made me shudder.

That night I sat at my desk and wrote a letter to Paul. I told him what had happened, in the hope that it would strengthen his decision to return to me.

I did not make a single mistake during the next concert. I played every note flawlessly, giving no one cause to suspect anything was wrong, but once again I did not see the music. I felt how soulless the sound of my violin had become.

This time, Carmichael didn't turn up to reproach me. For a whole week we communicated, when strictly necessary, through Mai, whose sympathy for me was disappearing rapidly. Carmichael had presumably told her about my condition.

I played concert after concert, each time losing a piece of my soul as I played. Deep inside, I felt that everything would be better when Paul returned. A few times I imagined I saw him in the audience, and on those occasions my playing improved so that, even though I no longer saw the images floating in my mind's eye, a little of my soul returned to the melodies.

The pit I was falling into grew deeper when I would realize at the end of the concert that I had been mistaken—he was not there. I felt as though I had wasted valuable energy, and so I shunned my admirers, and if conversation with them was absolutely unavoidable, I kept it as short as I could.

"Well, it's coming back," Carmichael felt obliged to say when, after two weeks, he came into my dressing room once again. No—I was still not playing any wrong notes, but my playing was as flat and cold as a slab of marble. Week after week, venue after venue, I waited for word from Paul. I imagined that if he had wanted he could have reached me, that if he really loved me he would have made a reckless journey around the world. But that did not happen. If he appeared, it was only in dreams that reduced me to hours of weeping.

The day came when my condition could no longer be concealed, as the curve of my belly could be seen beneath my dress, even though I wore the loosest one I possessed.

It was an illusion to think I could fool anyone. I was overcome by deep despair as I looked at myself in the mirror. That which would have brought most women delight caused me ever greater fear.

I told myself it would all be right if Paul appeared. If he made me his wife as he had promised.

Carmichael was grinding his teeth more and more. The chance to take me to an abortionist had long passed. The idea of having to look after a baby was a nightmare to him, but I was as determined as ever that it should live—after all, it was my child, mine and Paul's.

Then, one day, my agent came to me. Until that moment I had not given a thought to where I should go. My mother's house was no longer there for me; she was in the jungle, in Magek, a place that was nothing but a faint childhood memory for me, a place where demands would be made of me for which I was insufficiently prepared. And when Paul returned, he would never find me there.

Carmichael turned out to be prepared to help, even though I never asked him. As I was no longer of use to him, he could easily have dropped me, but he didn't. He used the contacts we had made during the previous months to find someone who would be prepared to accommodate me.

And so, just a week later, I found myself shamefully facing Piet van Swieten. There was regret in his eyes, as though his own daughter had committed this error, not me. He, too, had probably held me up as an angel, an ethereal, supernatural being free from all earthly desires, but now he had to concede that even I was human, weak and corrupt.

But of course he did not say so. Instead he offered me the annex to his house, which he called the guesthouse. That day I moved in there with Mai and my luggage, since I had no more possessions than what I carried with me in my suitcase.

I waited for four long months. Day after day I sat at the window and waited. I looked out on the dreamlike garden, which I came to know in all its moods. Sometimes I would even sit there at night, especially during the rainy season when the dull gray darkened my soul. I had no one but Carmichael and Mai. The servants of the house had been instructed to keep out of sight. Even the master of the house stayed away from me. I knew that I had fallen from his favor, that his agreement to allow me to lie low there was nothing more than an act of Christian charity, which he undertook without any true understanding of me.

The annex at Welkom could nevertheless have been a place of peace and relaxation for me. The beautiful garden could have strengthened my soul, could have enabled me to trust in the belief that I could manage with my child and that, despite all my disgrace, I could find my way back.

But my optimism diminished daily. As the date of the birth approached, I cried almost every day and wished that the thing in my womb would finally be out. Sometimes I even regretted not having decided to visit the abortionist.

Carmichael saw my despair and felt obliged to act without first asking for my permission.

"Van Swieten is offering to hand over the child to a very respectable family here in Padang for you," he declared one day. "They will raise it while you pick up your career again."

The words passed through me like a biting wind, but I remained unperturbed.

"Is there any mail?" I asked, as if I had not heard, as if I had lost my capacity to understand.

In truth, I was trying to come to a decision.

"No," Carmichael replied flatly, with perhaps a tinge of sympathy. "No mail."

My agent put the governor's offer to me another three times before I realized one morning that Paul would not be coming. He'd had almost nine months to visit me, and even without my letter, that should have been enough time for him to return—or at least to send me word to assure me that all would be well. I briefly toyed with the idea of sending a messenger to the plantation owner to ask whether the transaction between him and Paul had come about, but how would I feel if the message came back that he and his charming wife were already there for a visit and amusing themselves in style?

I told Carmichael to let the governor know that I consented.

The birth itself was one of the most dreadful things I had ever experienced. I lay in agony for hours, wishing only for release. With hindsight I'm glad that my memory has blocked out most of the details of the event. All I remember is the moment when the baby slipped from me, and I felt a wonderful sense of relief. The local midwife, who was clearly unaware of the arrangement, put the crying baby to my breast but quickly snatched it away again after the doctor whispered something in her ear that I did not catch.

But that moment was enough. I had seen that sweet face, a face that was still too new to show any real family likeness but that was nevertheless wonderful. And I had also seen that she was a girl. I had a little daughter!

But it was too late to turn back. The child had been promised to another family, and the birth had weakened me to such an extent that I was unable to protest. She was taken away, and I had nothing but my memories of the birth—a week of the deepest mental anguish and innumerable tears—leaving me emotionally scarred and with a deeply wounded heart.

Although it had caused a stir that I had vanished for so long from the stage, my audience forgave me for my absence and welcomed me, freshly recovered from childbirth, back into the limelight. I should have enjoyed my return to the role of admired musician, but I could not enjoy the applause, since I was firmly of the opinion that I did not deserve it.

Carmichael did not care. He organized concert after concert for me. The concert halls grew smaller, and the interest of the people grew less, but I played on—playing without soul, playing for no other reason than to silence my guilty conscience. In the evenings, after my performances, an empty shell would gaze back at me from the mirror, and at night I would be plagued by nightmares in which I saw a blood-smeared child's face that reproached me for giving her away.

But in the mornings I would don my mask again, and after a while I had gotten so used to it that I believed I was the old Rose again, the one who lived for nothing but music. I may have succeeded on the outside, but the fact that it was mere deception was clear to me from the way the images refused to return when I played.

Then, a few years later, I met Johan de Vries, a plantation owner from the vicinity of Padang. He appeared at one of my concerts, and although the bloom had gone from my cheeks and the light from my eyes, he came shyly to the door of my dressing room with a bouquet of dark red roses that looked fiendishly expensive.

At that moment, as he stood there scarcely daring to look at me, I knew that he might be my salvation—that, through him, I could save my soul.

I won't call it love—Paul had taken that away over the sea with him and, laughing, had thrown it overboard to be eaten by the sharks.

In contrast to my relationship with Paul, it took time for Johan and me to grow close. Roses in the dressing room, brief conversations, letters, walks. He was devoted, making every effort to satisfy my wishes, and I accepted his gifts graciously. As my eyes were not clouded by love, I recognized that he was my chance to restore my honor.

One day he went down on one knee before me to ask for my hand in marriage. I hardly hesitated before accepting. This was anything but acceptable to Carmichael, since it meant that I would never tread the stage again and was not going to end my days as a violinist in the dives of Jakarta. I paid Carmichael off with a generous sum of money and assured him of my friendship. I also entrusted Mai to his care, as I no longer needed her.

I could have created a stir of a different kind with a grand wedding, but I asked Johan for a quiet marriage with an unassuming celebration among a tiny circle of friends and family. I did not want to remind the world of what I had once been but to withdraw quietly and without fuss. There was not even an announcement of the wedding in the paper—at my request. In his adoration of me, Johan did everything I wanted.

I hardly recall our wedding night, or any of the other nights we spent in our marriage bed. He was not a thoughtless lover; on the contrary, he was gentle, considerate of me, moving carefully and making every effort not to cause me pain. But it was as though his devotion fell on stony ground. I let it all wash over me, and only if I closed my eyes and thought of Paul was it any better than merely bearable.

As it turned out, I became pregnant in no time, which caused great joy among my husband's family. I gave the appearance of being pleased, too, and I bore the aches and pains with good grace. It came all the easier to me since there was no audience, and no impatient agent, waiting for me. I still played the violin every now and then, but only because I convinced myself that the baby inside me would perhaps be musical and that I was doing some good by transmitting the sounds to it.

That birth, too, was awful, but this time I was given strength by the knowledge that I would keep the baby, and maybe it would be consolation for the loss of my firstborn. The midwife placed a little boy to my breast, every bit as beautiful as the child I did not know.

This time I did not recover so quickly. I had childbed fever and lay there, delirious, for days. I have no idea what I said during that time. At my worst I may have called out for Paul, again and again, begging him to come back to me. When I finally awoke, my first thoughts were of him, but fortunately I was sufficiently awake to realize that it was not Paul bending over my bed but Johan, who was ill with worry.

"You're back with me!" he said with relief as he stroked my hair and kissed me. "I thought I was going to lose you too."

He had chosen his words rather thoughtlessly, as they immediately aroused my suspicion.

"What's the matter with our son?" I asked weakly as fear froze my blood.

Johan appeared to recognize his mistake. He bit his lip and realized that lying would help nothing. "Our son . . . is dead," he said dully, drawing me into his arms.

If the loss of my daughter had already deeply wounded my heart, these words finally broke it in two. As I found out later, my boy had a heart defect, which he must have inherited from his father's family, since Johan had two sisters who had also died of the same cause.

I was immediately overcome by a strange weakness. It was thought at first to be caused by the melancholy I was feeling as a grieving mother, but when I broke down one day at the foot of the stairs, Johan called the doctor, who sat down by me with a serious expression.

"Mevrouw de Vries, I'm afraid I don't have good news for you. Your heart has been seriously weakened by the childbed fever. You must take great care of yourself during the coming months; otherwise I'm afraid of the consequences."

The words dried up in his throat, but I knew what he meant. If I did not look after myself, I would die. At only twenty-nine years of age!

After the doctor left, Johan came to me and took me silently in his arms. I could sense how much love lay in his touch, how much despair there was in his tears, but I felt nothing.

I was sure of only one thing, that it was not the childbed fever that had damaged my heart. No, the loss of my two babies had broken it, and I felt that if I did not at least find my daughter again, I would be condemned to eternal damnation after my death.

February 13, 1910

The day has now come. I'm to meet with the detective. I'm incredibly nervous, something my doctor warned me against as my weak heart can no longer withstand excitement, and my ailing veins could burst at any time. I refuse to believe that God is so cruel as to take away my life before I can discover where my daughter lives. I know I have sinned, but all human beings have a right to earn forgiveness, don't they?

Later . . .

I can hardly describe how I felt as I stood outside the detective agency. My rapid heartbeat had made me breathless, and at first I could not walk a step farther. My body was trembling from head to toe, and one or two concerned passersby asked if I was unwell. I sent them away with the excuse that the hot climate didn't suit me, which didn't particularly surprise them as I give a good impression of being an Englishwoman. (Paul's fiancée had complained constantly about the heat.) I finally managed to enter the building where Cooper Swanson had his office. In addition to his unattractive appearance, he also had a rather dubious past, according to the rumors that surrounded him. One such was that he had previously served in the British army in India but had to flee from there after a fight with a fellow soldier. Another version claims that he had been involved with Chinese bandits, ransacking English villas in India. I have no interest in whether there is any truth in either or both of these versions. I wanted only one thing: an answer to the question I had put to him weeks before.

He received me with a look of concern, probably because my lips had turned blue as they always did when I was under great stress.

"Your case has been a challenge for me, Mrs. de Vries," he began, sinking down into the old leather chair behind his desk. "But I have some positive news for you."

He pushed a thin black folder across the desk. I opened it cautiously, arming myself mentally against the unknown yet still unprepared for what I was about to see.

The photo showed a girl, around seven years old and such a spitting image of how I used to look that I could not help gasping in shock. There was no doubt that this was the child whose face I had seen lying against my breast so long ago!

"I had to bribe a few people, but it paid off," Swanson remarked smugly, as he could sense that I considered he had done his work satisfactorily. "The girl is in the care of James and Ivy Carter, a very respectable family in Padang. You will find the address beneath the photo. You can now decide whether you would like any further . . . services from me. I will say that the security at their house is hardly substantial."

At first I wondered what he meant, but then it dawned on me.

February 15, 1910

I can hardly believe it! The girl, that little girl with the amber eyes! The detective was right; it really was her. And I've spoken to her. I have no idea what I was like as a child, but this girl is so open, so sympathetic. All these years I've been imagining what she would be like. I've wondered which of us, her father or me, she would resemble. And now I've seen her.

There's hardly a trace of me or my ancestors in her; her eyes are shaped like her father's, and her skin is very white. No one would know that the blood of the Minangkabau flows in her veins. But the color of her eyes—they're like mine and my mother's. My mother, whom I haven't seen since she set off back to her village. She would have been so incredibly proud of her granddaughter. And I'm proud of my daughter, although I know that I've sinned deeply against her . . .

All my life I've never believed in any god, but I thank whoever granted me the mercy of seeing her, of speaking to her, from the bottom of my heart. Even though that heart has shown me all the more clearly today how weak it is.

March 27, 1910

After a month of illness and weakness that almost deprived me of the confidence to keep my promise, I can finally go and see her again!

As my heart fought to keep on beating, I imagined my little girl standing behind the wrought-iron gates. No, I didn't see them as a prison; they looked more like the gates to Heaven, a Heaven from which I was excluded. But I'm grateful that I can at least catch another glimpse.

Later . . .

My little Helen now has the violin, and I somehow feel as though I'm with her, day and night, to watch over her. We have agreed to meet regularly so that I can teach her to play.

How I would love to take her and have her with me, but I cannot. She would be made an orphan in just a few months, and then there might be no one who would look after her as well as the Carters.

But there are still two things I have to do before I close my eyes forever.

The first is already done—I've written a letter to Paul.

My resentment against him has faded now, and I've even come to understand that he could not have acted otherwise back then. Yes, I still refuse to accept that he acted out of spite. He had probably hardly set foot back on English soil when he was beset by so many obligations that he had no other choice.

I nevertheless recently asked Carmichael, with whom I have still had sporadic contact over the years despite the termination of our business relationship, to pass on this last message from me. Paul should know what has become of our child. Perhaps the years have also changed him, and he will now be prepared to accept the responsibility. Even if he doesn't, I know she's in very good hands; the Carters are a caring family, and their wealth will be of great benefit to her.

And now I'm sitting down at my desk once again to compose a letter to my mother, whom I have not seen for so long.

The fact that I did not tell her about my pregnancy, that I didn't invite her to my wedding, are two more sins that weigh heavily on me. I wanted at all costs to prevent the adat from having a claim on me, so I forgot that it wouldn't be an imperious old woman waiting for me there but my mother, my mother who loves me and who could perhaps have helped me to make a different decision . . .

28

By the time Lilly awoke it was almost noon. She blinked sleepily in the dull daylight that fell through the window.

It was not until a few minutes had passed that she realized she had spent the whole night reading Rose Gallway's diary. The little book lay on her pillow and had left an impression on her face.

But she had slept better than she had for ages. What a story! Gabriel would be delighted to have the diary in his hands. And now she had a lead! Rose Gallway had disappeared because she was no longer called Rose Gallway but Rose de Vries. Perhaps Lilly could find the name somewhere. In any case, she had been the wife of a plantation owner, and someone must know when she died.

As she had now lost half a day, she took a quick shower and decided that the first thing to do was to contact Verheugen and tell him about the diary.

A message from him was waiting for her downstairs at the hotel reception desk.

You're probably exhausted after our trip yesterday, but I should be delighted if you would come to a small party this

evening. The person I told you about has finally returned,
and I would very much like to introduce you two.

Yours sincerely,
D. V.

His girlfriend's back, Lilly thought, and a smile flitted across her face. She really did look forward to meeting this woman.

Since her honesty was stronger than her self-interest, she took the diary to a copy shop she had seen not far from the hotel. She then took the diary itself to the museum, where she handed it over to the deputy curator, who leafed through it in amazement.

"This is a valuable document. It's possible that the Faraday School of Music may approach you with a view to acquiring it," Lilly said.

Iza Navis gave her a gentle smile before handing the little book back. "Then please take it to the school with my best wishes. I'm proud that a daughter of our country has connections with England, and perhaps it may give rise to further connections between us."

"That's very generous; thank you very much," Lilly said in astonishment. Then she had an idea. "Could I perhaps have a look at the newspapers and registers of deaths for the years between 1910 and 1915? The diary has given me a new lead for my search."

"Of course. I'll have the documents fetched for you," the deputy curator replied. She led Lilly to the door of the reading room.

At first Lilly was a little overwhelmed by the heap of papers placed on the desk by an assistant, but her curiosity was soon aroused. She had the feeling that Rose's mystery was still missing a piece of the puzzle. Perhaps it would lie somewhere in these pages.

As she leafed through, she couldn't stop thinking about Helen. Had she discovered who her mother was? There had been no mention in the diary of whether Rose had told her. Lilly could imagine the bewilderment such a discovery could have caused her.

Although Lilly could not understand the meaning of the Dutch articles in the newspapers, she finally came across a picture that spoke for itself.

Aardbeving, the caption read. Earthquake. The photo showed collapsed houses and upended cranes. People gazed with shocked expressions at the sea of rubble. Lilly looked for a date and finally found it: June 6, 1910—only a few months after Rose had found Helen.

She suddenly felt uneasy. She skimmed through the foreign words, some of which were similar to the familiar German. No name. She turned the page feverishly, looking for death notices or the like. There were a few, but no Rose de Vries. Then she came across a long list of names. A list of victims.

She felt a dreadful tingling inside. Fearfully, she ran her finger down the list. They were mainly Dutch and local names, but there were a few English ones.

"Oh my God!" she said suddenly, pressing her hand to her mouth.

There it was. Rose de Vries, wife of Johan de Vries.

She had to lean back when she saw it. Rose had died in the major earthquake. Had she been on her way to visit her daughter? Had Helen been her final thought before she was struck by falling debris and killed?

Tears sprang to Lilly's eyes. Not only because of Rose's tragic end, but because of the life she had led. Could any individual have had such bad luck?

When her tears had dried up, she felt a little relieved and almost happy. Gabriel came back into her mind. He would be absolutely delighted to hear the solution to the mystery of Rose Gallway and her connection with Helen Carter. She looked forward to seeing his eyes light up, to watching the smile spread across his face. She missed him so much! Almost more than Ellen.

After turning a few more pages, she finally found Rose's obituary. Her husband may have had to do without announcing the wedding publicly, but his lengthy report of the loss of his wife would seem to indicate how much he had loved Rose. Had he ever known that her heart really belonged to another?

Lilly eventually left the museum with copies of the article about the earthquake, the list of victims, and the obituary, which she would ask Verheugen to translate for her. In the bright sunlight that was breaking through the thick clouds, her melancholy smile soon turned to a joyful one. Perhaps Rose could now rest in peace, she thought. Even if I never get to know why the violin found its way to me, I can live with that, now that I know what happened to its owners.

In the evening Lilly arrived at the address Verheugen had given her. She felt a little uneasy. She had not been able to rid herself of the feeling that he was more interested in her than she would have liked. What if his message was merely a pretext? No, that's ridiculous, she told herself. A man who wears his heart on his sleeve like he does wouldn't need that kind of pretense.

From quite a distance away she could hear the partygoers, which triggered her inhibitions. She wondered if these people really would welcome her. How would she explain to whoever opened the door that Verheugen was expecting her? Fortunately he was the one who answered.

"So, did you sleep well?" he asked with a broad smile as he invited her in. "When I asked for you at the hotel, they said the 'Please Do Not Disturb' sign was still hanging on your door. As I'm a man who goes in for positive thinking, I didn't immediately assume that anything had happened to you but imagined that you were simply tired."

"That's exactly how it was." Lilly smiled and followed him past a number of other guests into the house. "I sat there reading a document for a very long time last night."

"I hope you found it worthwhile."

"I certainly did. And I went back to the museum today, where I made an amazing discovery—Rose Gallway had a daughter, Helen

Carter, who also went on to become a famous violinist. I'll tell you about it later if you like."

"That's an offer I'll happily take you up on," Verheugen replied. "But first I'd like to introduce you to someone."

He excused himself from her and approached a group of men. He spoke briefly with one of them, then returned with him. He was a very handsome, muscular man with black hair and dark brown eyes.

"May I introduce you? This is Setiawan, my partner. Setiawan, this is my new friend, Lilly Kaiser."

Lilly raised her eyebrows in surprise and was pleased that her rational mind responded before her reaction could be misunderstood.

"I'm very pleased to meet you."

"The pleasure is all mine," the man replied.

"Setiawan works for a large computer firm and delivers seminars throughout the country."

Verheugen smiled proudly, and his partner nodded a little shyly.

"That sounds like a job with a lot of responsibility," she said. "Unfortunately I'm not very good with computers, though I need to know a certain amount. Until recently I never thought I'd need one for my shop."

"I believe I could advise you if you like," Setiawan replied. "But first you should get something to eat and meet a few people."

"Setiawan is Minangkabau," Verheugen explained to Lilly later, when he joined her after they'd had some food. He smiled at his boyfriend, who had turned to him and looked as though he was silently asking him for an excuse to leave the other men. "I met him ten years ago while here on vacation, and it was love at first sight."

"You're very lucky," Lilly replied a little wistfully. "It's difficult to find someone who loves you and you can love them back."

"Do you not have anyone like that?"

"Yes, maybe I do. But somehow . . . I still think about my husband a lot, and I don't feel as ready for a new relationship as I'd like."

"Just because you enter into a new relationship doesn't mean you need to forget your husband—far from it. He would surely give you his blessing for a new relationship."

"I know, but even so . . ."

"You should always follow your heart. Look at me and Setiawan. For a while we kept our relationship a secret from fear of what his family would say, but I was made completely welcome by them. In Aceh there are some radical factions who would like to make homosexuality a punishable offense, but it's accepted in most parts of the country. I believe that things often make us more afraid than they should. So go back to your new man and give it a go. You may be surprised at how easy it is."

Lilly nodded and lost herself in thought for a few moments.

"Setiawan is visiting his sister's family here and wants to go to his home village, where the rest of the family live. If you like, and have the time, we'd be pleased to take you with us so you can see the traditional houses firsthand."

"That would be lovely, but I've only got two more days here."

"No problem. I'll bring you back in good time. You simply must see these villages!"

Lilly nodded enthusiastically.

"A friend in England discovered that Rose Gallway herself was half Minangkabau. That means her daughter was a quarter."

She still found it difficult to believe that Helen was Rose's child and that Rose had really succeeded in finding her.

"Perhaps both women had a claim to an inheritance," Verheugen said. "Property is passed down the maternal line—provided there are any descendants, that is."

"There aren't, unfortunately," Lilly replied a little sadly. "Helen's ship was attacked, and she was killed with her family."

"That's really sad." Verheugen was clearly moved. "Do you know which village they belonged to, at least? It would make a wonderful end to your journey if you could see the village Rose's mother came from."

"Yes, I found out that the village is called Magek."

"That can't be true! Setiawan is also from Magek—his sisters, his mother, even his grandmother live there! Perhaps people in the village know of the two women."

Lilly shook her head. "I doubt it. Rose didn't think much of adat. She didn't want to step into the shoes of her forebears."

But perhaps they'll know of Adit, she thought. She did go back to the village, after all. Perhaps there will even be some relatives who can tell me a bit about her.

"Magek is a good day's drive away from here, so we should leave as soon as possible," Verheugen continued. "Or did you have plans for tomorrow?"

"No, not really."

"Do you want to see the village?"

"But won't your partner mind?"

"He'd be delighted to show you around. His relatives will be so pleased to see him again. He can only go twice a year because of his business commitments."

"Are you sure I won't be taking up too much of your time? Perhaps you should ask Setiawan first."

"I know what he'll say," Verheugen replied with a broad smile. "He'll say he'd be happy to show you his village and that people there will make you very welcome."

***

Lilly hardly slept a wink that night from excitement and anticipation. Fleeting images of the previous night merged with what she had found out about Rose Gallway and Helen Carter, and she could hardly believe all she had discovered in such a short time.

When morning came, she rose and sat by the window, watching the city gradually come to life. What would she find in the jungle? Would there be a "moonlit garden" there?

By the time Verheugen and Setiawan arrived outside the hotel in their car, she had already been sitting in the lobby for two hours, rereading the copies that she no longer needed.

"Here, have these," she said to Verheugen, handing him the pages. "This is the diary I told you about yesterday. And copies of the articles about the earthquake."

The evening before, she had not only told him about the earthquake and Rose's death but, full of guilt, had also told him that she had taken something from the governor's house without showing it to him. Verheugen had raised his eyebrows, but his astonishment was soon forgotten as Lilly told him the story of the diary and that she had been given it to keep by the museum's curator.

"I assume you need my help to translate the article and the obituary," Verheugen said.

"Yes, that would be very kind—but only if it's no trouble."

As they spoke, it occurred to Lilly again that she was still waiting for news from the man who was supposed to be examining the sheet music for a code. If anything had turned up, Ellen would surely have let her know. But what secret—if any—could the music be hiding?

"Trouble?" Verheugen laughed out loud. "You must know me well enough by now. It's no trouble; it's fun." He gave her a wink. "You must have thought I was crazy at first, didn't you?"

Lilly smiled playfully as she tucked a lock of hair behind her ear. "Only a little. But in truth, I'm so pleased I've met you."

A little later they were on their way into the jungle. The roads were pretty good, although every now and then they had to negotiate some rutted track that shook them around. After a few hours' drive, they finally reached Magek, which lay in the heart of the mountains, just behind the country's second-highest mountain, Gunung Singgalang.

The village in the middle of the jungle looked like something straight out of a fairy tale. Large houses crowned with buffalo horns rose out of their green surroundings, painted in different colors to indicate different families.

Completely enchanted, Lilly looked around in wonder at the buildings as well as the plants that flourished in abundance here and would surely make this a botanist's paradise.

Setiawan was given a very warm welcome by his family, as if he had been away for years.

"A Minangkabau man's standing is increased in the eyes of his family if he spends a lot of time in *rantau*, abroad. I'm sure that one day they'll give Setiawan the title of *Datuk* and make him the family's spokesman. At the moment his uncle still holds that position, but as you can see, Setiawan is very popular."

"Does he want the title?"

"Of course! Being Datuk means that you represent your family's interests publicly. It's a very great honor for the men here, one which doesn't exclude a computer expert, especially since it wouldn't affect his work in the slightest."

After all Setiawan's relatives had greeted him warmly, and finally also Verheugen, they introduced Lilly. Some of the women spoke English very well, and she discovered that some of them had also studied at the university. Lilly did not know how it would have been a hundred years ago, but she sensed that Rose's fear of the Minangkabau had been unfounded. Her family group would surely have taken her in and allowed her and her child to live together among them.

Lilly was finally also taken to see the headwoman, a very old woman who was introduced to her as Indah. Her clothes were very colorful, and to celebrate the special day, she and many of the women were wearing headdresses that, like the houses, resembled buffalo horns—although these had less sweeping curves and were formed from fine rolled fabric.

The woman eagerly asked about the reason for her trip, and Lilly told her that she was trying to trace two women who also had their origins in this village. She talked about Rose and Helen, but soon became aware that their names did not mean much to the people.

"Could you ask them, please, if they knew a woman called Adit? She was Rose's mother, who returned to the village."

Setiawan, who was acting as interpreter, nodded and asked the elderly woman. She inclined her head briefly, then smiled and said something.

"It seems that Indah does know of her. She says that the elder Adit was ruling the village at the time she was born. She must have been in her late seventies at the time."

Lilly felt her cheeks begin to glow. "That's wonderful! Could you please ask her what Adit was like? Why she came back to the village?"

In answer to her question Lilly found out that Adit had been a very strict but good headwoman, although it had taken a long time to persuade her to accept her obligations. But once she finally did, she was very conscientious and took great care to ensure that her tribe's fortunes increased.

"It was said that she went on a journey to London to look for her granddaughter," Setiawan said. "She found her, too, but just like she herself had once done, the young woman refused to go with her. But Adit later received letters from her in which her granddaughter promised to come to her. Unfortunately it didn't come to pass, because she and her family were killed during the war."

At last Lilly had found the connection with the information that Gabriel had already discovered about Helen Carter—the reason why the musician, who lived in London, had wanted to travel to Sumatra was Rose's mother. The circle was complete, and Lilly was now certain that Helen had known who her mother was.

Later, Lilly stood three terraces above the garden and recalled the melody of "The Moonlit Garden." If Rose had composed the piece, she could only have had this place in mind.

The garden before her was not the work of human hands like the one at the governor's house. Here, nature herself had achieved a perfect balance. This garden had trees and shrubs, flowers and grasses, and was radiant with all possible colors. Not even a fairy garden in a legend could have been more beautiful.

How often had Rose stood here and gazed out over it? How often had she walked among the flowers? It was such a shame that Adit was dead and Lilly couldn't tell her about Rose. At that moment Lilly felt remarkably close to her.

Perhaps I should come back and see the garden in the moonlight, she thought, and took a few photos so she could show Ellen how beautiful it was.

She was on her way back into the village when she saw Verheugen and Setiawan coming toward her.

"We've been looking for you!" Verheugen called, waving.

"I was just looking at the garden from above," Lilly said. "A marvelous sight. It's a shame I won't be able to see it in the moonlight."

"I'll send you a photo. And perhaps you'll come back one day and spend more time here." Verheugen gave her an encouraging smile. "But you should come back now. Indah would be extremely offended if you didn't enjoy a good meal before you leave."

29

London, 1920

The days after the accident were a blur of delirium. Helen had occasional lucid moments when she realized she was in the hospital and in great pain, but then she would sink back into unconsciousness, trapped in a chaotic world of weird dreams. She saw a village she knew she had never been to. Strange roofs with gables like buffalo horns pointed up into the sky.

After three weeks of semiconsciousness her thoughts began to get clearer, and she became aware of her body again. The doctors now spoke to her, trying to engage her in conversation. At first she found it difficult to give any answers, as her tongue refused to obey her brain's signals. When the doctors realized this, they explained that it was due to the opium she was being given to alleviate the pain of her fractures.

The last thing Helen could remember was the lights of the bus racing toward her and the dreadful hooting of its horn, the most horrible discord she had ever heard. Everything after that was a blur of light and shadow, heat and cold, silence and muffled sounds.

As her vision began to clear, she found she was looking up at a metal frame above her. At first her mind was too sluggish to know where she was, but then she realized that she could not move one of her hands.

When the nurse became aware that she was awake, she fetched the doctor on duty, a man with friendly blue eyes and graying hair.

"My violin, Doctor. What happened to my violin?" was the first question Helen asked.

A smile flitted across the face of the man who introduced himself as Dr. Fraser.

"You're obviously well enough to be thinking of music, then?"

Helen didn't fail to notice the hint of sympathy in his expression. It was destroyed, she thought, and although she had hated the instrument during the last moments before the accident, the thought that her treasure might have been destroyed caused her breast to tighten painfully. Or was that only her broken ribs? No, the pain was deeper than that.

"I can set your mind at rest regarding your violin. Miraculously it only suffered a few scratches, and a couple of strings snapped. Someone picked it up at the scene of the accident and sent it with you to the hospital. There are still some honest people in the world, even these days."

Tears sprang to Helen's eyes. The violin was safe. Even though she had put her career at risk with the accident, she would be able to play again.

Her delight in the thought of music paled when the plaster cast was removed from her arm, and Helen soon realized that something was wrong. Her thumb, index, and middle fingers were numb. At first she had assumed that this was due to the anesthetic, but Dr. Fraser was worried when she told him about her lack of sensation.

A few days later, the doctor appeared in her room with an X-ray plate. His dejected expression caused Helen's stomach to tighten. Until that moment she had not allowed herself to contemplate the dreadful thought—but now . . .

With a heavy sigh, Fraser stood by her bed and for a few moments said nothing, as if assessing his patient's condition to see whether she was strong enough for the news he had to break to her.

"It appears that some of your nerves were also affected by the accident," he began a little hesitantly. "I'm reluctant to make a definite prognosis, but I fear . . ."

"I'm never going to be able to play again, am I?" Helen's voice cut through her throat like glass.

Fraser sighed again. She could see clearly how much he wished he could tell her otherwise.

"At some stage . . . ," he began, but stopped again as if fighting for the right words. "Perhaps you will one day. Nerves sometimes knit together again, heal. If you train your hands, you might eventually manage it again."

The words of the old woman, the one who had claimed to be her grandmother, resounded in Helen's ears again. During the encounter in her dressing room they had led to Helen throwing the old woman out and ultimately running out into the street in a state of bewilderment.

"You're Rose's daughter," the old woman had said, her sharp eyes fixed on Helen.

"I don't understand," Helen replied in confusion. "My mother is Ivy Carter."

The old woman shook her head and then straightened her head scarf.

"No, Ivy Carter brought you up because your mother gave you away for music."

What was the old woman talking about? Helen felt a strange weight in her stomach. She had never doubted that Ivy was her mother, and now this old woman was claiming that her mother was actually a stranger.

"Look. Have you ever seen this woman?"

With trembling hands, the old woman took a photo plate from her bundle. The picture was stained, the plate slightly rusty, but the woman it showed was clearly recognizable.

Helen gasped. It was the woman who had spoken to her by the fence! The mystery lady who had given her the strange violin. After the earthquake she had never seen her again.

"This woman was called Rose. Rose Gallway. You probably won't know her name."

"Oh yes, I know it!" Helen cried in astonishment. "Twenty years ago she was one of the best solo violinists in the world!"

A bitter smile crossed the old woman's face.

"You're Rose's daughter," she said. "And I blame myself for not being there for you."

"You?"

"I'm Rose's mother, Adit. After the death of my husband I returned to my village to accept my inheritance—the inheritance of my forebears. I learned too late what happened to Rose." She sighed heavily and stroked her thumb lovingly over the plate. "I had hoped she would come to find me, that she would confide in me when she was in need, but she was obviously too proud for that. It was only later that I found out what had happened. That she had married and was among the dead following the earthquake. And that she had a daughter who grew up in another family."

Helen shook her head in disbelief. No, none of this had anything to do with her! The old woman was talking nonsense. Perhaps she was after money.

"You don't believe me," the old woman observed. "I didn't expect you to. But I'm old, and I'm going to die soon. I had no other daughter but Rose. You're my granddaughter, Helen. And it's up to you whether our maternal line will die out or remain."

Maternal line? Granddaughter? Helen's head was spinning. What did it all mean? Surely her mother was—

At once, she saw the face of the mystery lady before her. Amber eyes, exotically shaped. A strong chin, full lips. The years had eroded her recollection of the stranger but not fully erased it, and the photo now brought her mental image back into focus. How beautiful the woman had been.

"Go away!" she said, not noticing how harshly or hysterically her voice rang out in the room. "Leave me in peace!"

With a sad smile the old woman turned and left.

***

With a long sigh, Helen returned to reality in her hospital room. Bitterness spread through her heart. Despair. Perhaps the accident was fate's way of punishing her for failing to believe her grandmother.

Did she now have any other choice than to return to her roots? She was no longer able to live the glittering life of a musician. Maybe she would be able to play again one day—she was determined to succeed in that—but at best she would only be good enough to entertain the company at an evening function, who were bound to blather on about the tragic fate of Helen Carter, once such a bright star. The very thought made her stomach turn.

She looked regretfully at the violin case by her side until tears clouded her vision. Would my grandmother place such a curse on me? she wondered, then reached out her less injured hand to the case. As she fumbled to open the catches, a film of sweat coated her skin, making her nightshirt stick to her belly and back, but she refused to yield. She could have called for a nurse, but she had something to prove. To herself, and to the old woman who had so thoroughly turned her life upside down.

After she had finally raised the lid, she felt weaker than ever in her life. Her breathing hurt her ribs, and her unfeeling hand felt even number. She managed to grip the neck of the violin and take it from the case.

As if it were a child, she hugged it to her breast before sinking back against the pillow. The thought that she would never again be able to get a sound from it was almost unbearable, but her pain and sadness were subsumed by defiance. I will do it, she told herself. Somehow.

***

Helen was released a few weeks later. She was not sent home but to a sanatorium in Switzerland to convalesce after the trauma of her accident. Her agent had reacted with shock to the doctor's diagnosis but had assured her that he would not make the news public until it was definite that her hand would never recover.

Helen had her violin with her in the sanatorium and had discovered a piece of music in the lining of the case—a very unusual piece, one that may even have been composed by her mother.

She held the music tightly as she looked out at the garden. Which garden did her mother have in mind? Was the music really by her?

Her period of convalescence did not restore her ability to play the violin, but her courage to face life had grown. She had run through the conversation with the old woman again and again in her mind, and gradually a desire had crystallized: I must find out about my mother!

The number of questions she faced could have discouraged her, but she suddenly felt an inner strength, the like of which she had never known before. I mustn't give in! she thought.

Perhaps she could start over again. Perhaps being so far from London was not the worst thing that could happen to her.

Home, she thought. Sumatra is so far away from everything. It's my homeland; it was my mother's homeland, and that of my forebears. As soon as I get the opportunity, I intend to return.

30

London, 2011

The early spring sunshine was hot on Lilly's skin as she walked up the gravel path to Ellen's house. Its warmth did not compare to the heat Lilly had experienced on Sumatra, but it felt very good for European conditions.

Once she had reached the house, she looked in vain for the gardener, but there was no sign of him except for the snowdrops and crocuses adorning the beds alongside the path. Was Rufus ill, or had she merely missed him?

Ellen's car sitting outside the house indicated that her friend must have arrived home just before her. Although Lilly had deliberately not given her a precise time of arrival, since she never liked to distract her from her work, Ellen clearly seemed to have a sixth sense.

"The happy wanderer returns!"

Lilly jumped as Ellen appeared beside her. She was wearing gardening gloves and carrying a bundle of birch twigs, which she probably wanted to add to a bouquet of flowers. The two women fell into one another's arms.

"How lovely to see you! I've missed you so much this week!"

"I've missed you too! You should have come with me; I've discovered so much."

"Well, come in and tell me. I can't wait!"

In the living room, over tea and cakes, Lilly gave Ellen a detailed report of everything she had done in Indonesia and all she had found out about Rose and Helen. The diary and the photocopies were on the table, radiating a strange energy, as if they were dying to get into Gabriel's hands and be back where they belonged with Rose and Helen, even though they were little more than shadows of the past in the music school.

"So they were mother and daughter." Ellen shook her head in disbelief. "I don't understand how a mother could bring herself to give her child away."

"Times were different then," Lilly said, although she knew she would never be able to grasp it either. "The only way of really escaping from the scandal would have been to return to her mother in Magek. But Rose was afraid of that, afraid of losing her self-determination. But she paid a high price for it."

Ellen thought for a moment in silence before saying, "I'm really glad I live now, in a time when women no longer have to decide between family and career."

"You're right there," Lilly agreed and sank into her own thoughts. How would it have been for Rose in my situation? Could she have loved again if Paul had died? Paul had abandoned her, and despite what she had written, she had probably harbored a tiny spark of hope that she might see him again before she died. Whereas I've lost Peter forever. Rose couldn't open her heart to anyone else, but I can.

"Anyway, it seems the earthquake saved her from prolonged suffering," Ellen said sadly as she picked up the copy of her obituary. "No wonder she was thought to be missing without a trace. Historians would have looked in vain without the knowledge that she was married."

"Exactly. I'm so pleased that I had the help of that enthusiastic Dutchman. At first I thought he was after something from me, but no, he had already found the love of his life." Lilly paused to get her thoughts in order, then asked, "Have we received any mail from Italy?"

Ellen shook her head.

"No, I'm afraid not. The day you set off I sent Enrico an e-mail, but I only got a brief reply to say that his friend still hadn't been in touch. He probably needs a while longer."

"Yes, probably. Or he hasn't been able to find anything."

"Could be. But as it turns out, there's nothing left for him to find, is there?"

"I guess you're right—I've solved the puzzle of Rose and Helen, apart from the mystery of how the violin came to me. I suppose the music can't really help me with that last piece of the jigsaw, can it?"

"Probably not, unless one of the women could see into the future." Ellen paused briefly before giving an enigmatic smile. "Well?"

"Well what?" Lilly asked, although she could guess.

"I'm sure Gabriel will be delighted to hear all this."

"You bet!" Lilly replied with a smile.

"Well, don't leave him on tenterhooks. You were supposed to be having a meal together, weren't you?"

"Yes, we were. And . . ." It occurred to Lilly that with all the things she had experienced in Padang, she had forgotten to tell Ellen that Gabriel had come to find her before her flight. "He came to meet me."

"In Padang?"

"No. Well, kind of. I thought about him a lot. He came to find me at the airport before I left. I'd called him, but the last thing I expected was for him to appear. But he did, and he brought me a letter in which Rose asked one Paul Havenden to look after their daughter. That was the catalyst that set the ball rolling."

"And you kept all that secret from me? Shame on you!" Ellen laughed. "You know what this means?"

"That Havenden abandoned her?"

"That's not what I meant. I mean Gabriel. You know he wouldn't do something like that if he wasn't crazy about you, don't you? And that means your fears about his ex-wife were completely unfounded."

Lilly lowered her head, slightly embarrassed. "I know." She looked up with a smile. "And I'm sure about him myself now."

"Then pick up the phone! Do I have to keep telling you?"

"No, I don't think you do."

Lilly got up and went over to the telephone table, but Ellen couldn't help giving her a final piece of advice.

"Take him to the restaurant we went to. And wear your green dress—I'm sure the sight of you in it will floor him!"

***

Lilly looked out the window uncertainly. It was already half past seven. Perhaps she should have ordered a taxi. When she suggested it to Gabriel, he had protested.

"Surely you don't believe that I'd entrust my lady to a stranger's driving skills!"

Lilly had laughed. "I've accepted lifts from quite a few strange men recently—I'm sure I'd survive the journey to the restaurant."

"I don't doubt it, but I'd like the pleasure of spending a few more precious minutes with you. I'm not going to pass up that opportunity."

He was a bit late in giving himself that pleasure—where was he? After checking her hair and the fit of the green dress one more time, she heard the sound of an engine. As she looked out the window, she saw headlights shining through the twilight. There he was!

She grabbed her purse and ran toward the living room, her heart thumping. Dean and Ellen were sitting on the sofa watching TV, a sight that made Lilly smile. One day, will I sit there like that with Gabriel, happily spending such an ordinary evening?

"Gabriel's here, I'm off!" she called, and whirled out of the room again to fetch her coat.

"Have fun!" they chorused in reply. Ellen waved through the door.

Lilly felt as though she were going to the prom, or like Cinderella being whisked away by her prince.

"Make sure you don't only talk shop with him!" Ellen called after her, but Lilly was already out the door and only had eyes for Gabriel, who got out of the car and greeted her with a kiss.

"I can hardly believe you're finally coming to this meal with me!" He laughed as he held the passenger door open for her.

"Of course, what did you expect?" she replied with a smile as she fastened her seat belt.

"I'd better get going quickly before you change your mind."

"No fear of that. Anyway, it's not been entirely my fault that this dinner didn't happen sooner."

"OK, OK, I admit I've been guilty, too. So we'd better make sure we enjoy this evening. We've earned it, haven't we?"

On the way to the restaurant she told him all that she had found out about Rose. She only realized that she was chattering away without pausing for breath when she saw Gabriel's broad smile.

"It seems like it's made a real impression on you," he said when he could get a word in edgewise.

Lilly felt the blood shoot to her cheeks. Would that ever stop happening when she was with him?

"Yes, it has." *But something else has much more,* she added silently, glancing to her side.

The headlights of the oncoming vehicles constantly snatched his profile from the darkness. How handsome he was! Lilly suddenly felt a burning desire, a throbbing deep inside that she had not felt for a long time. She had almost lost her appetite; all she wanted was him. One step at a time, she told herself.

This time, too, the restaurant was very busy and, as if sensing what was going on between her and Gabriel, the waiter gave them a table for two with a lovely view of the Thames and the full moon sailing above it.

They sat there for several long moments simply gazing at one another. Once the waiter had finally taken their order, Gabriel said, "It feels so good to have you back. And you look amazing in that dress."

"Thank you. You haven't been worried, have you?" Lilly smiled uncertainly, running a hand over the silky fabric. The dress seemed to bring her luck, and she was delighted that Gabriel liked it.

"Of course I have, and only partly because I wanted you to get back safely. Clearly you haven't only solved the mystery of Rose Gallway, but it also seems the trip did you a world of good."

"Yes, that's true, although I confess I felt a little insecure at times."

"Insecure? You?"

"Yes, everything was so new and strange."

"That's what foreign places are usually like."

"It was nothing to do with the city or the country. It was because I was traveling alone. I've been hiding away the past few years. I think I was afraid of the world." She paused briefly before adding, "I'd like to tell you something. And I want to tell you because you're part of the reason why I've dared to come back into the world."

She took a shaky breath. Something had suddenly broken free inside her, like in the fairy tale of the Frog Prince in which loyal Henry lost the iron band around his heart. The words that followed were calm and emerged as if they were speaking themselves.

"Shortly before Peter died, he came around one final, brief time. It was a very strange moment, since the tumor had largely taken away his ability to speak, and most of the time he was in a semiconscious state so that I never knew whether he was aware of my presence at all. But in that moment he was completely lucid. He reached out his hand to me, stroked my face, and, speaking more clearly than he had for a long time, said, 'I love you.' I broke down in tears and kissed him. For a fraction of a second I believed that a miracle might happen. Promising to come and see him the next day, I said good-bye and left, feeling somehow . . . lighter. Lighter than on any day in the previous weeks. The call came the next morning. They told me that Peter had died peacefully in his sleep that night . . ."

She had to stop, as her mind was suddenly full of all the images she had locked away inside, suppressed for so long. And with the images came a realization.

"His death pulled away the ground from beneath my feet," she continued. "But I knew he loved me. And when I saw you, as I got closer to you, I knew that you could free me."

Many minutes of silence followed. Lilly wiped the tears from her cheeks and looked at Gabriel, whose eyes were also gleaming moistly. He was looking at her intently, and his expression told her that her words had moved him deeply.

"I want you to know something," he said. "It wasn't only Peter who loved you. I love you too. Even though this is only our first real date, I feel strongly that we . . ."

He didn't get any further, since Lilly rose and moved around to him, not caring whether the whole restaurant was watching. She cupped his face in her hands and kissed him.

"I love you too, Gabriel. And yes, I also believe that we have a future!"

***

Hours later she was gazing at Gabriel's bedroom ceiling and smiling at what fate had given her. She still found it difficult to believe that something like this could happen to her. Gabriel was lying there by her side, his soft breathing filling the peace of the room, and her body was still on fire from his kisses, his touch, and the way their bodies had moved together in passionate mutual understanding. How she had missed making love! And how she had enjoyed having Gabriel so close to her, so close that not even a feather could have passed between them. He's the one, she thought. He's the man who's right for me. I know that for sure now.

Perhaps Peter had even had a hand in it from above. Until then she hadn't believed in supernatural forces or angels, but now she was tempted to. Whatever the cause, she would never let Gabriel go, even though her time in London was almost up and she would have to go home.

There must be ways of being together. Somehow. Who said that Berlin was the only place for an antiques shop?

The next morning, after a phone call with Sunny in which she discovered that the video, securely packaged, was waiting for her in the shop, Lilly felt as if she were walking on air.

"I'll be flying back tomorrow," Lilly told Ellen that evening. "The video's ready, and I feel so damned close to finally solving the mystery of our violin."

Ellen hugged her.

"I really hope that your mother or whoever else recognizes the man in the video. It all depends on him now."

"I'll find him—you can bet your life on that. And I'll call you as soon as I know!"

"Don't forget to tell Gabriel as well. He'll probably lie in wait for you at the airport and try and persuade you to stay."

"I'll be back," Lilly laughed. "And he'll be waiting for me. At least I hope so."

Of course Ellen had wanted to know how the evening had gone, down to the last detail. There were a few things Lilly had kept to herself, but no words were needed for her friend to see that at that moment she was the happiest woman in the whole of London. Ellen had an eye for such things.

"At last! I knew you'd let someone into your heart one day. He's the right one, believe me."

Lilly believed it with all her heart.

***

The next morning, as the plane landed in Berlin Tegel airport, Lilly felt not only excitement and anticipation, but also a warm feeling of coming home. Not to mention heartfelt gratitude toward Ellen, which she had made quite clear as they said their farewells.

"Just don't wait forever to come see me again," Ellen had admonished her at the end, hugging her tightly.

The heaps of snow had dwindled to slush, but the small shop looked just as it had when Lilly left. Most of the stubborn items were still there, but with a few gaps where Sunny must have sold some. As she entered, the bell rang out above the door, and she saw Sunny at the counter, bent over a large pile of books and photocopied notes.

"Lilly!" she cried. "You're here!"

"Yes, I am. Our phone call made me realize that I can't lose any more time. I'd like to show the video to my mother today."

She didn't fail to notice the way Sunny was looking at her in amazement.

"You look good. Have you been on the tanning beds?"

"No, in Indonesia," she replied as casually as if she were remarking on the weather. "Where's the DVD?"

During the flight Lilly had decided not to stay in Berlin for long. Her mother would probably be flabbergasted when she appeared at the house, but something was pushing her on, and she wanted to show her the clip that day at all costs.

Sunny's eyes widened even further. She dug out the DVD from where it was stashed beneath a pile of papers, and asked, "Indonesia? Really? I thought you were going to London?"

"I did. But I've also been to Cremona and Padang."

"Way to go!" Sunny leaned eagerly over the counter. "Tell me all about it."

"Later. We can sit down to supper together. First, I've got to go see my mother."

Lilly stowed the DVD in her bag, and without giving Sunny the chance to respond, she was out the door and on her way to the station.

After a little over two hours on the train, she reached Hamburg-Eppendorf. The street where her parents lived consisted of a row of more or less identical houses, distinguished only by the colors of their roofs.

The taxi driver, who had seemed very quiet in comparison with the London cabbies, unloaded her suitcase, accepted the fare, and drove off. Lilly allowed herself a moment's pause to slip back into her memories of her childhood spent in this house, before entering through the garden gate. Suddenly, she realized how silent it was.

Normally her father would be puttering around outside, especially with the weather as mild as this. But there was no one to be seen. The house looked almost abandoned.

"Mama?"

Lilly's voice echoed uneasily around the entrance hall. No one had answered the bell when she rang, so she had let herself in. A nasty feeling spread through her stomach. Of course her parents didn't play loud music or sit in front of the TV all day, but one of them would always react to the doorbell ringing.

And her mother could sense her coming home hours in advance.

As Lilly entered the living room, she was shocked by what she saw. Her mother lay on the sofa, her face bright red and her eyes closed. Her arms were wrapped around her belly as if she was in agony.

"Mama?"

Lilly hurried over to her. She placed a cool hand on her mother's brow and felt a raging fever. Her mother's eyes fluttered open.

"Lilly." Her voice sounded scratchy, and her lips were cracked.

"Mama, what's the matter? Where's Papa?"

"He's gone away," she sighed, and her face twisted.

"What's wrong with you?" Lilly asked in panic, forcing herself to stay calm. Whatever it was, she needed to call an ambulance, but it would be better if she knew what her mother's symptoms were.

"My stomach," she groaned. "I've got these dreadful pains there!"

Lilly didn't need to know more. She whipped out her cell phone and dialed the emergency number.

After hanging up, she went into the kitchen to fetch a thermometer, a bowl of cold water, and a clean handkerchief, which her mother still kept in the same drawer she always had. She moistened it and returned to where her mother was lying.

"Mama, what's going on?" As she cooled her mother's brow, Lilly looked at her watch. It was still showing English time; she would reset it later, when her mother was in the hospital. "How long have you been like this?"

"Two days, I think. At first I thought it was a simple stomach upset, but then the pains got worse."

"Why didn't you phone the doctor? And where's Papa?"

"He's gone away with a few friends from the sailing club."

"Did you have these pains when he left?"

It would be typical of her to say nothing because she didn't want to spoil her husband's vacation.

"No, it started a couple of days ago."

"How much longer is he away for?"

Lilly was sure her father would reproach himself when he found out that his wife had been ill while he was away.

"A week."

"A week?" Lilly exclaimed in shock. "Why didn't you call anyone? Why didn't you tell anyone?"

Or was there a message waiting for her on her answering machine at home? Before her mother could reply, the ambulance arrived, to Lilly's relief.

***

There were only a few people in the waiting room at that time. Most of those waiting were patients who had been brought in an ambulance or people accompanying them. Since the doctors' offices in town were still open for their regular consulting hours, the emergency room wouldn't get busy until the evening.

Lilly paced nervously around a recess where a snack and coffee machine stood. She was shielded here from the looks of the nurses, who had already asked her twice to be patient.

Lilly had no idea how to tell them that she was not pacing up and down out of impatience.

How lovely it was on Sumatra, she thought suddenly, but quickly suppressed the thought. She was glad that she had acted on her impulse and come straight to Hamburg. She didn't believe in the supernatural, but somehow she was sure that it was some instinct that had brought her here, planting the impatience to view the video in her heart.

"Ms. Kaiser?"

Lilly turned and jumped when she saw the nurse standing so close to her.

"Yes, what is it?" she asked, a little bewildered.

"Dr. Rotenburg would like to speak to you."

These words caused all trace of tiredness to vanish. She grabbed her bag, and her wallet fell to the floor. Lilly scooped it up with shaking hands but didn't bother to put it back, hurrying off as she was, wallet in hand, after the nurse. The sight and smell of the patients she saw through the open doors of the emergency room cubicles made Lilly's stomach churn.

The nurse stopped outside a frosted glass door, announced Lilly, and indicated for her to enter.

"Oh, that's nice, you're going to pay me immediately!" Dr. Rotenburg laughed as she entered the consulting room.

Lilly didn't understand his joke at first and stared at him in confusion until she realized her wallet was in her hand. She blushed.

"Excuse me, I . . . It . . ."

"Don't worry, I didn't really think you were about to pay me. Fortunately your mother's health insurance will cover it."

The doctor motioned for her to sit down, then reached for his notes.

"But I'm sure you haven't come here to listen to my weak attempts at humor. When you've been on duty for twenty hours, you tend to lose your ability to make a good joke, and gallows humor takes over. So, without further ado, I'll tell you straight out that your mother has come through it all very well."

Once again, Lilly felt grateful for her sense of duty toward the shop and Sunny, who had pressed the video into her hand. It didn't bear thinking about what would have happened otherwise.

"We'll be keeping your mother in the emergency room for monitoring for a few hours more. If everything's all right then, she can go to her room."

"When can I see her?"

"When she's awake. It will be a little while yet. In any case, it looks as though she'll be with you for plenty of time to come."

31

"Hi, Ellen, it's me, Lilly."

Back home, Lilly had decided to call her friend. The visit to her mother had shaken her, since she had never seen the strong woman who had brought her up looking so helpless. Even though it was clear that her mother was already feeling better, Lilly felt the need to speak to someone and share her cautious relief.

"Lilly!" Ellen cried. "Are you OK?"

"Yes, I'm fine, no need to worry."

"Well, do you have any news?"

"Yes, I do," Lilly replied. "My mother's been taken to the hospital."

"What? For God's sake, what's the matter with her?"

"Appendicitis. But she's had the operation, and she's come out of it well."

"You're only telling me now? You could have called me."

"I could have, but I was all over the place. I'm in Hamburg at the moment, looking after the house. My father's away; he's on a sailing trip with his club. He'll really be shocked when he hears what's happened."

"How is she now?"

"Getting better already."

"Do you need anything?" Ellen asked after a pause. "A little moral support, perhaps? I could come to Hamburg for a few days."

Lilly was surprised by this offer, but she was overjoyed inside. Things wouldn't seem as difficult with Ellen there, and her mother was crazy about her friend. A visit from Ellen would be bound to do her good. It would also mean she could show her the video with the mysterious old man.

***

The next morning, as Lilly was watching the video on her laptop at the kitchen table, the doorbell rang. She looked up in surprise and caught sight of Ellen through the window.

Delighted, she ran to the door and opened it, then fell into Ellen's arms.

"You know how to cause a stir," Ellen said reproachfully as she rubbed her back.

"Not me, my mother! Believe me, when she's back on her feet, I'll be giving her a piece of my mind. But come in, I've got some coffee brewing."

As they sat at the kitchen table, Lilly had to give a detailed account of what had happened and how she had found her mother.

"I've never been so scared, not even on the flight to Padang," she added.

"It's just as well you flew home when you did."

"I don't know why I did, either. Must have been some sixth sense," Lilly replied thoughtfully. "At first I thought my impatience was because I just had to show her the video. But what if it was because I sensed she was ill?"

"I'd bet it was a mixture of the two. My foster mother always used to say that blood's thicker than water, and I think there's some truth in it."

That afternoon they took the suburban railway to the hospital. "I feel like I'm sixteen again," Ellen said. "Do you remember how we'd take the train into the city in the afternoons?"

"Oh, I certainly do. And I also remember how we managed to get the wrong train more than once."

Ellen nodded. "Once, my foster mother was on the verge of calling the police because she thought we'd been kidnapped."

"Yes, she got my mother into a real state while we were there asleep on the train. We didn't wake up until we'd reached the other side of the city, and it took us ages to get back."

Before Lilly could say anything else, an announcement sounded through the car to tell them they had arrived.

"I've never been able to bear the smell of hospitals," Ellen said as they walked the corridors toward Lilly's mother's room.

"Same here."

The door of the room stood open, and as they entered they saw a nurse bending over her mother's arm, taking a blood sample.

"Wait a moment," she said as she saw the visitors. "Are you Jennifer Nicklaus's daughters?"

"I'm her daughter, and this is my friend Ellen," Lilly said.

"That's fine. You can come in now; I've finished."

She patted her patient's arm a final time and drew out the needle.

"Lilly, darling." Her mother held out her arms for a hug. The hospital bed made her look fragile, but despite all the tubes she seemed much better. "It's lovely to see you. And you've brought Ellen!"

Ellen smiled, then offered her hand. "I'm pleased to see you're getting better, Mrs. Nicklaus. When Lilly called to tell me you were in the hospital, I was shocked, I can tell you."

"Don't worry, I'm fine. It was only appendicitis. Lilly must have made it out to be worse than it was."

"People only go to the hospital when it's bad, Mama," Lilly said defensively.

"It's nothing to worry about. Appendicitis isn't dangerous these days." She turned back to Ellen. "You look really grown up now, if I may say so. The last time I saw you, you'd just turned twenty, and you'd met that nice young man. Dean, isn't it?"

Ellen gave her a big smile. "That's right, Dean."

"How long have you been married now? It must be almost twenty years."

"Fifteen years," Ellen corrected her. "We lived in sin the rest of the time."

"It's half an age, anyway. Marriages that last that long are all too rare these days. But I'm sure you haven't come here to listen to me rambling about the state of marriage today. What's on your mind, Lilly? The fact that you've brought Ellen suggests that it must be something important. You always have her with you when you want to tell me something important."

Lilly smiled, a little embarrassed, but it was true. If ever she didn't trust herself to own up to her mother, she had taken Ellen along for moral support.

"I wanted to show you a video. That's the real reason I came to Hamburg."

"Not to see your old mother? You've hurt my feelings."

"But, Mama—"

"Oh, don't worry, I was only pulling your leg. Show me, then!"

Lilly got out the laptop and booted it up.

"A few weeks ago a man came into my shop and gave me something," Lilly explained briefly.

"What was that?"

"A violin. He said it belonged to me. But he didn't tell me why, what his name was, how he came to that conclusion, or anything. I wanted to ask you if you recognized him. Of course it could have been someone from Peter's family, but I only want to go down that road if you're sure you don't know him."

She started the video. There was no sound, but the man could clearly be seen as could she. At the point where the old man gave Lilly the violin, her mother suddenly turned pale.

When Lilly noticed, she quickly stopped the video. "Are you OK, Mama? Is something up?"

"No, no," she replied, sounding a little bewildered. "I'm fine. It's just . . ." She fell silent.

Lilly looked helplessly at Ellen, toying with the idea of ringing for the nurse, but her mother roused herself from her paralysis. As she looked at them, it seemed as though she had returned from a trip far back down memory lane.

"I do know that man," her mother said after a long pause.

"Are you sure? Do you want to see the clip again?"

She shook her head.

"No, I don't think that's necessary. I met him many years ago, when you were still a little girl. He was much younger then, as I was."

"So how did he get the idea that the violin belongs to me?"

"I can't tell you, since I sent him away back then. But he gave me his name and his address."

"You sent him away?" Lilly looked at Ellen in confusion, but she clearly had no more idea herself.

"Yes, I sent him away. I didn't want to know about it. How could the violin have done me any good? I had a husband and a daughter, and I was afraid of finding something out that could shake my world to the core. Sometimes it's better to let ghosts rest in peace."

Was that really true? Lilly wondered. If so, then it was too late for her, as the ghosts had already been set free, and she already knew the secrets of some of them. What else was she about to discover?

"Do you remember the address?" Ellen asked.

Lilly's mother nodded. "Even though I didn't want to accept what the man was offering me, I never forgot his name."

32

The thatched house in a suburb of Hamburg was in need of renovation, and at first sight it gave the impression that the owner was not at home. Sprays of forsythia by the wall bloomed in bright yellow magnificence, and in the front garden snowdrops nodded their heads, and purple crocuses peered cheekily out from among the thin grass.

Lilly opened the garden gate a little hesitantly, but she hardly dared to step onto the flagstone path.

"What if he isn't in?" she asked.

"Then we'll come back another time," Ellen replied. "Come on now. You want to know whether it's him, don't you?"

As they walked up the path, Lilly saw a magnolia tree in full bloom in the backyard. The pale pink flowers were also part of the Berlin landscape, but they had a special meaning for her now. Magnolias also grew on Sumatra . . .

On the front door hung a weathered blue-and-white wreath. Lilly pressed the bell, her heart thumping, and felt for Ellen's hand. She squeezed it briefly and gave Lilly an encouraging nod. It felt like an eternity before anything happened. At last they heard footsteps. Ellen let go Lilly's hand as if to tell her, This is up to you, and you can do it.

The door opened and Lilly was in no doubt that this was the man who had brought her the violin. His surprise lasted for only a moment.

"Mrs. Kaiser!"

"Mr. Hinrichs? My mother gave me your address."

A smile flickered across the man's face.

"I wondered when you'd turn up here," he said and stepped aside. "Do come in."

"This is my friend Ellen Morris. She's been helping me to reconstruct the history of the violin."

"I'm pleased to meet you. Morris sounds English. Is that where you're from?"

"My husband's English. I'm from Hamburg myself."

"So you know something about violins?"

Ellen grinned. "A little."

***

"Come in to the best room."

Karl Hinrichs's house looked like a set from a historical seafaring movie. The blue-painted walls with white skirtings were hung with oil paintings of old ships, and shelves contained various ships in bottles and ancient measuring equipment. The grandfather clock by the window, which Lilly estimated to be at least one hundred and fifty years old, ticked away leisurely. When the pendulum swung to the left, it was caught by a ray of sunlight that made it shine momentarily.

"You must want to know how I came by the violin," he said after leading them to a living room set that, like much in the house, must have been at least fifty years old.

"I'm even more interested in why you think I should have the violin," Lilly replied. "And why you shot off so quickly without explaining anything."

"Well, it's a long story." An enigmatic smile creased his weather-beaten face. "What about a cup of tea? I've just made a fresh pot, and you have to admit that it's a great accompaniment to any conversation."

"Yes, please," Lilly said after an affirmative nod from Ellen.

The old man disappeared into the kitchen, leaving Lilly and Ellen to look at their surroundings. Lilly was really glad her friend was with her. This is the last piece of the jigsaw, she thought.

After a few minutes Hinrichs returned with the tea. The white porcelain cups reminded Lilly of a tea service her parents-in-law used to own.

"I was a fresh-faced young sailor when I signed up on a merchant ship sailing the Indian Ocean to avoid conscription," he began after pouring the tea. "In 1945, shortly before the German capitulation, there was a Japanese attack on a passenger steamer heading for Sumatra. We hurried to their aid but could only watch as the ship sank. Among the few who were saved were two children, two girls, one of them nine years old, the other only two. The older one was holding on to a violin case."

Lilly felt her hands go cold.

"They said their mother and father had been with them on the ship, but even after an extended search, their parents were never found. Their family name was Rodenbach, though their mother was also known by her stage name, Helen Carter, and the two girls were called Miriam and Jennifer."

Lilly looked at Ellen, who seemed to be able to guess what she wanted to say. They both stayed silent and let the old man continue.

"The two girls were taken in by a Christian mission. I kept the violin, intending to give it back to them, but they vanished before I got a chance. I couldn't rest, so I did some research and found that, after the end of the war, the girls had been brought to Germany.

"Little Jennifer went to the Paulsen family in Hamburg, and Miriam to a family called Pauly."

"That's impossible!" said Ellen, who had turned as white as chalk.

"It's true," the old man replied with a smile. "After adoption, Jennifer and Miriam Rodenbach became Jennifer Paulsen and Miriam Pauly."

Lilly and Ellen looked at one another in amazement. Miriam Pauly. Lilly had not heard that name for a long time. She had never really associated it with a person, but she knew the name, even though it was that of a ghost. A ghost who was inseparably bound up with her best friend, Ellen.

She glanced at Ellen, whose gleaming eyes betrayed her emotion. She had many more associations with the name of Pauly. After all, it was her maiden name, since her foster parents had not adopted her. And Miriam . . . Miriam was her mother—her mother who had died in an accident so long ago. Miriam Pauly and Jennifer Paulsen.

The next moment it struck Lilly like an arrow. If her mother and Ellen's were sisters, then they were . . . cousins! And descendants of Rose and Helen! It couldn't be true.

"A long time ago I tried to find Miriam to give her the violin, which had been lying in my mother's house for many years," Hinrichs continued. "I have no idea why the girl hadn't taken it with her. But in Germany I discovered that Miriam had been killed in an accident a short time before. So I turned my attention to the second girl, Jennifer, who was also married by then. I told her about her sister, which surprised her. She sent me away, swearing up and down that she didn't have a sister and it was all a mistake. And no wonder, since she was only two when the shipwreck happened, and her adoptive parents had obviously never told her about her sister. I wrote her a letter and tried to tell her all I knew, but I never received a reply. I knew that I was never going to get anywhere with her. I was about to give up once and for all when I found that sheet of music in the lining. And that made me decide to try again—with you, Mrs. Kaiser."

Silence followed his words. Each of them appeared to be sunk in their own thoughts.

"Will you please tell me one more thing," Lilly began eventually. "Why did you disappear after bringing me the violin? You could have told me the whole story there and then!"

The man took a drink of tea, then smiled mischievously.

"People learn from experience," he said. "I didn't want to hold on to the violin any longer, and I didn't want you to give it back to me after I'd gone to so much trouble to find you. So I ran for it. I hope you'll forgive me."

***

Not wanting to go straight home after their conversation with Hinrichs, Lilly and Ellen walked for a while along the banks of the Alster. They were silent at first; then Lilly ventured, "Why do you think our mothers were never in contact with each other?"

"Jennifer, your mother, was very young at the time. She probably didn't remember that she had a sister. And Miriam . . ." Ellen frowned. She bit her bottom lip for a moment, then said, "Perhaps she did try to make contact with her sister."

"Do you think so?"

"Your mother and mine were adopted, weren't they?"

"Yes."

"Perhaps our adoptive grandmothers tried to prevent any contact between them."

"What makes you think that? My mother was only two; she wouldn't have remembered having a sister," Lilly said.

"But my mother must have remembered. I wonder if she ever tried to find her sister."

"Who knows what her adoptive parents told her. It would have been impossible for a child to look for her sister. The authorities wouldn't have released any information to her." Lilly shrugged helplessly. "The best thing would be for us to go back to see my mother tomorrow and ask her. If anyone can answer this final question for us, she's the one."

The next day, Lilly sat by her mother's hospital bedside, trying to tell the story as calmly as possible, although the questions were boiling inside her. She still could not believe that she and Ellen were cousins.

Lilly's mother folded her hands on the sheet and listened in silence as Lilly and Ellen took turns sketching out the story of the two unfortunate musicians. When they had finished, silence hung over them for several long minutes, each of them lost in her own thoughts. Lilly looked at her mother's familiar face. She had never known her whole story before. Would she reject this story as she had the violin?

"Did my mother, your sister, ever try to make contact with you?" Ellen said, finally breaking the silence.

Lilly's mother sighed and remained silent for a few more moments.

"Yes, she did," she replied eventually. "Lilly, when you get home, look in the bottom drawer of the chest of drawers in my bedroom. There's a letter right at the back. Show it to Ellen, would you?"

Lilly nodded and glanced at Ellen, who was tensely gnawing her bottom lip.

"Ever since I was very little, I had a certain memory," her mother continued, her gaze fixed on an empty spot on the opposite wall. "We were on a ship, and my parents and sister were with me. I didn't remember anything else. I was far too little. It was like a photo I carried around with me, a single snapshot. I don't remember anything of the attack itself, or anything that followed. Only that I once had a family—father, mother, sister." She paused briefly before continuing. "Over time I came to believe that my family had been killed. Or that I had merely imagined them. And then one day this old man appeared, claiming that I had a sister. I sent him away because I believed he was crazy. And then I did some research of my own. I've never forgotten the words of the letter I received as a result. It was dated August 14, 1973, and it was from the registrar, informing me that I was adopted—and that in fact I had had a sister, who had been put into the care of another foster family."

Lilly saw that Ellen had tears in her eyes.

"My mother died in an accident on February 22, 1973. The road was icy. She skidded and crashed into a tree. My foster parents didn't tell me until I was sixteen. Apart from that, they had never made a secret of the fact that I'd had another mother."

"My parents never told me anything about my background," Jennifer said. "I confronted them with the letter, which led to a falling-out and us not speaking for over two years. I continued my research, and the outcome was sobering. I was told that Miriam Pauly had died in an accident. I traced her grave and discovered that her little son was buried with her. Since she wasn't married, I assumed there was no other family. The people who adopted Miriam were no longer alive. Because I believed there was no one else left in my family whom I could ask, I let the matter lie and never told anyone about it. If I'd known that you were my niece . . ."

"My mother couldn't tell me that I had an aunt," Ellen said. "The youth welfare office knew nothing about it and simply put me in the care of foster parents."

"No one could have known, Mama," Lilly said, laying her hand on her mother's arm. Growing up with Ellen would have been wonderful, but no one sitting around that bed could have done anything to change the situation.

"I should have looked up this Karl Hinrichs and told him he was right, but I could never bring myself to do it. Although I didn't know my sister, I grieved for her. Then I looked at you and told myself that, despite everything that had happened, my life hadn't been in vain. And now, thanks to the two of you, I know the whole story."

33

The call reached Lilly as she was leaving the hospital and on her way to the train. Ellen's time in Hamburg was unfortunately coming to an end. She was due to leave the following afternoon, to return to Dean and her girls and tell them that their Aunt Lilly really was related to them—a cousin once removed, strictly speaking, but a family member all the same.

"So, how's Hamburg?" Gabriel's voice.

A smile came to Lilly's face. "Fine, thanks. And London?"

"How's your mother?"

After returning from their visit to Karl Hinrichs, she had sent Gabriel a long e-mail in which she told him the story of herself, Ellen, and the violin.

"She's getting better—even well enough to be making jokes. If all goes well, she'll be coming out the day after tomorrow. My father's beside himself. He'll be back tomorrow."

"I can understand it. I'd be similarly shocked myself."

Lilly smiled to herself. It did her good to feel the love growing ever greater in her heart, like a plant sending out shoots and buds. And it was good to know Gabriel felt the same.

"When will I see you again?" he asked after a comfortable pause.

"I'd love to say I was flying over to London this minute, but I have to see to the shop first. I can't keep Sunny there for much longer; she's already done so much for me."

"Have you considered the idea that you could also sell antiques here? You could specialize in items from Germany. Cuckoo clocks are all the rage, with locals and tourists alike."

"What a shame that I don't deal in cuckoo clocks," Lilly said, thinking back to their first night together when the same idea had crossed her mind.

"You should get some in as a matter of urgency. But that aside, what do you think? Would you consider it?"

"If I think of you, I definitely would," she said. "Perhaps I might even consider moving to London at some stage. But my parents are here, and they aren't getting any younger."

"There are such things as airplanes," Gabriel said.

Lilly sensed he was in earnest. "Yes, there are. We'll talk about it soon."

"About airplanes?"

"No, about the possibility of moving to London. I've only known you for a few weeks. Maybe you'll get fed up with me sooner than you think."

"That's unlikely. I'm not someone who gives my heart away as easily as that, but I understand what you mean. I should make more effort to sell myself to you."

"Even more effort? Is that possible?"

"I'll think of something, you can bet on that!"

They said their good-byes, and Lilly switched off her cell phone, gazing up happily at the sky. A few areas of blue were showing in the patchwork of clouds, a beam of sunshine reaching down to the earth. Who would it land on? With a sigh of happiness she stowed her cell phone in her bag and boarded the train.

When she arrived at her parents' house, she noticed a strange car parked in front. The plate number indicated a rental car. Did she have a visitor? Or had Ellen rented a car? Why would she do that?

She stepped through the garden gate, breathing in the spring air mingled with the scent of moist soil. She felt more at peace now that she had solved the mystery of the violin. And the fact that Ellen was not just her best friend but also her cousin was one of the best things that had happened to her that year. What more could she want?

As she entered the house, she heard voices. Ellen was talking to a man . . . She knew that laugh!

She raced toward the living room and stood rooted to the spot in the doorway.

"Gabriel?"

He leapt up. His smile was more outrageous than she had ever seen it.

"Yes, it's me."

"But we were just on the phone. How could you—" Before she could finish her sentence, it dawned on her. "You're using a travel SIM card, aren't you? That's why I didn't see the number."

Gabriel laughed. "That's right."

"But how?" She looked across at Ellen, who was grinning broadly.

"An airplane, Lilly, flying. One of the best human inventions ever. And Hamburg has an excellent airport."

Lilly was bowled over. A thousand butterflies had begun to flutter in her stomach.

"So was that conversation we just had all for nothing?"

"No, not at all. It made my wait at the traffic lights pass much more quickly."

"Why didn't you tell me?"

"Because I assumed that the new Lilly could take it."

He took her in his arms and kissed her.

***

"Well, all we need to know now is why Lord Havenden broke his word and simply abandoned his pregnant lover," Ellen said thoughtfully as they sat at the kitchen table over coffee and cakes that Ellen had bought from a nearby baker's.

A look of triumph crossed Gabriel's face.

"You've found something else out in the meantime," Lilly guessed.

He nodded.

"After finding that letter at the Carmichaels', I looked up the Havendens. It wasn't an easy task, since the name died out some time ago. But after a little digging around, I managed to locate his sister's daughter, who now lives in Devon, with live-in care, of course. The old lady didn't know Paul Havenden personally—she wasn't born until 1920. But she still remembers well the stories her mother told. According to her, Paul Havenden and his wife, Margaret, were killed in a shipwreck in the Indian Ocean."

"What?" Lilly's hand flew to her mouth in shock.

"I checked it out, and it's true that in 1902 a passenger steamer sank after colliding with a mail steamer. It would be called human error today—the captain of the mail steamer had miscalculated the route."

"So perhaps he had intended to marry Rose after all?"

"Possibly, who knows? But he never got the chance to put his honesty to the test."

It took a while to sink in with Lilly.

"Did Paul's niece know anything about the letter Rose sent to his ancestral home?"

Gabriel shook his head. "No, I don't think she did. And I assume that the letter I found at the Carmichaels' never reached Havenden Manor. Carmichael would have discovered that Paul was no longer alive."

"So he let Rose believe that he had simply forgotten her?" Ellen shook her head indignantly. "He could have told her what had happened."

"Maybe he wanted to protect her."

"Protect her?" Lilly was agitated now. "What could be worse than believing that he never really loved her? I'm sure the news of Paul's death at sea would have hit Rose hard, but at least she could have hoped that he had truly loved her. And if she'd known, perhaps she might have made a different decision about her baby. And maybe she would have had the chance to know love again."

At that moment Ellen's cell phone rang. She jumped in surprise, fished the buzzing device from her bag, and disappeared with it into the kitchen.

"That has to be a sign," Gabriel remarked, and drew Lilly toward him again and kissed her. This time it was a much longer, more passionate kiss than when Ellen had been there.

"What will my cousin think of us?" Lilly asked reproachfully.

"That we're madly in love with one another?"

Lilly gave him a broad smile. "OK, you're right. I hope you've got time to stay here in Germany for a while. I'd like to show you my shop."

"I'm not so sure about that if you don't have any cuckoo clocks . . ."

Epilogue

Sunlight flooded into Lilly's apartment on Berliner Street as the sound of the phone ringing tore her abruptly from her sleep. Muttering to herself, she opened her eyes and reached for the bedside phone.

"Kaiser."

"You won't believe this!" came Ellen's voice on the line.

"Ellen?" Lilly rubbed her eyes. The previous night had been later than she had intended, and now a glance at the alarm clock told her that it was already after ten. "What won't I believe? Have you won the lottery?"

"No, we've received a letter."

"A letter?"

At that time of the morning her mind was still too sluggish to grasp what Ellen meant and why she was so excited.

"Enrico's written. You remember?"

As she gradually shook off her sleepiness, she had a mental image of the station in Cremona and the wonderful palazzo. And of course its good-looking occupant.

"Yes, I remember." And at once the scales fell from her eyes. "Oh my God, he hasn't—"

"Yes, he has. Or his friend, more like. He's finally completed his analysis of the music."

"So?" Lilly was wide awake now. After all she had discovered during the last few weeks, she was beyond surprise.

"Your dream wasn't too wide of the mark concerning the mystery." Ellen paused for effect.

"Come on, don't keep me in suspense!"

"There really was a kind of code in the music that ultimately spells out a name."

"What's the name? And how did Enrico's friend work it out?"

"Enrico goes on at length in his letter about complicated calculations. His friend wrote it all out on the sheet music, but it's all Greek to me. All we need to know is that his calculations led him to a four-letter name."

Lilly felt like crawling down the telephone line and shaking her friend, who was clearly reveling in her impatience.

"Adit?" she asked.

"No. Rose."

"What?"

"Rose."

"That can't be true!"

"Why not?"

"So it means that Rose didn't compose the piece?"

"Not necessarily. Either Helen used it to refer to her mother, or Rose immortalized her own name in the music. It could also be possible that Enrico's friend played around with the possibilities so much that he had to come up with something. Perhaps it's all nothing more than a huge coincidence."

"Perhaps," Lilly replied, but her momentary disappointment soon vanished. She had solved the biggest part of the puzzle and in so doing had reunited her family. Could she wish for more?

"Is Gabriel still with you?" Ellen asked.

"Yes, he is."

"Give him my regards."

"I certainly will." They both hung up.

Lilly put the phone back on the bedside table, then turned to her side. It looked as though the phone ringing had not disturbed Gabriel's peaceful sleep. Lilly allowed herself a moment to gaze at him. Although she had done so many times during the last few days, she still thought she saw something new every time. After he had given her such a surprise by turning up like that, she had managed to persuade him to stay for two whole weeks. Their time was coming to an end the next day, and she was already dreading seeing him leave. It would not be for long, though, as she was going to visit him soon. Her plans to move to London were far from definite, but Lilly had begun to consider it seriously. But first she wanted to get her thoughts in order, reorganize her life. She would need some time for that. But she had not felt such energy and optimism for a long time. She could do this! Together with Gabriel.

"Gabriel," she whispered, smiling gently and brushing a lock of hair from his face.

"Hm." Even her touch seemed unable to rouse him from his sleep. She leaned over and kissed him on the cheek, but to no effect. It wasn't until she kissed him on the lips that his arm shot up and grabbed her. With a cry of delight Lilly snuggled up to his chest.

"Ellen says hello. She's received a letter from Enrico di Trevi."

"I heard. At least that Ellen called."

"So you weren't asleep?"

"Who could sleep through a phone ringing?"

"I thought you might be sunk too deeply in your dreams."

"That only happens when I'm dreaming of you. Any other time I can quite easily snap out of dreamland. Fortunately I don't have to dream of you at the moment, because I have you here."

They kissed again; then Gabriel looked at her expectantly.

"Any news?"

"Only that the music probably does contain a code. One that produces just a single word: *Rose.* We still don't know who composed 'The Moonlit Garden.'"

"Do we need to know?" Gabriel replied with a huge yawn.

"Says the man who's been researching these women's lives for such a long time." Lilly nudged him gently.

"Well, if we want to find out when the music was written down, we can have the paper analyzed. Then we'd have the date it was produced and would know for certain. But that would be incredibly unromantic, don't you think? Let's leave them with this one little secret and let people puzzle over who wrote 'The Moonlit Garden.'"

He drew her back into his arms and kissed her.

About the Author

Photo © Hans Scherhaufer

Bestselling author Corina Bomann was born in Parchim, Germany. She originally trained as a dental nurse, but her love of stories compelled her to follow her passion for writing. Bomann now lives in Berlin.

About the Translator

Photo © 2014 Sandra Dalton

Alison Layland is a novelist and translator from French, German, and Welsh into English. A member of the Institute of Translation and Interpreting and the Society of Authors, she won the 2010 Translators' House Wales / Oxfam Cymru Translation Challenge, as well as various short-story competitions for her own writing. Her published translations include a number of novels and nonfiction titles, and her own debut novel, *Someone Else's Conflict*, was published in 2014 by Honno Press. She is married with two children and lives in the beautiful and inspiring countryside of Wales, United Kingdom.